BIRTHRIGHT

VOLUME SIX
FATHERHOOD

IMAGE COMICS, INC.
Robert Kirkman *Chief Operating Officer*
Erik Larsen *Chief Financial Officer*
Todd McFarlane *President*
Marc Silvestri *Chief Executive Officer*
Jim Valentino *Vice President*

Eric Stephenson *Publisher*
Corey Murphy *Director of Sales*
Jeff Boison *Director of Publishing Planning & Book Trade Sales*
Chris Ross *Director of Digital Sales*
Jeff Stang *Director of Specialty Sales*
Kat Salazar *Director of PR & Marketing*
Drew Gill *Art Director*
Heather Doornink *Production Director*
Branwyn Bigglestone *Controller*

www.imagecomics.com

SKYBOUND
www.skybound.com

Robert Kirkman *Chairman*
David Alpert *CEO*
Sean Mackiewicz *SVP, Editor-in-Chief*
Shawn Kirkham *SVP, Business Development*
Brian Huntington *Online Editorial Director*
June Alian *Publicity Director*
Andres Juarez *Art Director*
Jon Moisan *Editor*
Arielle Basich *Associate Editor*
Carina Taylor *Production Artist*
Paul Shin *Business Development Coordinator*
Johnny O'Dell *Social Media Manager*
Sally Jacka *Skybound Retailer Relations*
Dan Petersen *Director of Operations & Events*
Nick Palmer *Operations Coordinator*

International inquiries: ag@sequentialrights.com
Licensing inquiries: contact@skybound.com

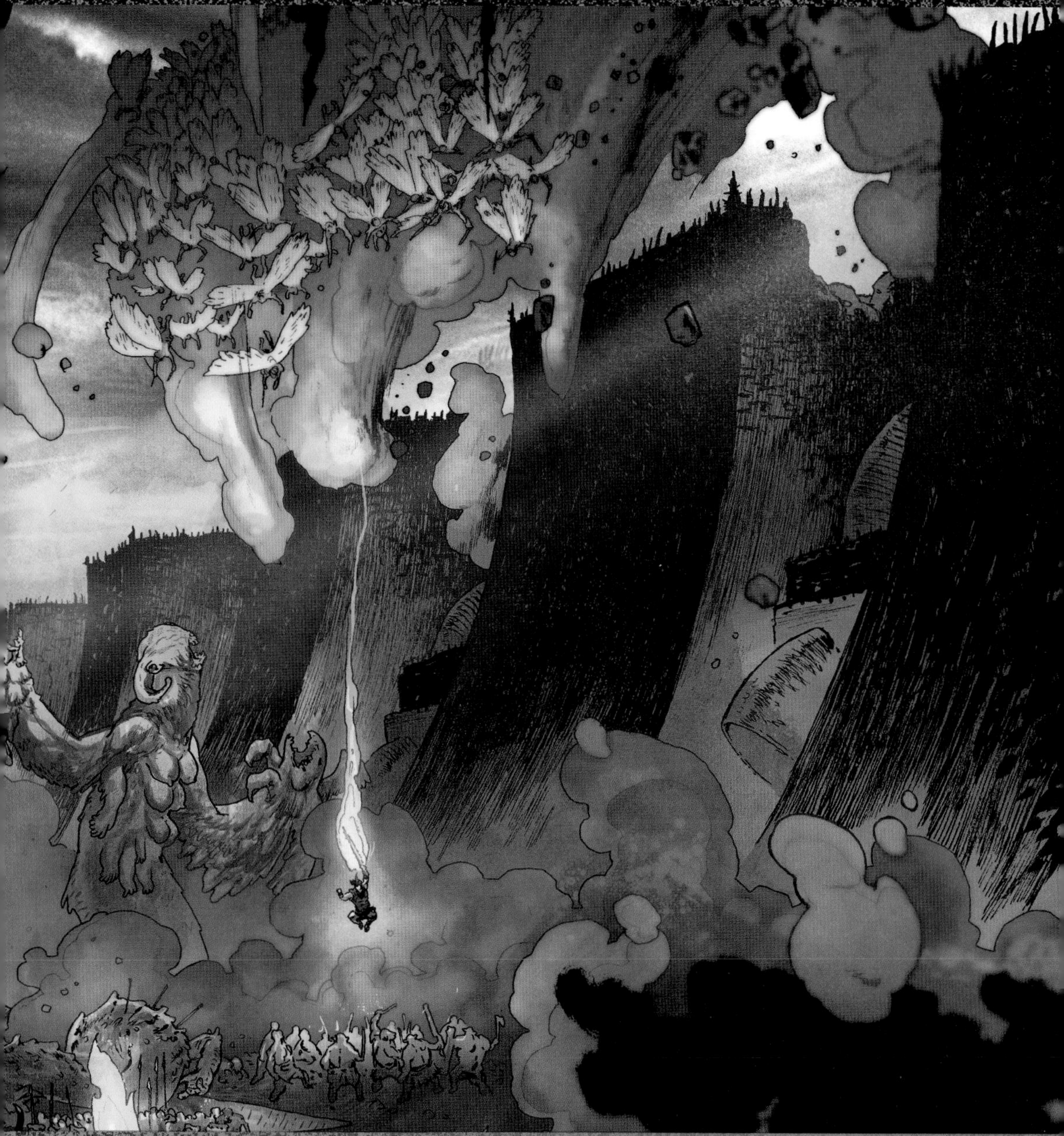

Joshua Williamson
creator, writer

Andrei Bressan
creator, artist

Adriano Lucas
colorist

Pat Brosseau
letterer

Arielle Basich
associate editor

Sean Mackiewicz
editor

logo design by **Rian Hughes**

cover by **Andrei Bressan** *and* **Adriano Lucas**

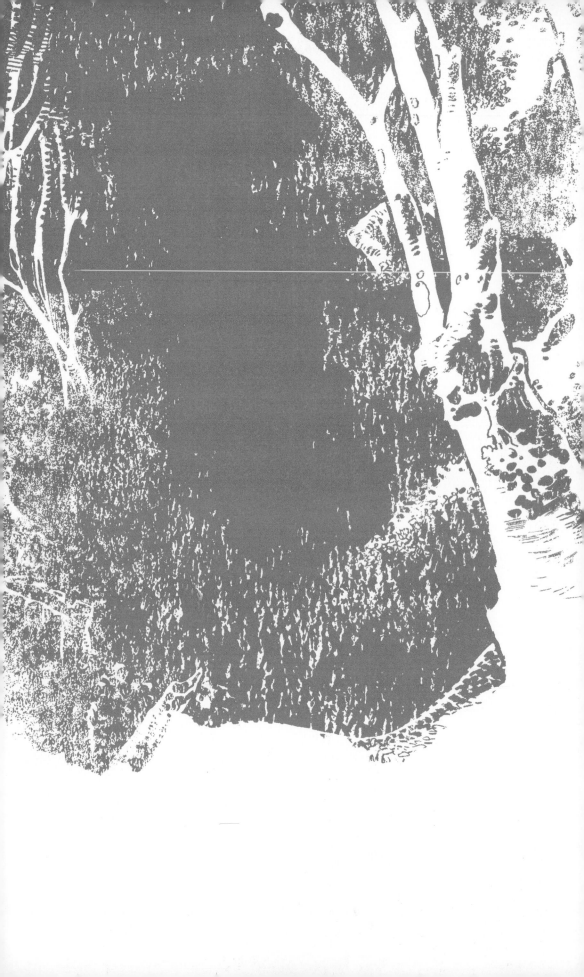

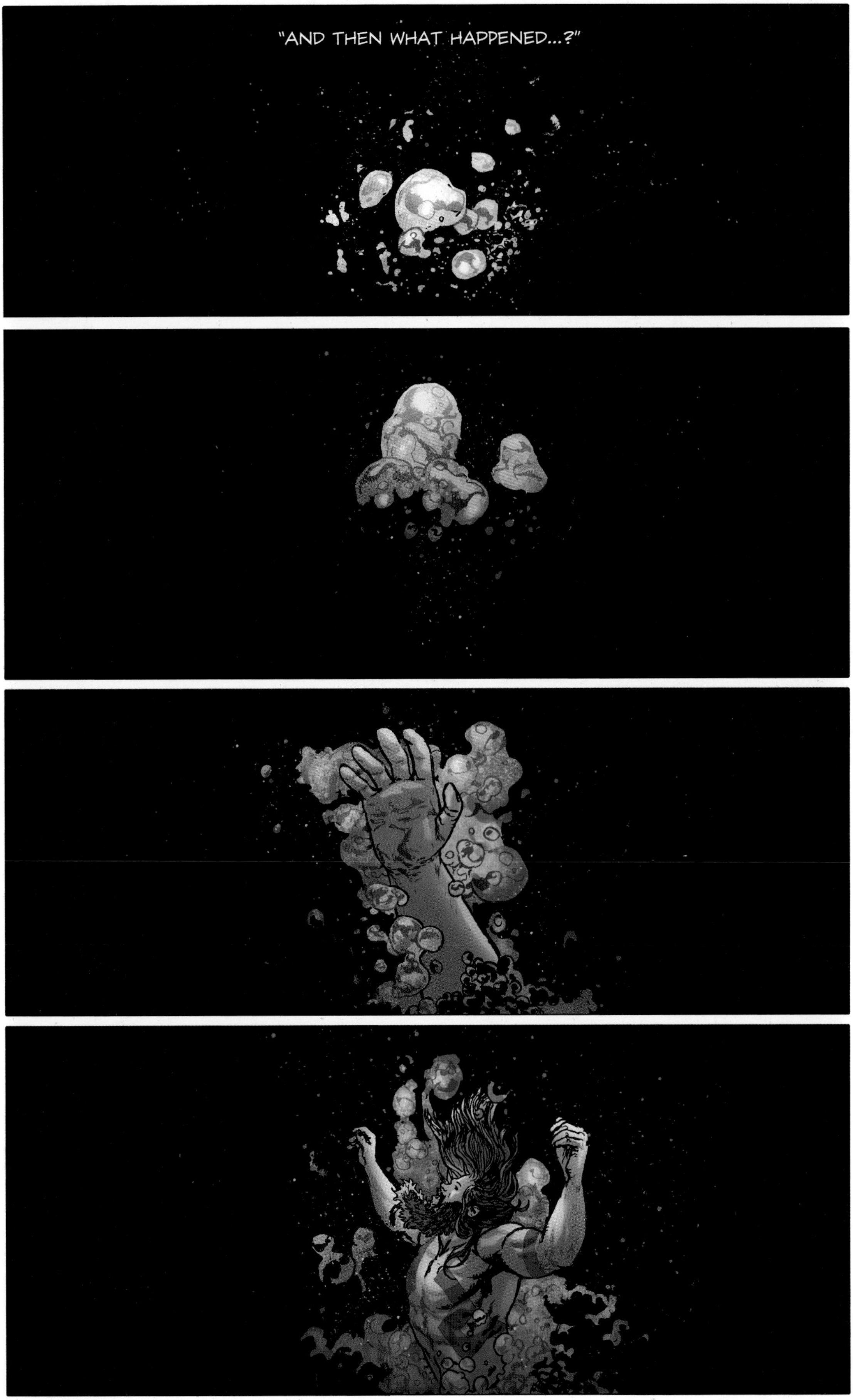
"AND THEN WHAT HAPPENED...?"

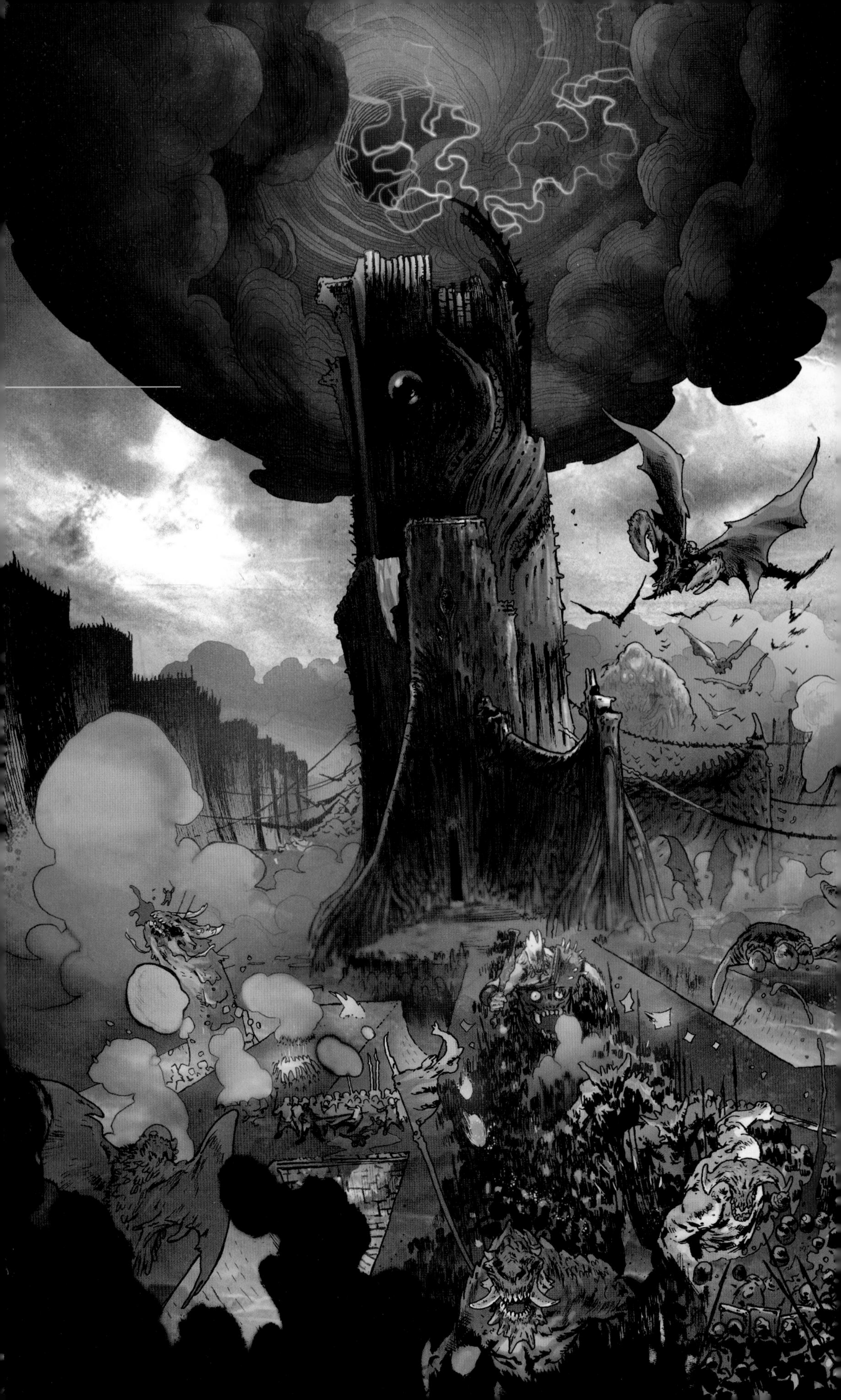

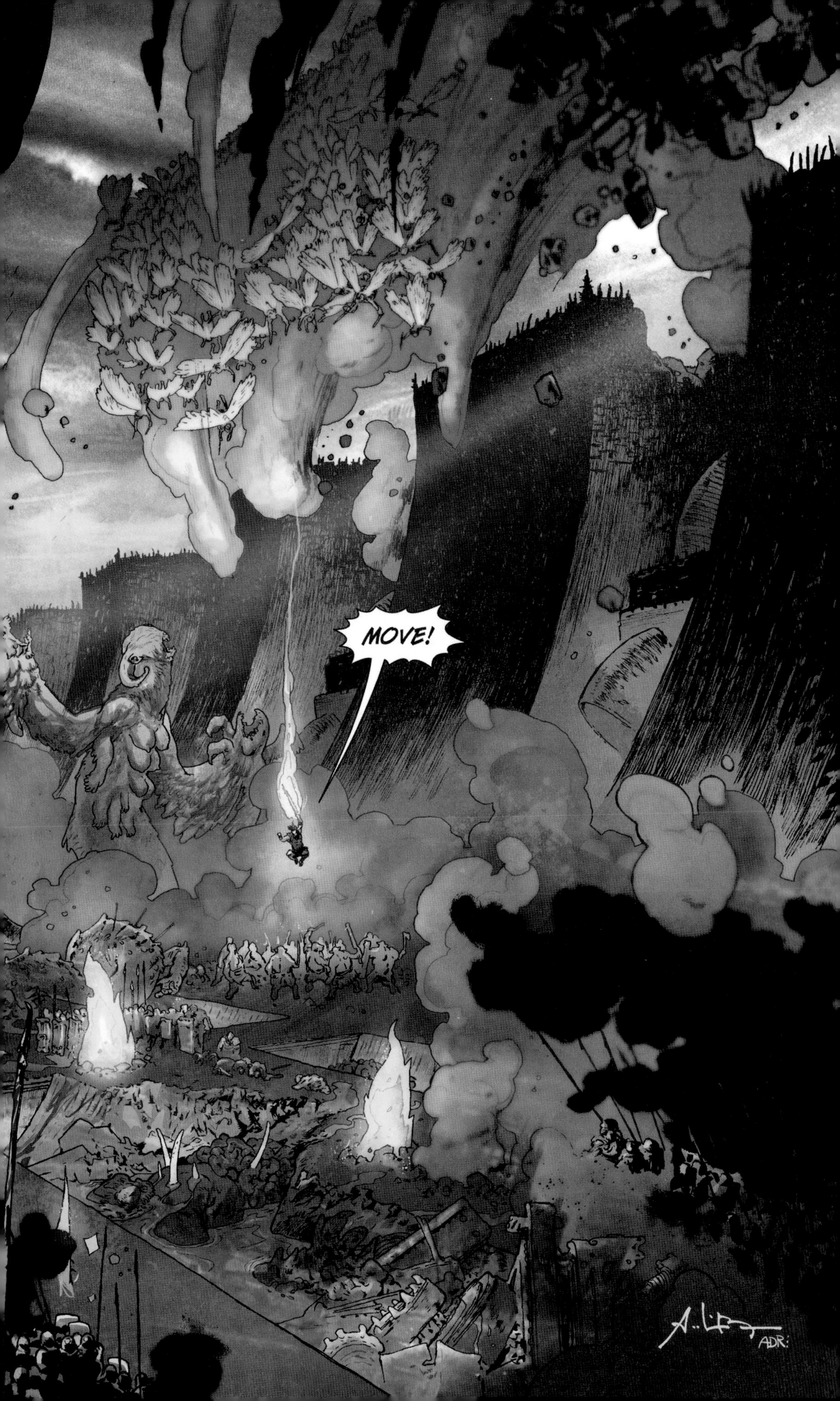
MOVE!

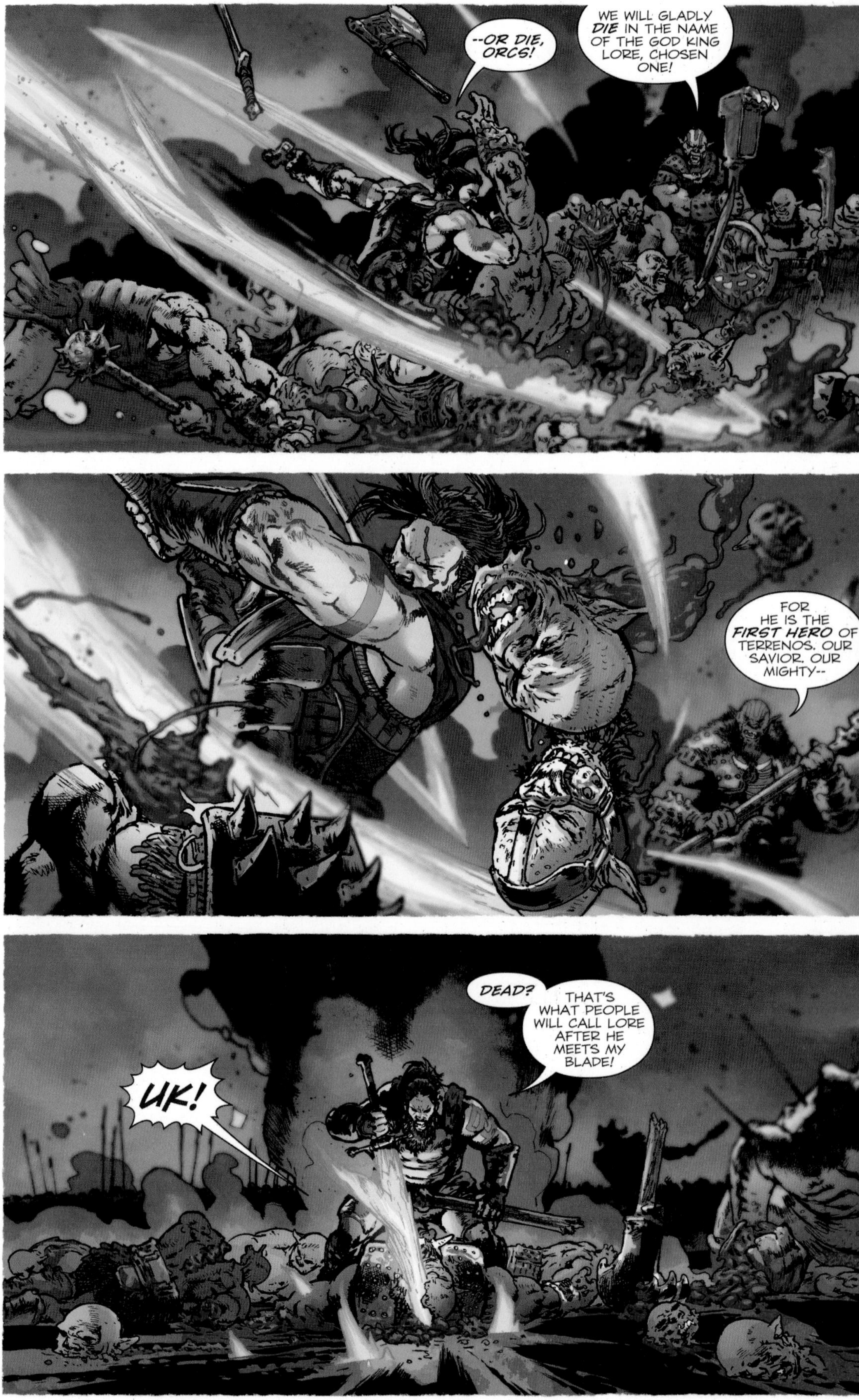
--OR DIE, ORCS!
WE WILL GLADLY DIE IN THE NAME OF THE GOD KING LORE, CHOSEN ONE!
FOR HE IS THE FIRST HERO OF TERRENOS. OUR SAVIOR. OUR MIGHTY--
DEAD?
THAT'S WHAT PEOPLE WILL CALL LORE AFTER HE MEETS MY BLADE!
UK!

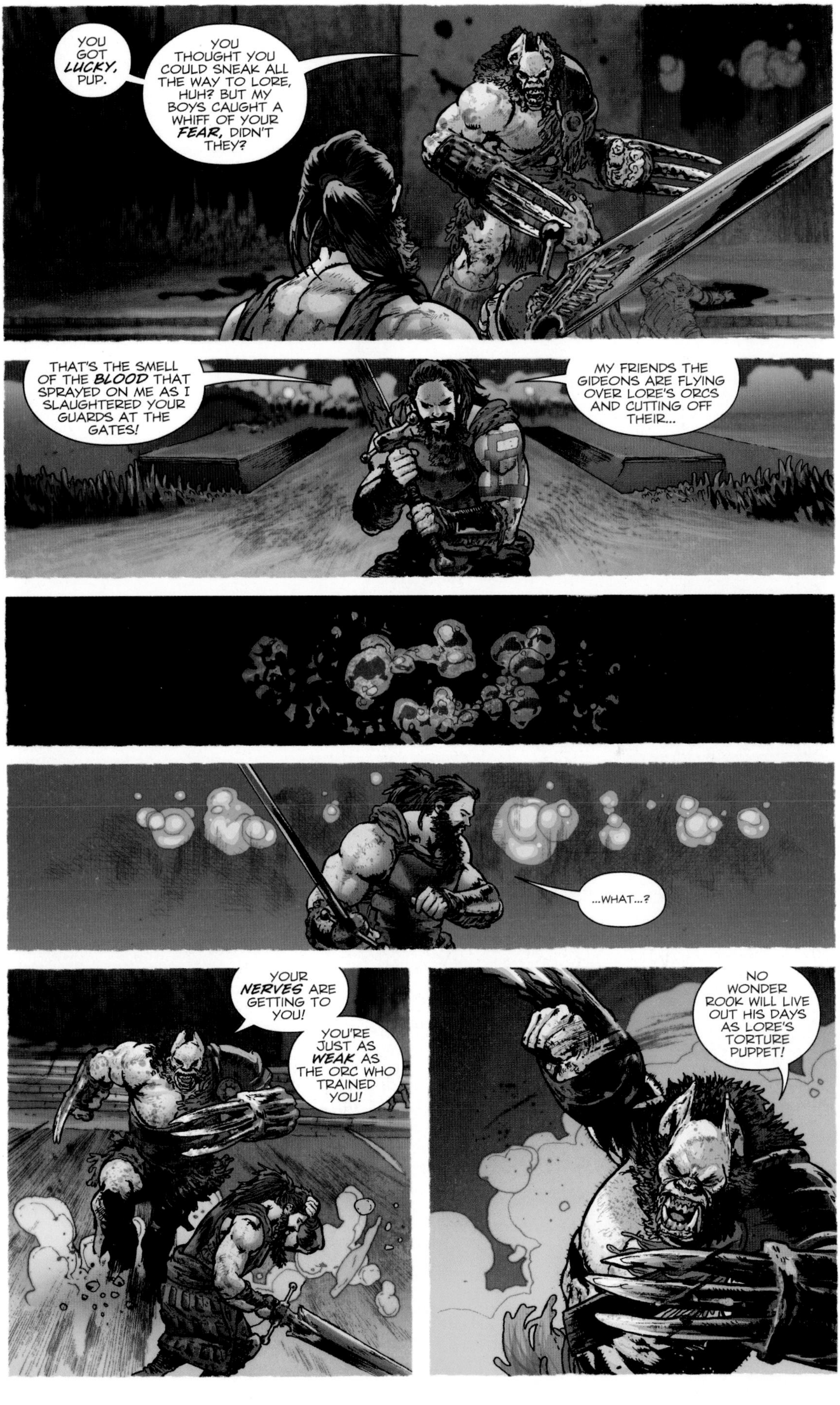
YOU GOT LUCKY, PUP.
YOU THOUGHT YOU COULD SNEAK ALL THE WAY TO LORE, HUH? BUT MY BOYS CAUGHT A WHIFF OF YOUR FEAR, DIDN'T THEY?
THAT'S THE SMELL OF THE BLOOD THAT SPRAYED ON ME AS I SLAUGHTERED YOUR GUARDS AT THE GATES!
MY FRIENDS THE GIDEONS ARE FLYING OVER LORE'S ORCS AND CUTTING OFF THEIR...
...WHAT...?
YOUR NERVES ARE GETTING TO YOU!
YOU'RE JUST AS WEAK AS THE ORC WHO TRAINED YOU!
NO WONDER ROOK WILL LIVE OUT HIS DAYS AS LORE'S TORTURE PUPPET!

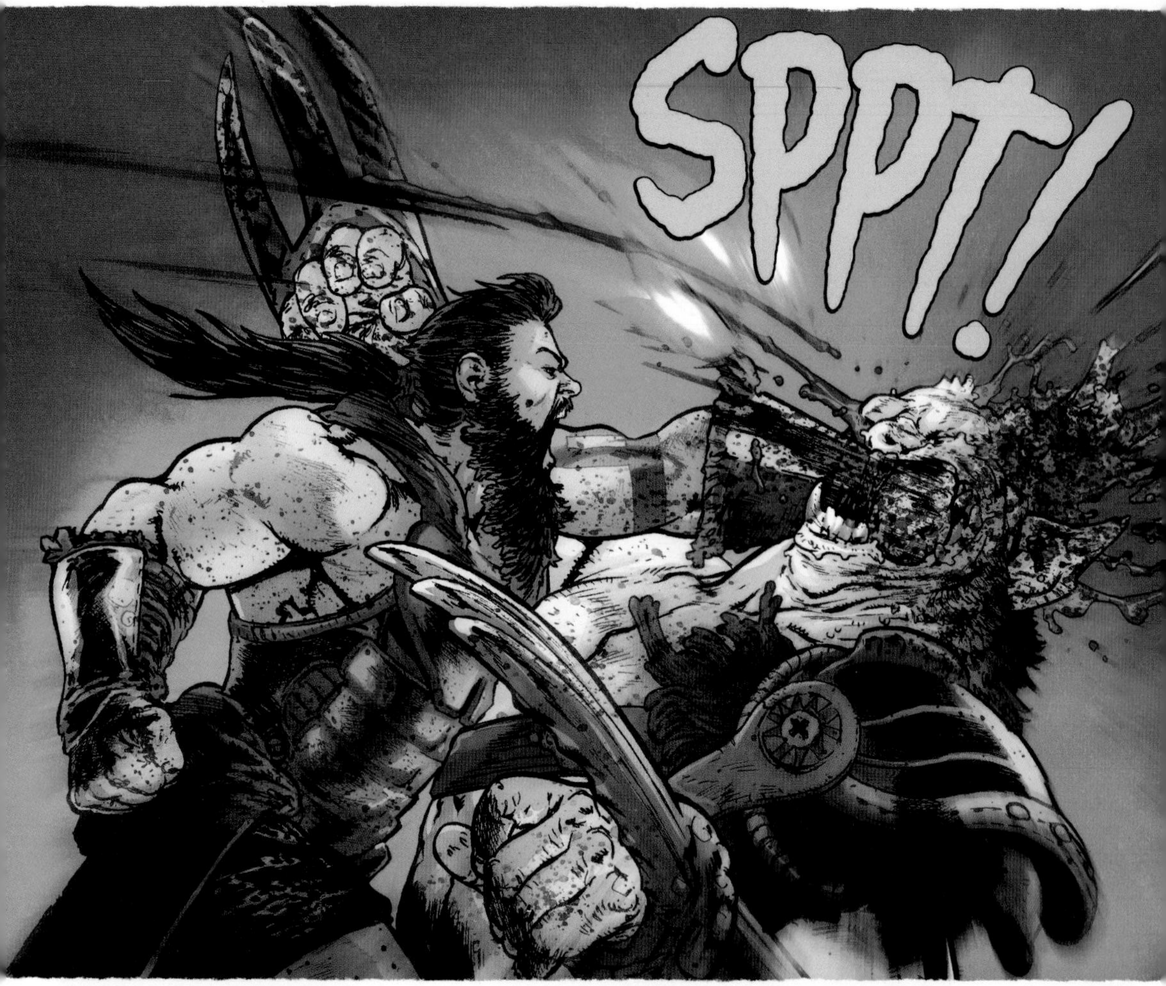
SPPT!!

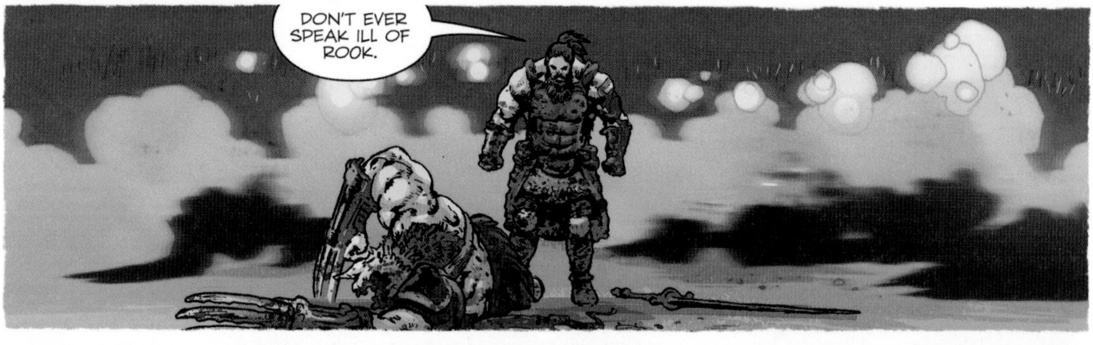
DON'T EVER SPEAK ILL OF ROOK.

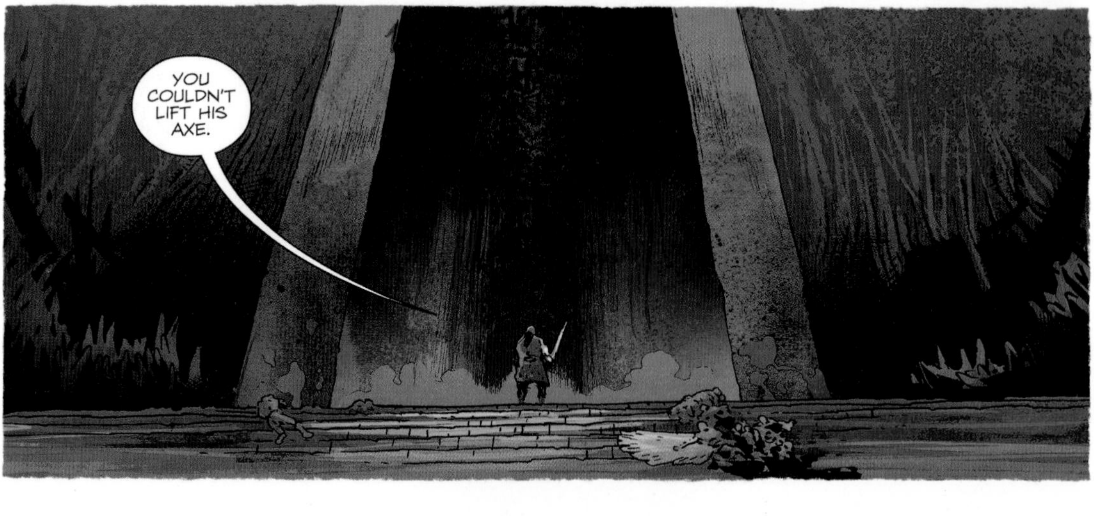
YOU COULDN'T LIFT HIS AXE.

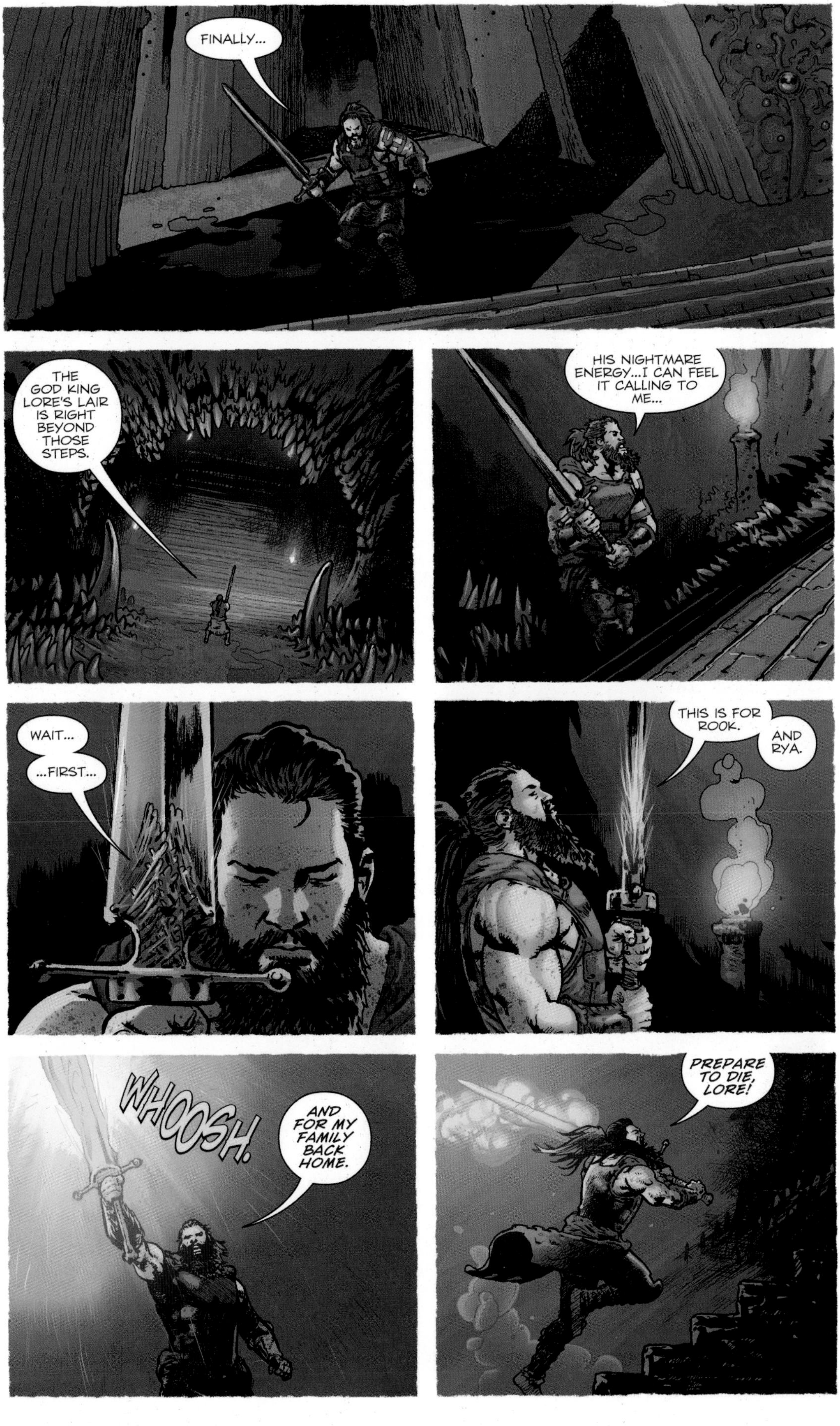
FINALLY...
THE GOD KING LORE'S LAIR IS RIGHT BEYOND THOSE STEPS.
HIS NIGHTMARE ENERGY...I CAN FEEL IT CALLING TO ME...
WAIT...
...FIRST...
THIS IS FOR ROOK.
AND RYA.
WHOOSH.
AND FOR MY FAMILY BACK HOME.
PREPARE TO DIE, LORE!

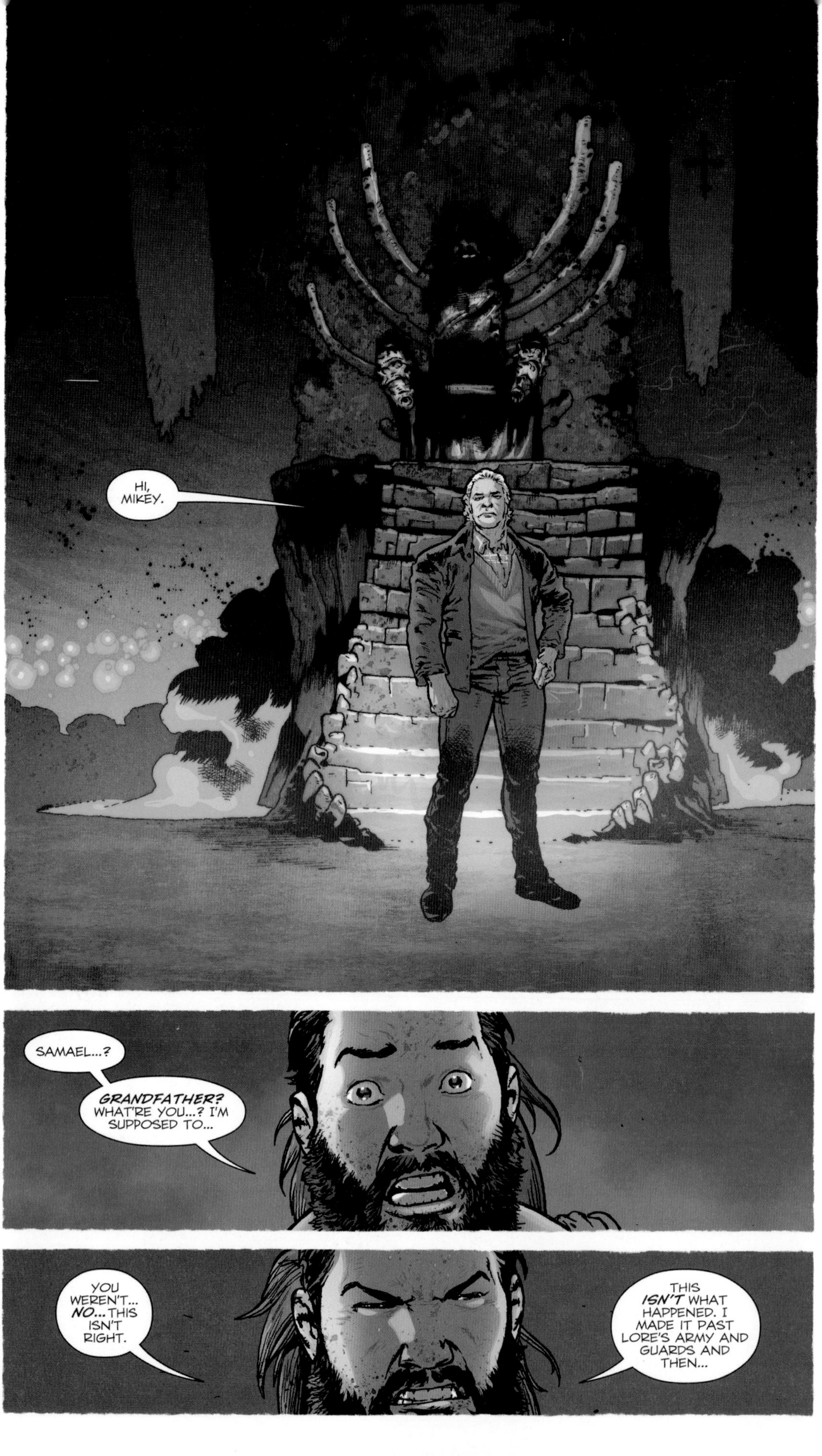
HI, MIKEY.
SAMAEL...?
GRANDFATHER? WHAT'RE YOU...? I'M SUPPOSED TO...
YOU WEREN'T... NO... THIS ISN'T RIGHT.
THIS ISN'T WHAT HAPPENED. I MADE IT PAST LORE'S ARMY AND GUARDS AND THEN...

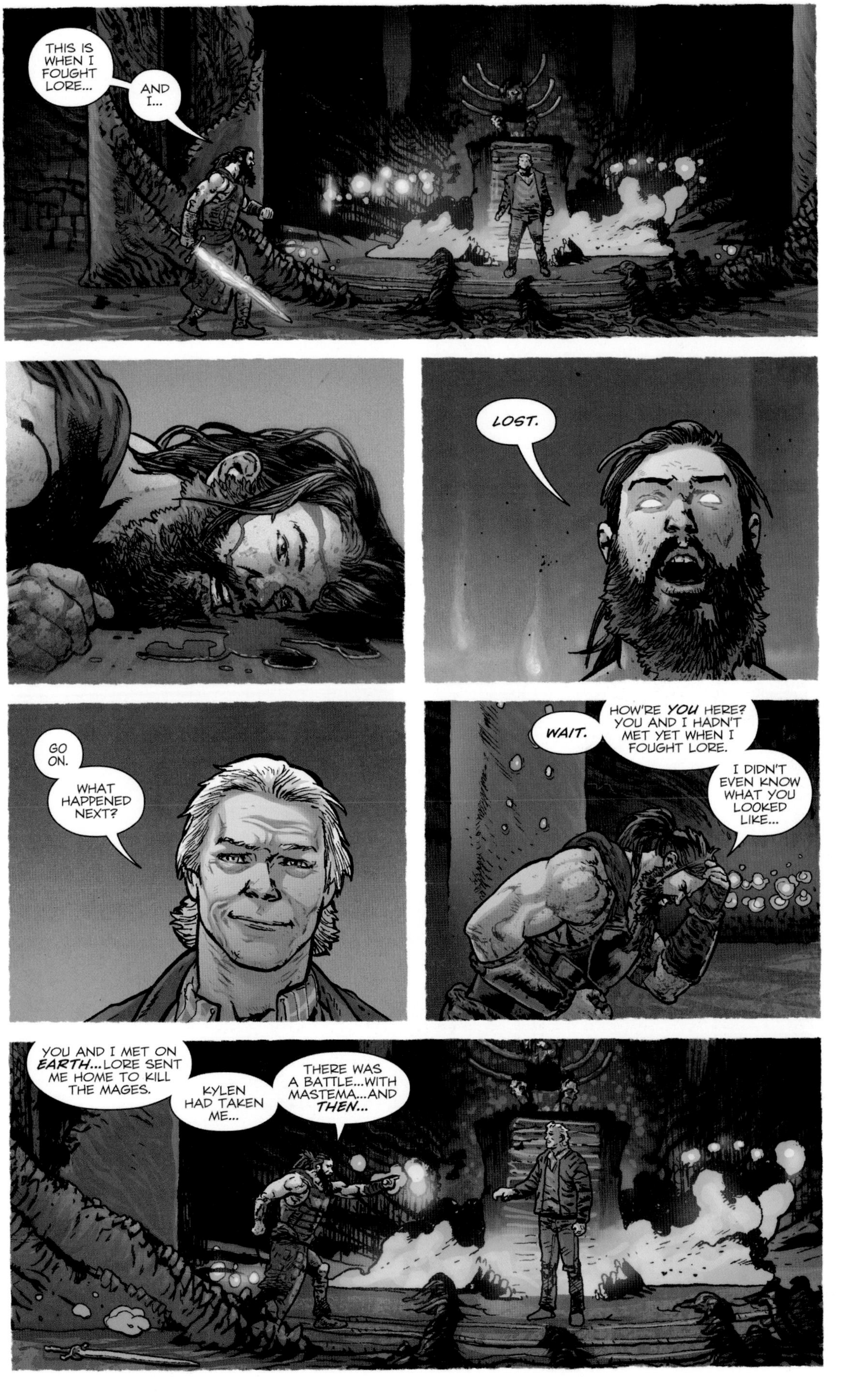
THIS IS WHEN I FOUGHT LORE...
AND I...
LOST.
GO ON.
WHAT HAPPENED NEXT?
WAIT.
HOW'RE YOU HERE? YOU AND I HADN'T MET YET WHEN I FOUGHT LORE.
I DIDN'T EVEN KNOW WHAT YOU LOOKED LIKE...
YOU AND I MET ON EARTH...LORE SENT ME HOME TO KILL THE MAGES.
KYLEN HAD TAKEN ME...
THERE WAS A BATTLE...WITH MASTEMA...AND THEN...

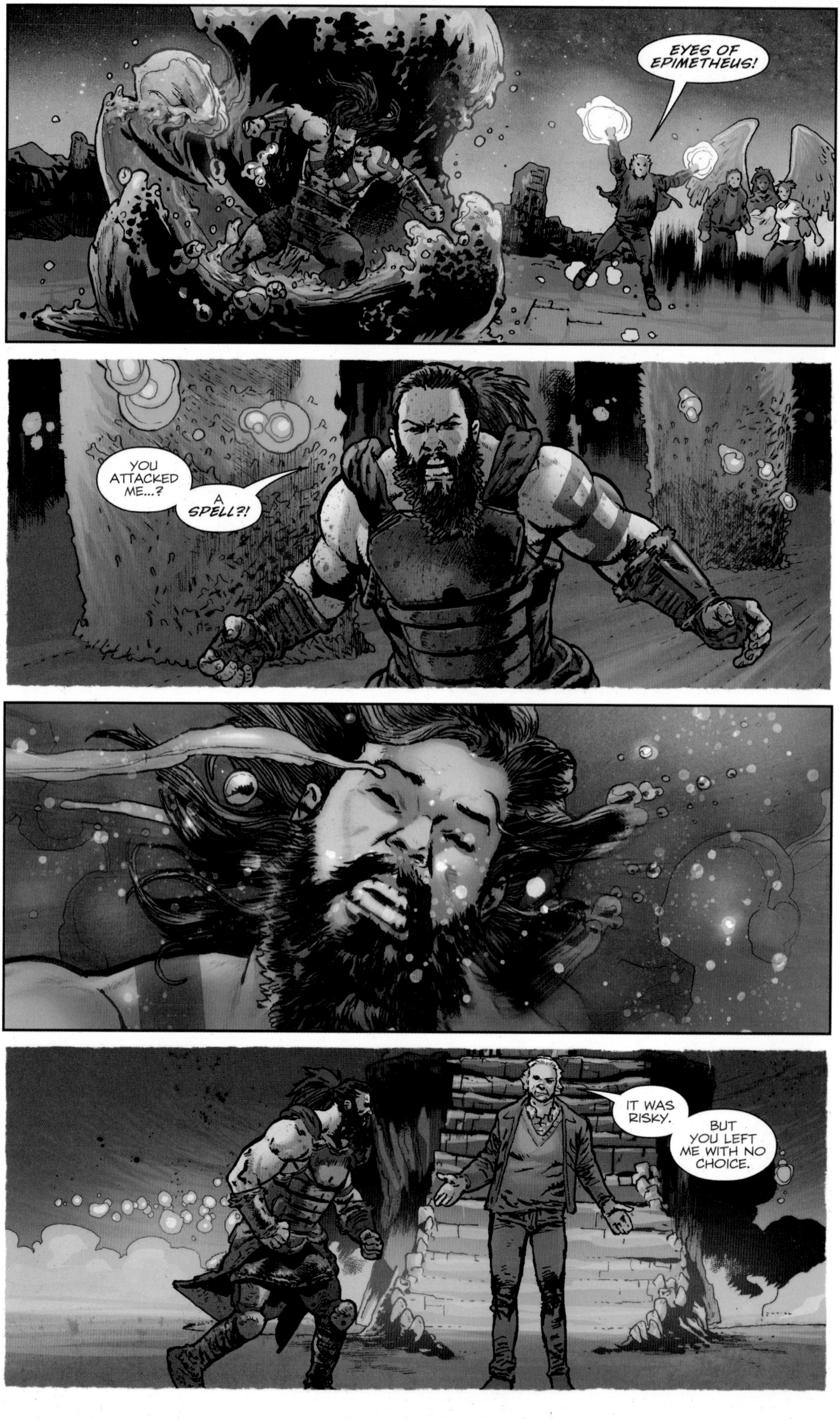
EYES OF EPIMETHEUS!
YOU ATTACKED ME...?
A SPELL?!
IT WAS RISKY.
BUT YOU LEFT ME WITH NO CHOICE.

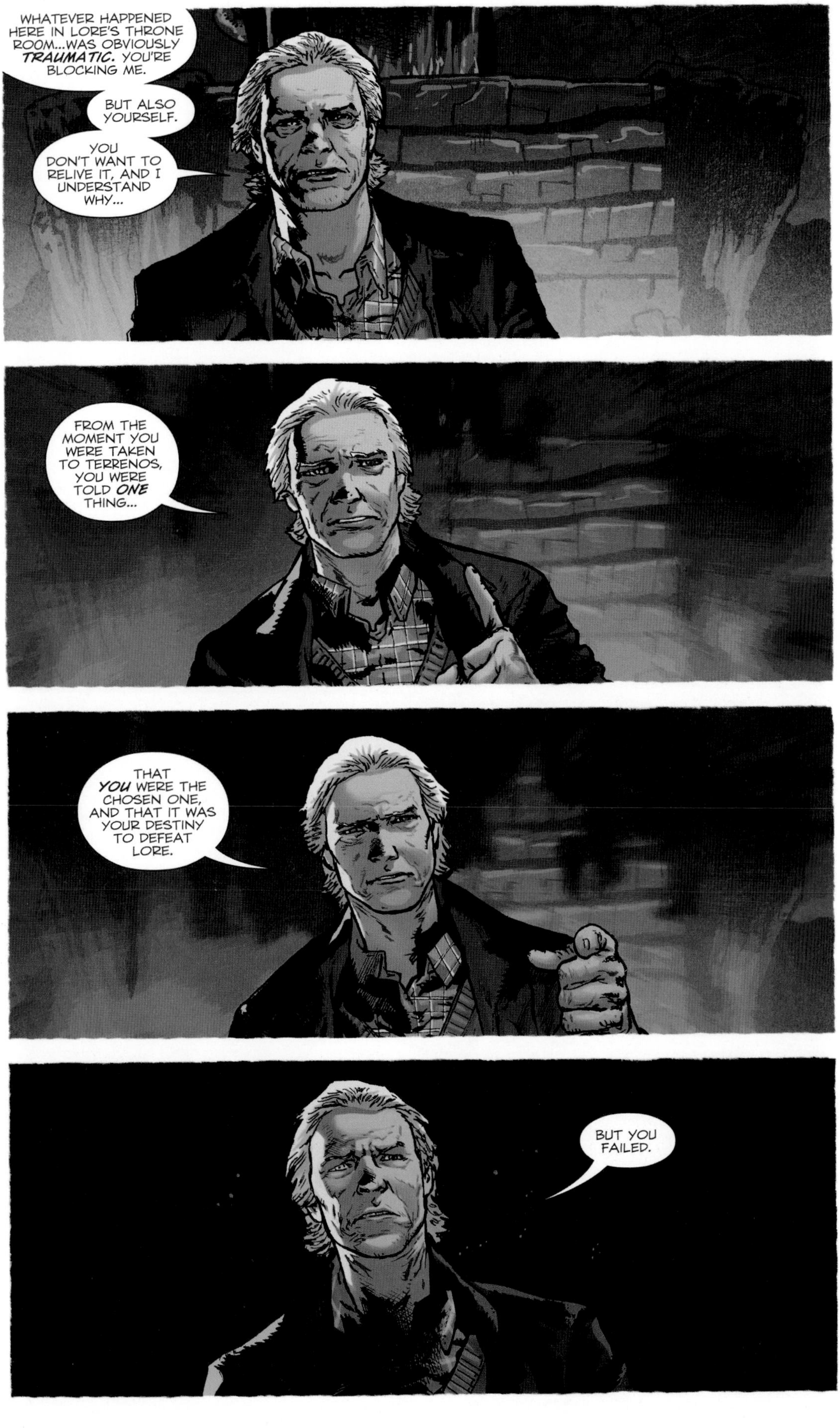
WHATEVER HAPPENED HERE IN LORE'S THRONE ROOM...WAS OBVIOUSLY TRAUMATIC. YOU'RE BLOCKING ME.
BUT ALSO YOURSELF.
YOU DON'T WANT TO RELIVE IT, AND I UNDERSTAND WHY...
FROM THE MOMENT YOU WERE TAKEN TO TERRENOS, YOU WERE TOLD ONE THING...
THAT YOU WERE THE CHOSEN ONE, AND THAT IT WAS YOUR DESTINY TO DEFEAT LORE.
BUT YOU FAILED.

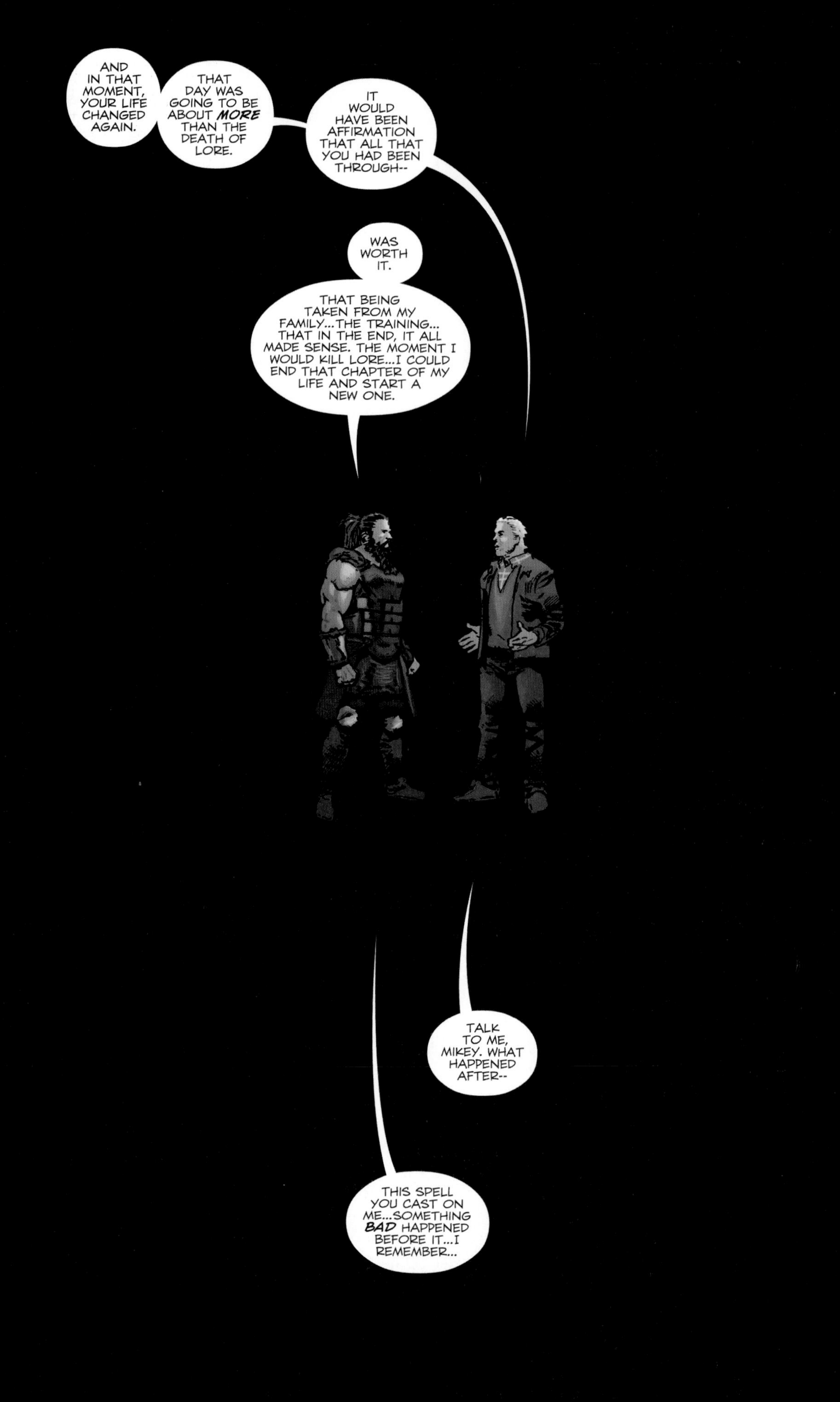
AND IN THAT MOMENT, YOUR LIFE CHANGED AGAIN.
THAT DAY WAS GOING TO BE ABOUT ***MORE*** THAN THE DEATH OF LORE.
IT WOULD HAVE BEEN AFFIRMATION THAT ALL THAT YOU HAD BEEN THROUGH--
WAS WORTH IT.
THAT BEING TAKEN FROM MY FAMILY...THE TRAINING... THAT IN THE END, IT ALL MADE SENSE. THE MOMENT I WOULD KILL LORE...I COULD END THAT CHAPTER OF MY LIFE AND START A NEW ONE.
TALK TO ME, MIKEY. WHAT HAPPENED AFTER--
THIS SPELL YOU CAST ON ME...SOMETHING ***BAD*** HAPPENED BEFORE IT...I REMEMBER...

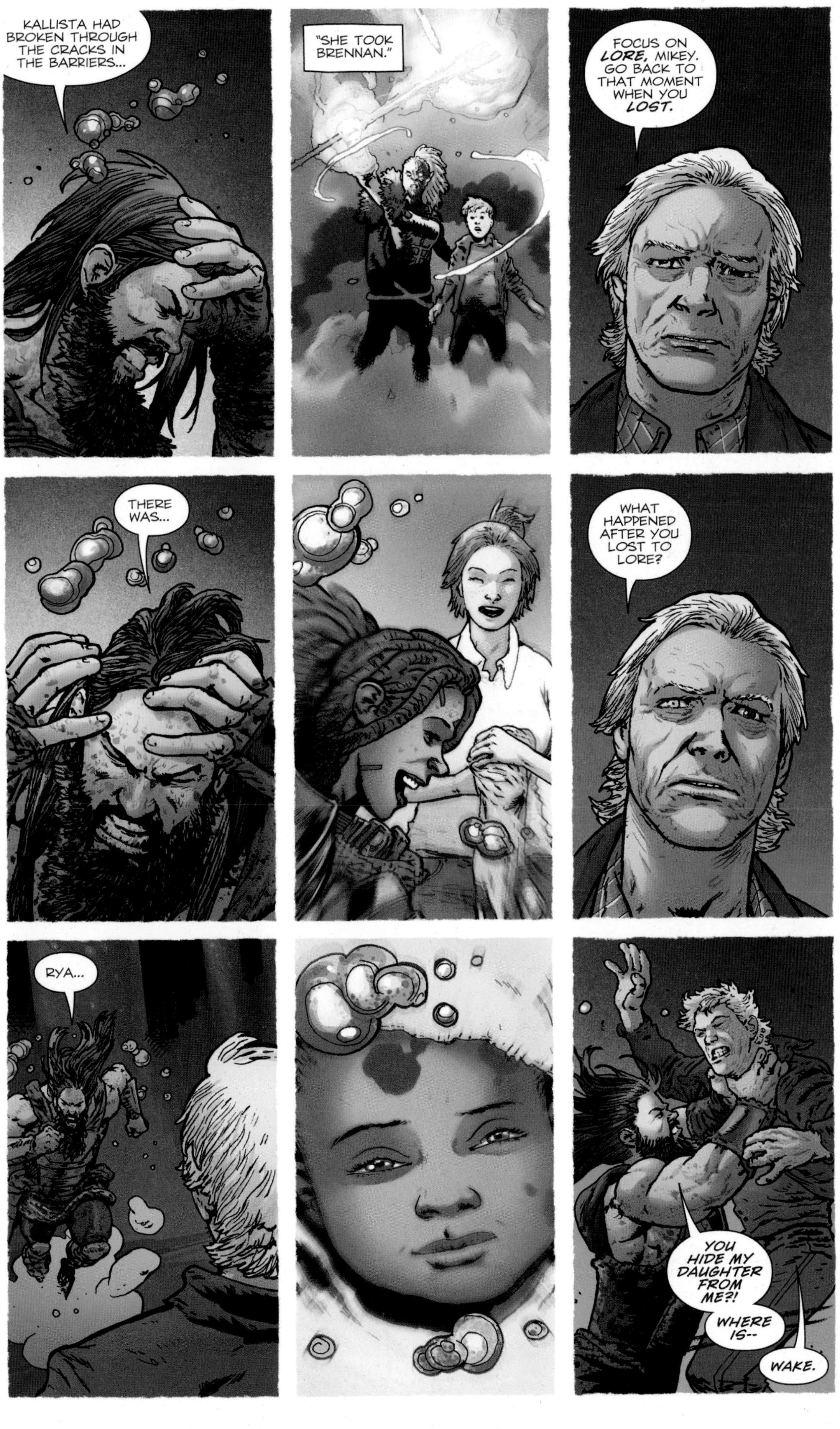
KALLISTA HAD BROKEN THROUGH THE CRACKS IN THE BARRIERS...
"SHE TOOK BRENNAN."
FOCUS ON LORE, MIKEY. GO BACK TO THAT MOMENT WHEN YOU LOST.
THERE WAS...
WHAT HAPPENED AFTER YOU LOST TO LORE?
RYA...
YOU HIDE MY DAUGHTER FROM ME?!
WHERE IS--
WAKE.

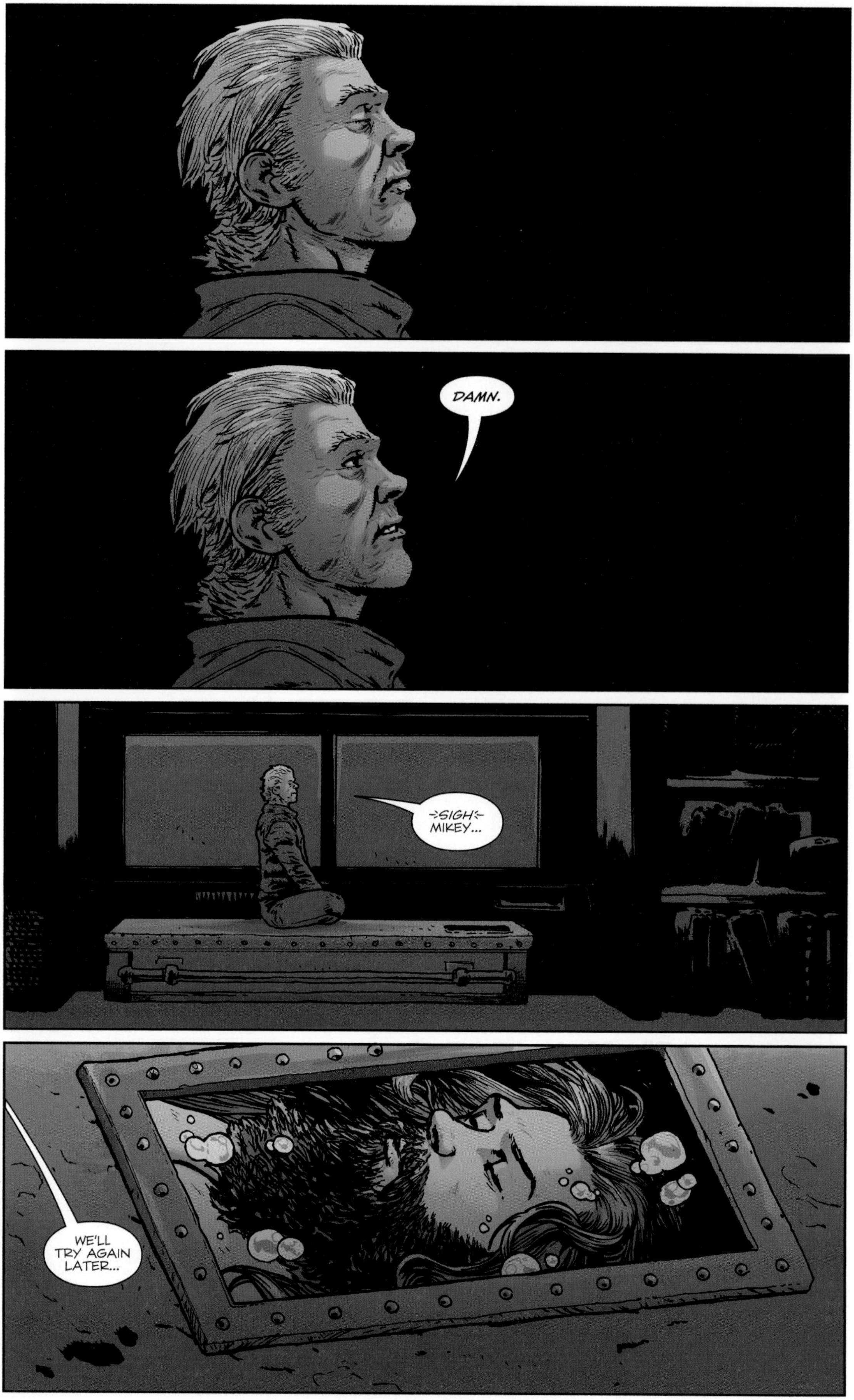
DAMN.
-SIGH- MIKEY...
WE'LL TRY AGAIN LATER...

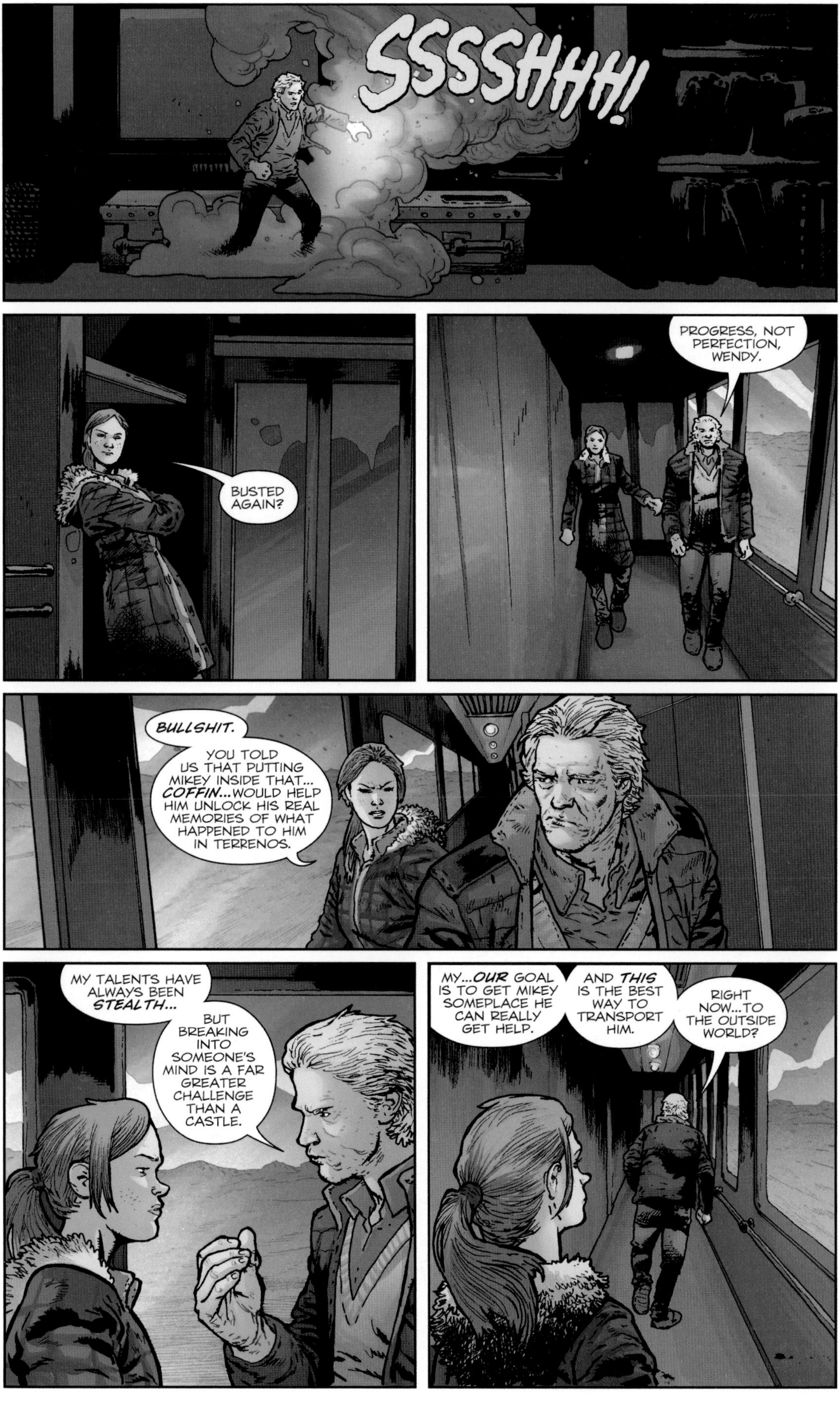
SSSSHHH!
BUSTED AGAIN?
PROGRESS, NOT PERFECTION, WENDY.
BULLSHIT.
YOU TOLD US THAT PUTTING MIKEY INSIDE THAT... COFFIN...WOULD HELP HIM UNLOCK HIS REAL MEMORIES OF WHAT HAPPENED TO HIM IN TERRENOS.
MY TALENTS HAVE ALWAYS BEEN STEALTH...
BUT BREAKING INTO SOMEONE'S MIND IS A FAR GREATER CHALLENGE THAN A CASTLE.
MY...OUR GOAL IS TO GET MIKEY SOMEPLACE HE CAN REALLY GET HELP.
AND THIS IS THE BEST WAY TO TRANSPORT HIM.
RIGHT NOW...TO THE OUTSIDE WORLD?

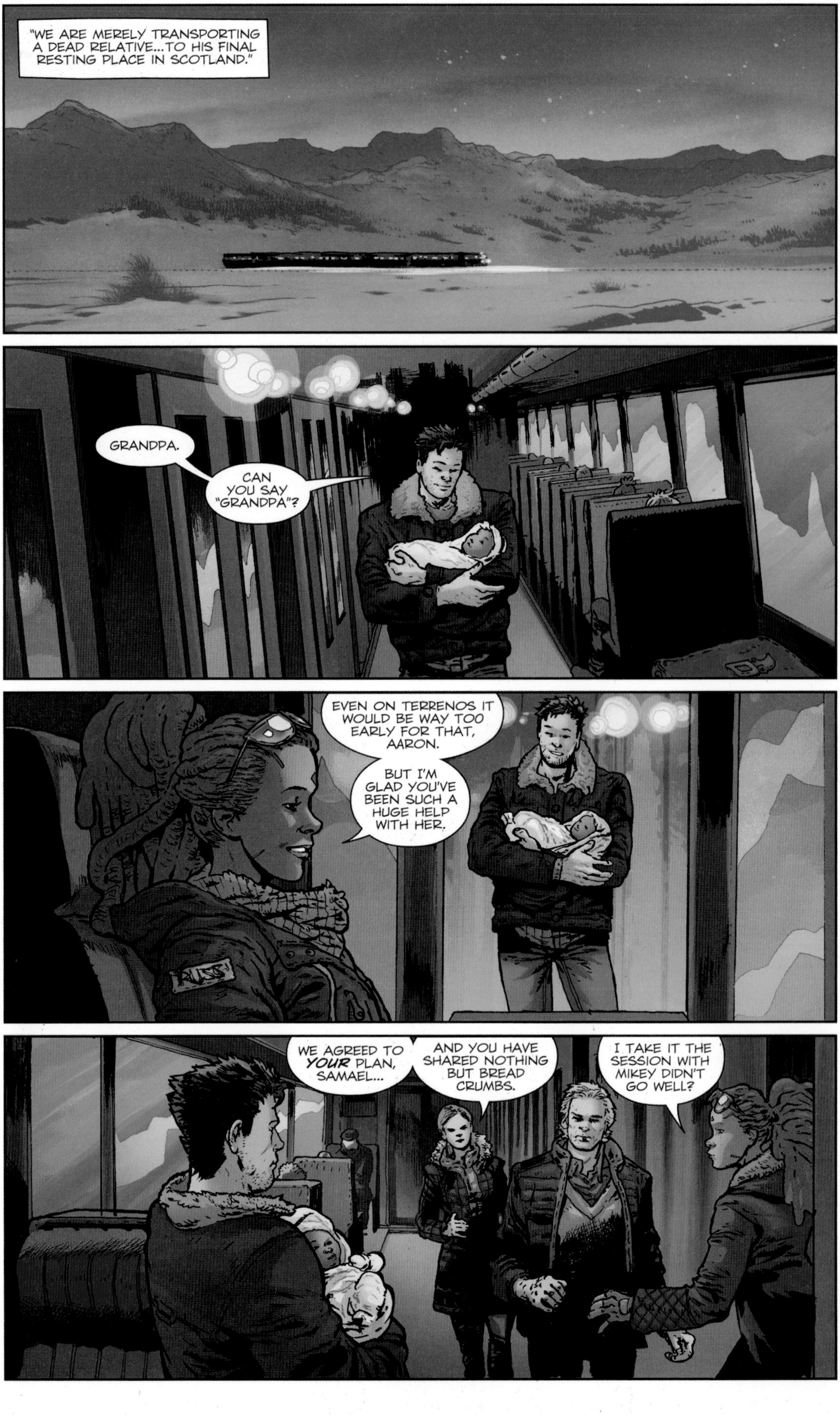
"WE ARE MERELY TRANSPORTING A DEAD RELATIVE...TO HIS FINAL RESTING PLACE IN SCOTLAND."
GRANDPA.
CAN YOU SAY "GRANDPA"?
EVEN ON TERRENOS IT WOULD BE WAY TOO EARLY FOR THAT, AARON.
BUT I'M GLAD YOU'VE BEEN SUCH A HUGE HELP WITH HER.
WE AGREED TO *YOUR* PLAN, SAMAEL...
AND YOU HAVE SHARED NOTHING BUT BREAD CRUMBS.
I TAKE IT THE SESSION WITH MIKEY DIDN'T GO WELL?

WE AGREED TO STAY TOGETHER AS A *FAMILY* TO HELP MIKEY...

AND YOU PROMISED THIS WOULD HELP US FIND KALLISTA AND *BRENNAN*, AS WELL.

AND WE WILL. I PROMISE YOU.

WE KNOW THAT MIKEY WAS SENT TO EARTH ON A MISSION BY LORE...TO KILL ALL THE MAGES.

BUT ONLY YOU AND MASTEMA ARE LEFT.

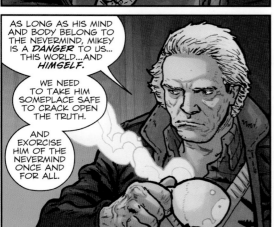

AS LONG AS HIS MIND AND BODY BELONG TO THE NEVERMIND, MIKEY IS A *DANGER* TO US... THIS WORLD...AND *HIMSELF.*

WE NEED TO TAKE HIM SOMEPLACE SAFE TO CRACK OPEN THE TRUTH.

AND EXORCISE HIM OF THE NEVERMIND ONCE AND FOR ALL.

AND THAT'S IN SCOTLAND?

BEFORE, WHEN I WAS ON TERRENOS, I TOLD THE OTHER MAGES THAT THERE WAS *NO* MAGIC ON EARTH.

BUT... *THERE IS.*

BECAUSE OF KNOWN LEGENDS AND MYTHS, I COULD ALREADY GUESS A FEW HERE AND THERE. SO, AFTER WE CLOSED THE PORTAL TO TERRENOS, I STARTED TO EXPLORE *THIS* WORLD.

MANY WERE *FALSE,* THEY REMAINED MYTHS. AND SOME WERE REAL.

AND THEN I FOUND A PLACE...

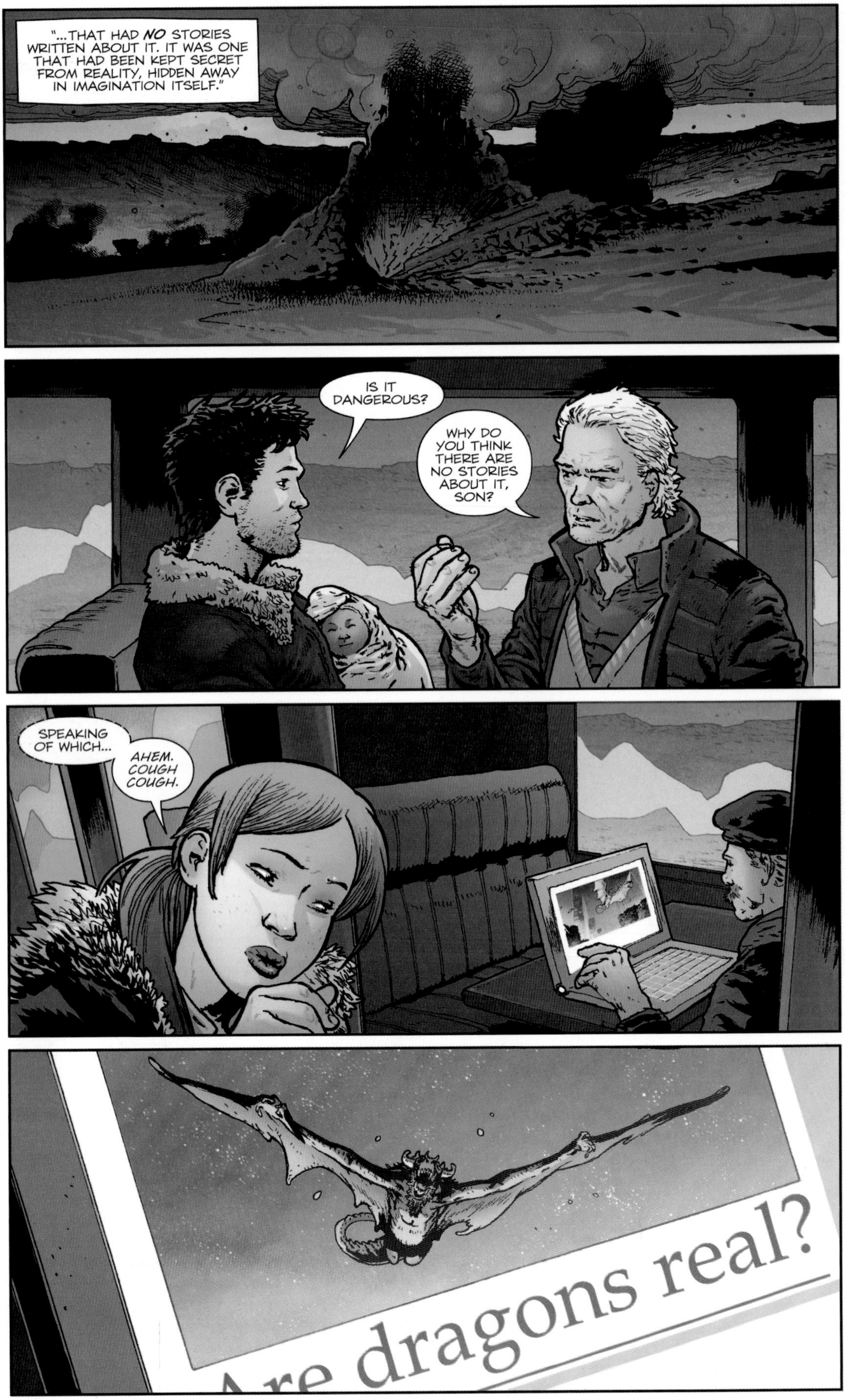
"...THAT HAD NO STORIES WRITTEN ABOUT IT. IT WAS ONE THAT HAD BEEN KEPT SECRET FROM REALITY, HIDDEN AWAY IN IMAGINATION ITSELF."
IS IT DANGEROUS?
WHY DO YOU THINK THERE ARE NO STORIES ABOUT IT, SON?
SPEAKING OF WHICH...
AHEM. COUGH COUGH.
Are dragons real?

YOUR WORLD IS CATCHING UP.

DOESN'T MATTER. IF PEOPLE FIND PROOF OF BIGFOOT, *THEN* WE WORRY.

ENOUGH OF THE BARRIER BETWEEN THIS WORLD AND TERRENOS STILL STANDS.

I CAN PROTECT AND HIDE US FROM *MOST* MAGIC. I DID IT FOR YEARS IN MY BUNKER...

...IF *ANYTHING* MAGICAL TRIES TO COME AFTER US, MY DEFENSE SPELLS WILL LET ME KNOW *FAR* IN ADVANCE.

YOU SURE THAT'S THE TRAIN?

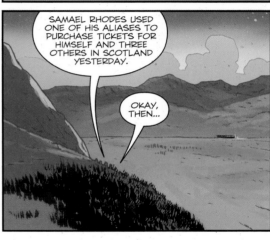

SAMAEL RHODES USED ONE OF HIS ALIASES TO PURCHASE TICKETS FOR HIMSELF AND THREE OTHERS IN SCOTLAND YESTERDAY.

OKAY, THEN...

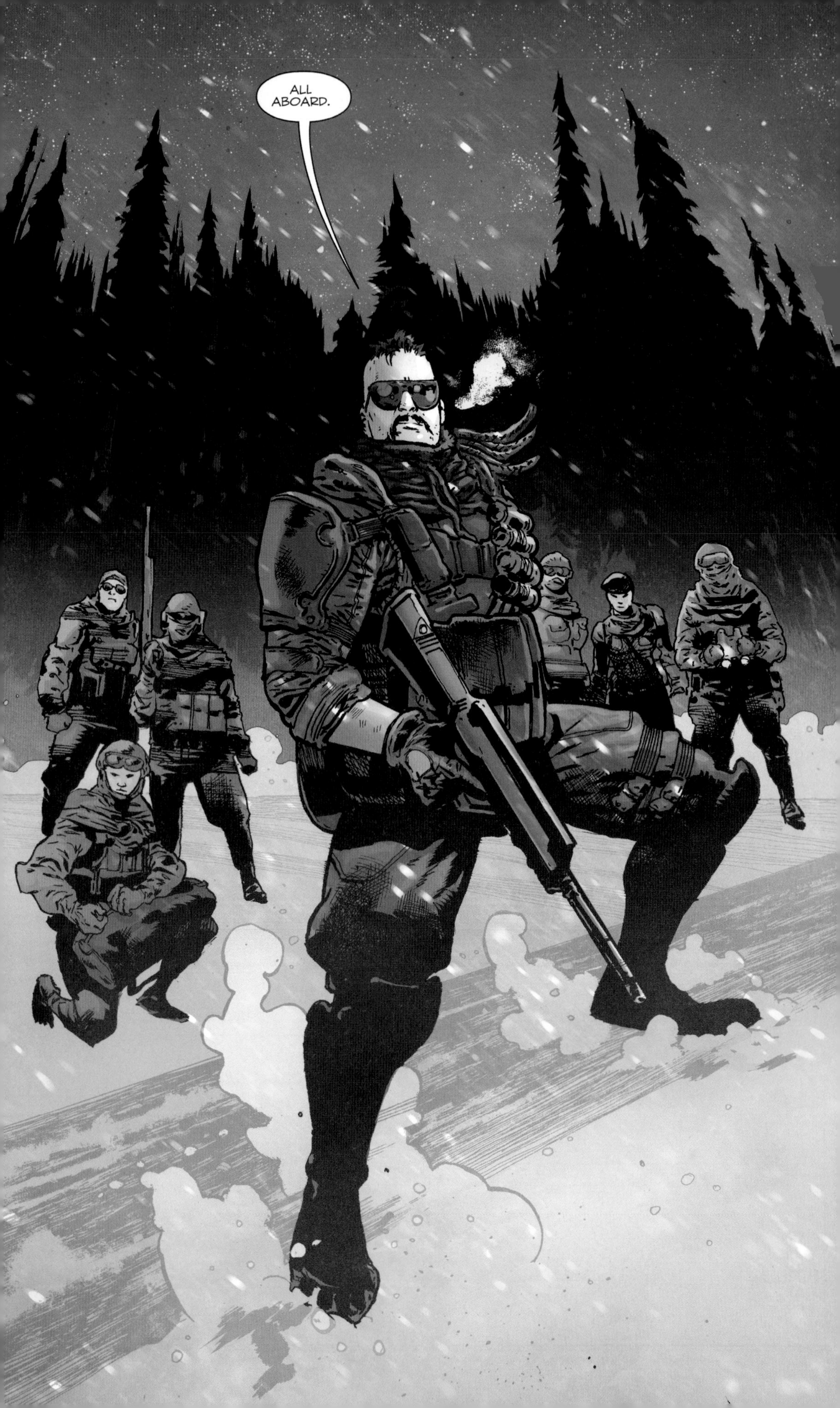
ALL ABOARD.

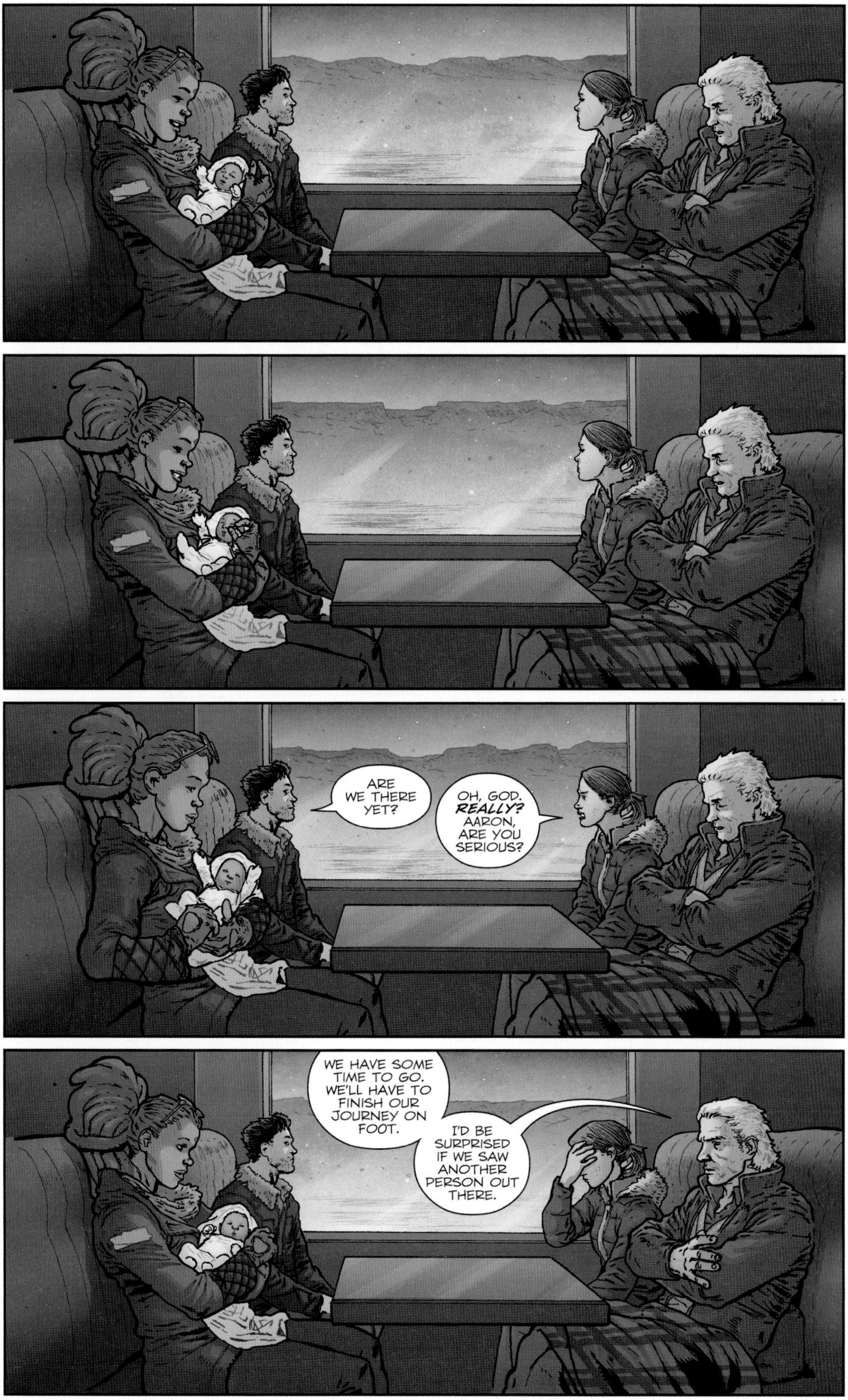
ARE WE THERE YET?
OH, GOD. *REALLY?* AARON, ARE YOU SERIOUS?
WE HAVE SOME TIME TO GO. WE'LL HAVE TO FINISH OUR JOURNEY ON FOOT.
I'D BE SURPRISED IF WE SAW ANOTHER PERSON OUT THERE.

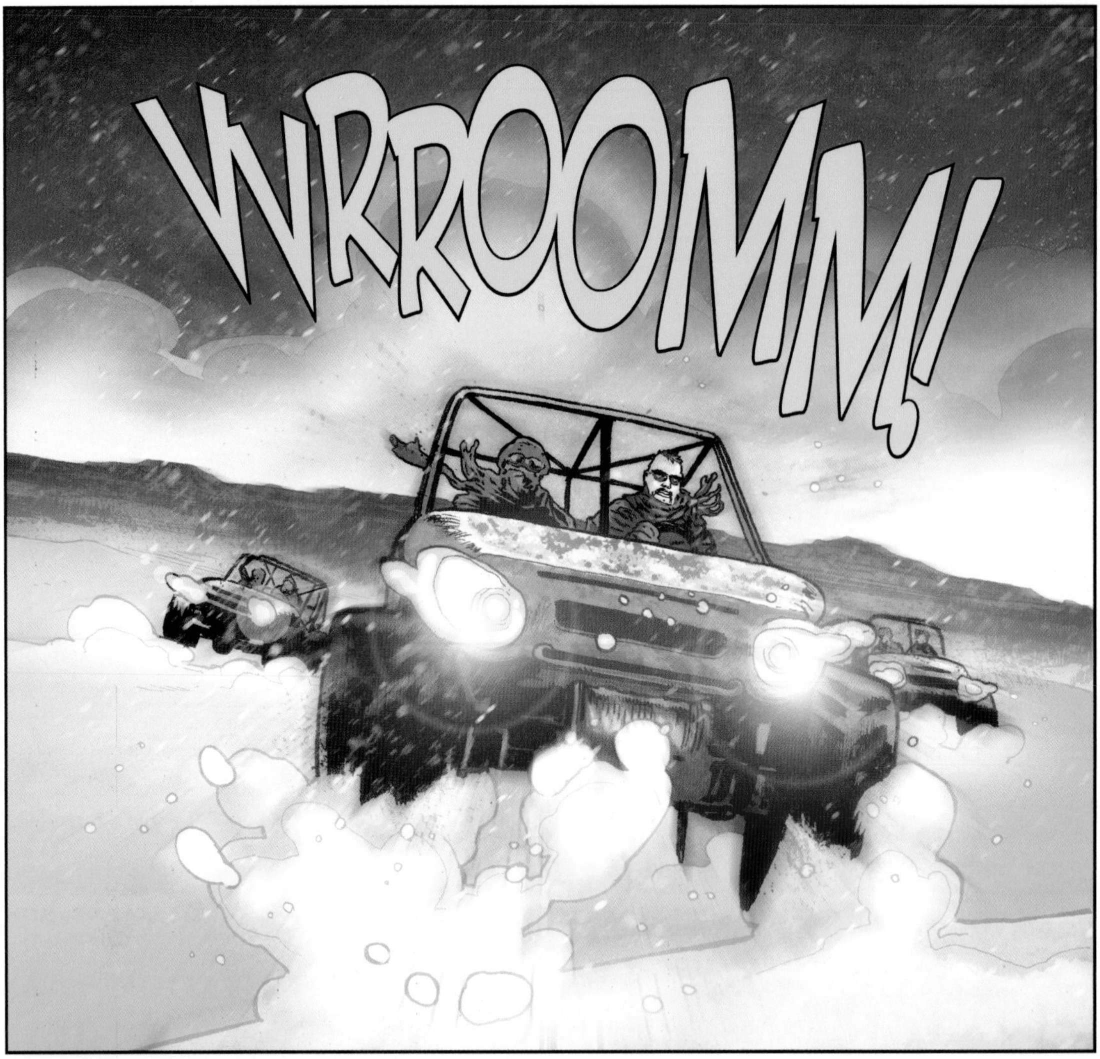
WRROOMM!

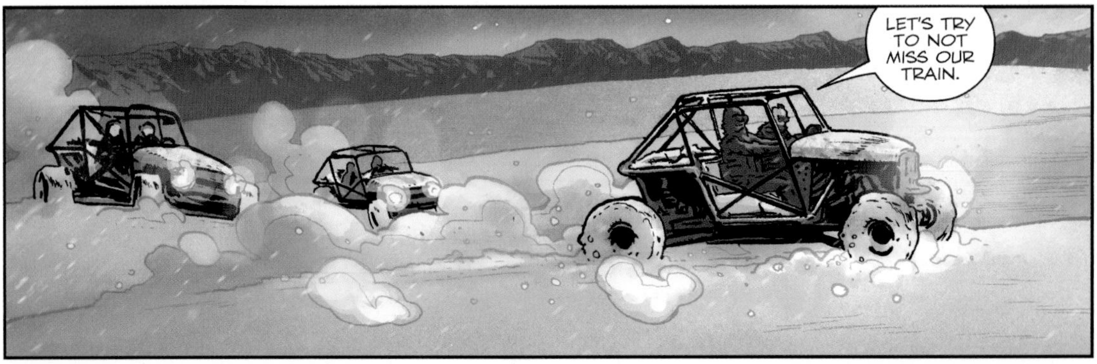
LET'S TRY TO NOT MISS OUR TRAIN.

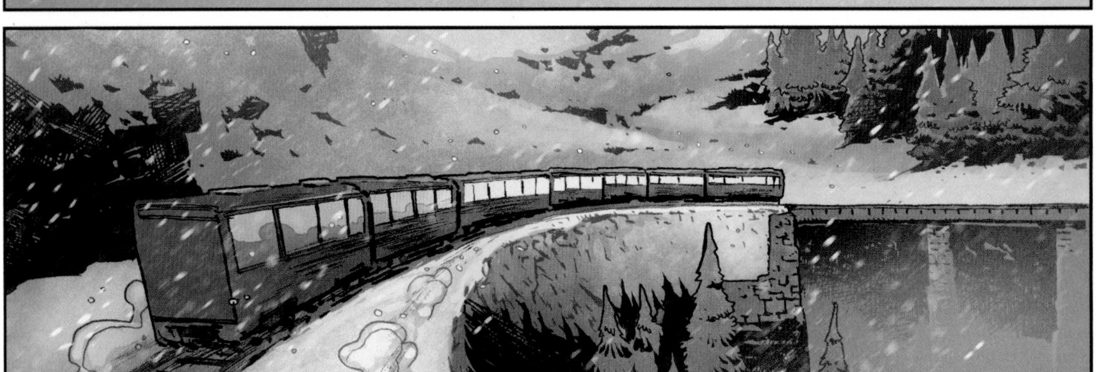

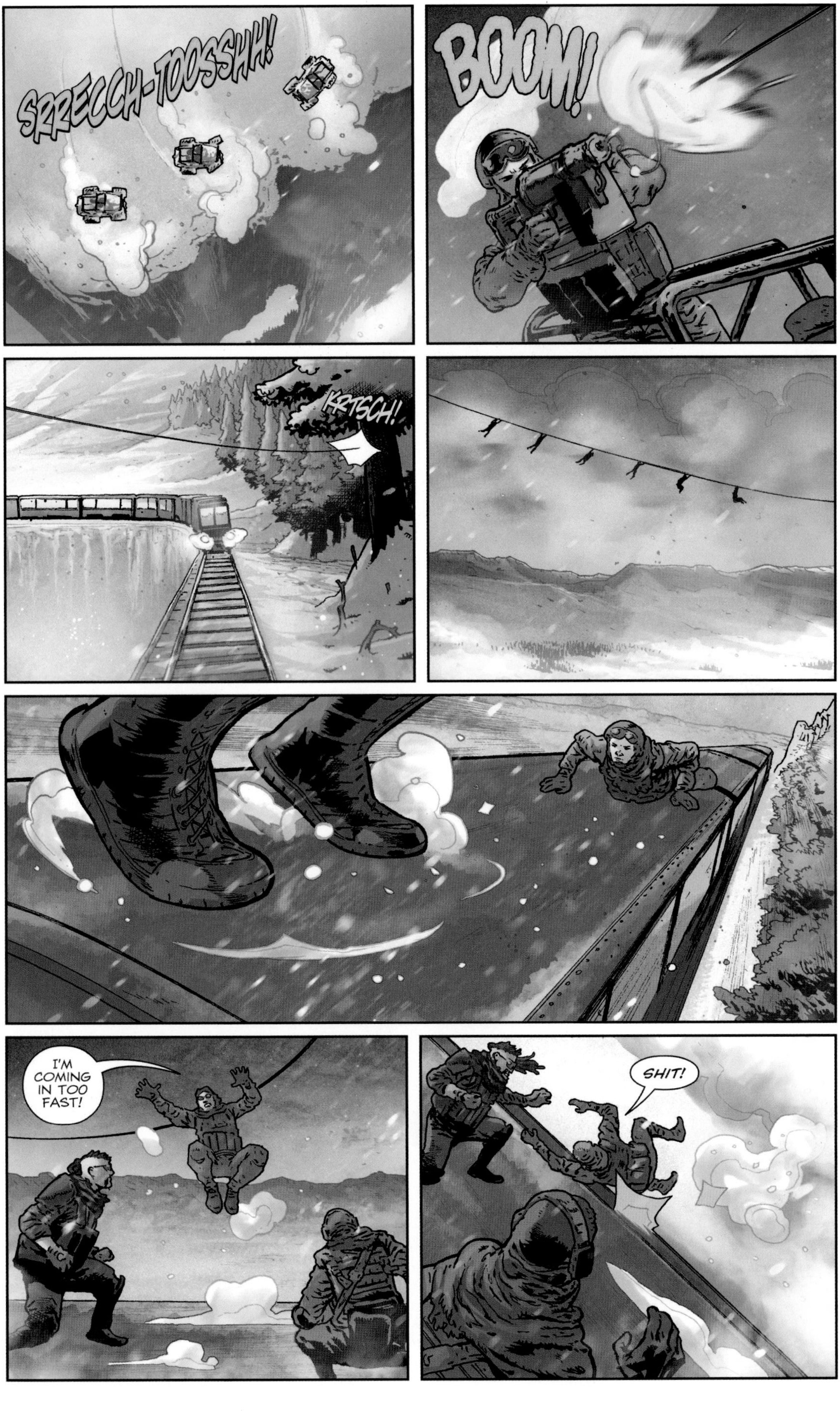
SRRECCH-TOOSSHH!
BOOM!
KRTSCH!
I'M COMING IN TOO FAST!
SHIT!

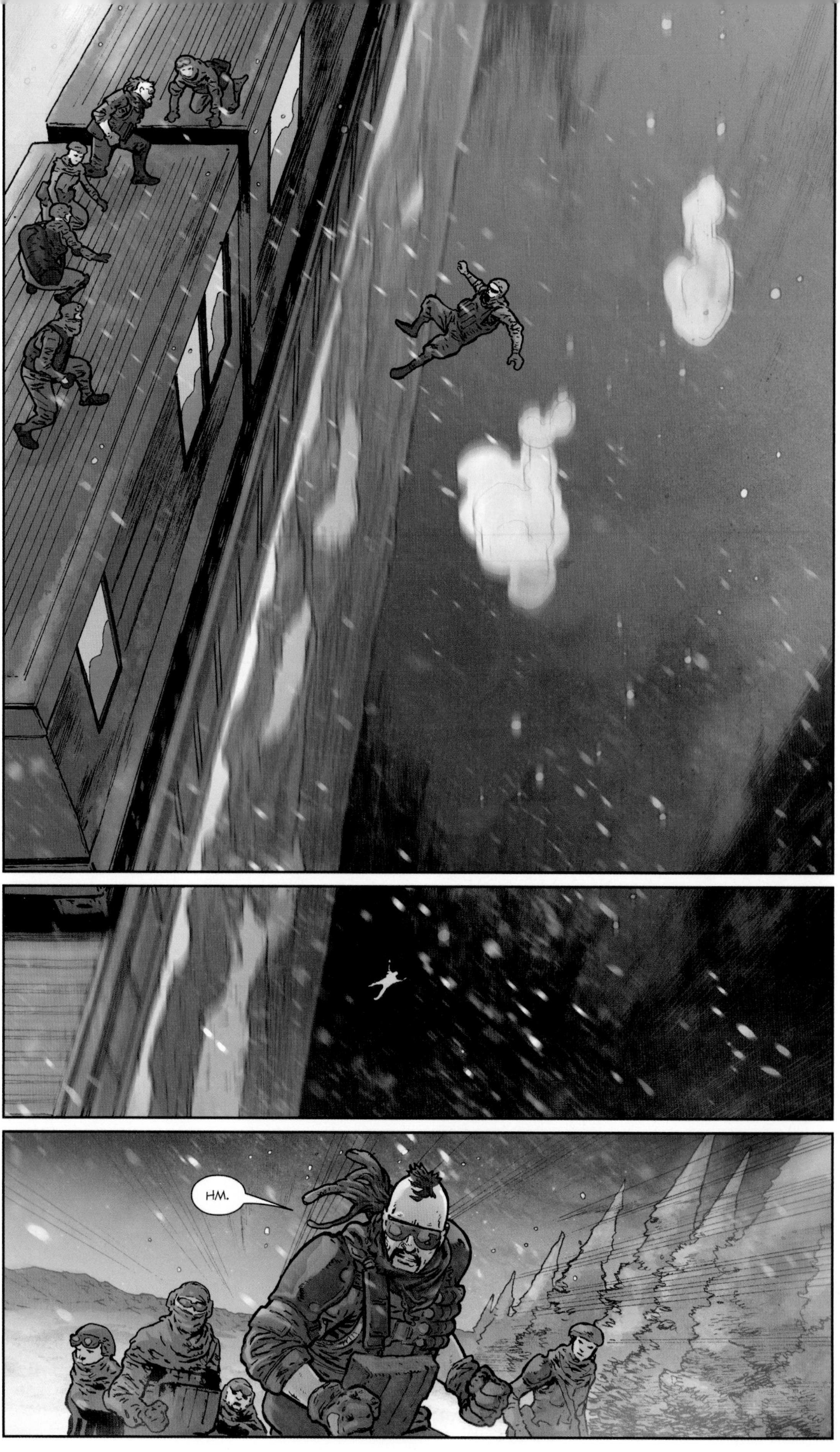
HM.

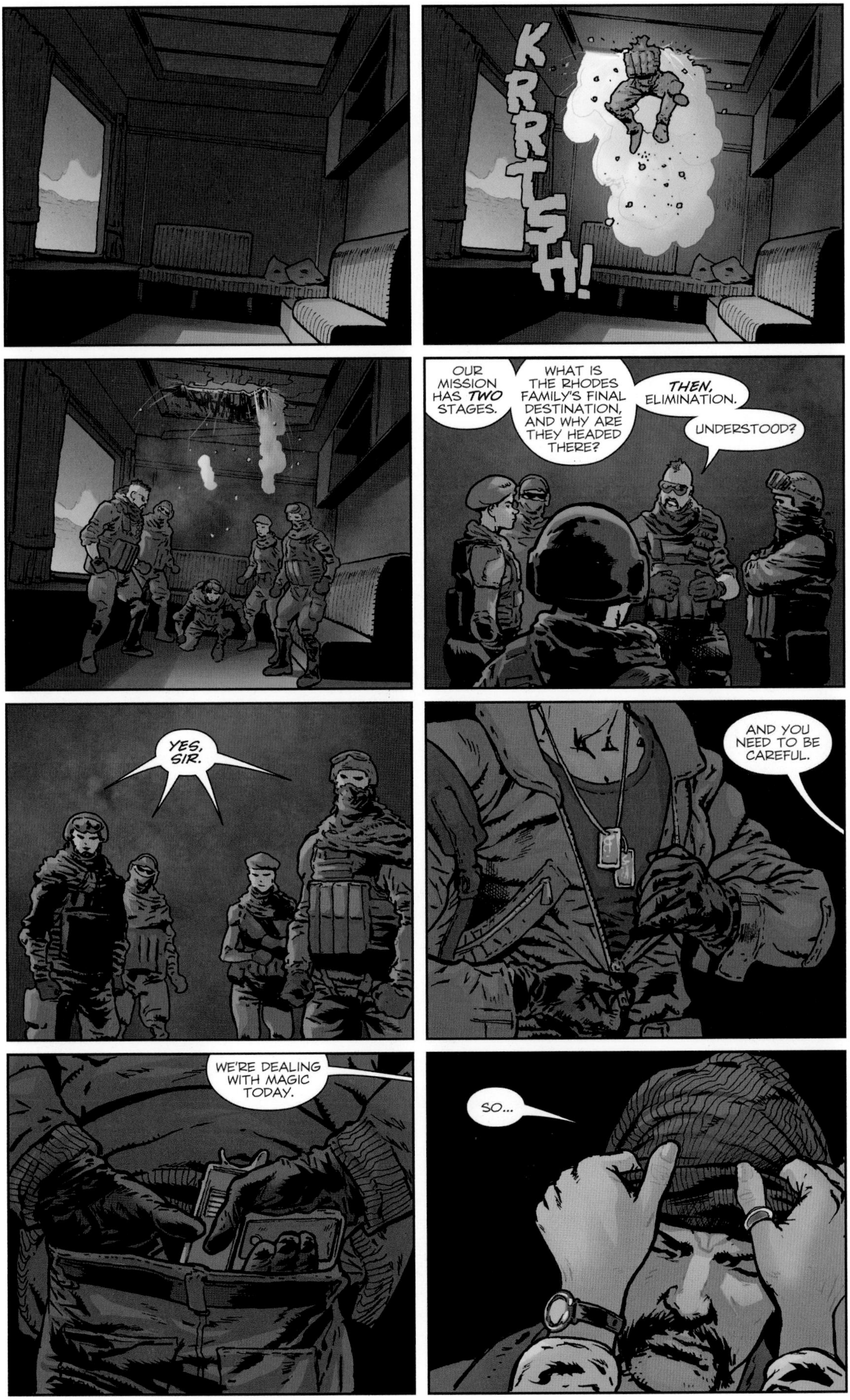
KRRTSH!
OUR MISSION HAS TWO STAGES.
WHAT IS THE RHODES FAMILY'S FINAL DESTINATION, AND WHY ARE THEY HEADED THERE?
THEN, ELIMINATION.
UNDERSTOOD?
YES, SIR.
AND YOU NEED TO BE CAREFUL.
WE'RE DEALING WITH MAGIC TODAY.
SO...

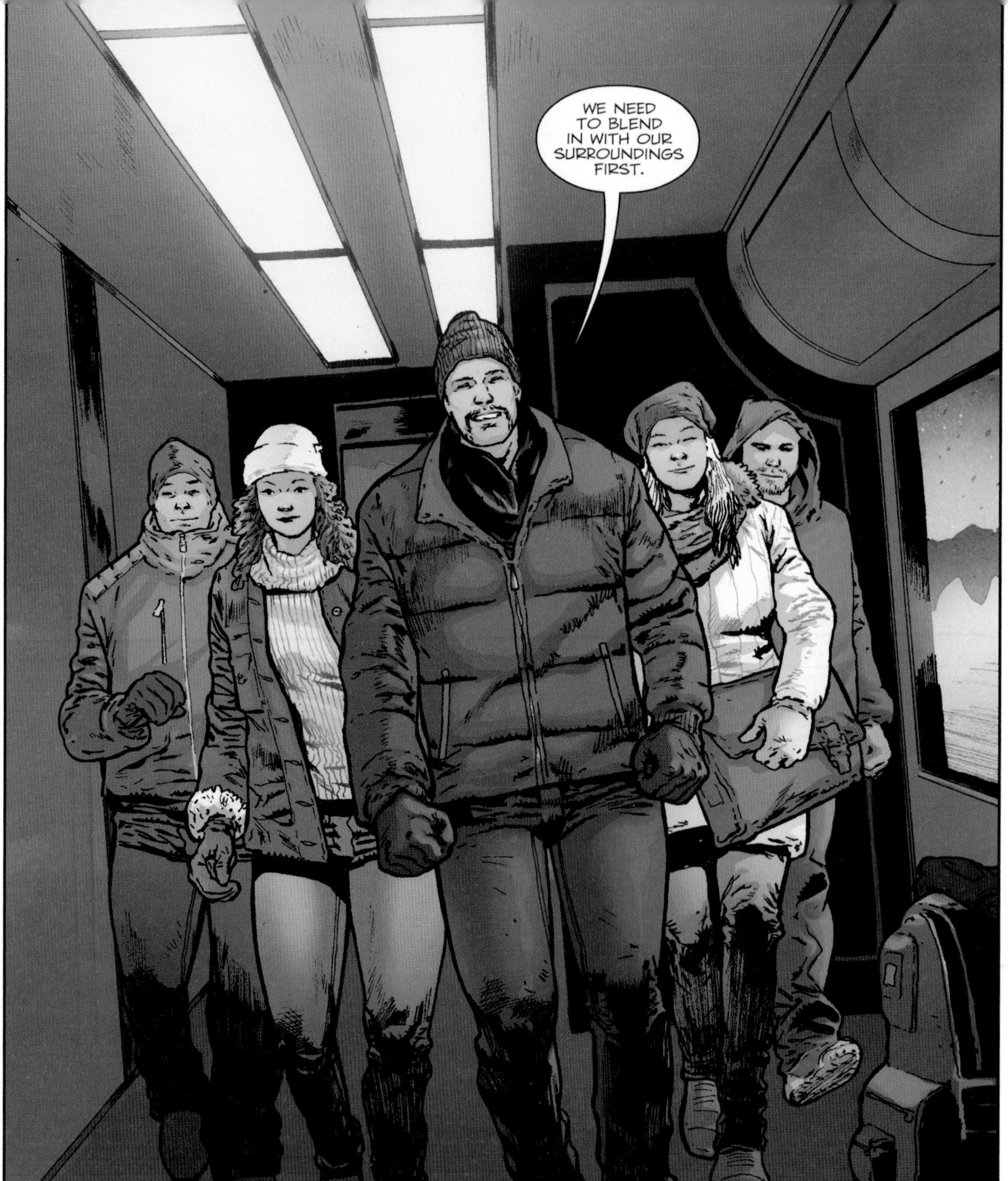
WE NEED TO BLEND IN WITH OUR SURROUNDINGS FIRST.

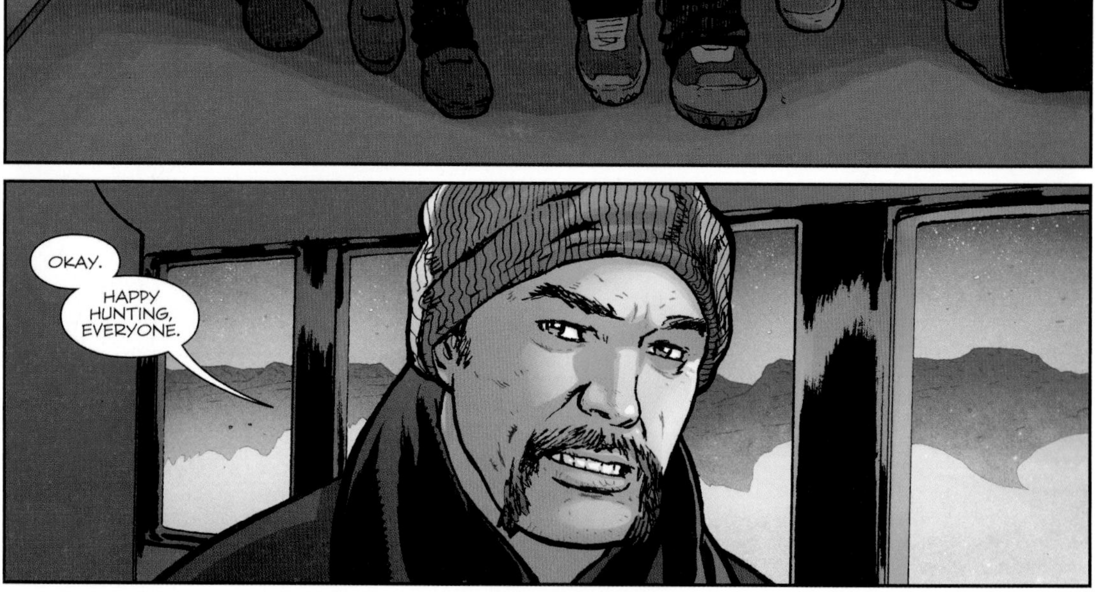
OKAY.
HAPPY HUNTING, EVERYONE.

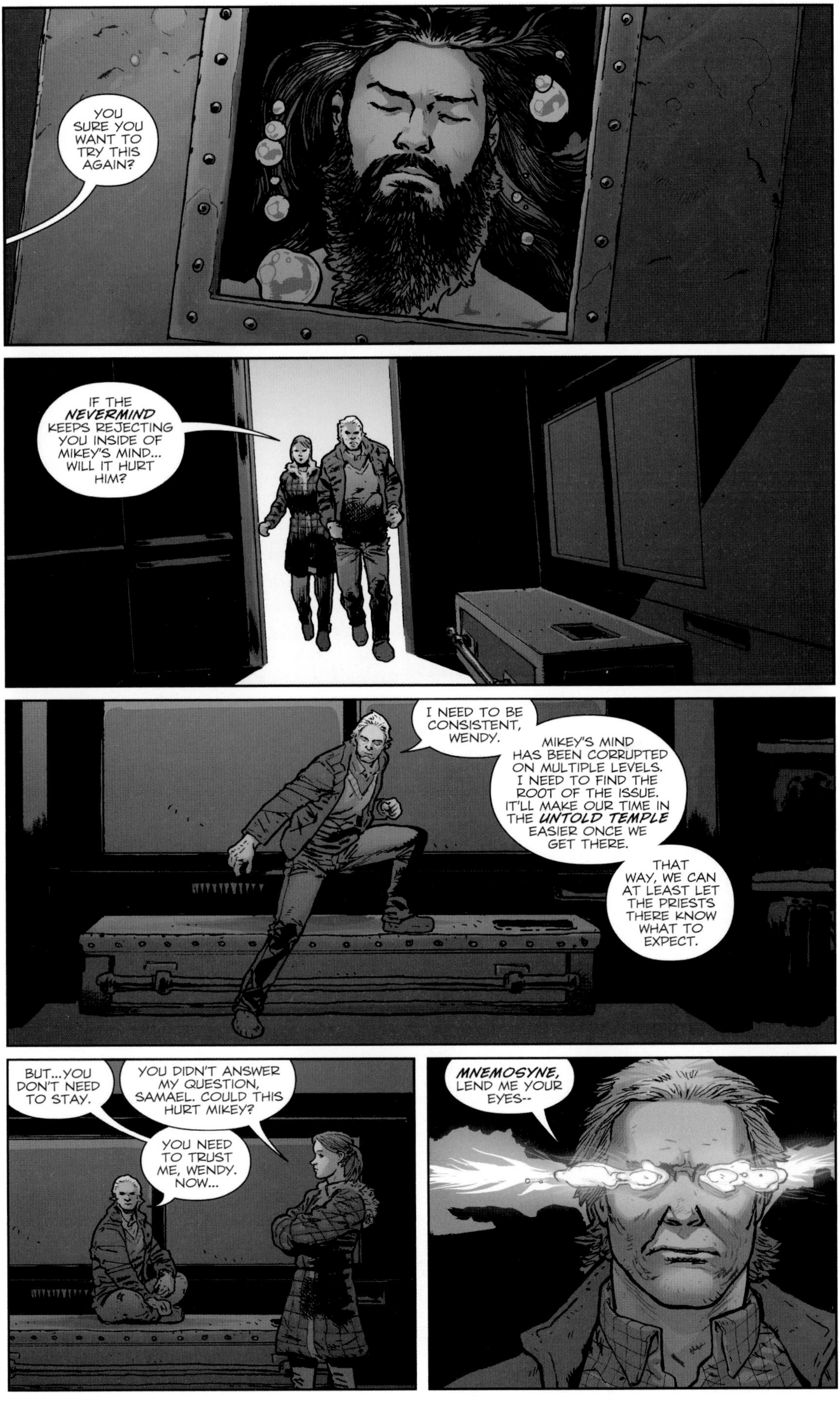
YOU SURE YOU WANT TO TRY THIS AGAIN?
IF THE *NEVERMIND* KEEPS REJECTING YOU INSIDE OF MIKEY'S MIND... WILL IT HURT HIM?
I NEED TO BE CONSISTENT, WENDY.
MIKEY'S MIND HAS BEEN CORRUPTED ON MULTIPLE LEVELS. I NEED TO FIND THE ROOT OF THE ISSUE. IT'LL MAKE OUR TIME IN THE *UNTOLD TEMPLE* EASIER ONCE WE GET THERE.
THAT WAY, WE CAN AT LEAST LET THE PRIESTS THERE KNOW WHAT TO EXPECT.
BUT...YOU DON'T NEED TO STAY.
YOU DIDN'T ANSWER MY QUESTION, SAMAEL. COULD THIS HURT MIKEY?
YOU NEED TO TRUST ME, WENDY. NOW...
MNEMOSYNE, LEND ME YOUR EYES--

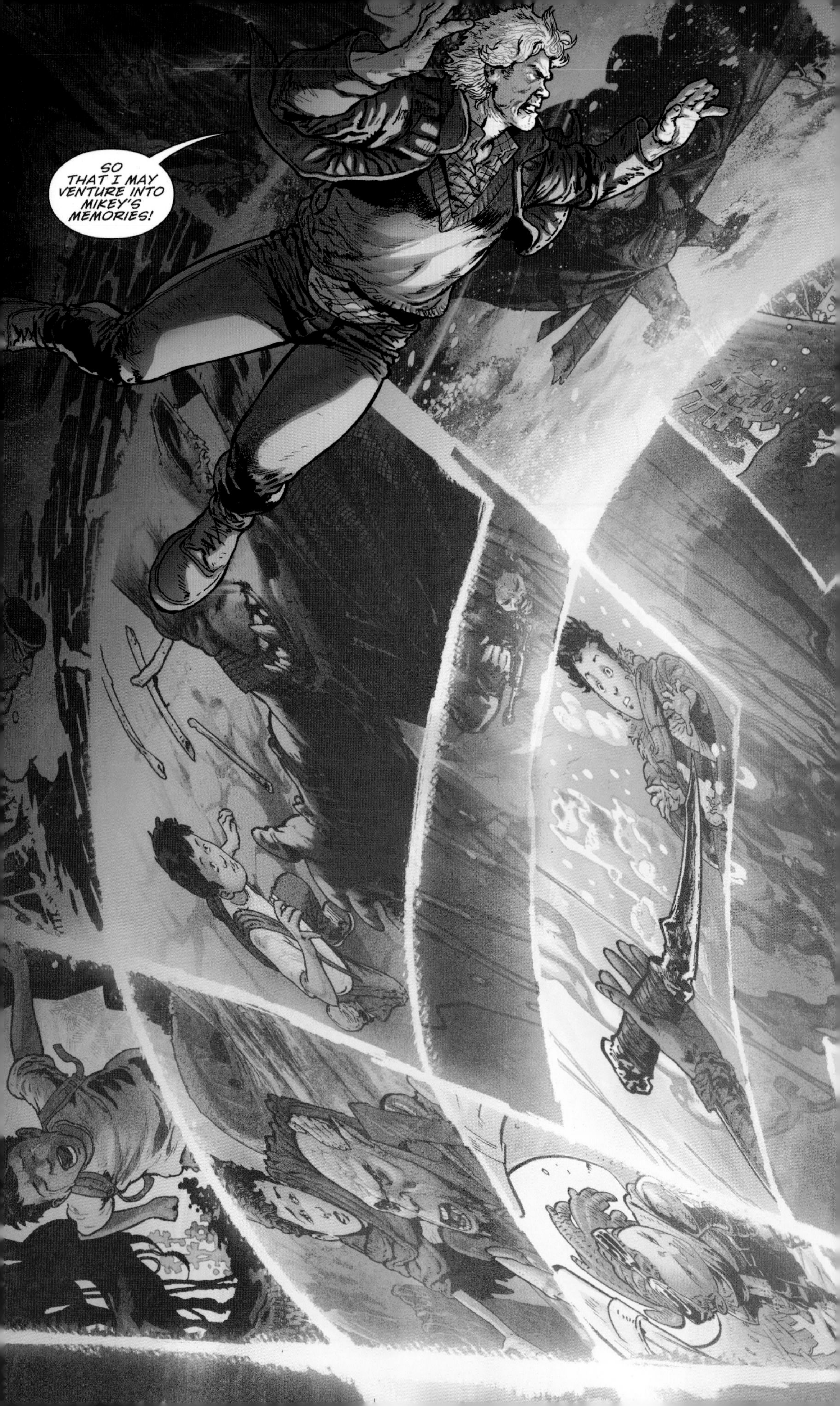
SO THAT I MAY VENTURE INTO MIKEY'S MEMORIES!

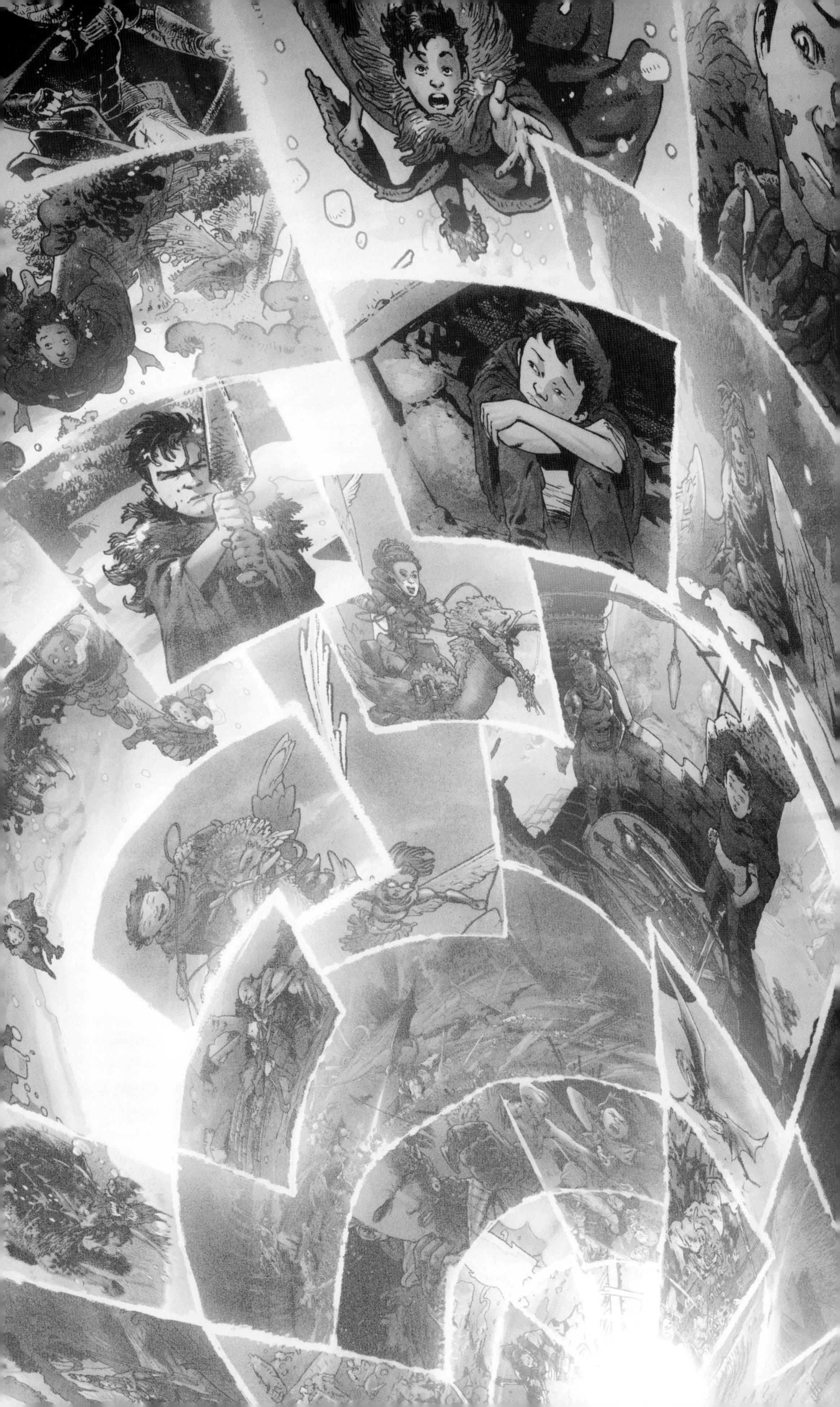

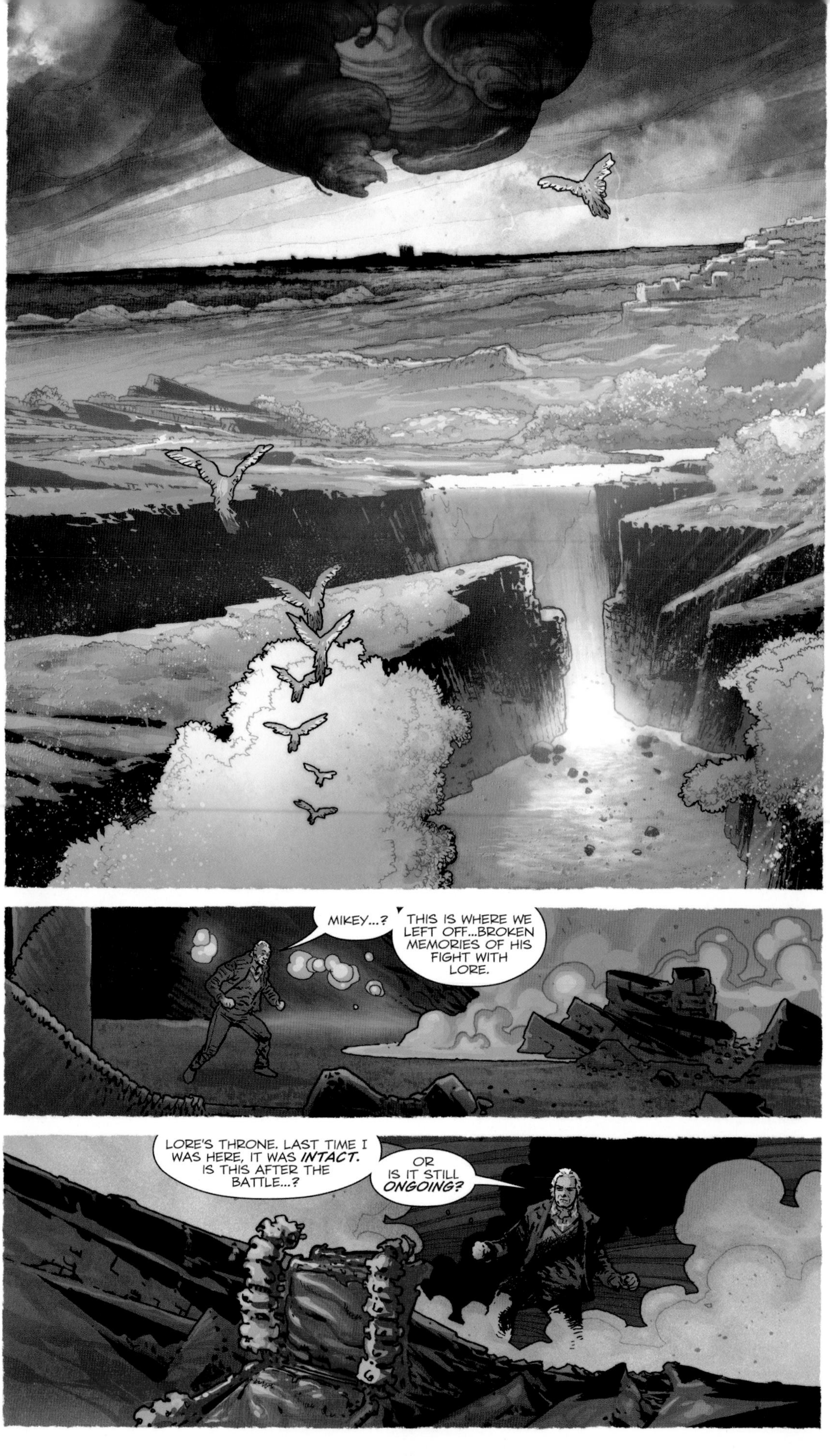
MIKEY...?
THIS IS WHERE WE LEFT OFF...BROKEN MEMORIES OF HIS FIGHT WITH LORE.
LORE'S THRONE. LAST TIME I WAS HERE, IT WAS *INTACT.* IS THIS AFTER THE BATTLE...?
OR IS IT STILL *ONGOING?*

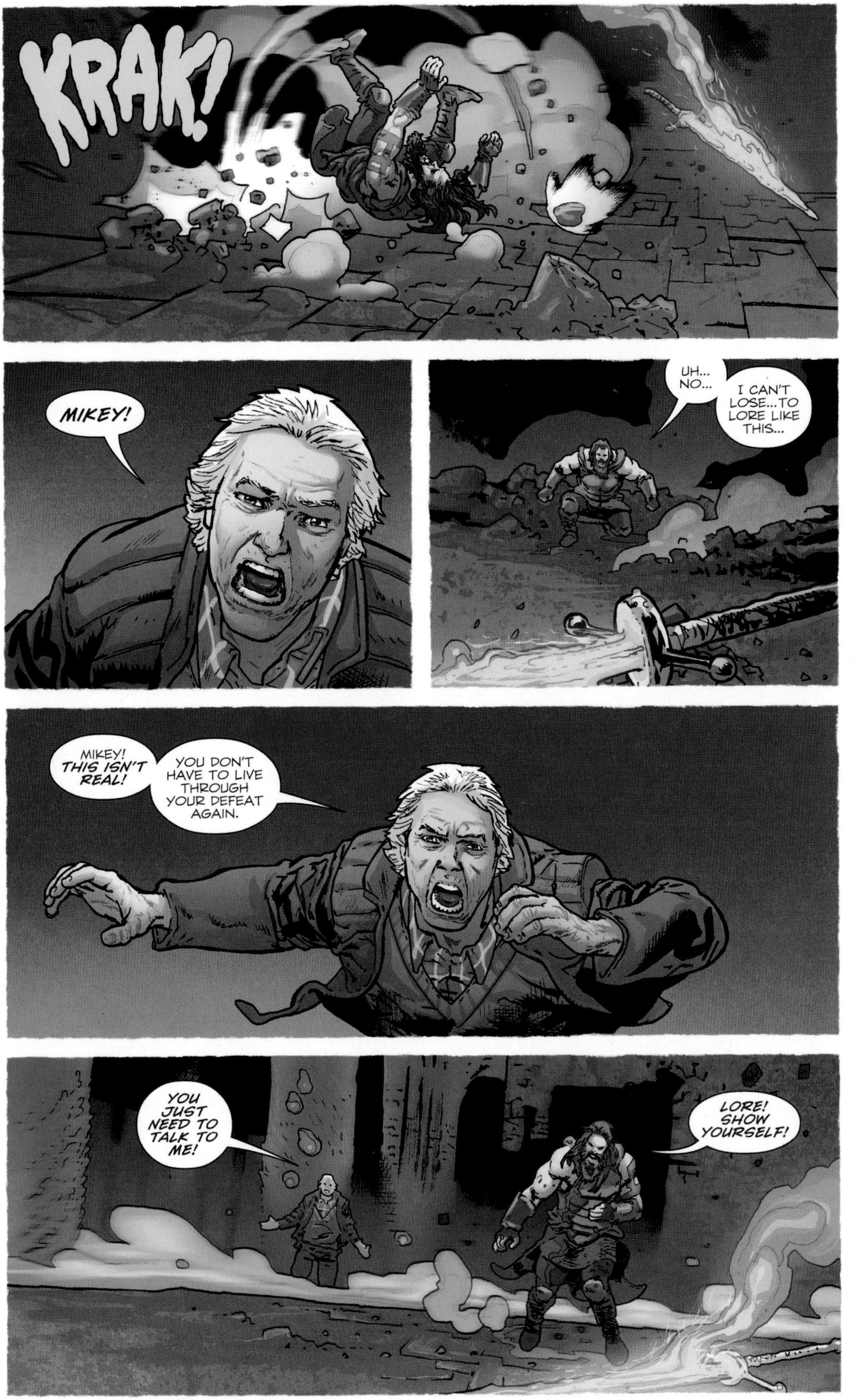
KRAK!
MIKEY!
UH... NO...
I CAN'T LOSE...TO LORE LIKE THIS...
MIKEY! THIS ISN'T REAL!
YOU DON'T HAVE TO LIVE THROUGH YOUR DEFEAT AGAIN.
YOU JUST NEED TO TALK TO ME!
LORE! SHOW YOURSELF!

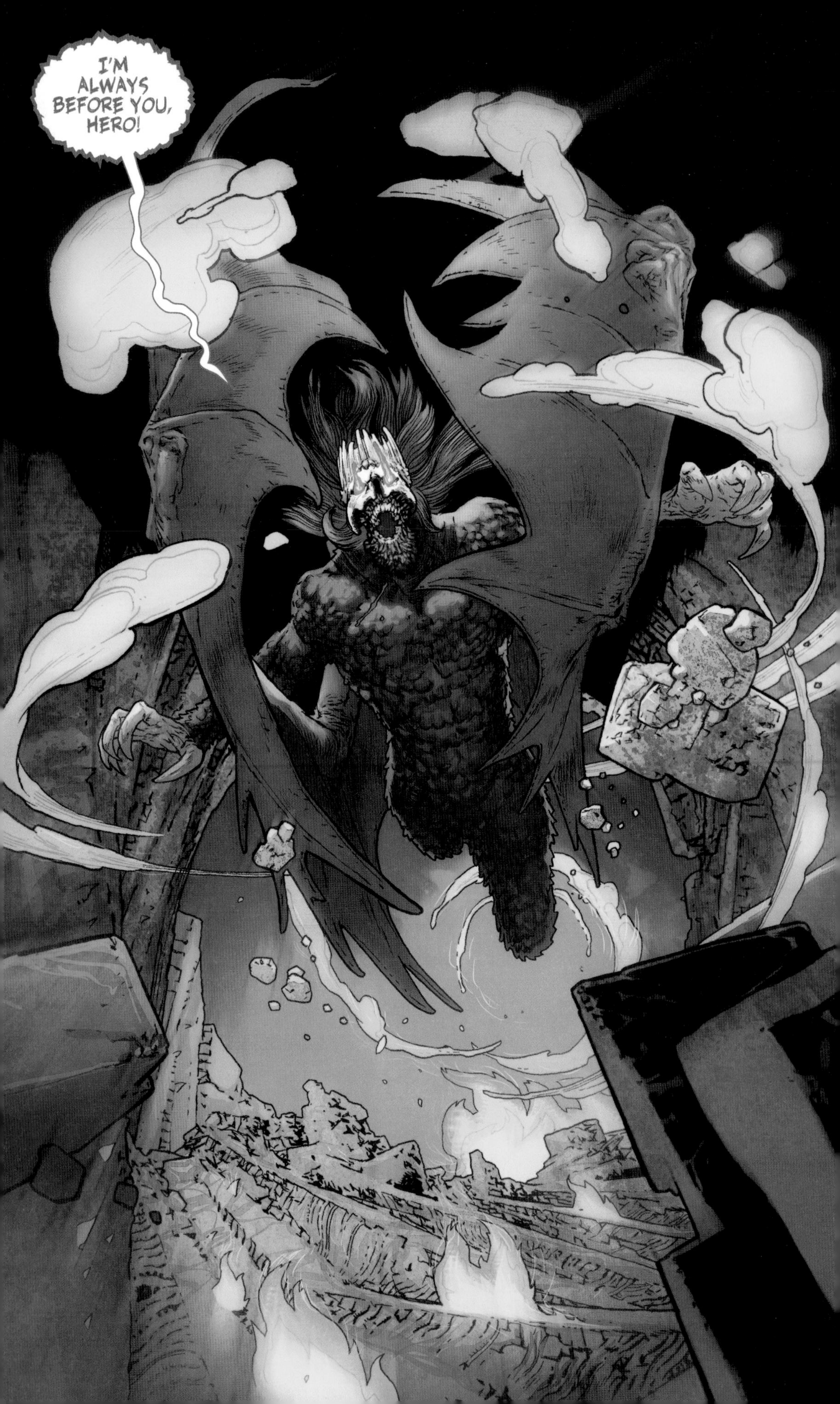
I'M ALWAYS BEFORE YOU, HERO!

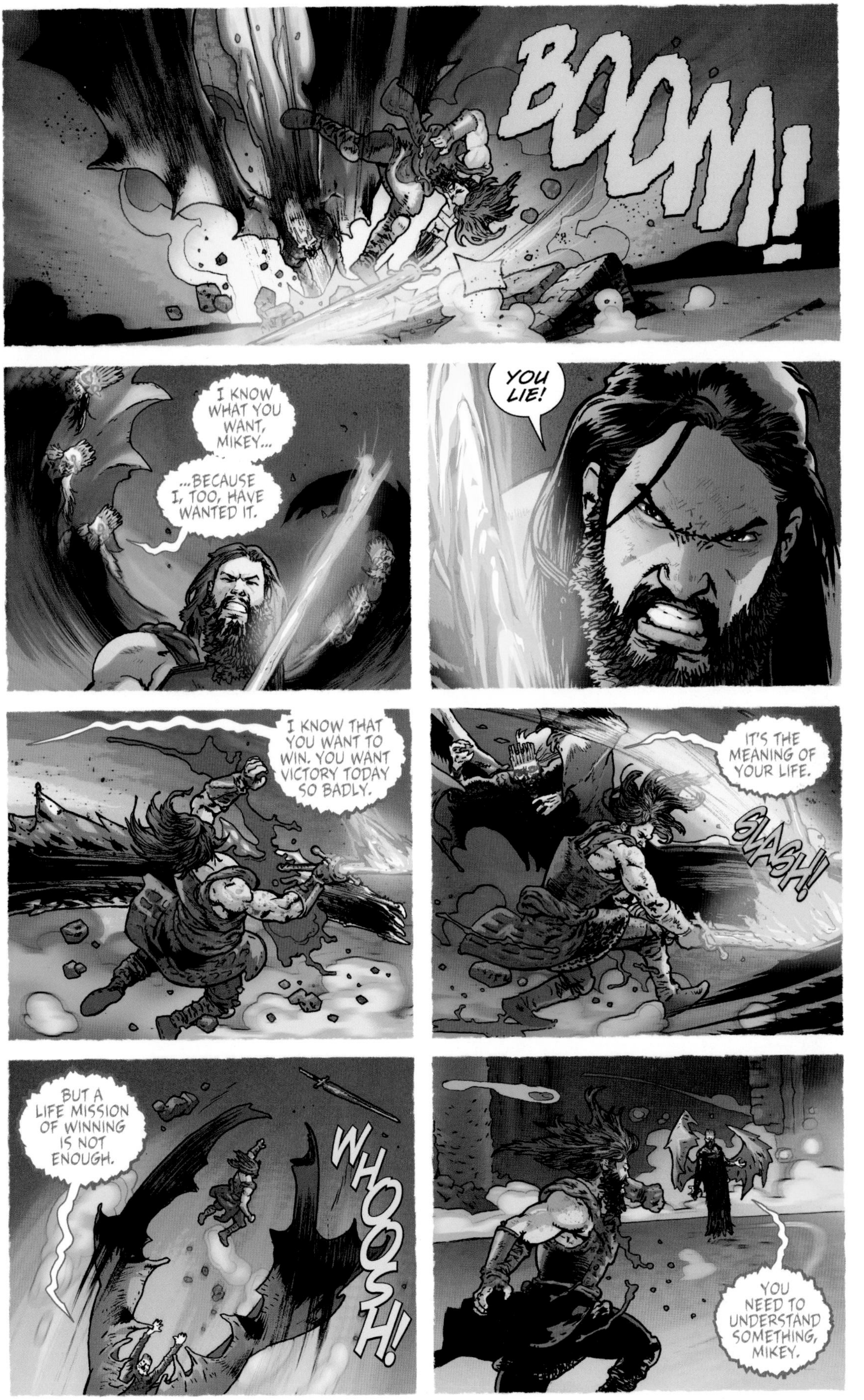
BOOM!
I KNOW WHAT YOU WANT, MIKEY...
...BECAUSE I, TOO, HAVE WANTED IT.
YOU LIE!
I KNOW THAT YOU WANT TO WIN. YOU WANT VICTORY TODAY SO BADLY.
IT'S THE MEANING OF YOUR LIFE.
SLASH!
BUT A LIFE MISSION OF WINNING IS NOT ENOUGH.
WHOOSH!
YOU NEED TO UNDERSTAND SOMETHING, MIKEY.

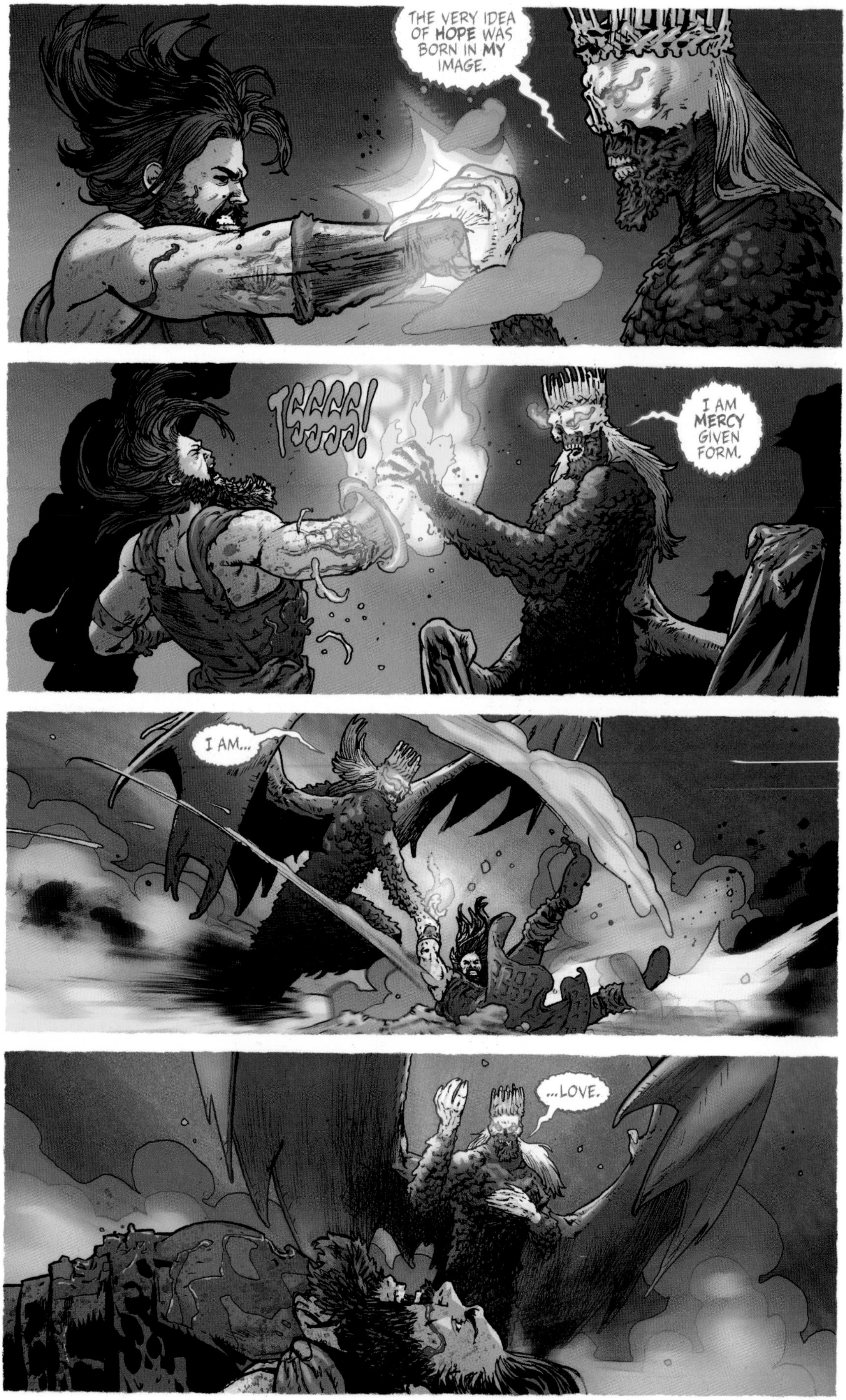
THE VERY IDEA OF HOPE WAS BORN IN MY IMAGE.
TSSSS!
I AM MERCY GIVEN FORM.
I AM...
...LOVE.

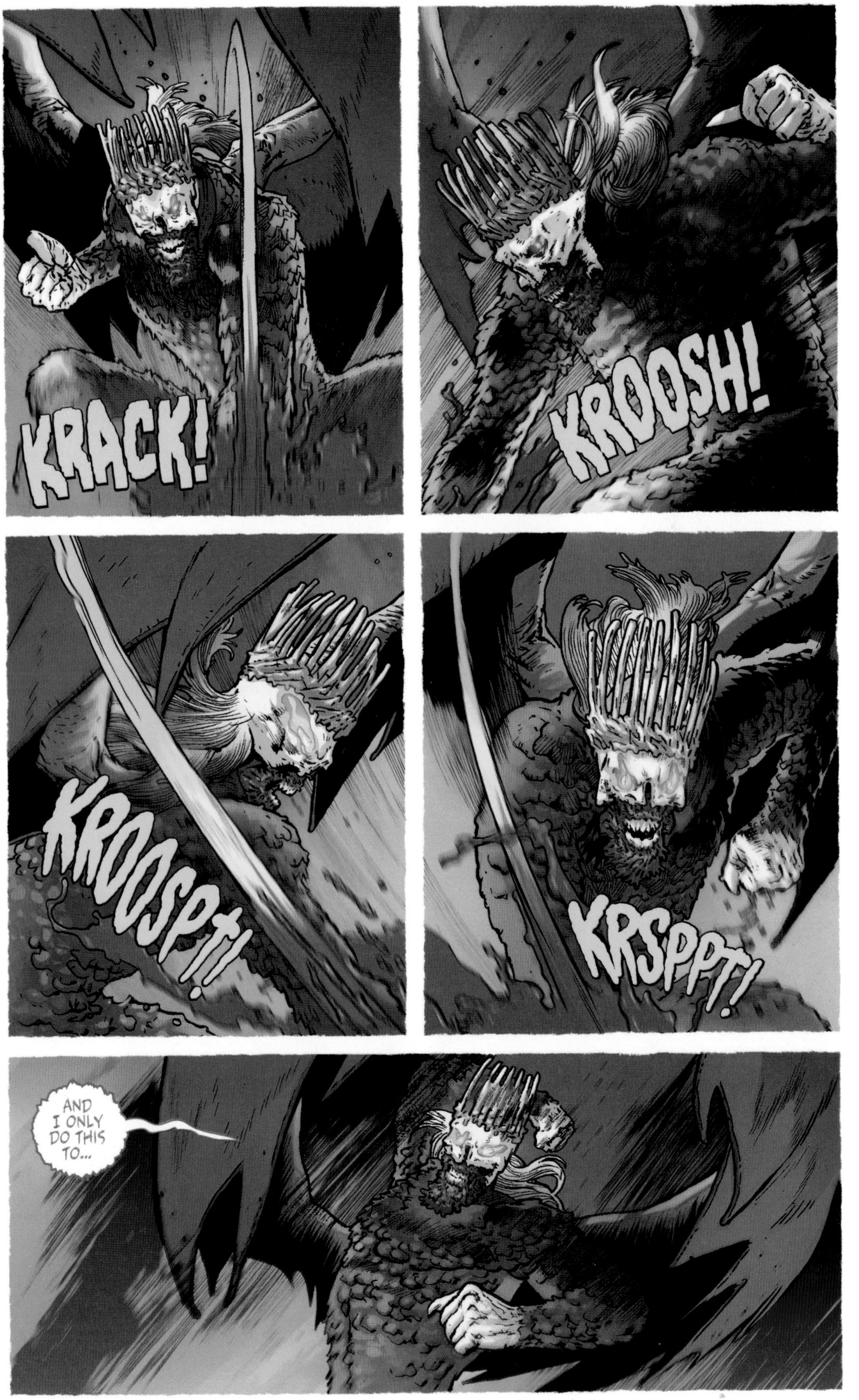
KRACK!
KROOSH!
KROOSPT!!
KRSPPT!
AND I ONLY DO THIS TO...

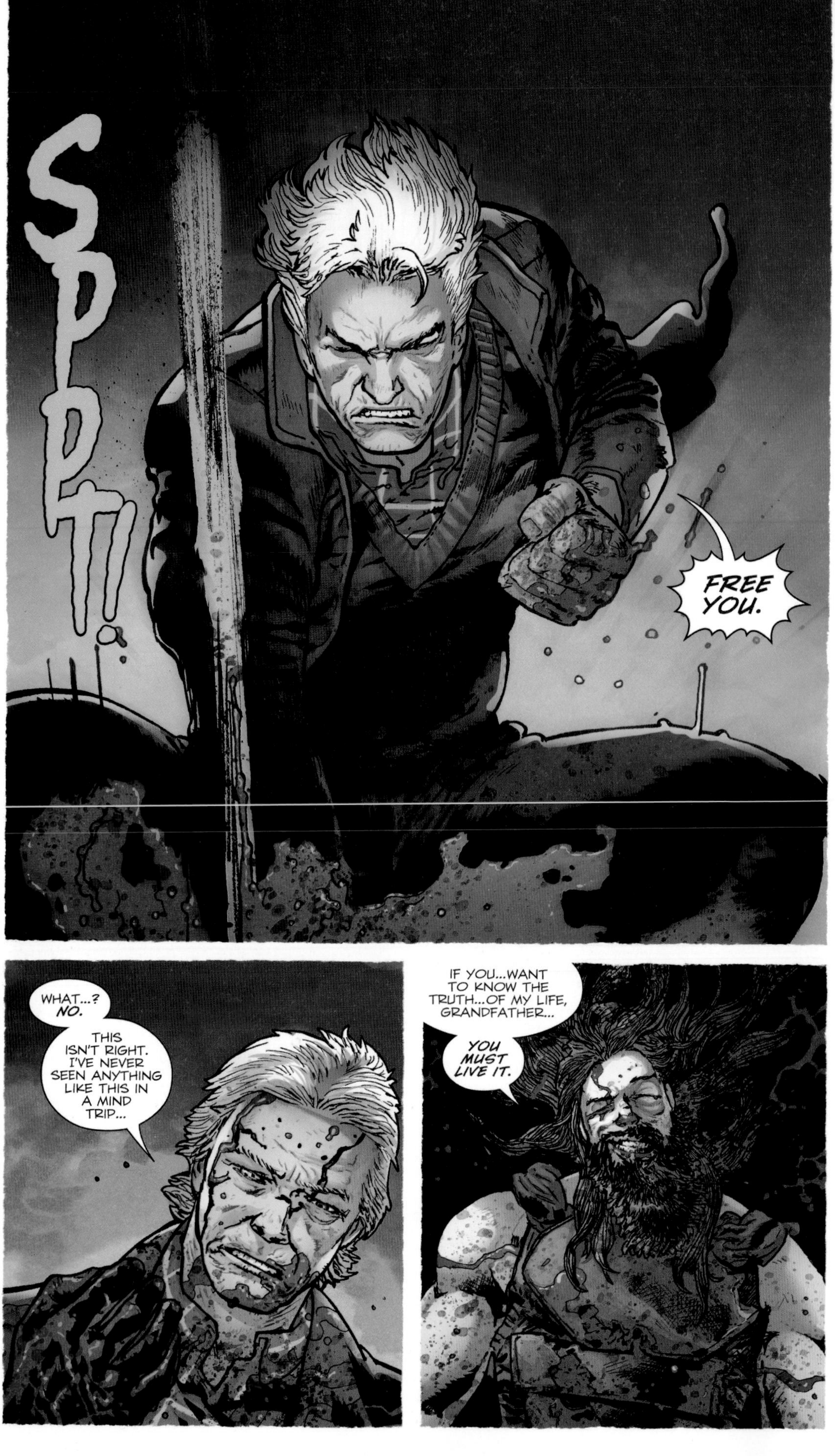
SPPT!!
FREE YOU.
WHAT...? NO.
THIS ISN'T RIGHT. I'VE NEVER SEEN ANYTHING LIKE THIS IN A MIND TRIP...
IF YOU...WANT TO KNOW THE TRUTH...OF MY LIFE, GRANDFATHER...
YOU MUST LIVE IT.

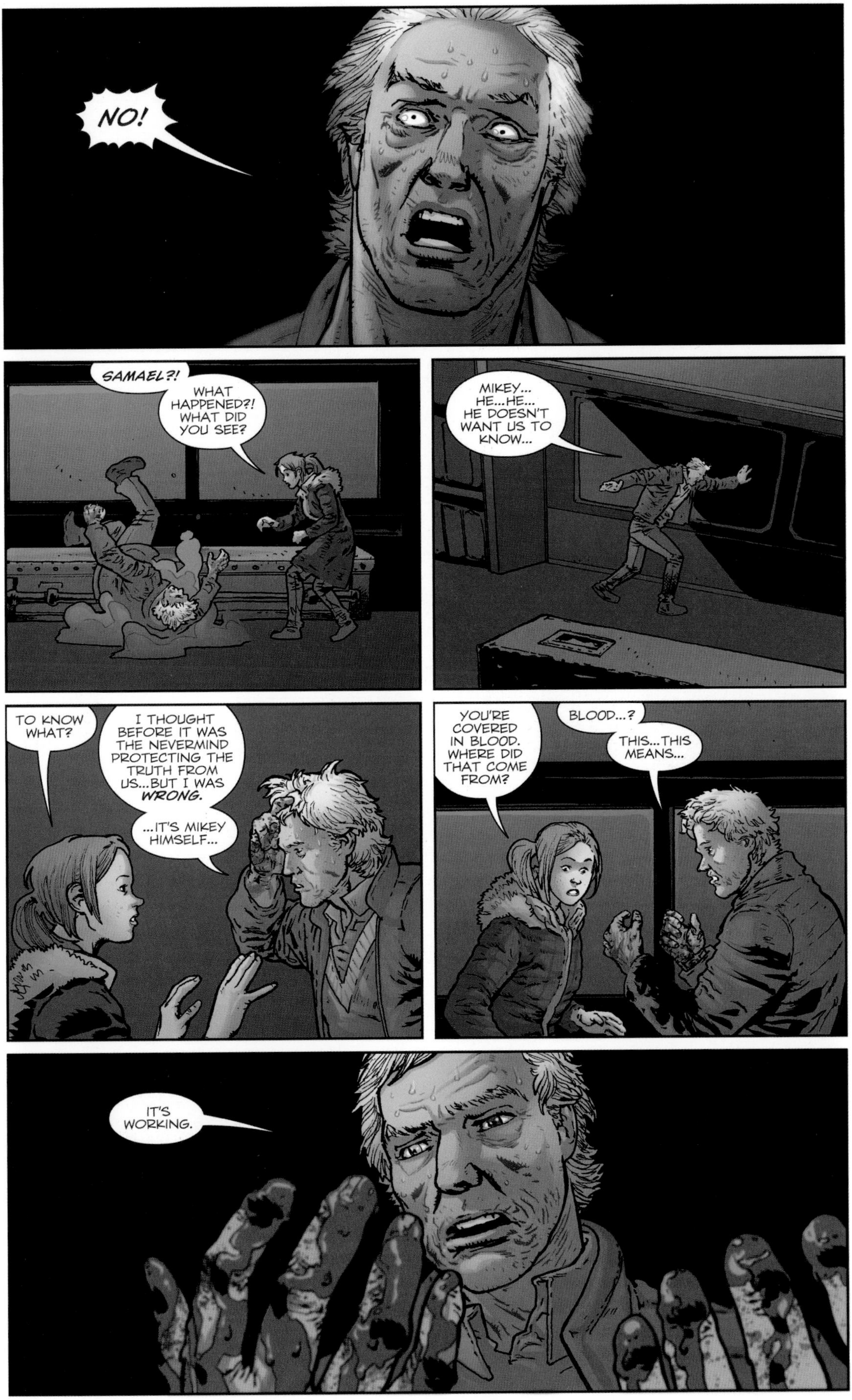
NO!
SAMAEL?!
WHAT HAPPENED?! WHAT DID YOU SEE?
MIKEY... HE...HE... HE DOESN'T WANT US TO KNOW...
TO KNOW WHAT?
I THOUGHT BEFORE IT WAS THE NEVERMIND PROTECTING THE TRUTH FROM US...BUT I WAS WRONG.
...IT'S MIKEY HIMSELF...
YOU'RE COVERED IN BLOOD. WHERE DID THAT COME FROM?
BLOOD...?
THIS...THIS MEANS...
IT'S WORKING.

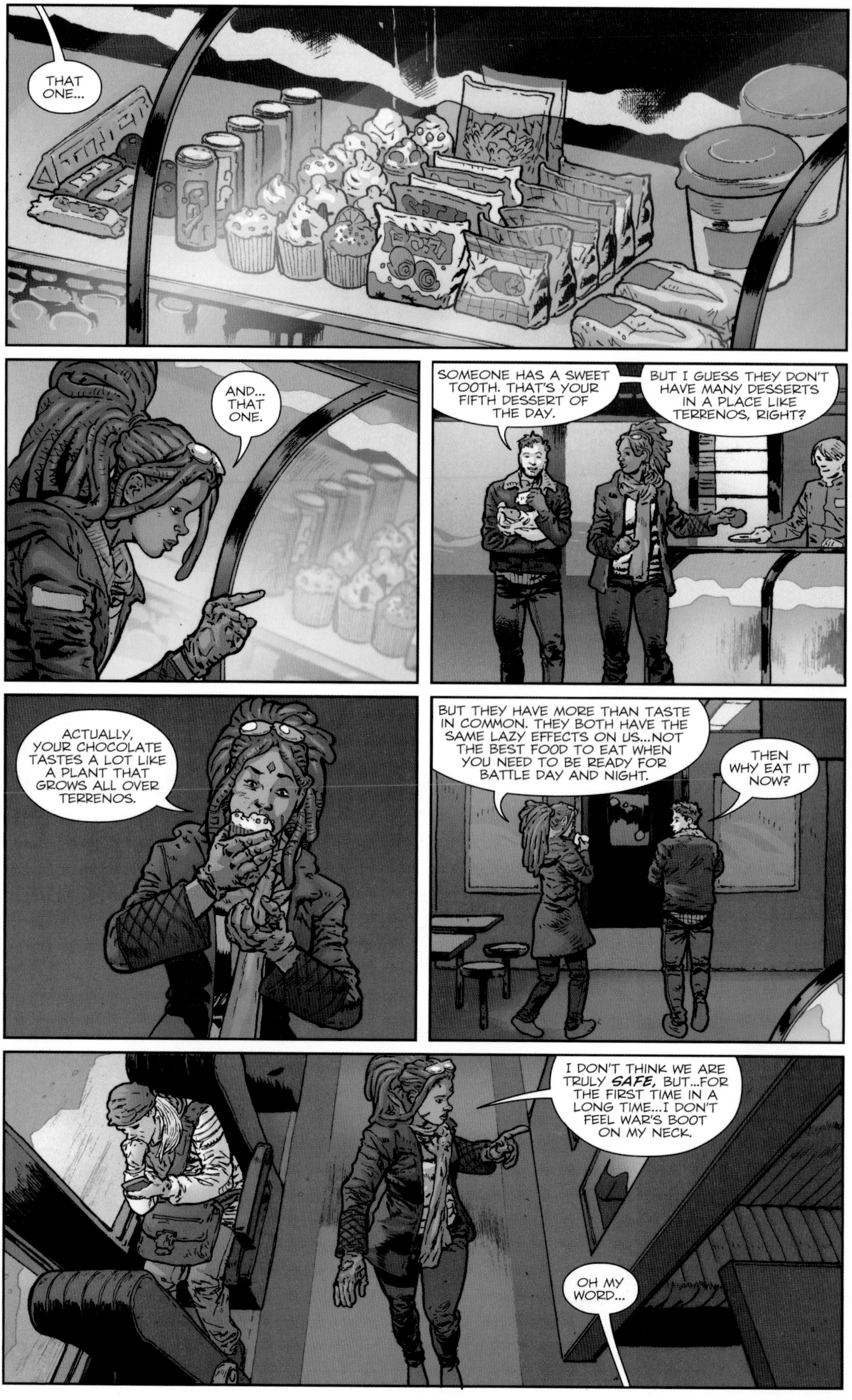
THAT ONE...
AND... THAT ONE.
SOMEONE HAS A SWEET TOOTH. THAT'S YOUR FIFTH DESSERT OF THE DAY.
BUT I GUESS THEY DON'T HAVE MANY DESSERTS IN A PLACE LIKE TERRENOS, RIGHT?
ACTUALLY, YOUR CHOCOLATE TASTES A LOT LIKE A PLANT THAT GROWS ALL OVER TERRENOS.
BUT THEY HAVE MORE THAN TASTE IN COMMON. THEY BOTH HAVE THE SAME LAZY EFFECTS ON US...NOT THE BEST FOOD TO EAT WHEN YOU NEED TO BE READY FOR BATTLE DAY AND NIGHT.
THEN WHY EAT IT NOW?
I DON'T THINK WE ARE TRULY *SAFE*, BUT...FOR THE FIRST TIME IN A LONG TIME...I DON'T FEEL WAR'S BOOT ON MY NECK.
OH MY WORD...

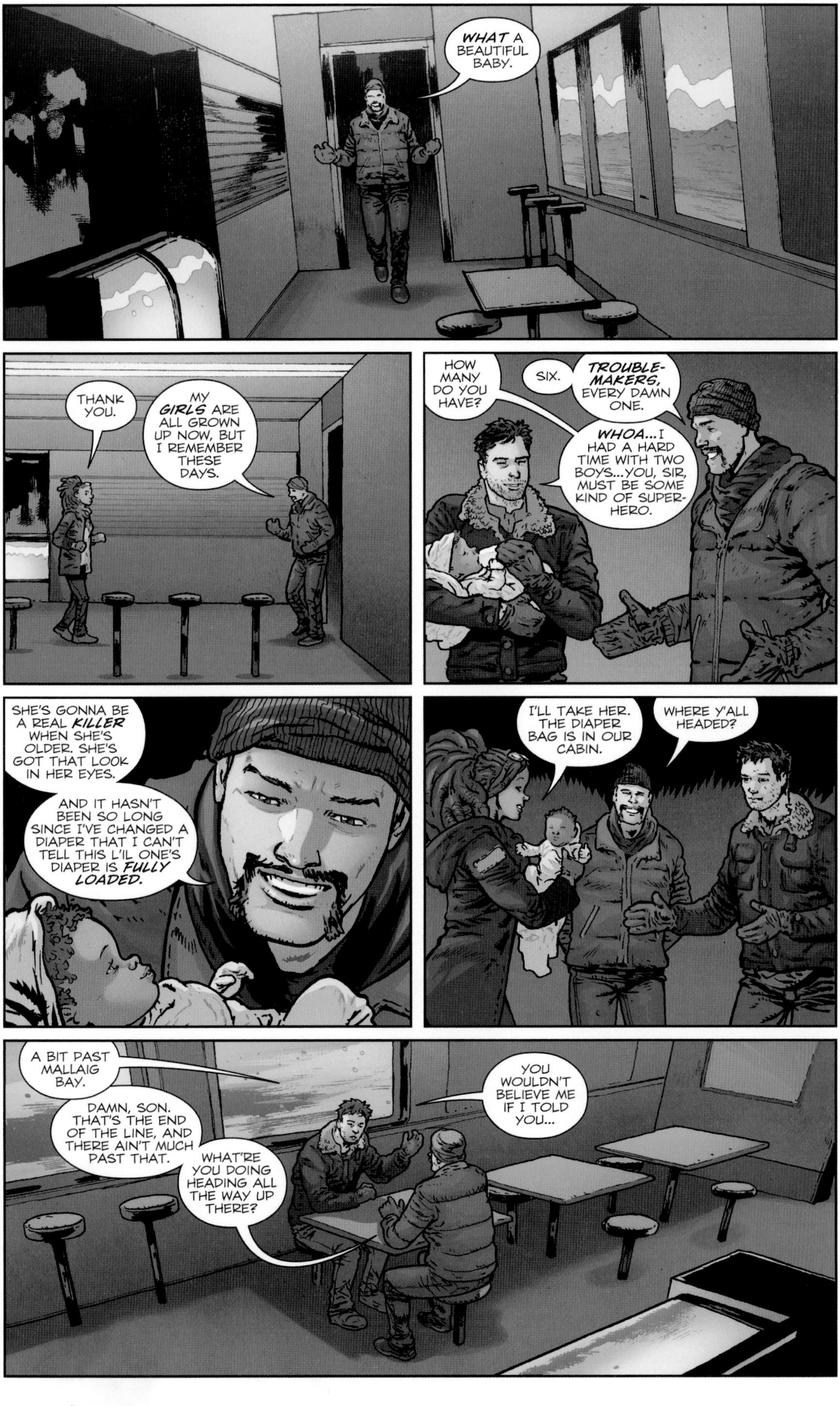

WHAT A BEAUTIFUL BABY.
THANK YOU.
MY GIRLS ARE ALL GROWN UP NOW, BUT I REMEMBER THESE DAYS.
HOW MANY DO YOU HAVE?
SIX.
TROUBLE-MAKERS, EVERY DAMN ONE.
WHOA...I HAD A HARD TIME WITH TWO BOYS...YOU, SIR, MUST BE SOME KIND OF SUPER-HERO.
SHE'S GONNA BE A REAL KILLER WHEN SHE'S OLDER. SHE'S GOT THAT LOOK IN HER EYES.
AND IT HASN'T BEEN SO LONG SINCE I'VE CHANGED A DIAPER THAT I CAN'T TELL THIS L'IL ONE'S DIAPER IS FULLY LOADED.
I'LL TAKE HER. THE DIAPER BAG IS IN OUR CABIN.
WHERE Y'ALL HEADED?
A BIT PAST MALLAIG BAY.
DAMN, SON. THAT'S THE END OF THE LINE, AND THERE AIN'T MUCH PAST THAT.
WHAT'RE YOU DOING HEADING ALL THE WAY UP THERE?
YOU WOULDN'T BELIEVE ME IF I TOLD YOU...

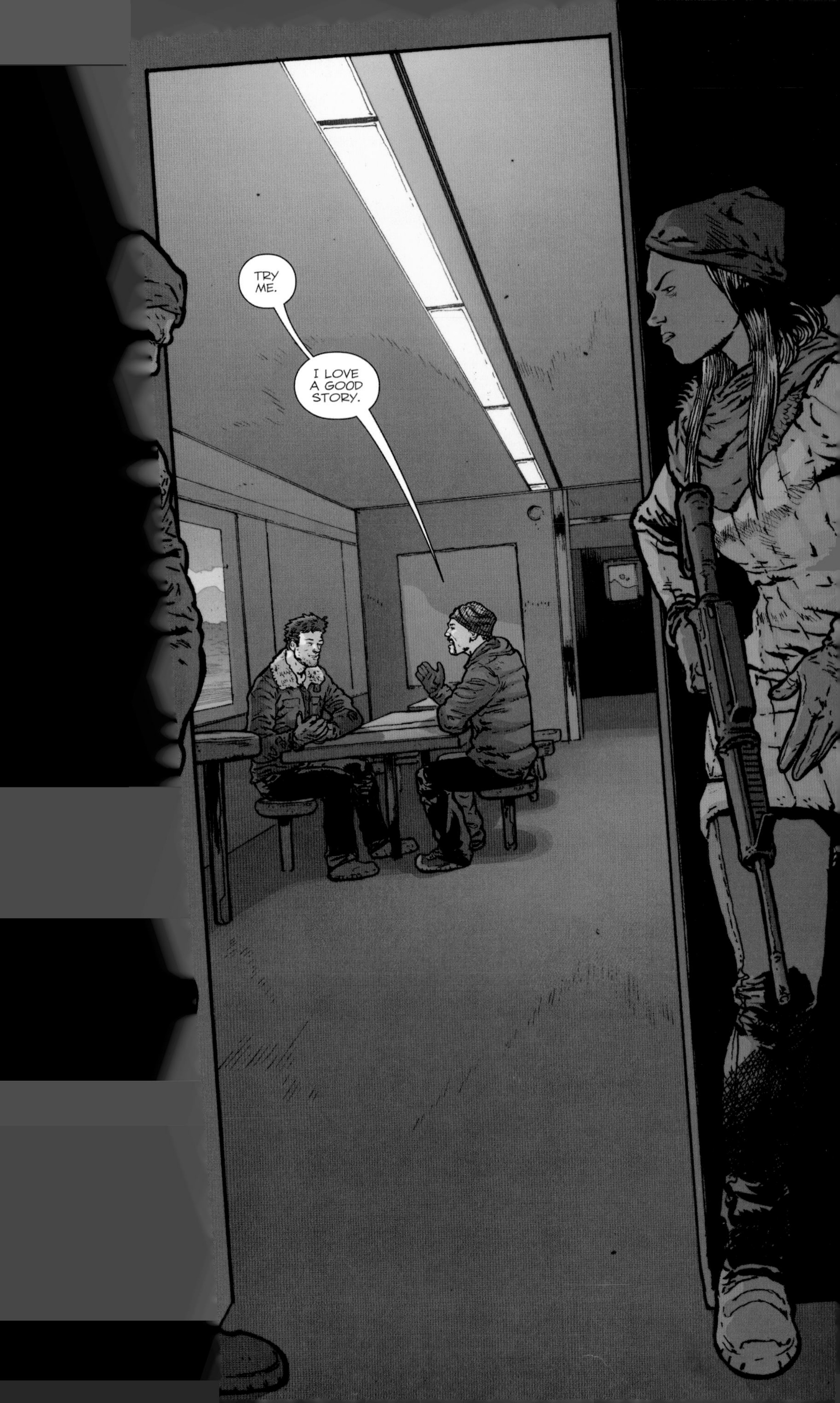
TRY ME.
I LOVE A GOOD STORY.

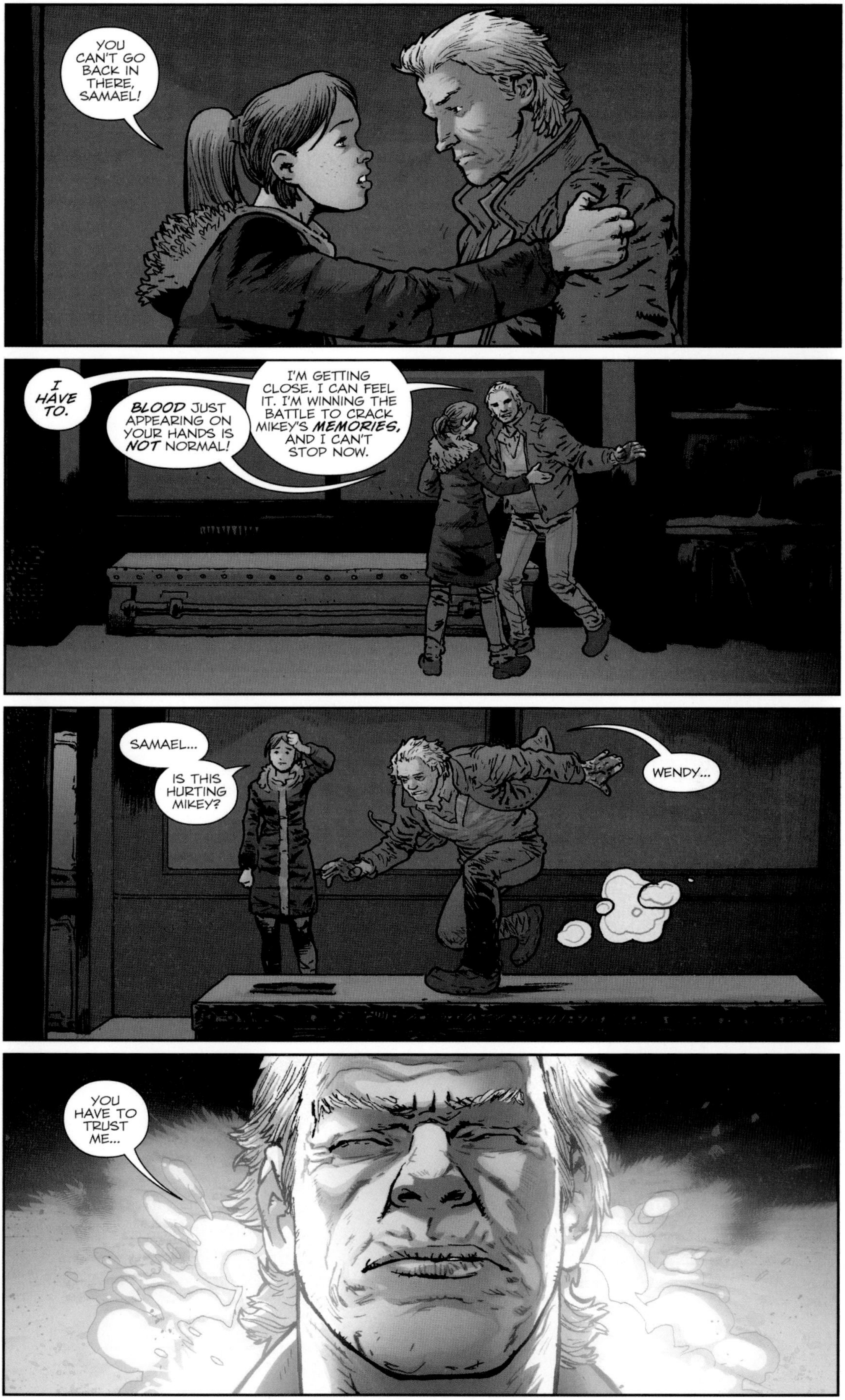
YOU CAN'T GO BACK IN THERE, SAMAEL!
I HAVE TO.
BLOOD JUST APPEARING ON YOUR HANDS IS NOT NORMAL!
I'M GETTING CLOSE. I CAN FEEL IT. I'M WINNING THE BATTLE TO CRACK MIKEY'S MEMORIES, AND I CAN'T STOP NOW.
SAMAEL...
IS THIS HURTING MIKEY?
WENDY...
YOU HAVE TO TRUST ME...

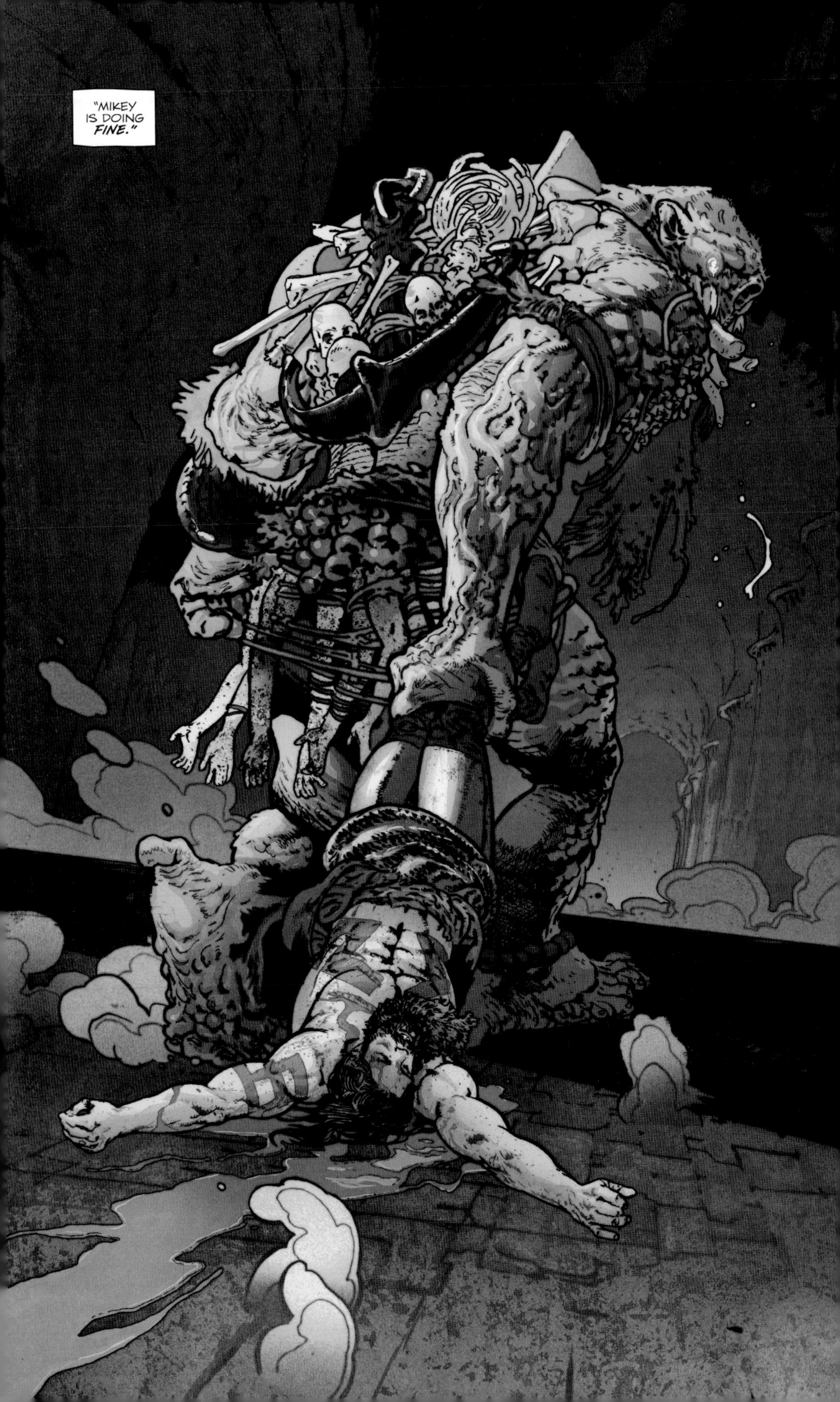
"MIKEY IS DOING *FINE.*"

SPLASH!

OOM OOM OOM OOM

SAVE YOUR *CHANTS* FOR SOMEONE WHO NEEDS THEM, PRIESTS!

NO MATTER HOW INJURED I AM, I STILL HAVE THE STRENGTH TO FIGHT MY WAY OUT OF HERE AND RIP YOUR--

OOM OOM OOM OOM

NO!

OOM OOM OOM OOM

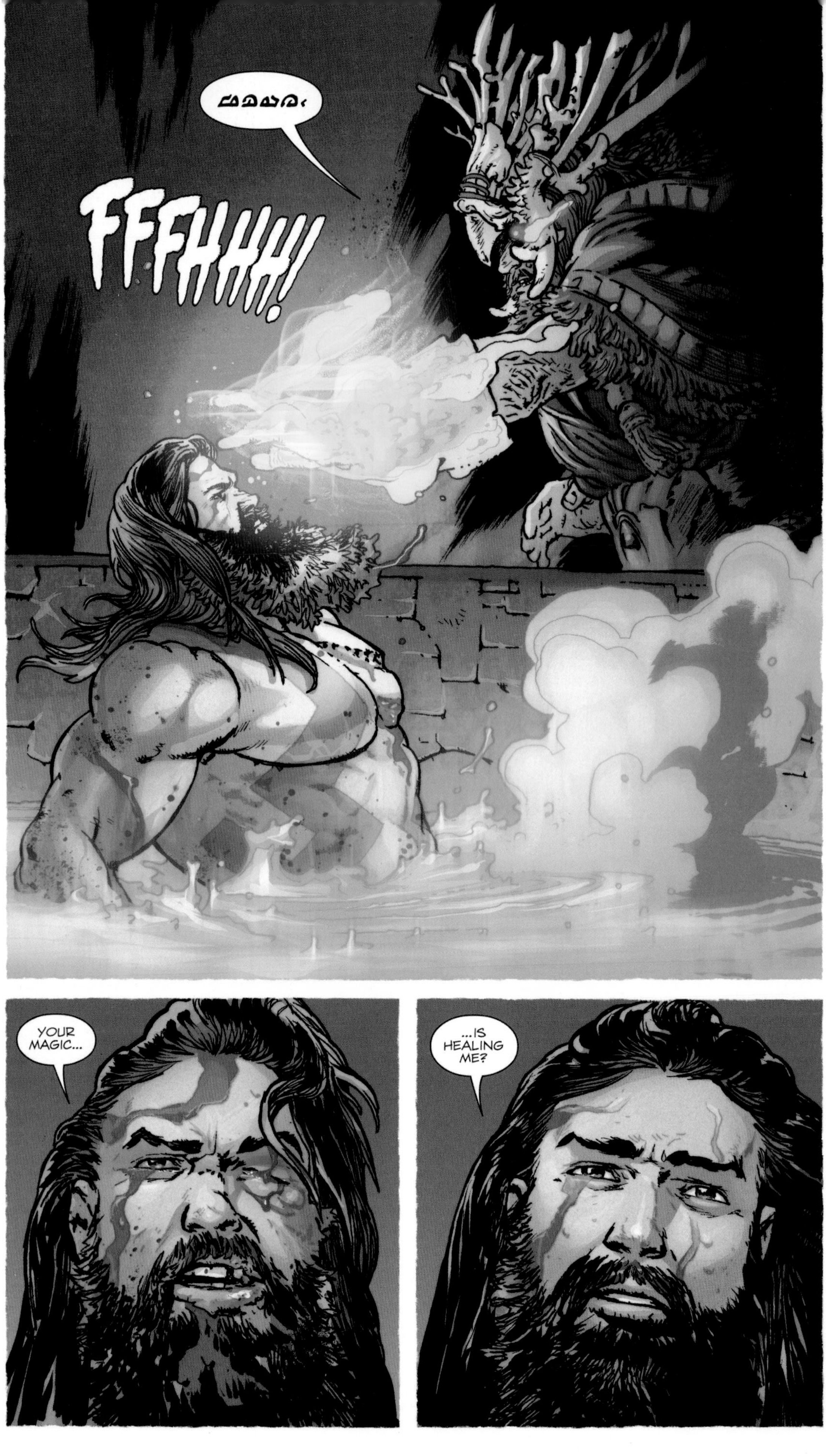
FFFHHH!
YOUR MAGIC...
...IS HEALING ME?

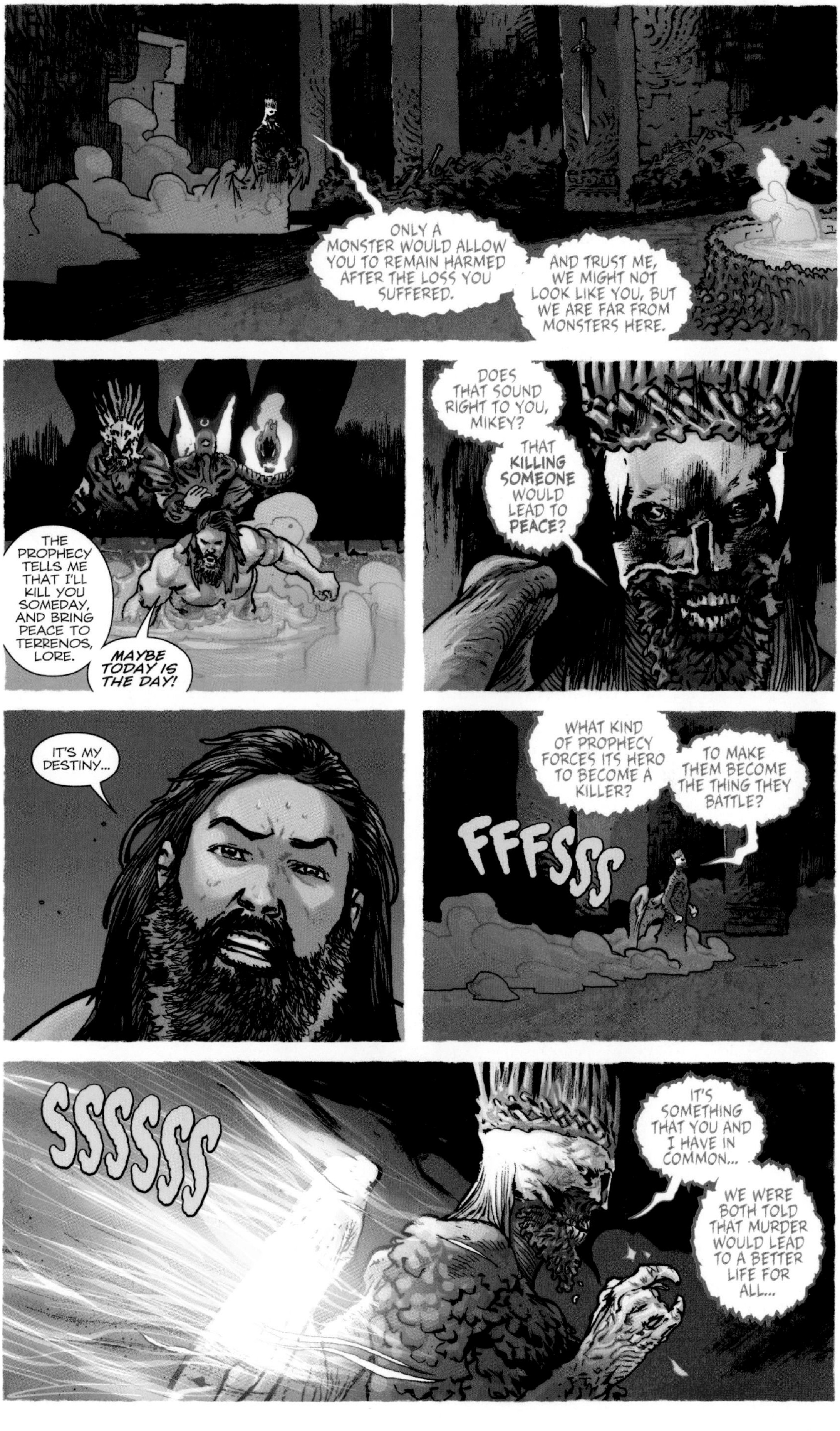
ONLY A MONSTER WOULD ALLOW YOU TO REMAIN HARMED AFTER THE LOSS YOU SUFFERED.
AND TRUST ME, WE MIGHT NOT LOOK LIKE YOU, BUT WE ARE FAR FROM MONSTERS HERE.
THE PROPHECY TELLS ME THAT I'LL KILL YOU SOMEDAY, AND BRING PEACE TO TERRENOS, LORE.
MAYBE TODAY IS THE DAY!
DOES THAT SOUND RIGHT TO YOU, MIKEY?
THAT KILLING SOMEONE WOULD LEAD TO PEACE?
IT'S MY DESTINY...
WHAT KIND OF PROPHECY FORCES ITS HERO TO BECOME A KILLER?
TO MAKE THEM BECOME THE THING THEY BATTLE?
FFFSSS
SSSSSS
IT'S SOMETHING THAT YOU AND I HAVE IN COMMON...
WE WERE BOTH TOLD THAT MURDER WOULD LEAD TO A BETTER LIFE FOR ALL...

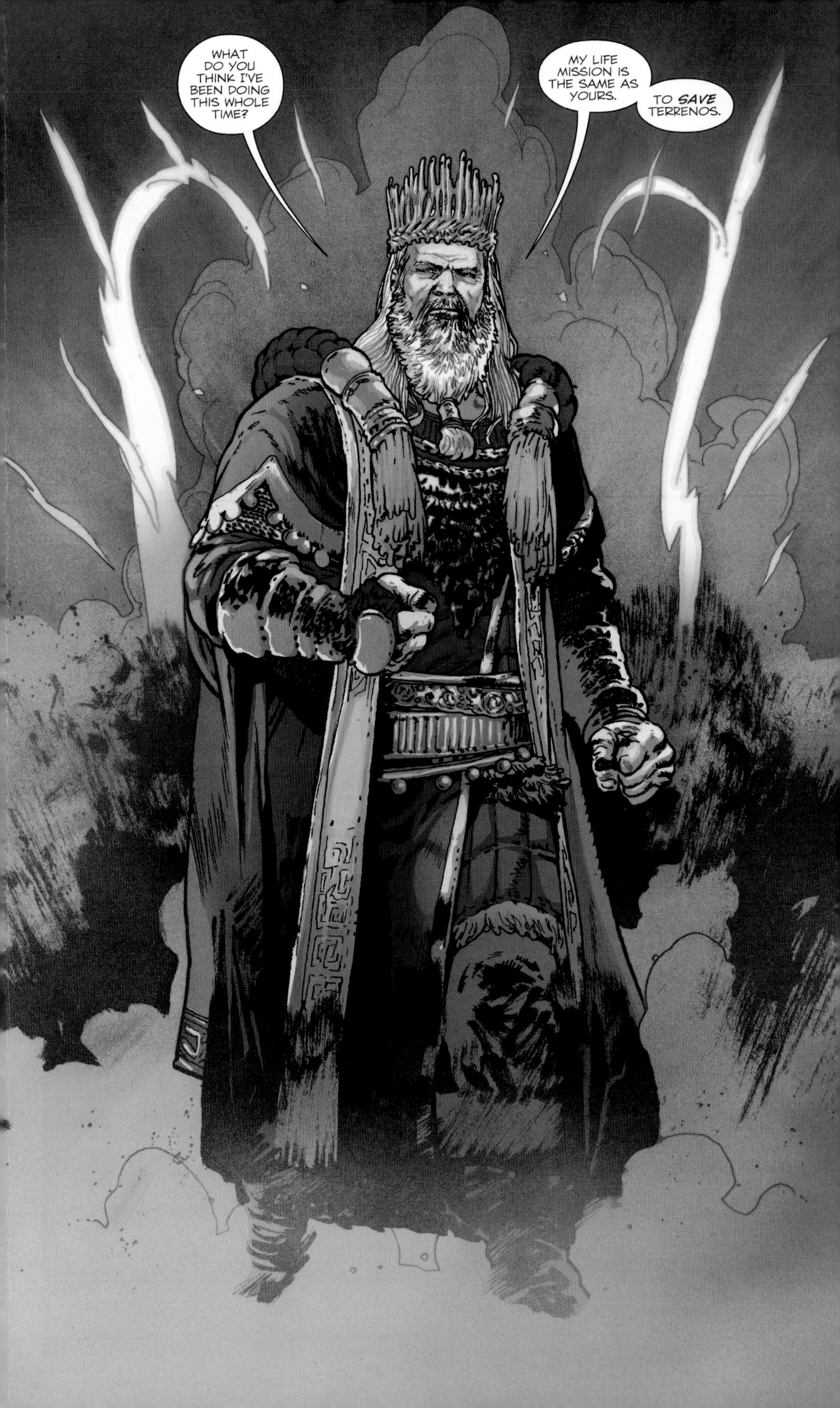
WHAT DO YOU THINK I'VE BEEN DOING THIS WHOLE TIME?
MY LIFE MISSION IS THE SAME AS YOURS.
TO SAVE TERRENOS.

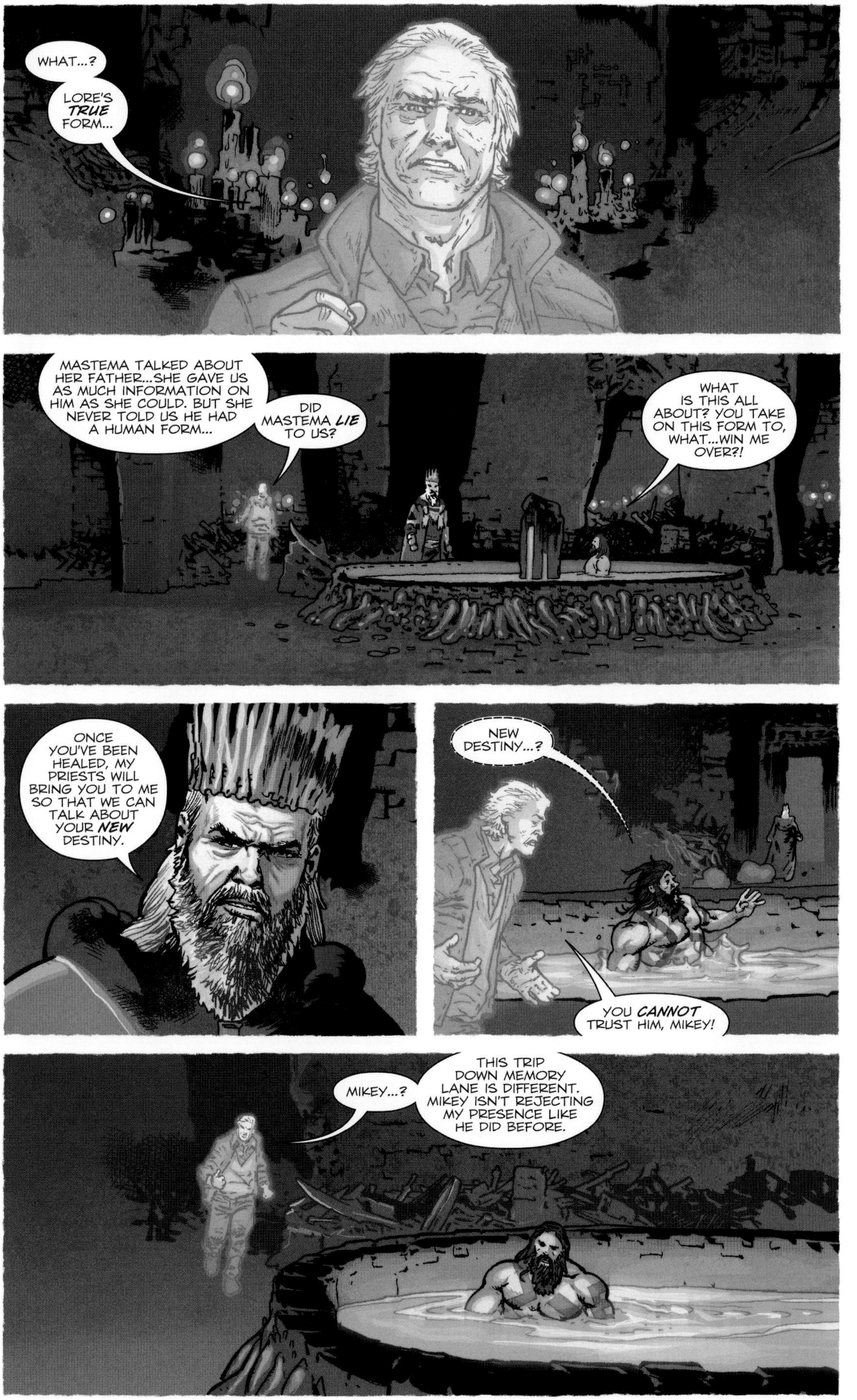

WHAT...?
LORE'S TRUE FORM...
MASTEMA TALKED ABOUT HER FATHER...SHE GAVE US AS MUCH INFORMATION ON HIM AS SHE COULD. BUT SHE NEVER TOLD US HE HAD A HUMAN FORM...
DID MASTEMA LIE TO US?
WHAT IS THIS ALL ABOUT? YOU TAKE ON THIS FORM TO, WHAT...WIN ME OVER?!
ONCE YOU'VE BEEN HEALED, MY PRIESTS WILL BRING YOU TO ME SO THAT WE CAN TALK ABOUT YOUR NEW DESTINY.
NEW DESTINY...?
YOU CANNOT TRUST HIM, MIKEY!
MIKEY...?
THIS TRIP DOWN MEMORY LANE IS DIFFERENT. MIKEY ISN'T REJECTING MY PRESENCE LIKE HE DID BEFORE.

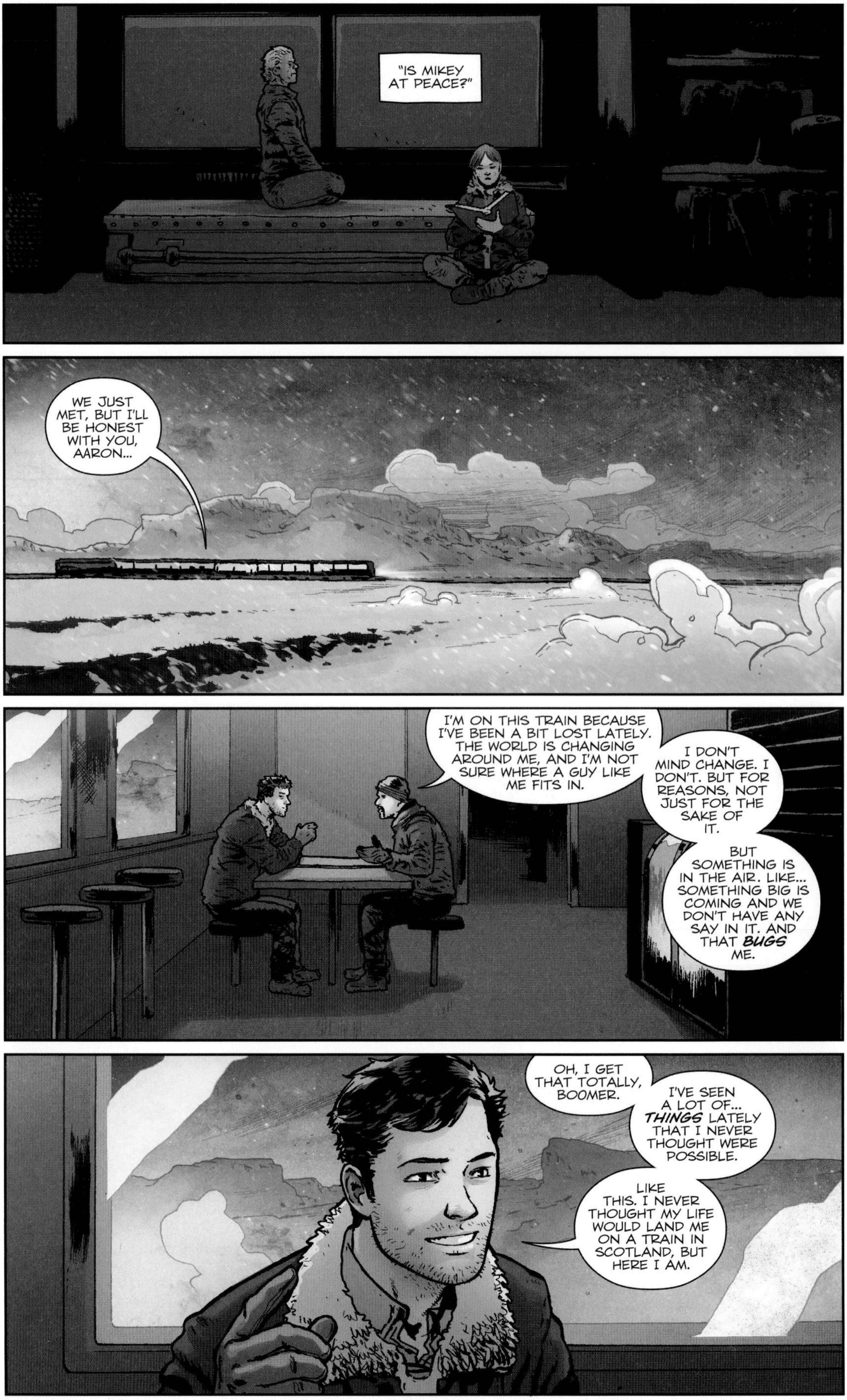

"IS MIKEY AT PEACE?"
WE JUST MET, BUT I'LL BE HONEST WITH YOU, AARON...
I'M ON THIS TRAIN BECAUSE I'VE BEEN A BIT LOST LATELY. THE WORLD IS CHANGING AROUND ME, AND I'M NOT SURE WHERE A GUY LIKE ME FITS IN.
I DON'T MIND CHANGE. I DON'T. BUT FOR REASONS, NOT JUST FOR THE SAKE OF IT.
BUT SOMETHING IS IN THE AIR. LIKE... SOMETHING BIG IS COMING AND WE DON'T HAVE ANY SAY IN IT. AND THAT *BUGS* ME.
OH, I GET THAT TOTALLY, BOOMER.
I'VE SEEN A LOT OF... *THINGS* LATELY THAT I NEVER THOUGHT WERE POSSIBLE.
LIKE THIS. I NEVER THOUGHT MY LIFE WOULD LAND ME ON A TRAIN IN SCOTLAND, BUT HERE I AM.

YOU NEVER SAID WHY *YOU* WERE HEADED UP ALL THE WAY TO THE TOP OF THE WORLD.

YOU TRYING TO FIND YOURSELF?

HA, NO. ONE OF MY BOYS...GOT INTO SOME TROUBLE AND WE NEED TO...

...BAIL HIM OUT.

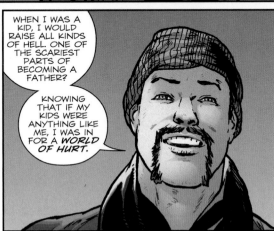

WHEN I WAS A KID, I WOULD RAISE ALL KINDS OF HELL. ONE OF THE SCARIEST PARTS OF BECOMING A FATHER?

KNOWING THAT IF MY KIDS WERE ANYTHING LIKE ME, I WAS IN FOR A *WORLD OF HURT.*

WELL, MY BOYS...THEY'RE A HANDFUL, BUT EVERY DAY I'M THANKFUL THEY GOT THEIR SMARTS FROM THEIR MOTHER.

YOU WERE RIGHT.

THE BABY HAD A *REALLY* MESSY DIAPER.

IT WAS SO *REPUGNANT* THAT I DIDN'T NOTICE...

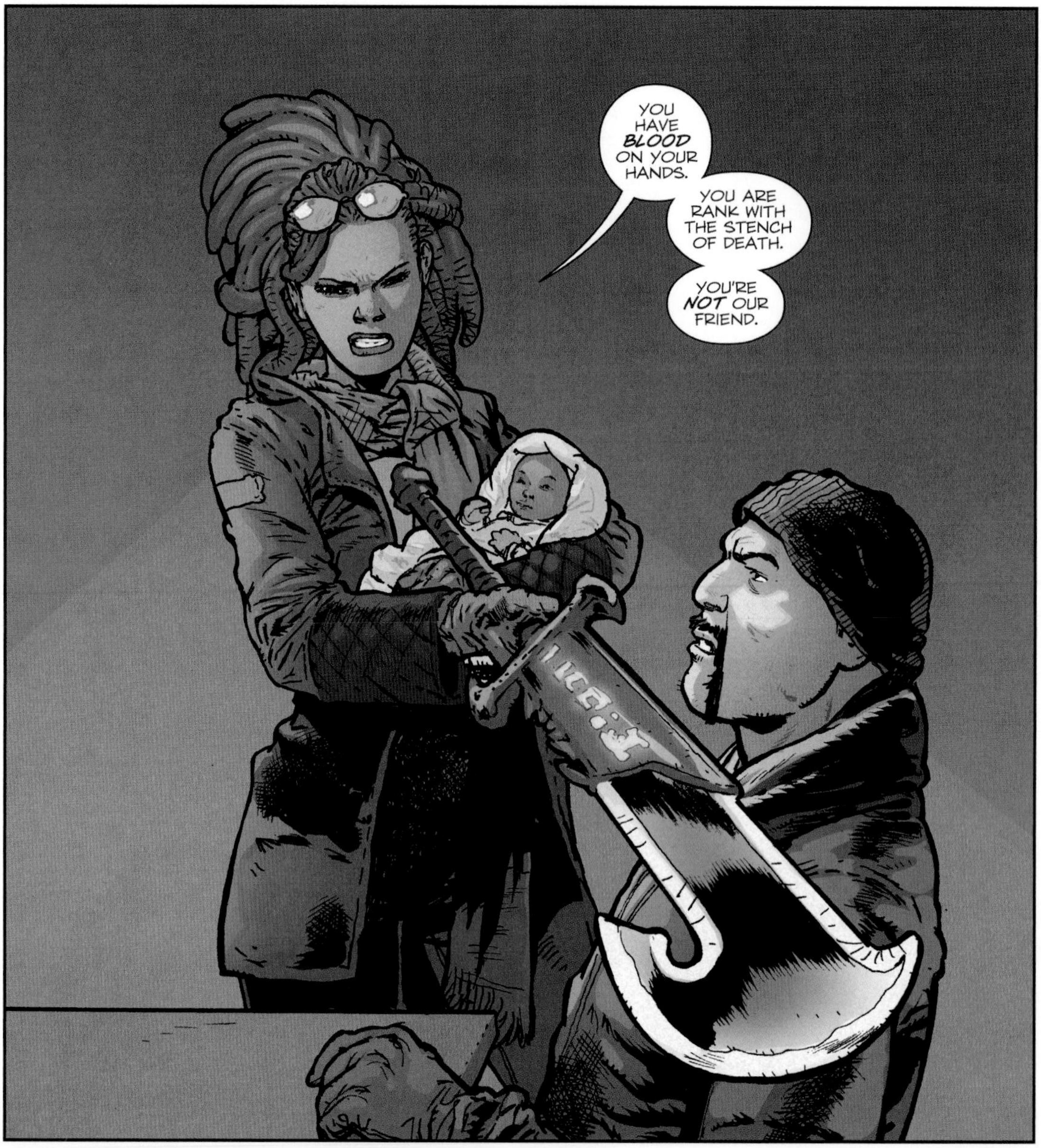
YOU HAVE BLOOD ON YOUR HANDS.
YOU ARE RANK WITH THE STENCH OF DEATH.
YOU'RE NOT OUR FRIEND.

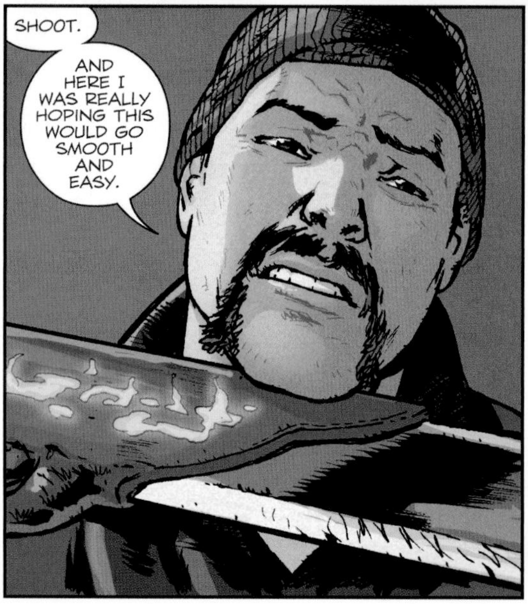
SHOOT.
AND HERE I WAS REALLY HOPING THIS WOULD GO SMOOTH AND EASY.

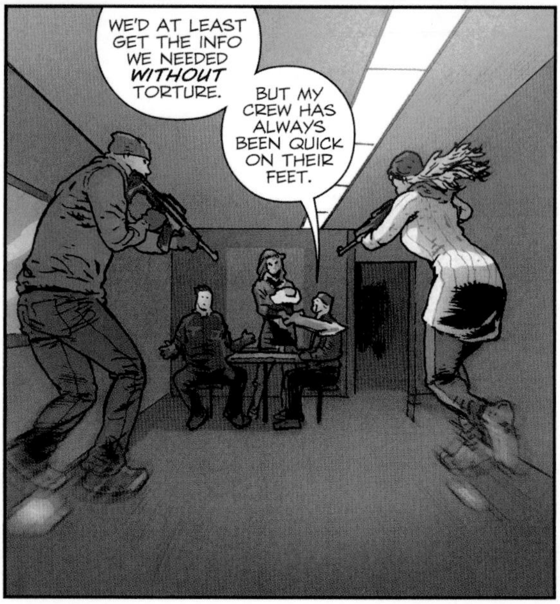
WE'D AT LEAST GET THE INFO WE NEEDED WITHOUT TORTURE.
BUT MY CREW HAS ALWAYS BEEN QUICK ON THEIR FEET.

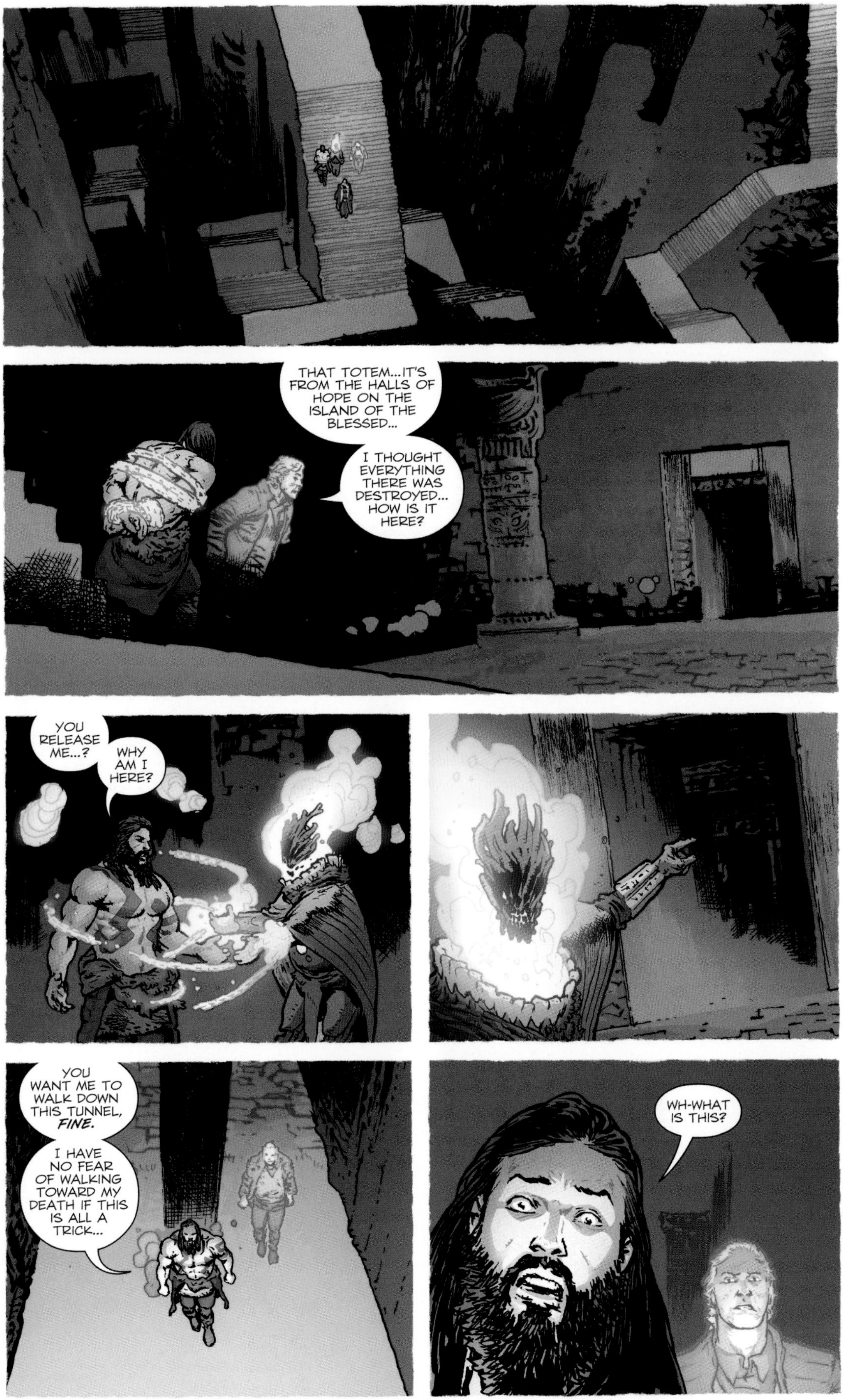
THAT TOTEM...IT'S FROM THE HALLS OF HOPE ON THE ISLAND OF THE BLESSED...
I THOUGHT EVERYTHING THERE WAS DESTROYED... HOW IS IT HERE?
YOU RELEASE ME...?
WHY AM I HERE?
YOU WANT ME TO WALK DOWN THIS TUNNEL, *FINE.*
I HAVE NO FEAR OF WALKING TOWARD MY DEATH IF THIS IS ALL A TRICK...
WH-WHAT IS THIS?

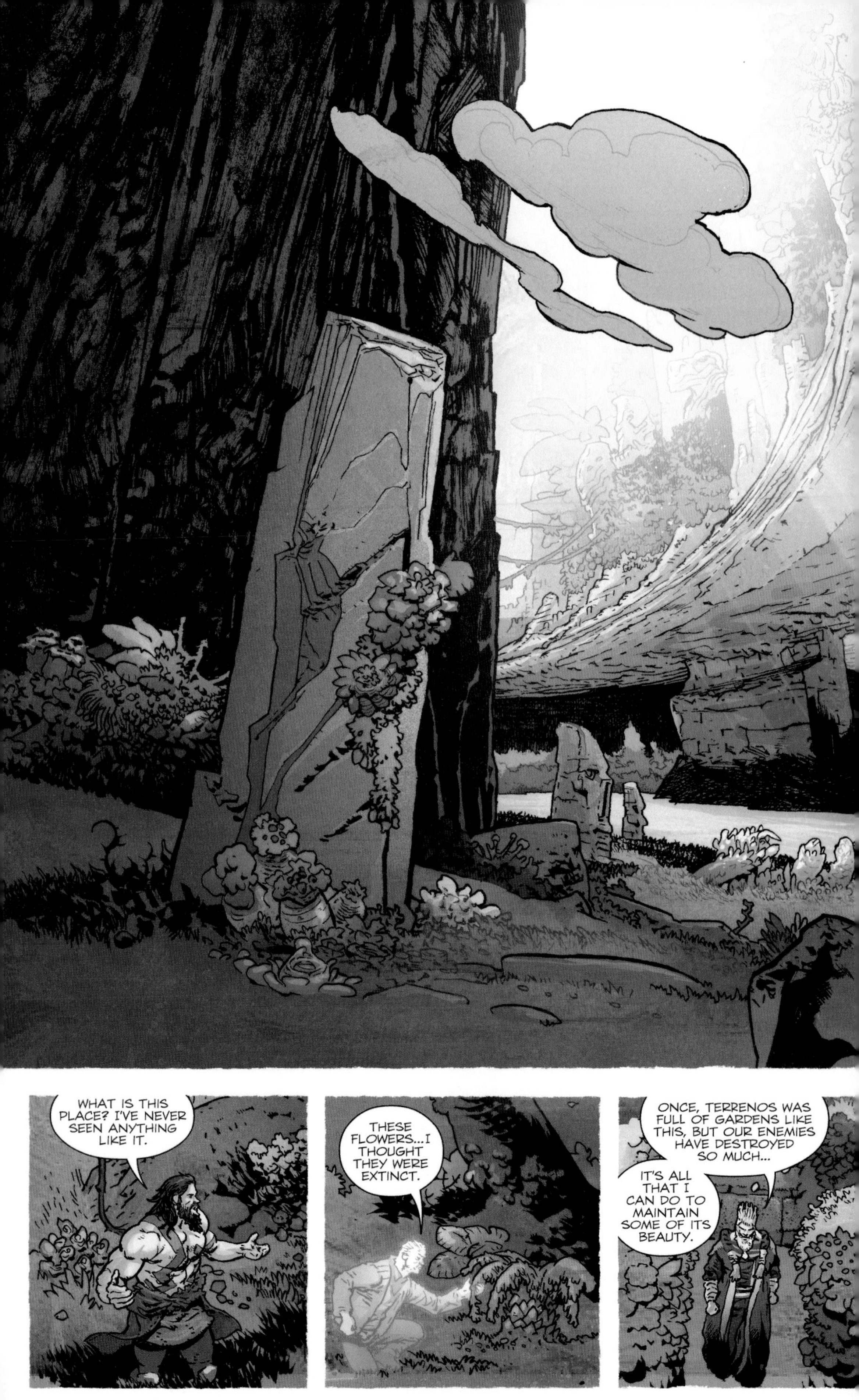
WHAT IS THIS PLACE? I'VE NEVER SEEN ANYTHING LIKE IT.
THESE FLOWERS...I THOUGHT THEY WERE EXTINCT.
ONCE, TERRENOS WAS FULL OF GARDENS LIKE THIS, BUT OUR ENEMIES HAVE DESTROYED SO MUCH...
IT'S ALL THAT I CAN DO TO MAINTAIN SOME OF ITS BEAUTY.

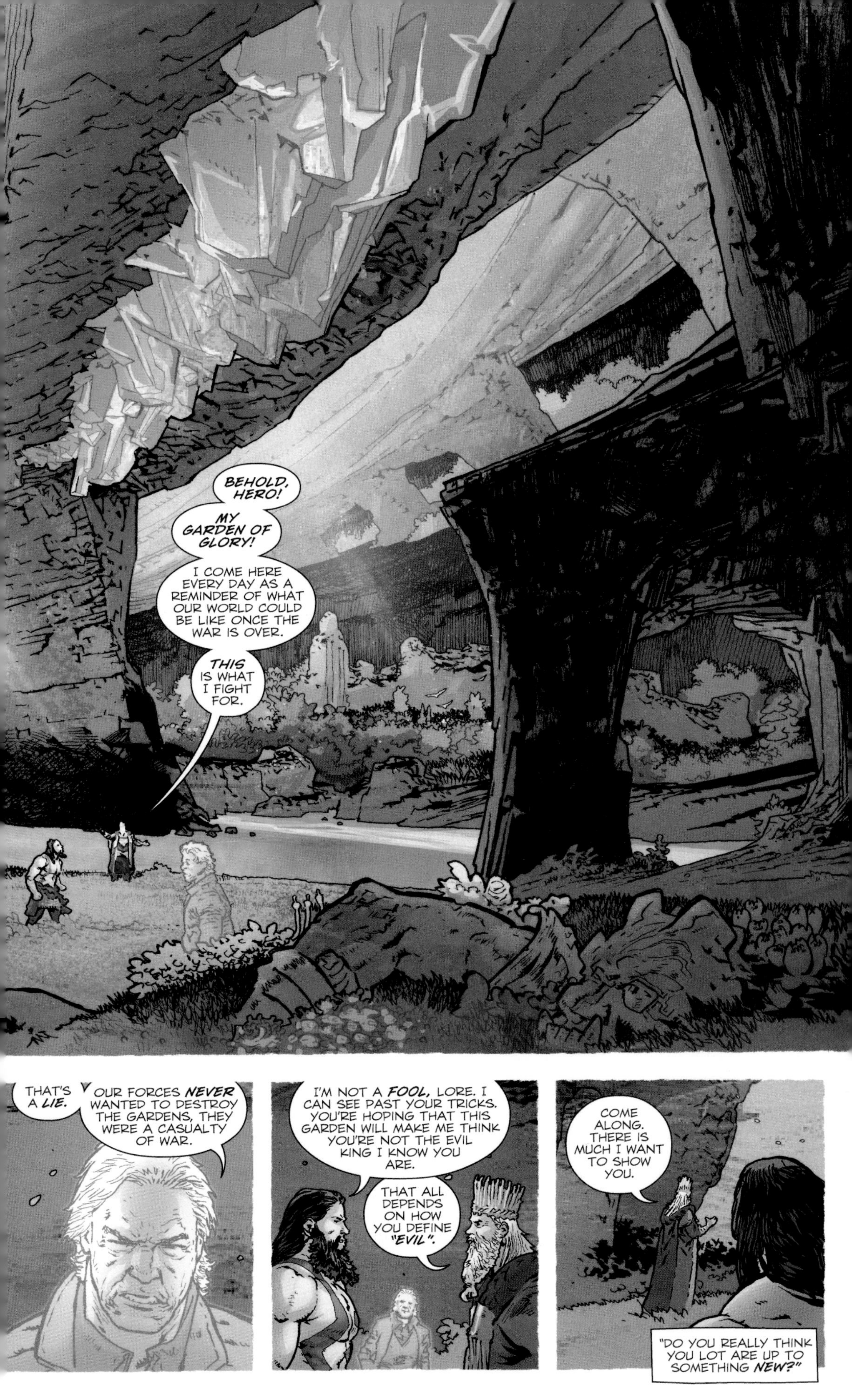
BEHOLD, HERO!
MY GARDEN OF GLORY!
I COME HERE EVERY DAY AS A REMINDER OF WHAT OUR WORLD COULD BE LIKE ONCE THE WAR IS OVER.
THIS IS WHAT I FIGHT FOR.
THAT'S A LIE.
OUR FORCES NEVER WANTED TO DESTROY THE GARDENS, THEY WERE A CASUALTY OF WAR.
I'M NOT A FOOL, LORE. I CAN SEE PAST YOUR TRICKS. YOU'RE HOPING THAT THIS GARDEN WILL MAKE ME THINK YOU'RE NOT THE EVIL KING I KNOW YOU ARE.
THAT ALL DEPENDS ON HOW YOU DEFINE "EVIL".
COME ALONG. THERE IS MUCH I WANT TO SHOW YOU.
"DO YOU REALLY THINK YOU LOT ARE UP TO SOMETHING NEW?"

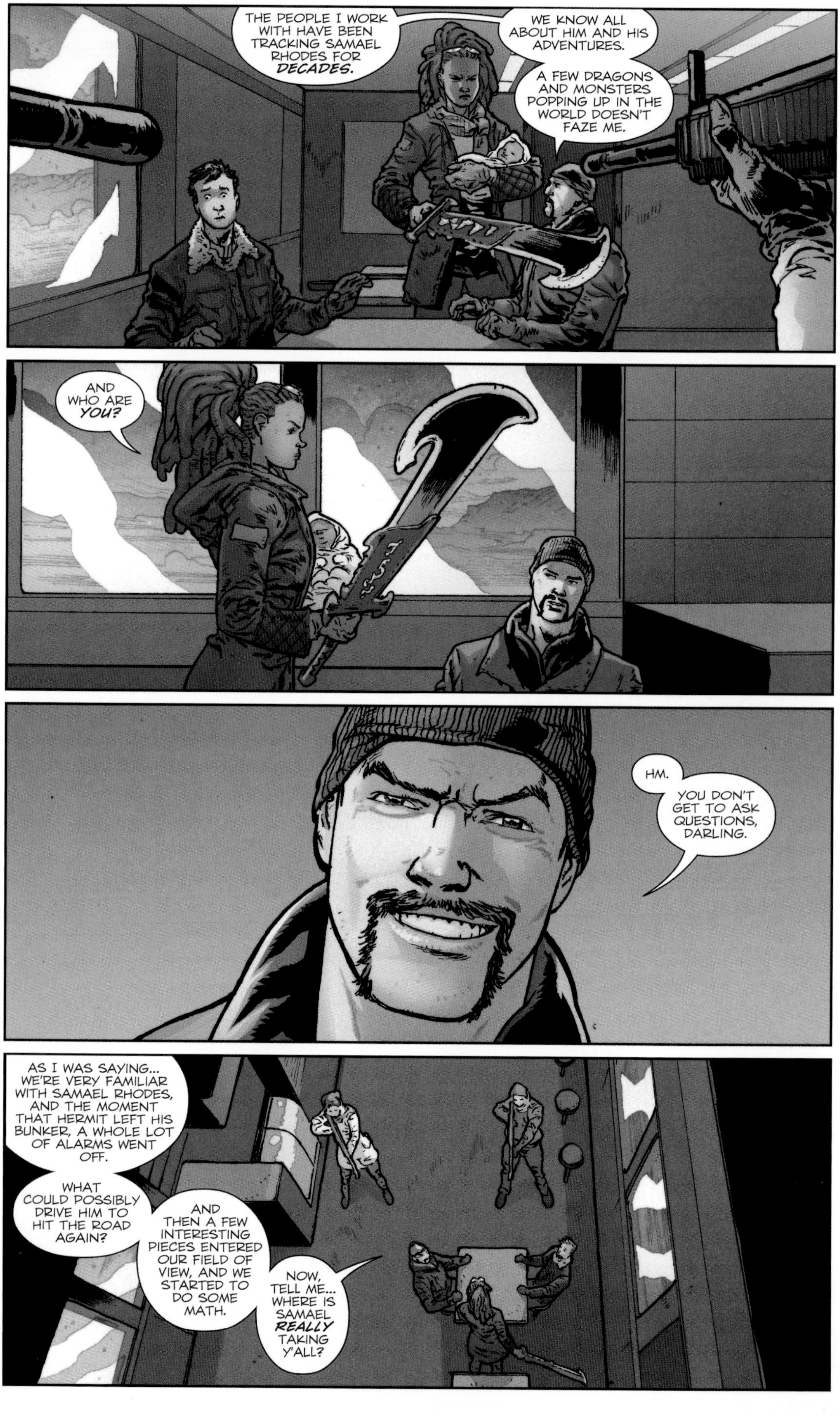
THE PEOPLE I WORK WITH HAVE BEEN TRACKING SAMAEL RHODES FOR *DECADES.*
WE KNOW ALL ABOUT HIM AND HIS ADVENTURES.
A FEW DRAGONS AND MONSTERS POPPING UP IN THE WORLD DOESN'T FAZE ME.
AND WHO ARE *YOU?*
HM.
YOU DON'T GET TO ASK QUESTIONS, DARLING.
AS I WAS SAYING... WE'RE VERY FAMILIAR WITH SAMAEL RHODES, AND THE MOMENT THAT HERMIT LEFT HIS BUNKER, A WHOLE LOT OF ALARMS WENT OFF.
WHAT COULD POSSIBLY DRIVE HIM TO HIT THE ROAD AGAIN?
AND THEN A FEW INTERESTING PIECES ENTERED OUR FIELD OF VIEW, AND WE STARTED TO DO SOME MATH.
NOW, TELL ME... WHERE IS SAMAEL *REALLY* TAKING Y'ALL?

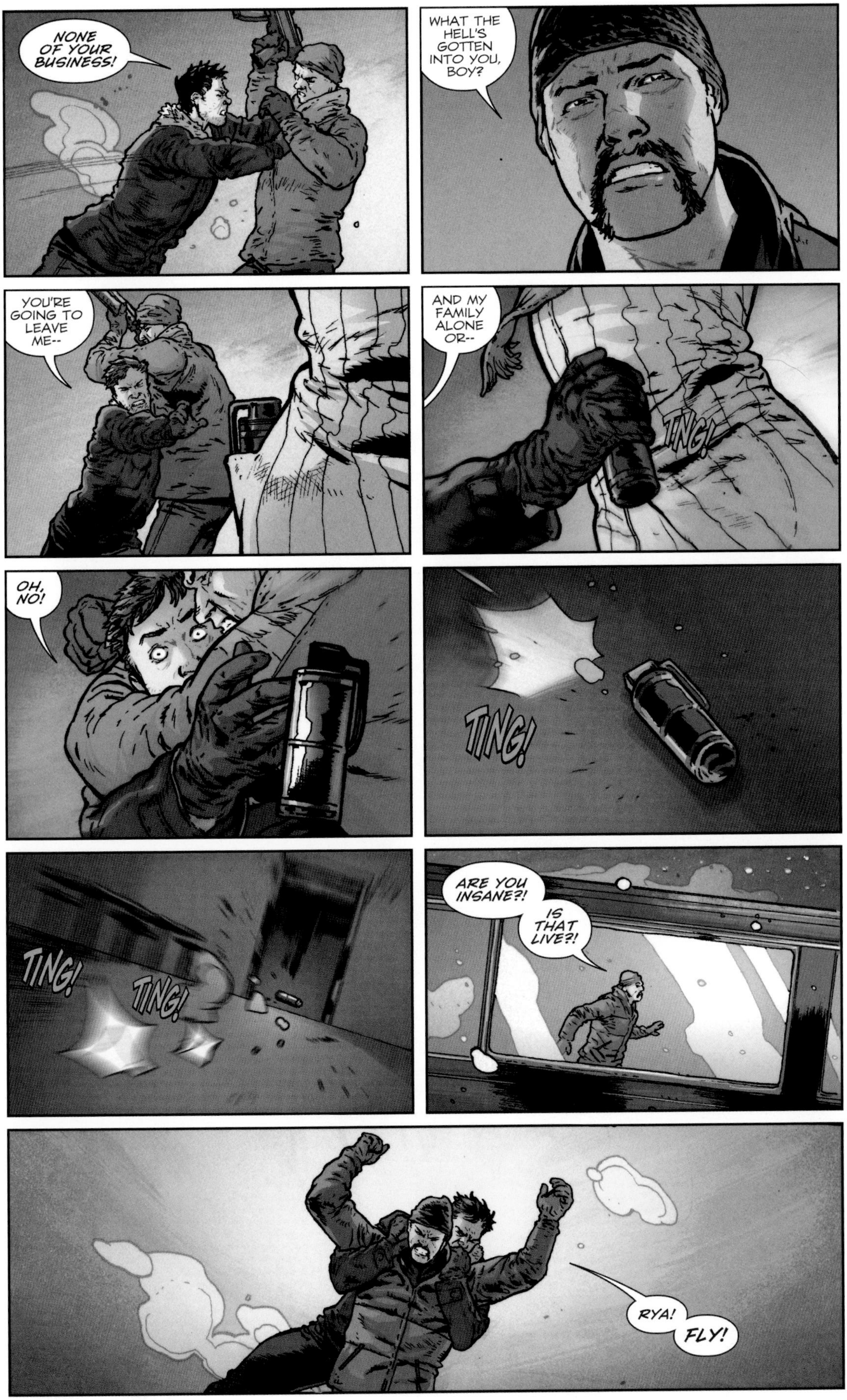
NONE OF YOUR BUSINESS!
WHAT THE HELL'S GOTTEN INTO YOU, BOY?
YOU'RE GOING TO LEAVE ME--
AND MY FAMILY ALONE OR--
TING!
OH, NO!
TING!
TING!
TING!
ARE YOU INSANE?!
IS THAT LIVE?!
RYA!
FLY!

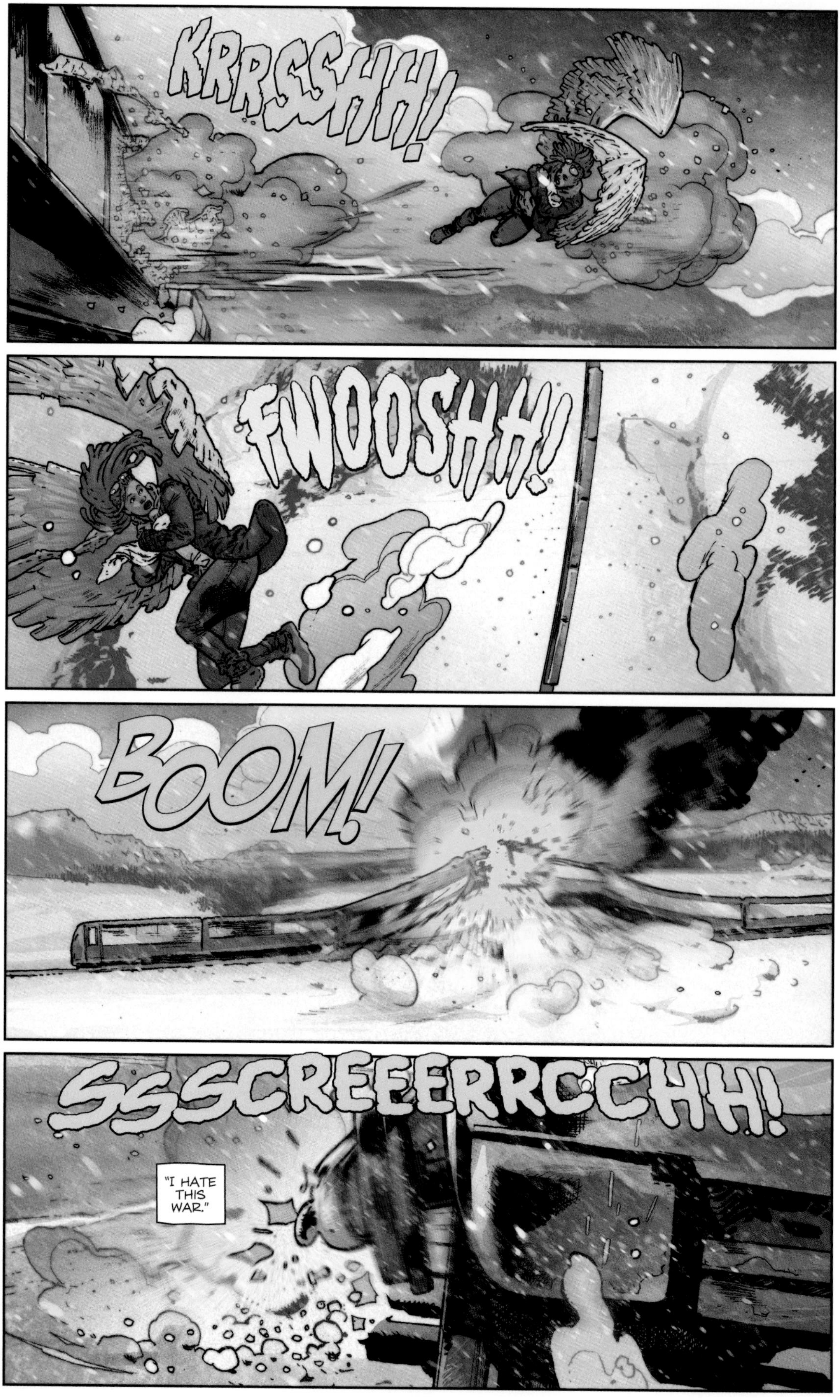
KRRSSHH!
FWOOSHH!
BOOM!
SSSCREEERRCCHH!
"I HATE THIS WAR."

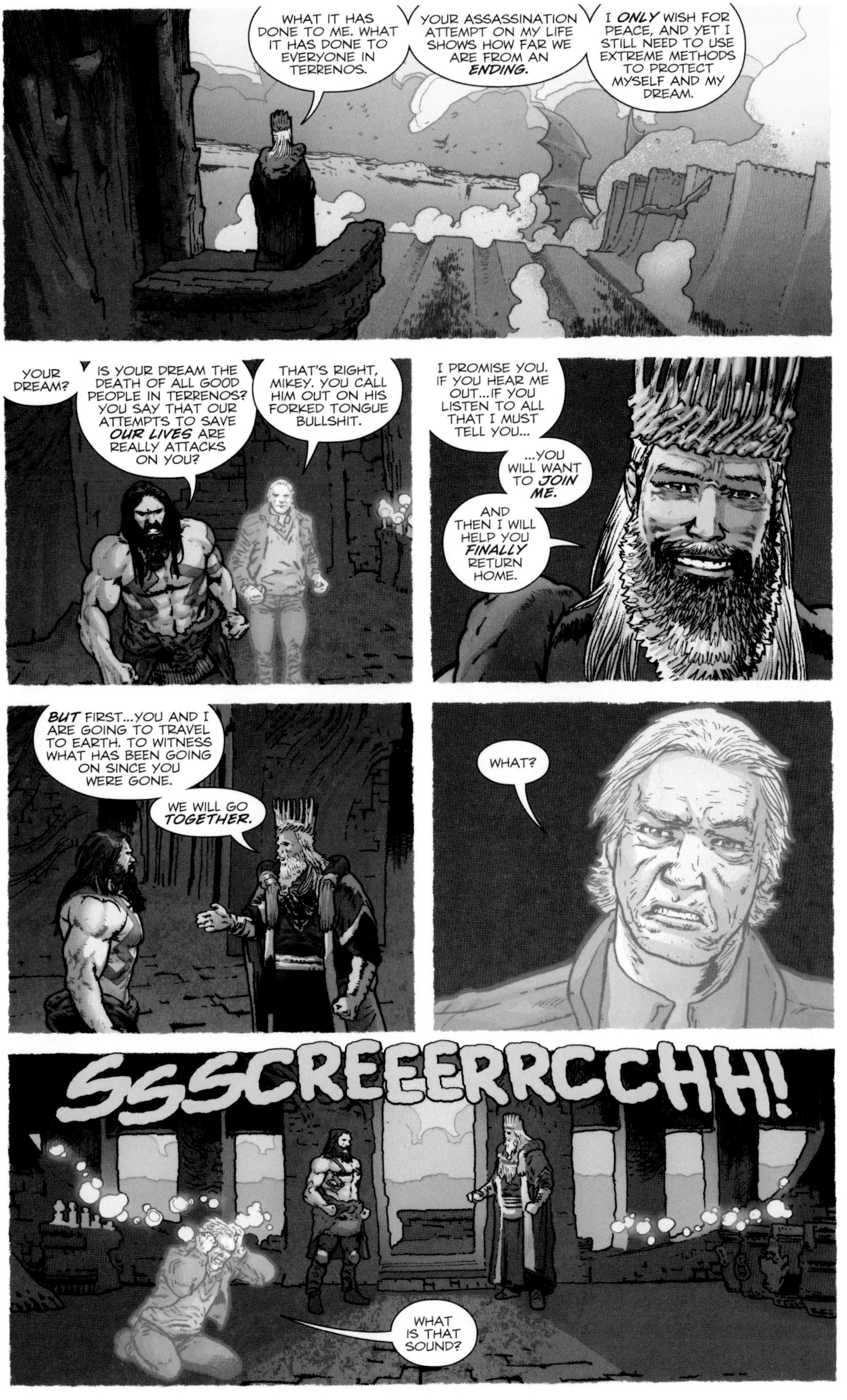
WHAT IT HAS DONE TO ME. WHAT IT HAS DONE TO EVERYONE IN TERRENOS.
YOUR ASSASSINATION ATTEMPT ON MY LIFE SHOWS HOW FAR WE ARE FROM AN ENDING.
I ONLY WISH FOR PEACE, AND YET I STILL NEED TO USE EXTREME METHODS TO PROTECT MYSELF AND MY DREAM.
YOUR DREAM?
IS YOUR DREAM THE DEATH OF ALL GOOD PEOPLE IN TERRENOS? YOU SAY THAT OUR ATTEMPTS TO SAVE OUR LIVES ARE REALLY ATTACKS ON YOU?
THAT'S RIGHT, MIKEY. YOU CALL HIM OUT ON HIS FORKED TONGUE BULLSHIT.
I PROMISE YOU. IF YOU HEAR ME OUT...IF YOU LISTEN TO ALL THAT I MUST TELL YOU...
...YOU WILL WANT TO JOIN ME.
AND THEN I WILL HELP YOU FINALLY RETURN HOME.
BUT FIRST...YOU AND I ARE GOING TO TRAVEL TO EARTH. TO WITNESS WHAT HAS BEEN GOING ON SINCE YOU WERE GONE.
WE WILL GO TOGETHER.
WHAT?
SSSCREEERRCCHH!
WHAT IS THAT SOUND?

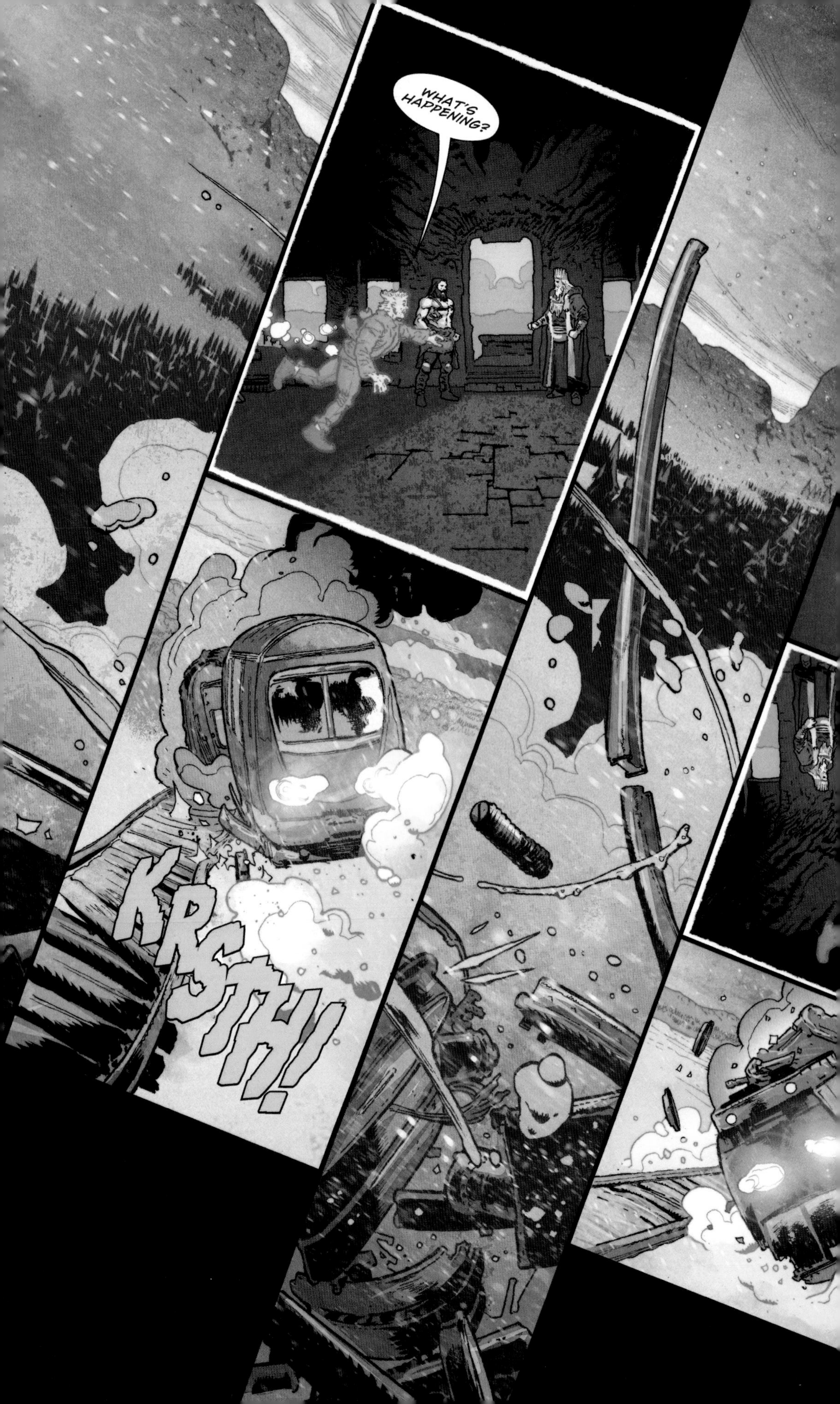

WHAT'S HAPPENING?
KRSSTH!

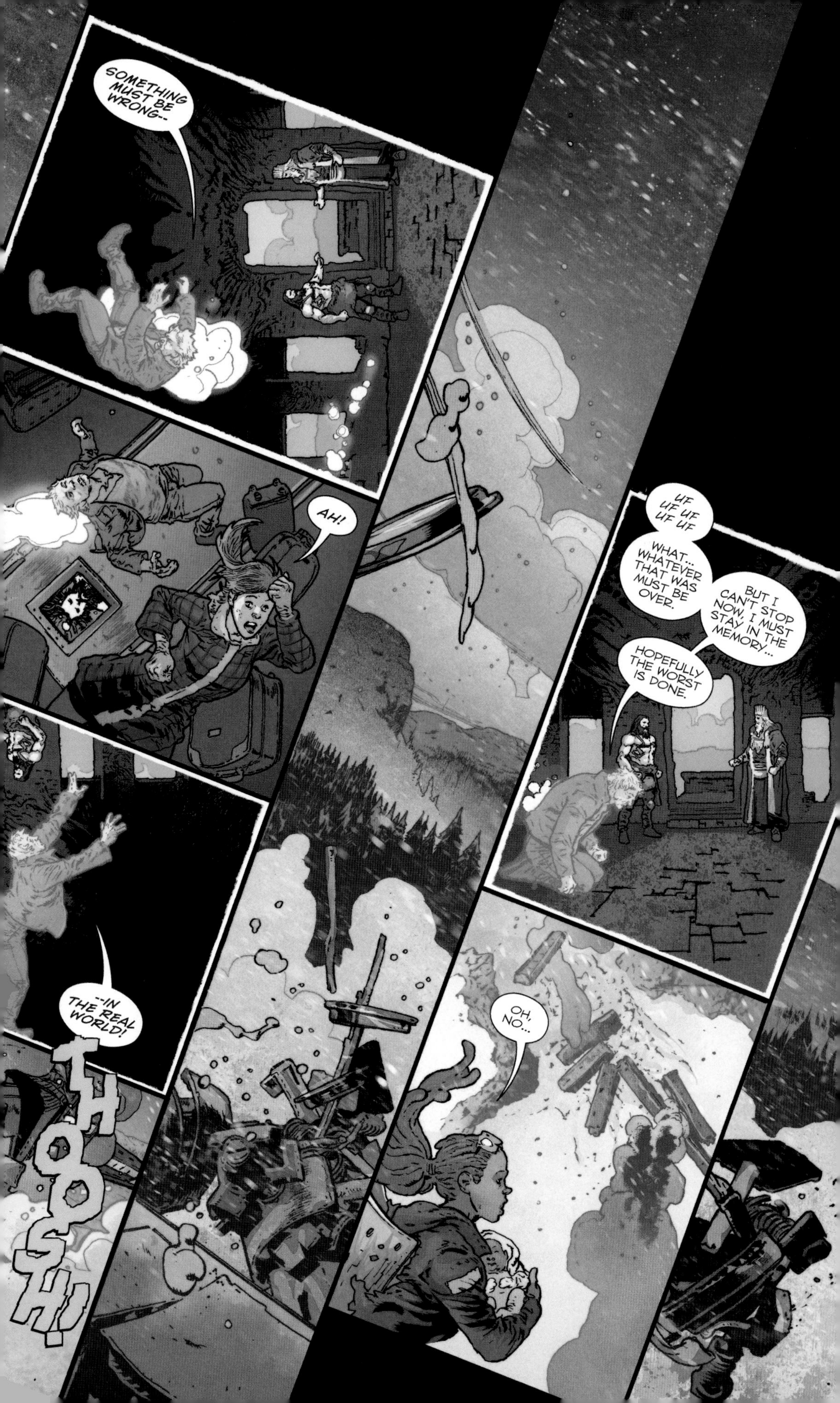
SOMETHING MUST BE WRONG--
AH!
--IN THE REAL WORLD!
THOOSH!
UF UF UF UF UF
WHAT... WHATEVER THAT WAS MUST BE OVER.
BUT I CAN'T STOP NOW, I MUST STAY IN THE MEMORY...
HOPEFULLY THE WORST IS DONE.
OH, NO...

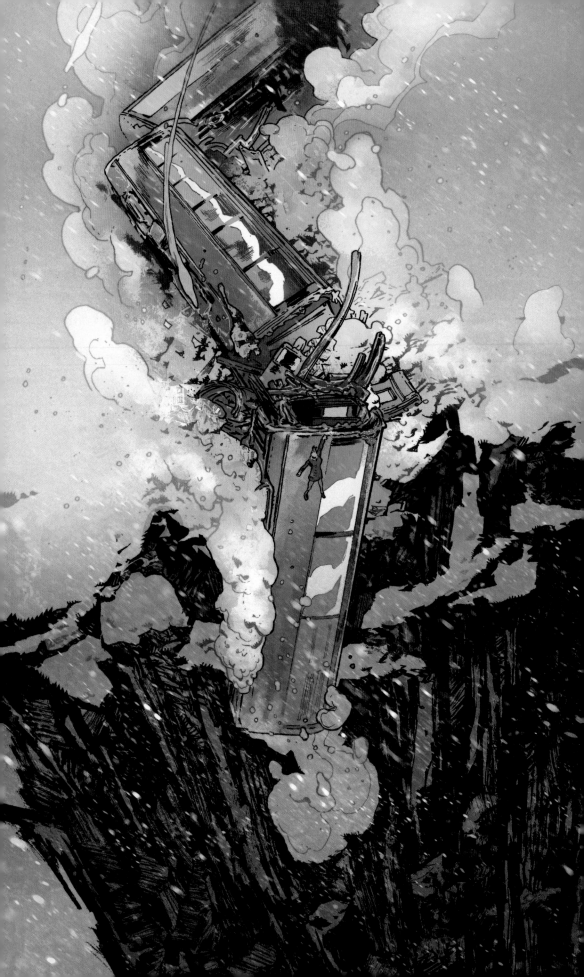

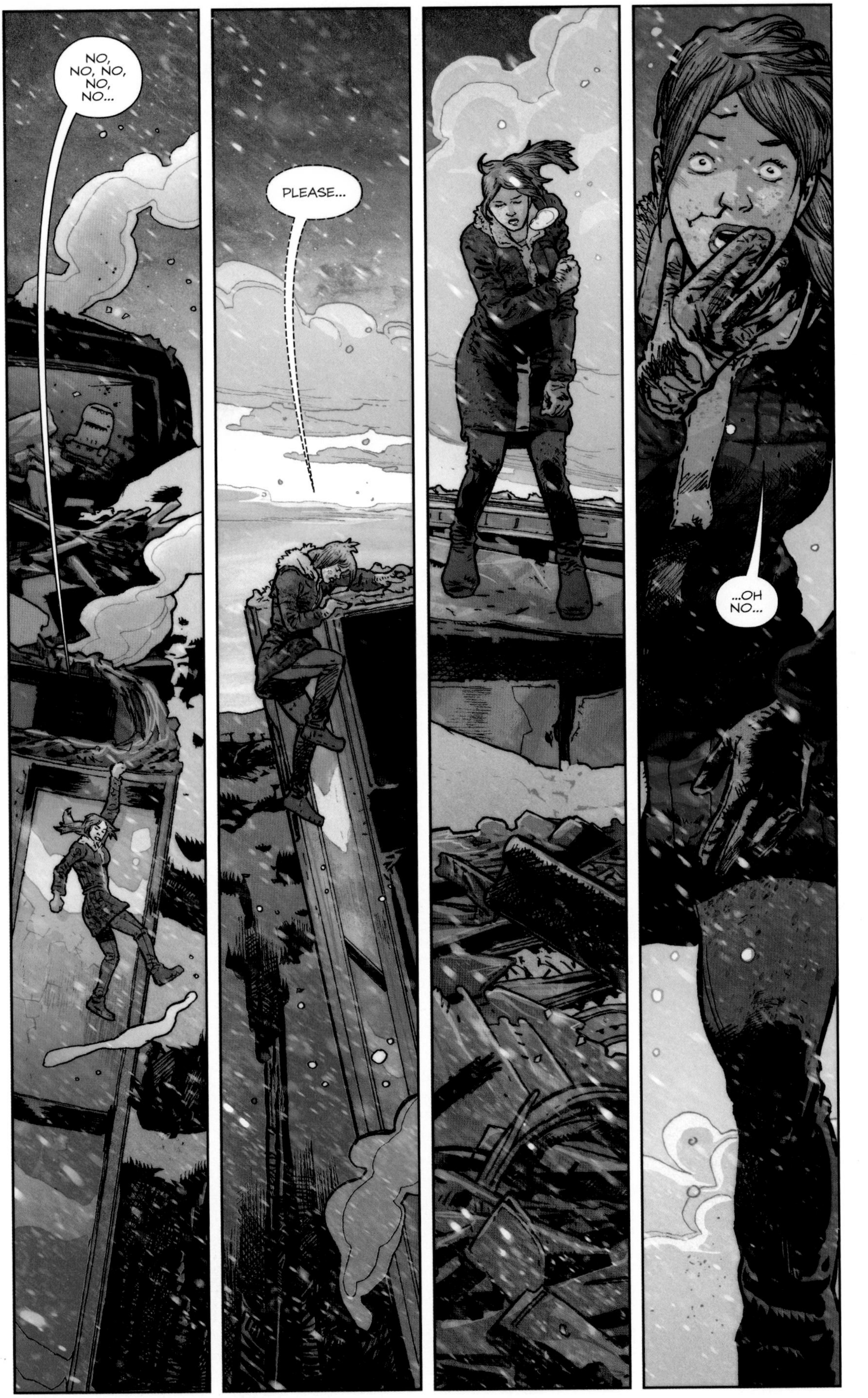

NO, NO, NO, NO, NO...
PLEASE...
...OH NO...

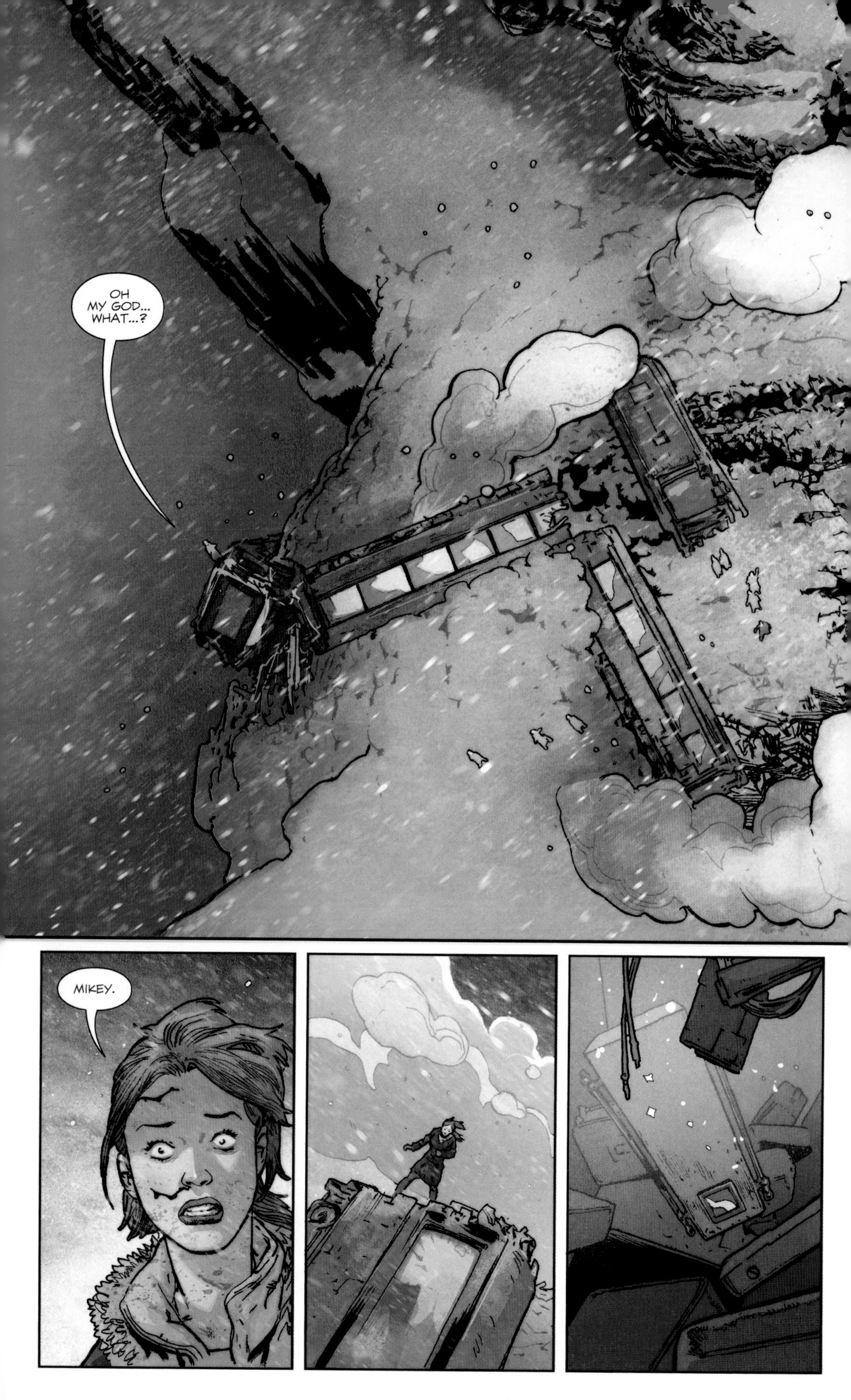
OH MY GOD... WHAT...?
MIKEY.

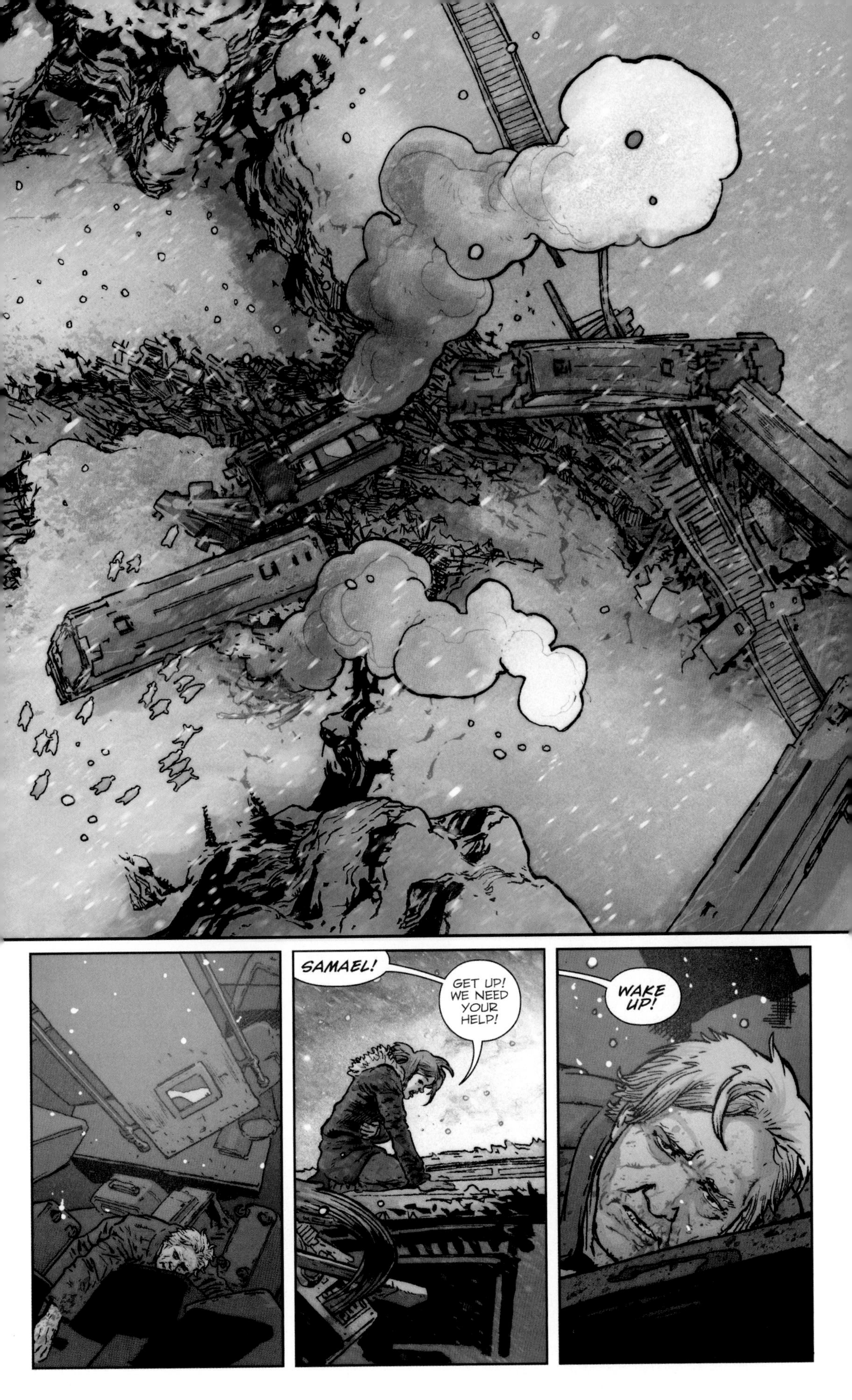
SAMAEL!
GET UP! WE NEED YOUR HELP!
WAKE UP!

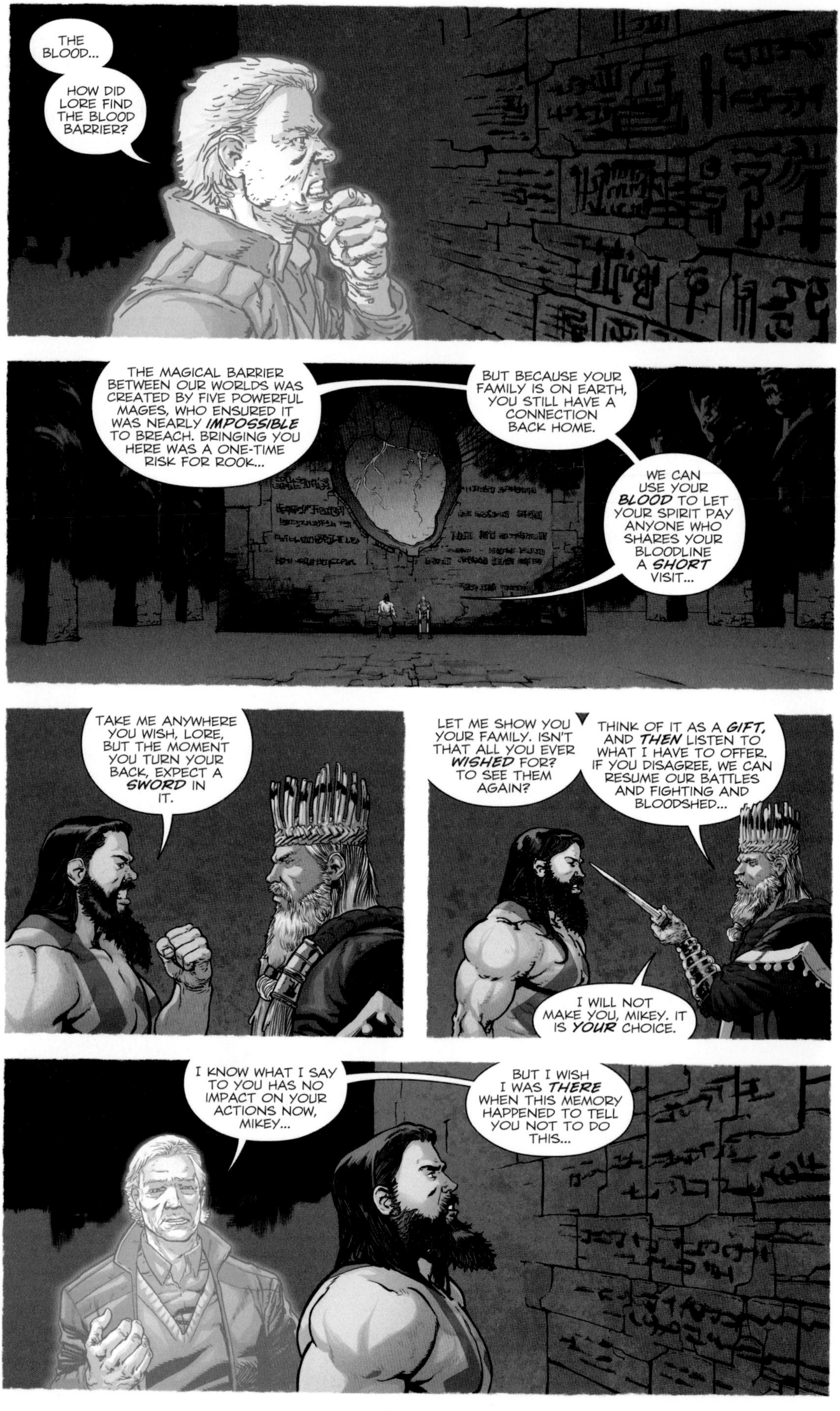
THE BLOOD...
HOW DID LORE FIND THE BLOOD BARRIER?
THE MAGICAL BARRIER BETWEEN OUR WORLDS WAS CREATED BY FIVE POWERFUL MAGES, WHO ENSURED IT WAS NEARLY *IMPOSSIBLE* TO BREACH. BRINGING YOU HERE WAS A ONE-TIME RISK FOR ROOK...
BUT BECAUSE YOUR FAMILY IS ON EARTH, YOU STILL HAVE A CONNECTION BACK HOME.
WE CAN USE YOUR *BLOOD* TO LET YOUR SPIRIT PAY ANYONE WHO SHARES YOUR BLOODLINE A *SHORT* VISIT...
TAKE ME ANYWHERE YOU WISH, LORE, BUT THE MOMENT YOU TURN YOUR BACK, EXPECT A *SWORD* IN IT.
LET ME SHOW YOU YOUR FAMILY. ISN'T THAT ALL YOU EVER *WISHED* FOR? TO SEE THEM AGAIN?
THINK OF IT AS A *GIFT*, AND *THEN* LISTEN TO WHAT I HAVE TO OFFER. IF YOU DISAGREE, WE CAN RESUME OUR BATTLES AND FIGHTING AND BLOODSHED...
I WILL NOT MAKE YOU, MIKEY. IT IS *YOUR* CHOICE.
I KNOW WHAT I SAY TO YOU HAS NO IMPACT ON YOUR ACTIONS NOW, MIKEY...
BUT I WISH I WAS *THERE* WHEN THIS MEMORY HAPPENED TO TELL YOU NOT TO DO THIS...

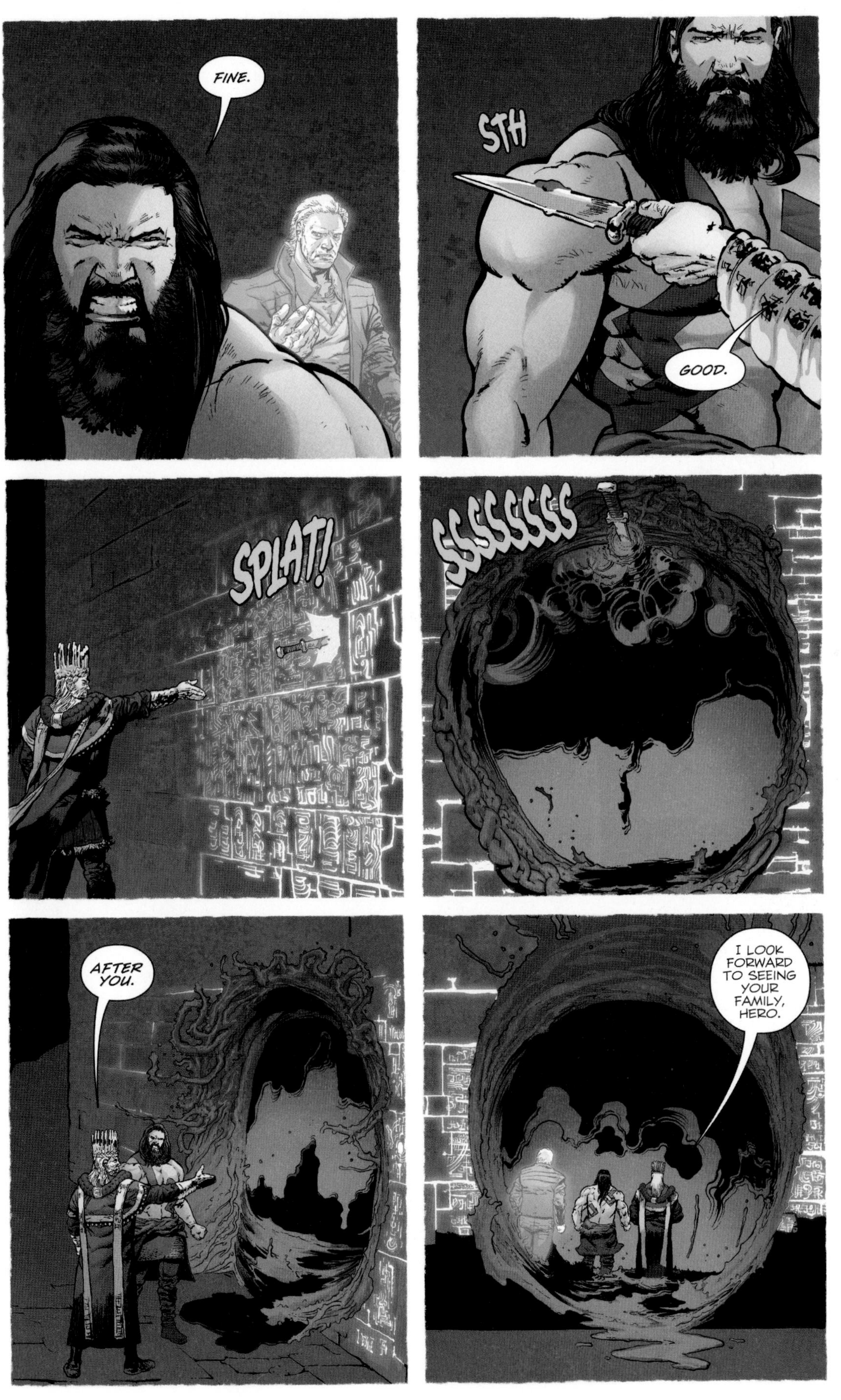
FINE.
STH
GOOD.
SPLAT!
SSSSSSSS
AFTER YOU.
I LOOK FORWARD TO SEEING YOUR FAMILY, HERO.

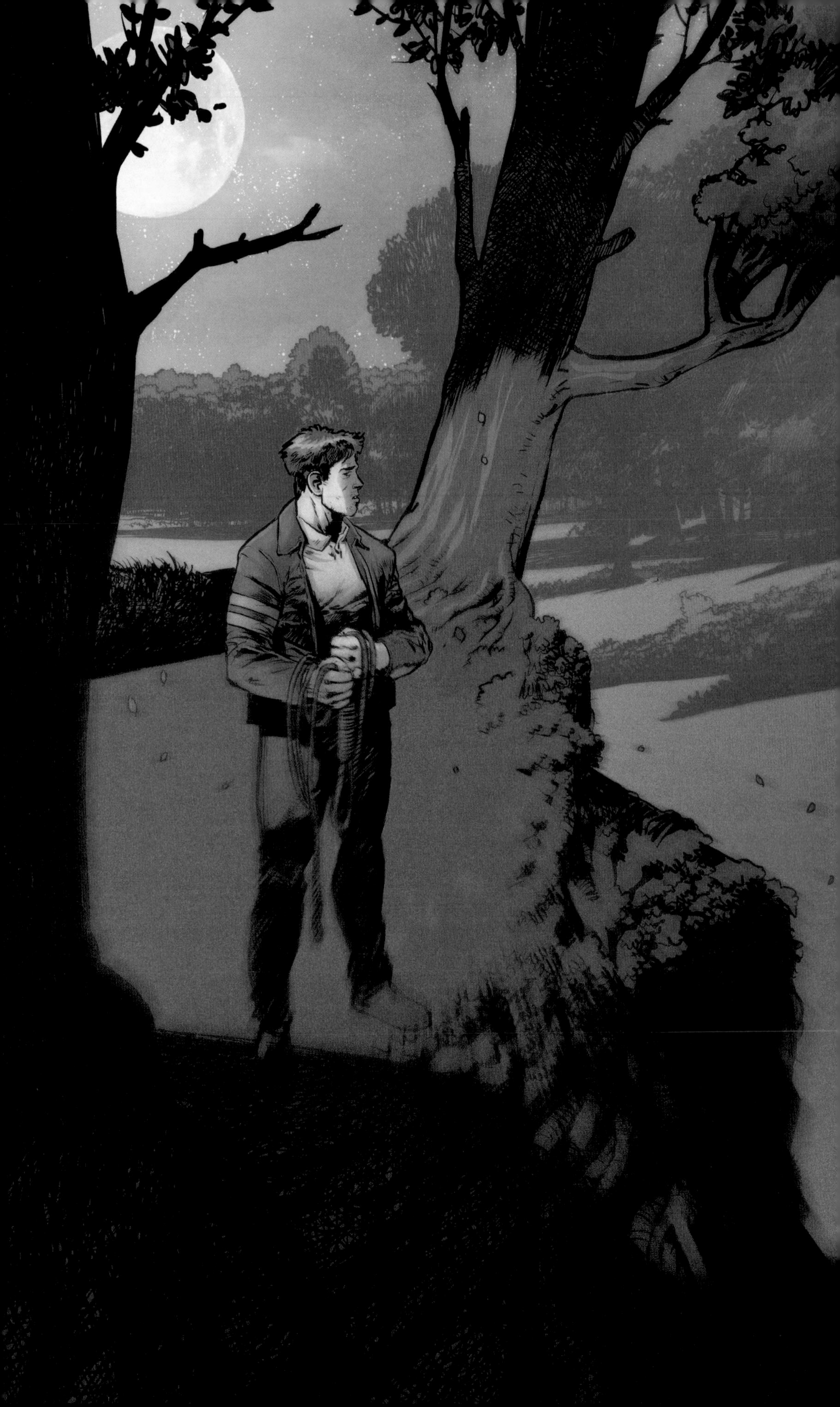

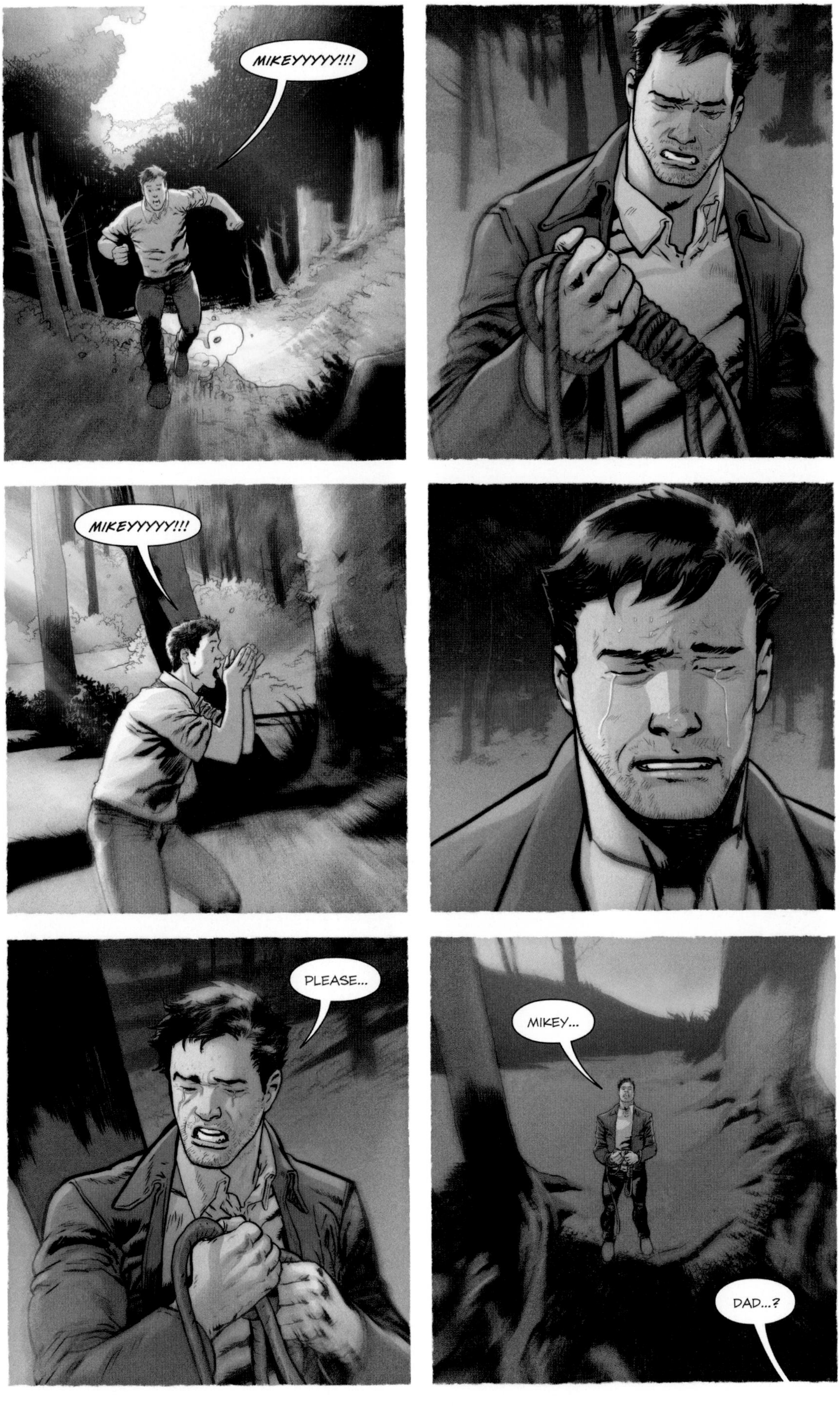
MIKEYYYYY!!!
MIKEYYYYY!!!
PLEASE...
MIKEY...
DAD...?

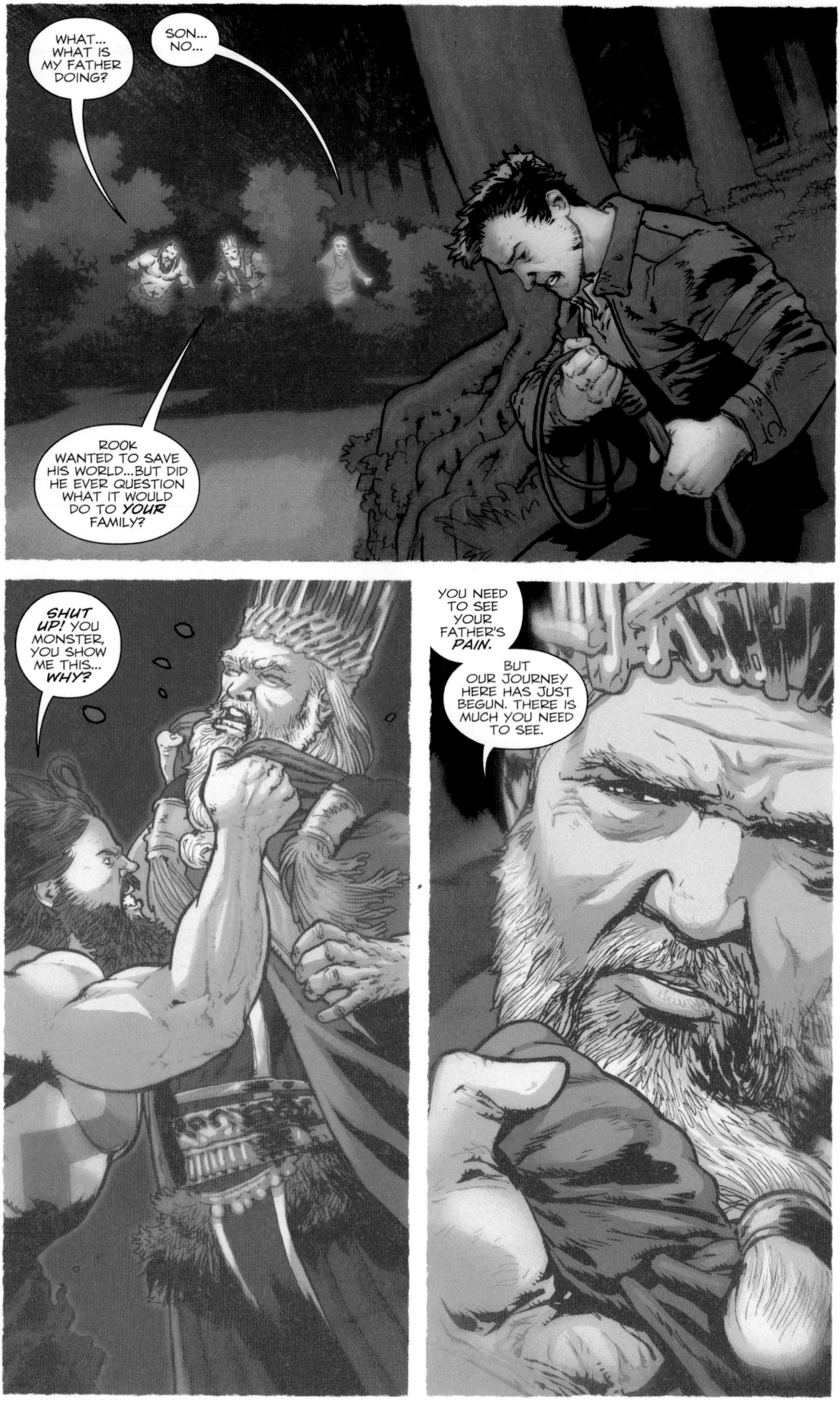
WHAT... WHAT IS MY FATHER DOING?
SON... NO...
ROOK WANTED TO SAVE HIS WORLD...BUT DID HE EVER QUESTION WHAT IT WOULD DO TO YOUR FAMILY?
SHUT UP! YOU MONSTER, YOU SHOW ME THIS... WHY?
YOU NEED TO SEE YOUR FATHER'S PAIN.
BUT OUR JOURNEY HERE HAS JUST BEGUN. THERE IS MUCH YOU NEED TO SEE.

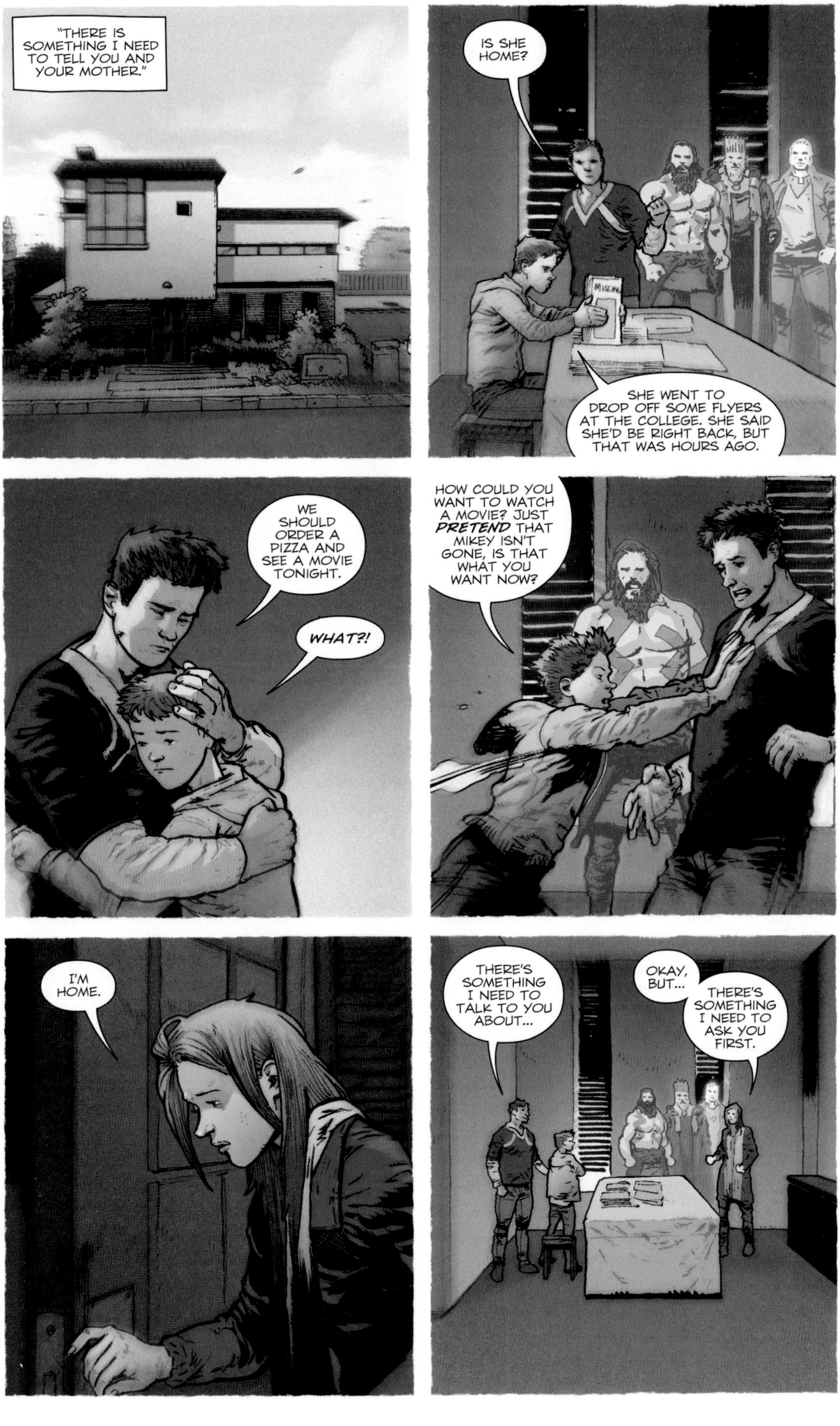
"THERE IS SOMETHING I NEED TO TELL YOU AND YOUR MOTHER."
IS SHE HOME?
SHE WENT TO DROP OFF SOME FLYERS AT THE COLLEGE. SHE SAID SHE'D BE RIGHT BACK, BUT THAT WAS HOURS AGO.
WE SHOULD ORDER A PIZZA AND SEE A MOVIE TONIGHT.
WHAT?!
HOW COULD YOU WANT TO WATCH A MOVIE? JUST PRETEND THAT MIKEY ISN'T GONE, IS THAT WHAT YOU WANT NOW?
I'M HOME.
THERE'S SOMETHING I NEED TO TALK TO YOU ABOUT...
OKAY, BUT...
THERE'S SOMETHING I NEED TO ASK YOU FIRST.

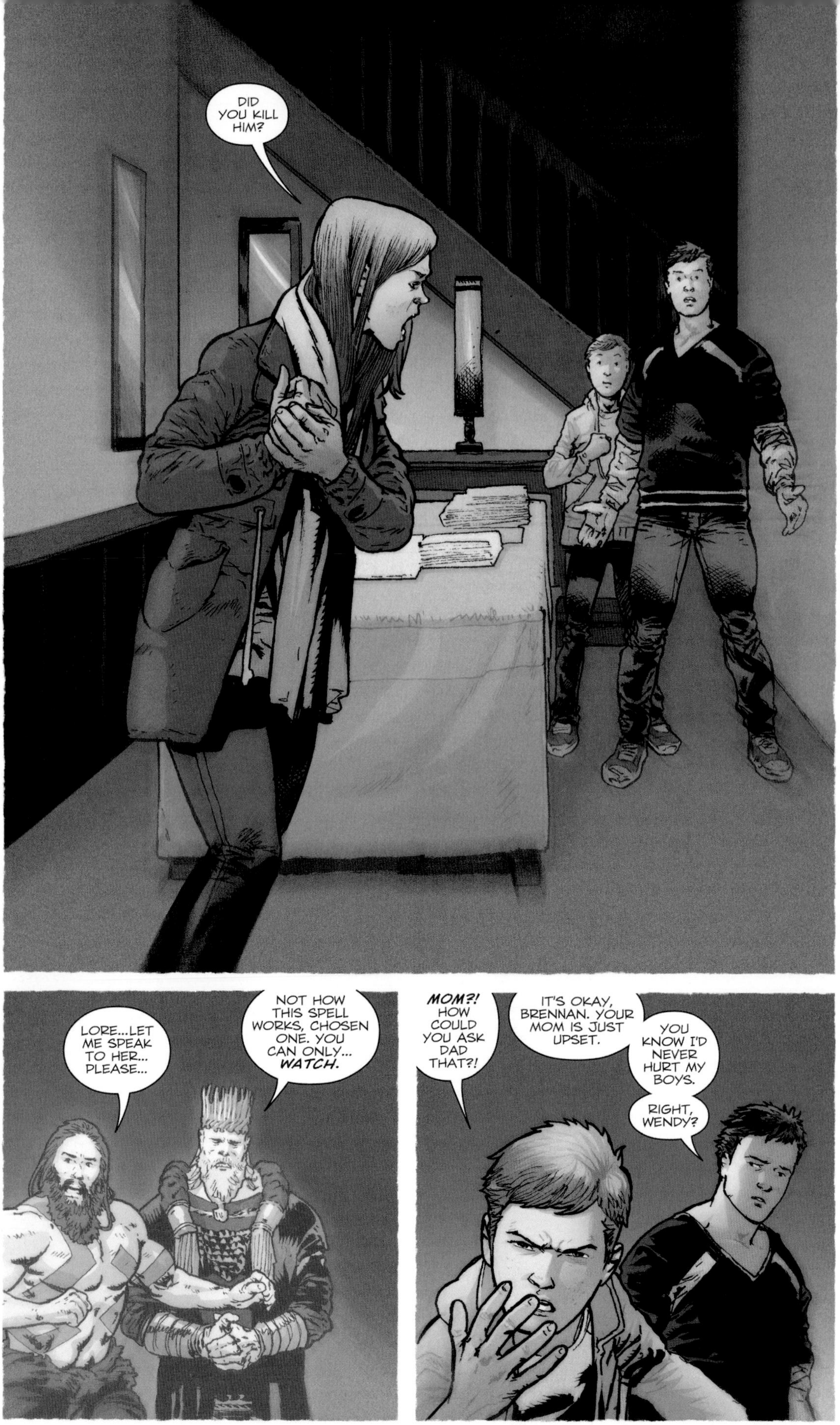
DID YOU KILL HIM?
LORE...LET ME SPEAK TO HER... PLEASE...
NOT HOW THIS SPELL WORKS, CHOSEN ONE. YOU CAN ONLY... ***WATCH.***
MOM?! HOW COULD YOU ASK DAD THAT?!
IT'S OKAY, BRENNAN. YOUR MOM IS JUST UPSET.
YOU KNOW I'D NEVER HURT MY BOYS.
RIGHT, WENDY?

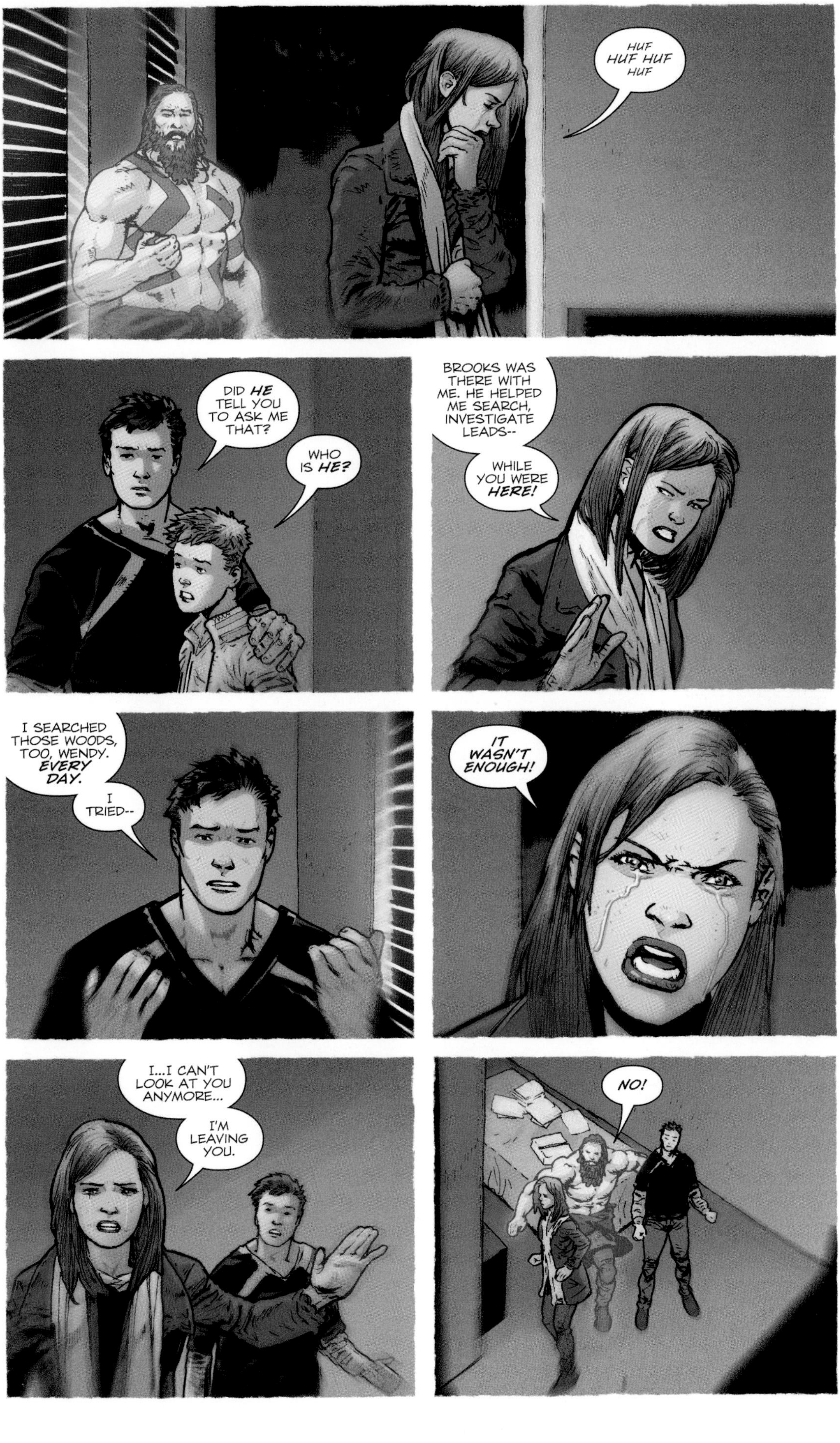
HUF HUF HUF HUF
DID HE TELL YOU TO ASK ME THAT?
WHO IS HE?
BROOKS WAS THERE WITH ME. HE HELPED ME SEARCH, INVESTIGATE LEADS--
WHILE YOU WERE HERE!
I SEARCHED THOSE WOODS, TOO, WENDY. EVERY DAY.
I TRIED--
IT WASN'T ENOUGH!
I...I CAN'T LOOK AT YOU ANYMORE...
I'M LEAVING YOU.
NO!

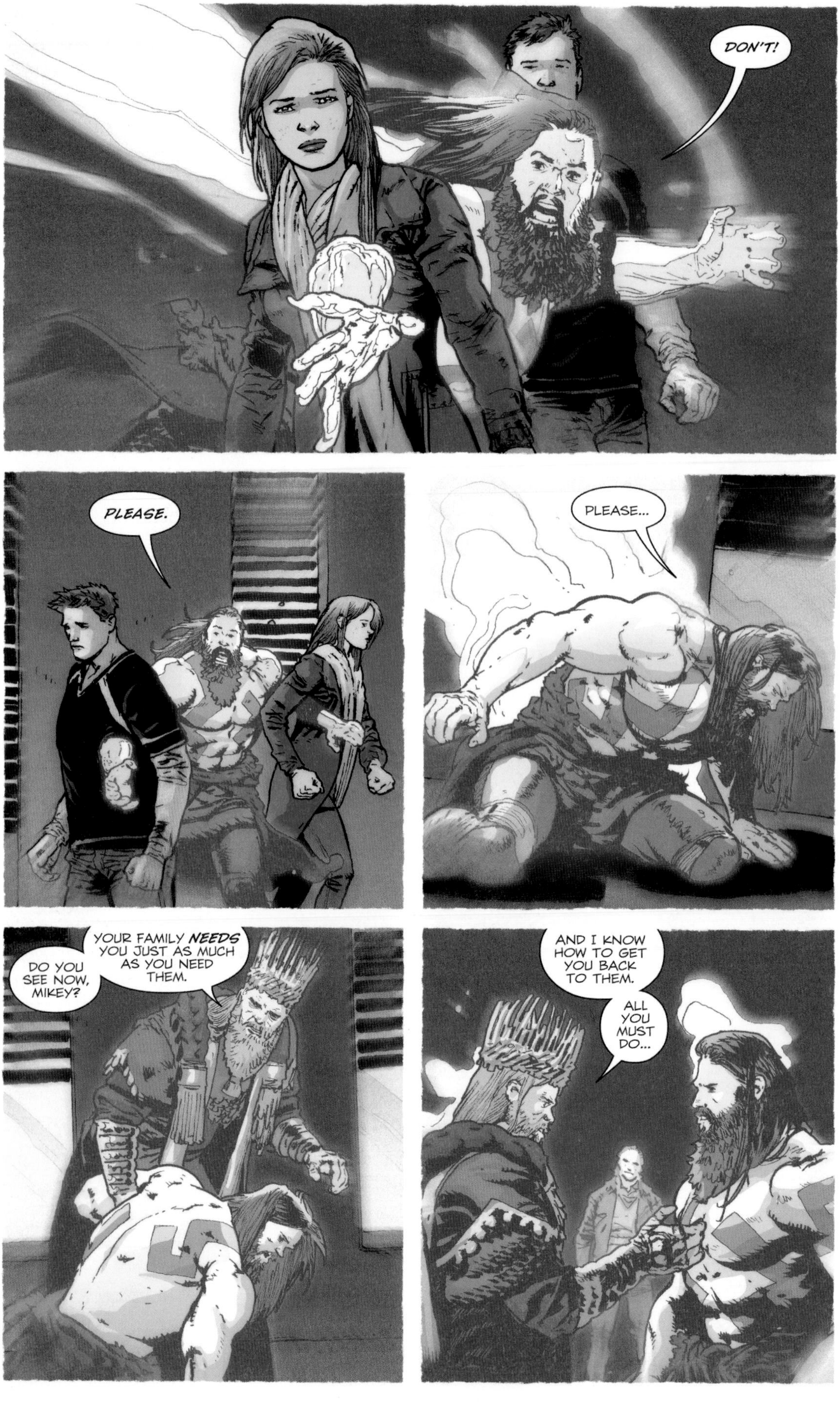
DON'T!
PLEASE.
PLEASE...
DO YOU SEE NOW, MIKEY?
YOUR FAMILY NEEDS YOU JUST AS MUCH AS YOU NEED THEM.
AND I KNOW HOW TO GET YOU BACK TO THEM.
ALL YOU MUST DO...

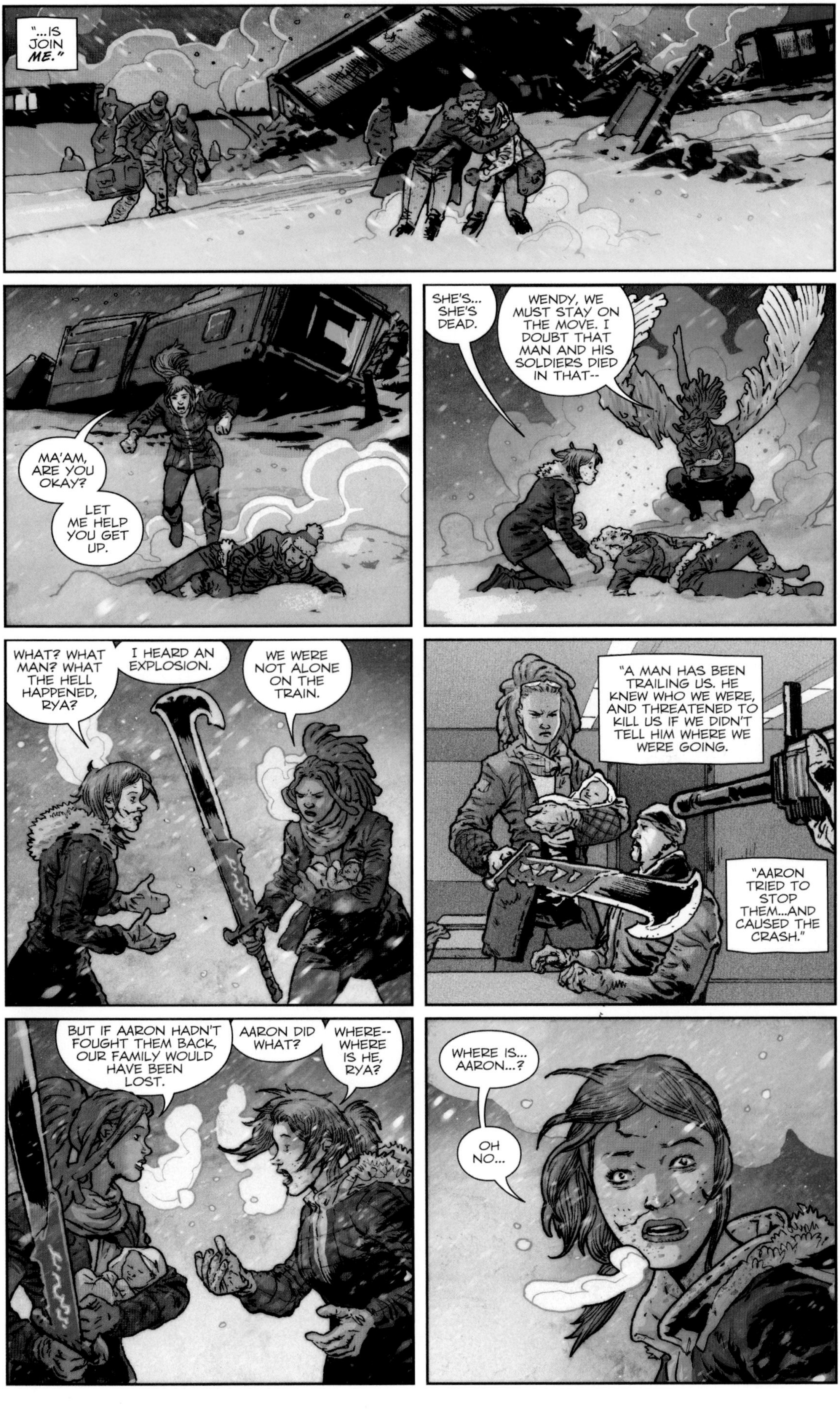

"...IS JOIN *ME*."
MA'AM, ARE YOU OKAY?
LET ME HELP YOU GET UP.
SHE'S... SHE'S DEAD.
WENDY, WE MUST STAY ON THE MOVE. I DOUBT THAT MAN AND HIS SOLDIERS DIED IN THAT--
WHAT? WHAT MAN? WHAT THE HELL HAPPENED, RYA?
I HEARD AN EXPLOSION.
WE WERE NOT ALONE ON THE TRAIN.
"A MAN HAS BEEN TRAILING US. HE KNEW WHO WE WERE, AND THREATENED TO KILL US IF WE DIDN'T TELL HIM WHERE WE WERE GOING.
"AARON TRIED TO STOP THEM...AND CAUSED THE CRASH."
BUT IF AARON HADN'T FOUGHT THEM BACK, OUR FAMILY WOULD HAVE BEEN LOST.
AARON DID WHAT?
WHERE-- WHERE IS HE, RYA?
WHERE IS... AARON...?
OH NO...

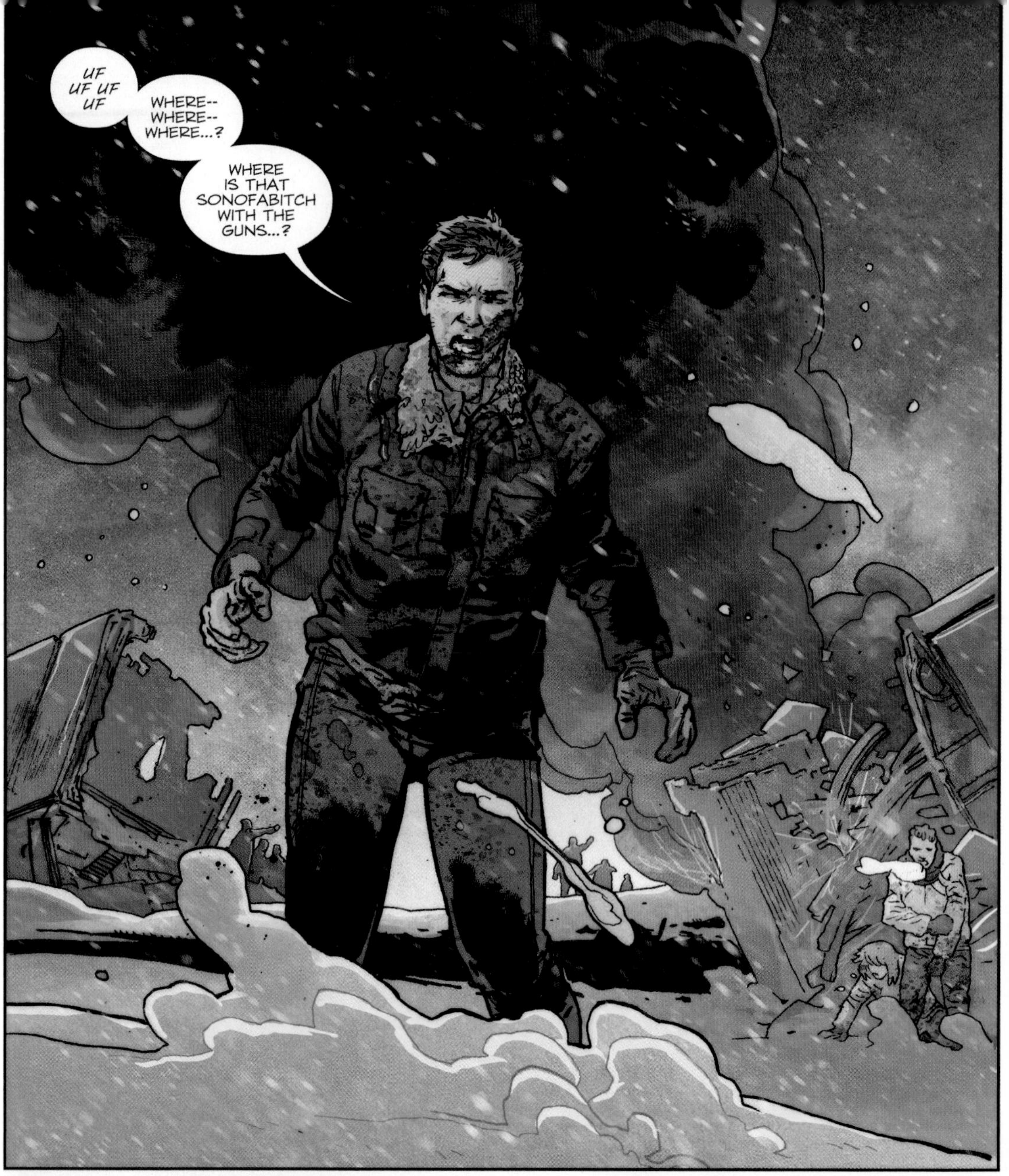
UF UF UF UF
WHERE-- WHERE-- WHERE...?
WHERE IS THAT SONOFABITCH WITH THE GUNS...?

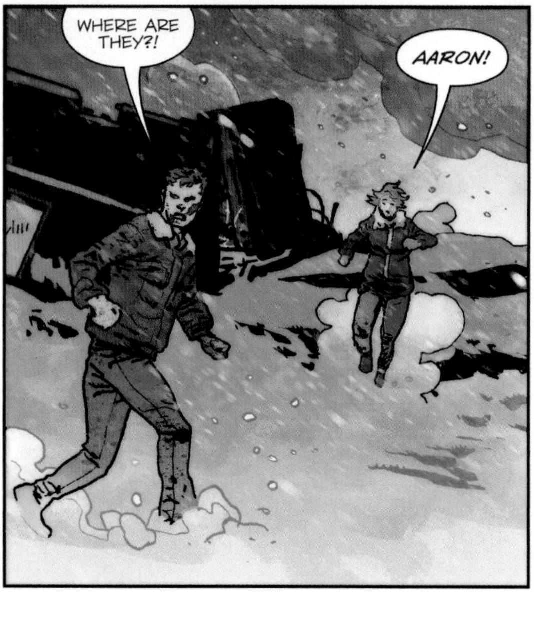
WHERE ARE THEY?!
AARON!

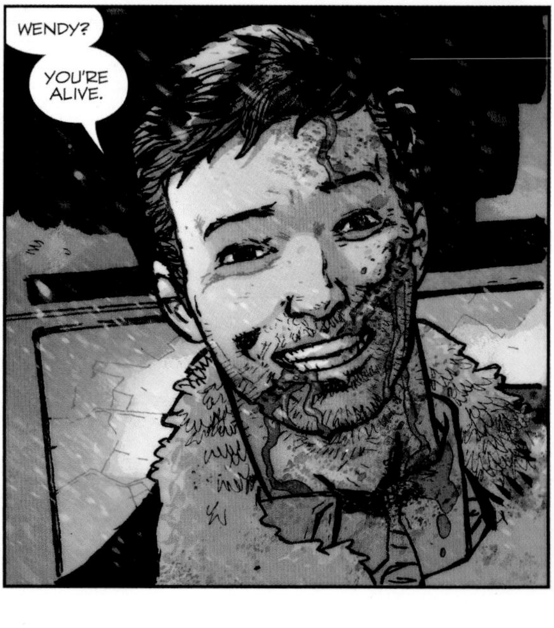
WENDY?
YOU'RE ALIVE.

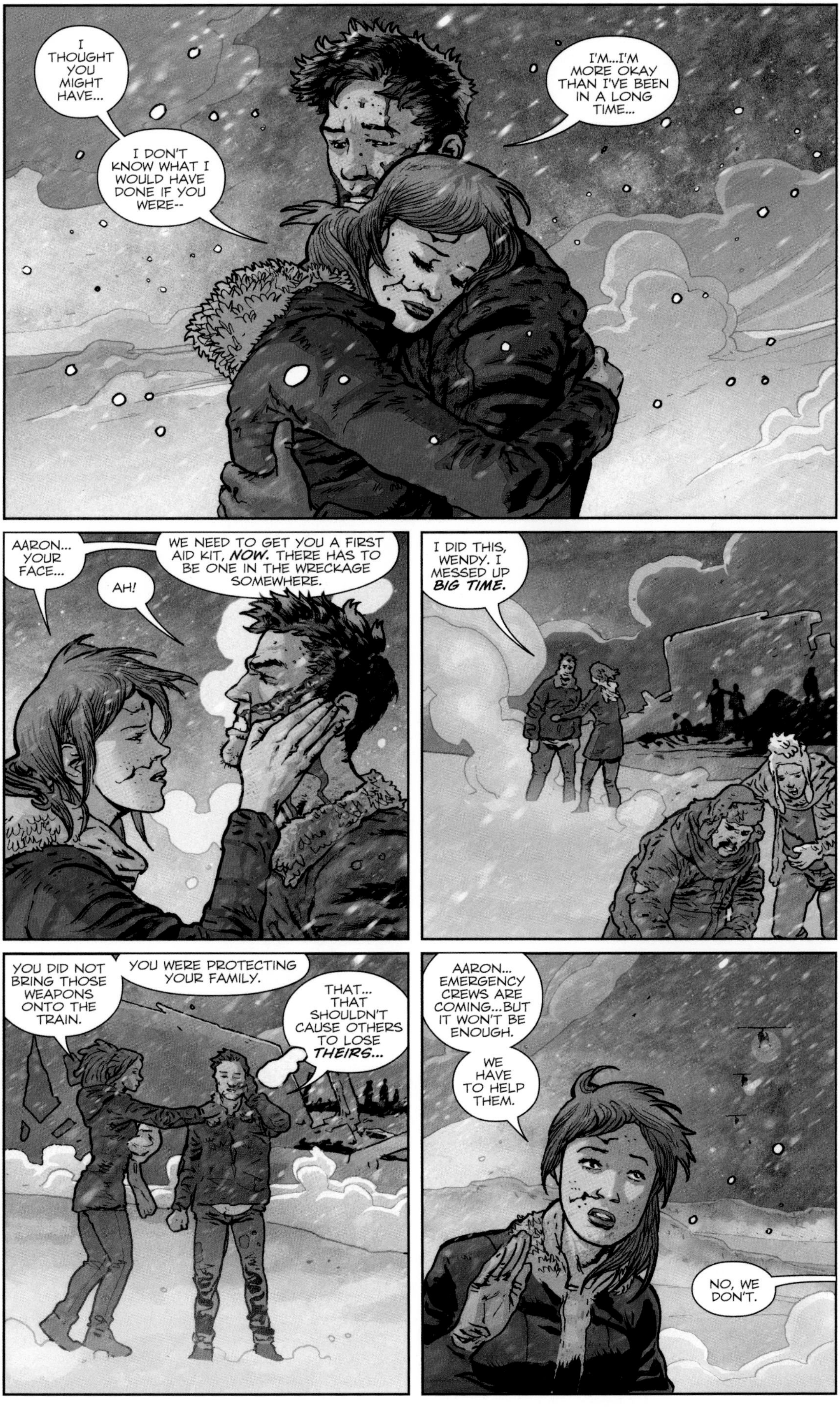

I THOUGHT YOU MIGHT HAVE...
I DON'T KNOW WHAT I WOULD HAVE DONE IF YOU WERE--
I'M...I'M MORE OKAY THAN I'VE BEEN IN A LONG TIME...
AARON... YOUR FACE...
AH!
WE NEED TO GET YOU A FIRST AID KIT, ***NOW.*** THERE HAS TO BE ONE IN THE WRECKAGE SOMEWHERE.
I DID THIS, WENDY. I MESSED UP ***BIG TIME.***
YOU DID NOT BRING THOSE WEAPONS ONTO THE TRAIN.
YOU WERE PROTECTING YOUR FAMILY.
THAT... THAT SHOULDN'T CAUSE OTHERS TO LOSE ***THEIRS...***
AARON... EMERGENCY CREWS ARE COMING...BUT IT WON'T BE ENOUGH.
WE HAVE TO HELP THEM.
NO, WE DON'T.

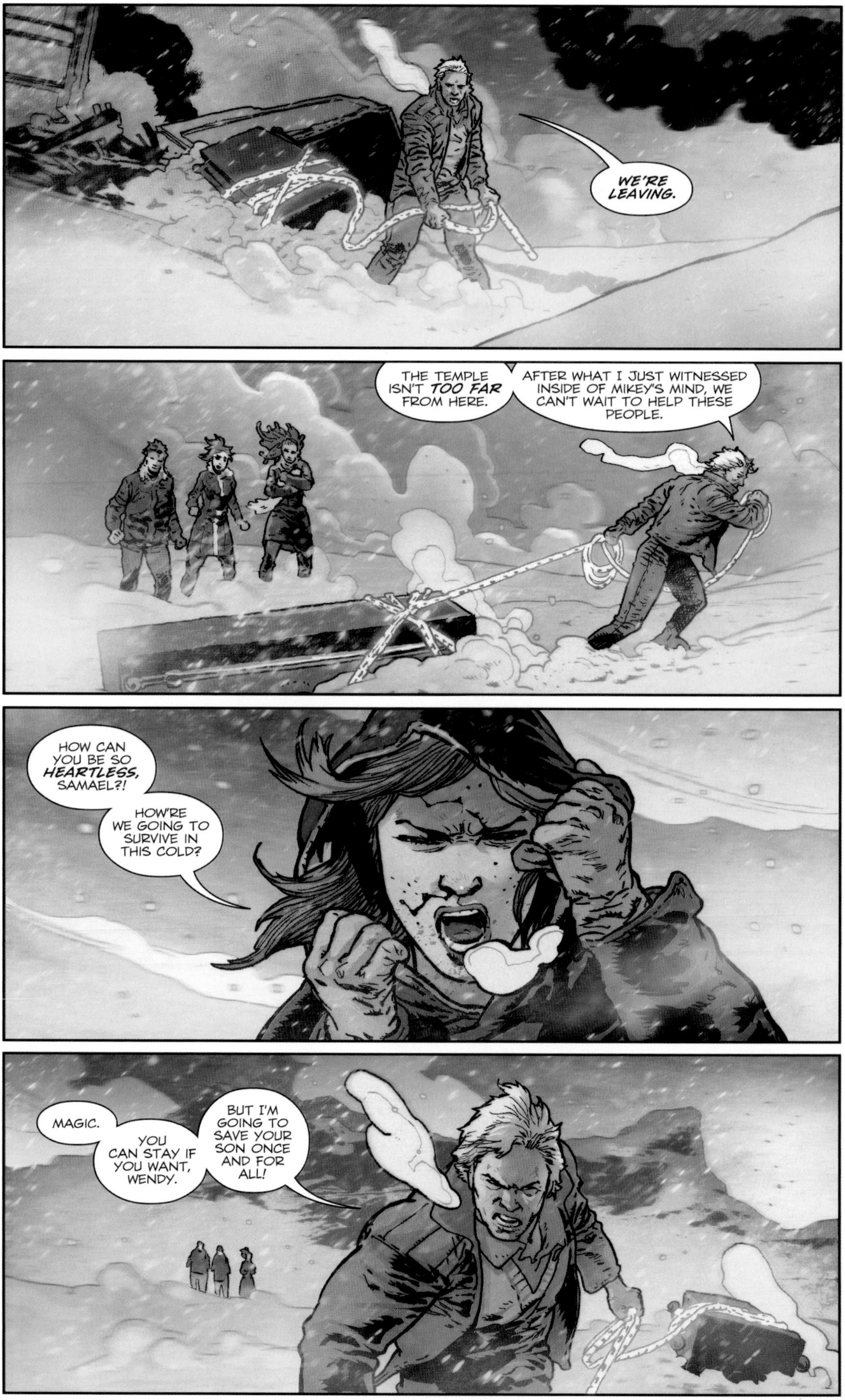

WE'RE LEAVING.
THE TEMPLE ISN'T TOO FAR FROM HERE.
AFTER WHAT I JUST WITNESSED INSIDE OF MIKEY'S MIND, WE CAN'T WAIT TO HELP THESE PEOPLE.
HOW CAN YOU BE SO HEARTLESS, SAMAEL?!
HOW'RE WE GOING TO SURVIVE IN THIS COLD?
MAGIC.
YOU CAN STAY IF YOU WANT, WENDY.
BUT I'M GOING TO SAVE YOUR SON ONCE AND FOR ALL!

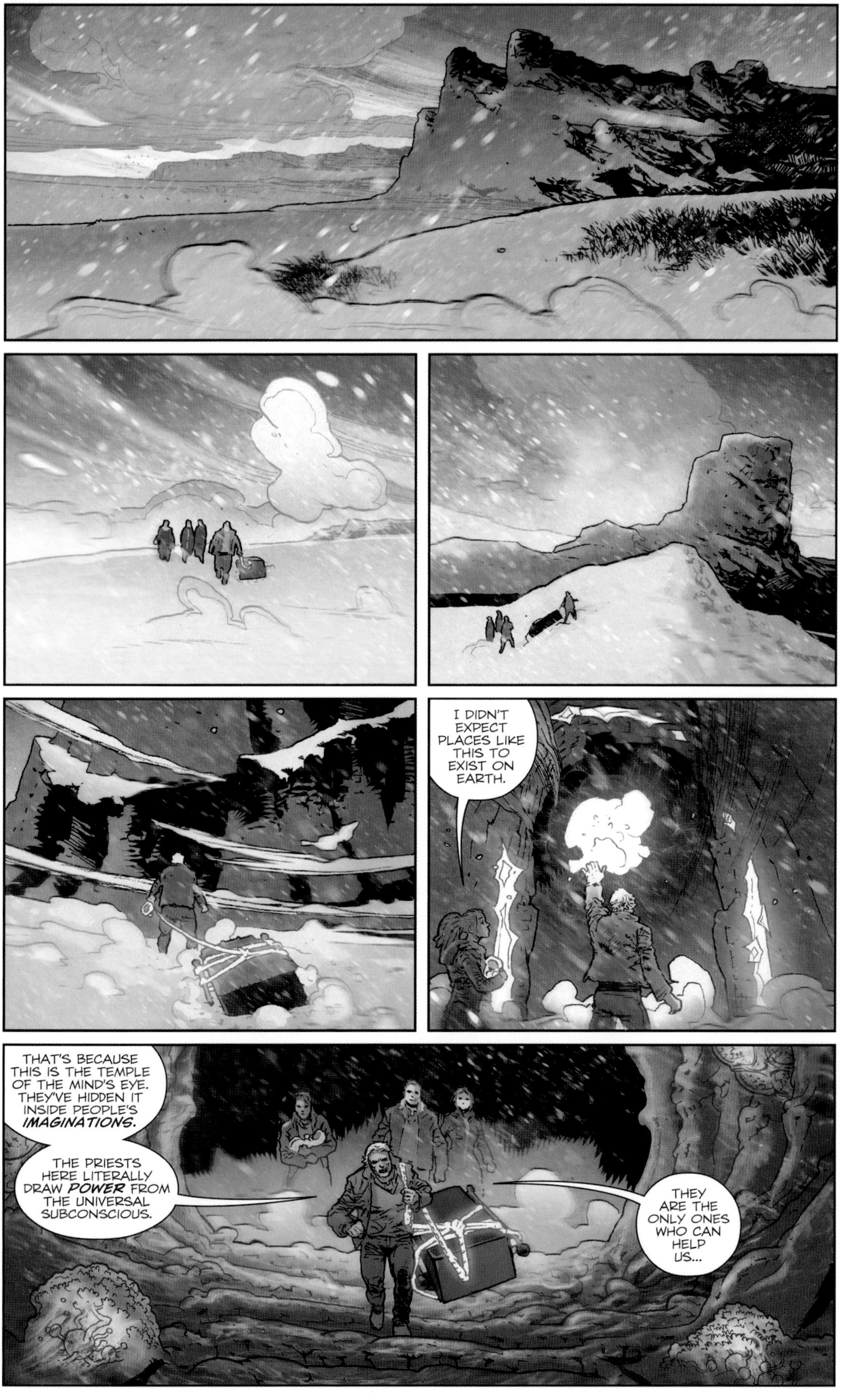
I DIDN'T EXPECT PLACES LIKE THIS TO EXIST ON EARTH.
THAT'S BECAUSE THIS IS THE TEMPLE OF THE MIND'S EYE. THEY'VE HIDDEN IT INSIDE PEOPLE'S *IMAGINATIONS*.
THE PRIESTS HERE LITERALLY DRAW *POWER* FROM THE UNIVERSAL SUBCONSCIOUS.
THEY ARE THE ONLY ONES WHO CAN HELP US...

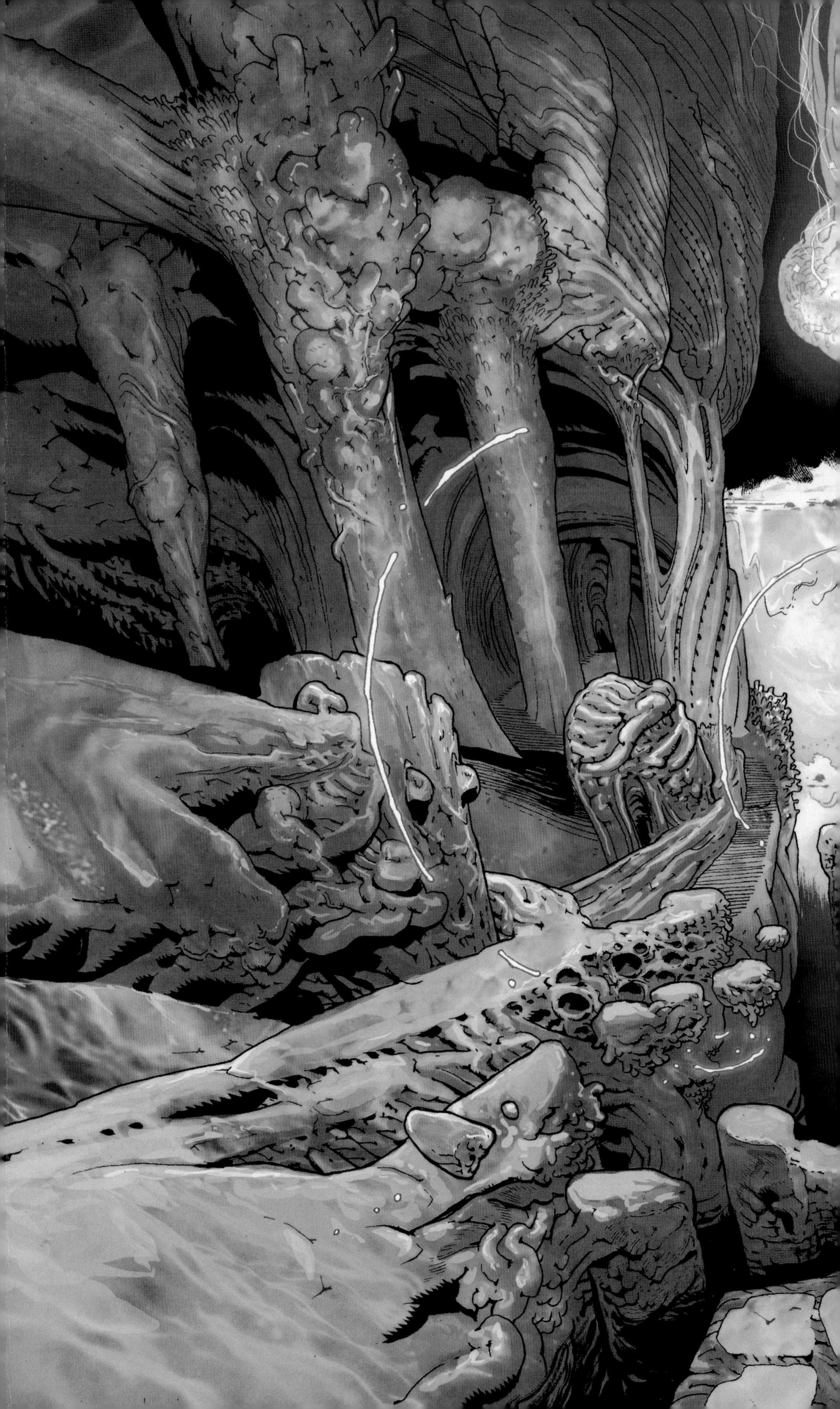

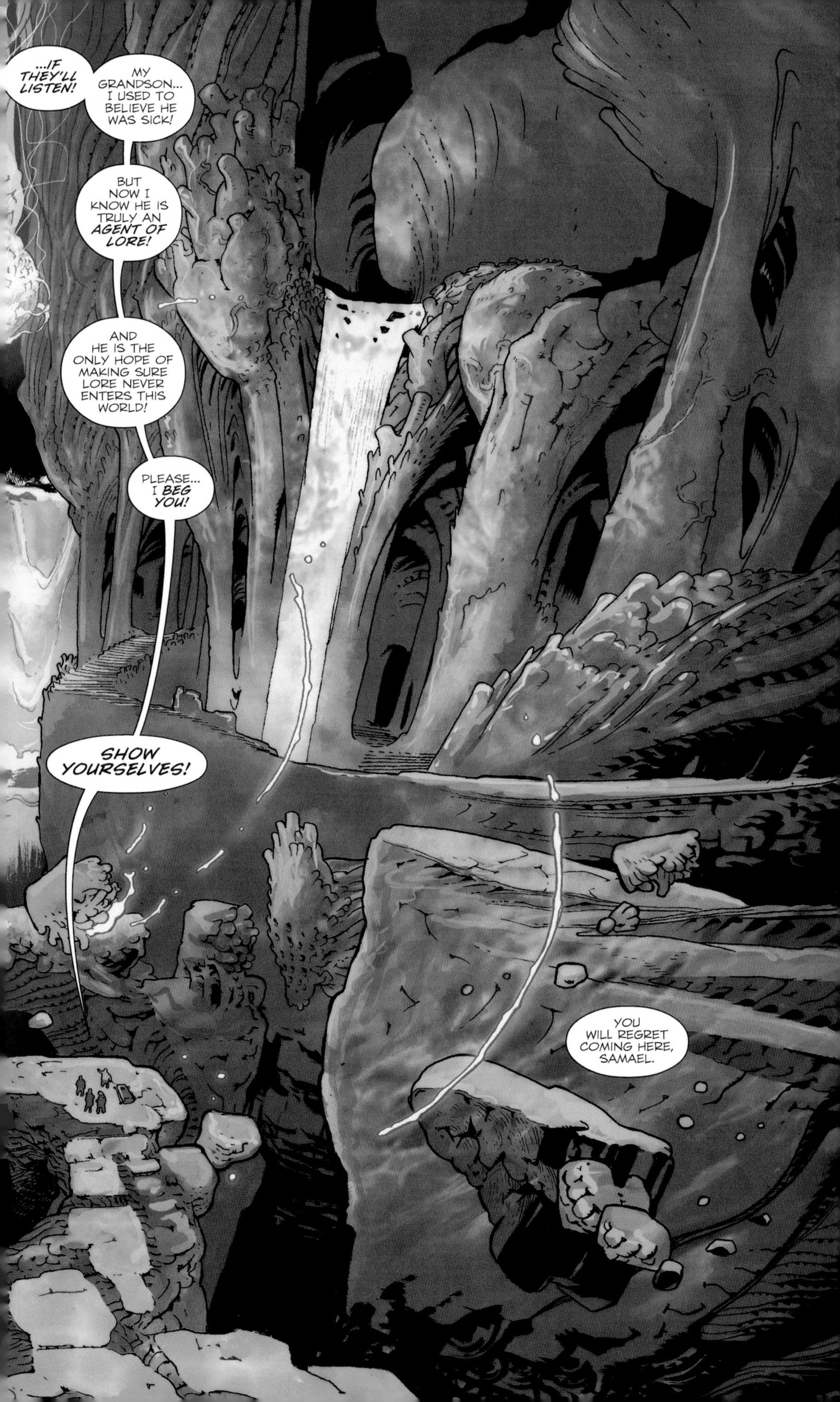
...IF THEY'LL LISTEN!
MY GRANDSON... I USED TO BELIEVE HE WAS SICK!
BUT NOW I KNOW HE IS TRULY AN AGENT OF LORE!
AND HE IS THE ONLY HOPE OF MAKING SURE LORE NEVER ENTERS THIS WORLD!
PLEASE... I BEG YOU!
SHOW YOURSELVES!
YOU WILL REGRET COMING HERE, SAMAEL.

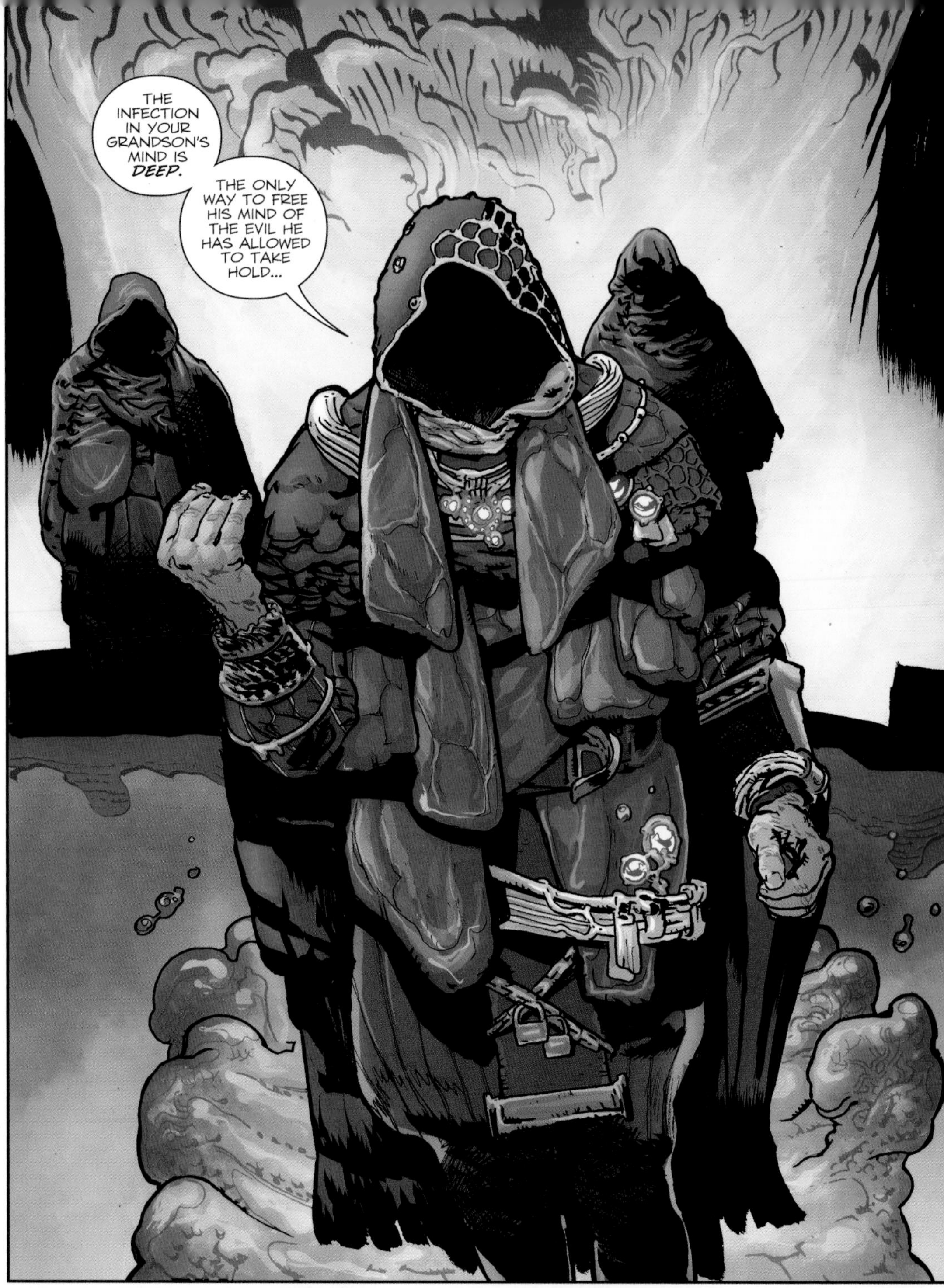
THE INFECTION IN YOUR GRANDSON'S MIND IS *DEEP.*
THE ONLY WAY TO FREE HIS MIND OF THE EVIL HE HAS ALLOWED TO TAKE HOLD...

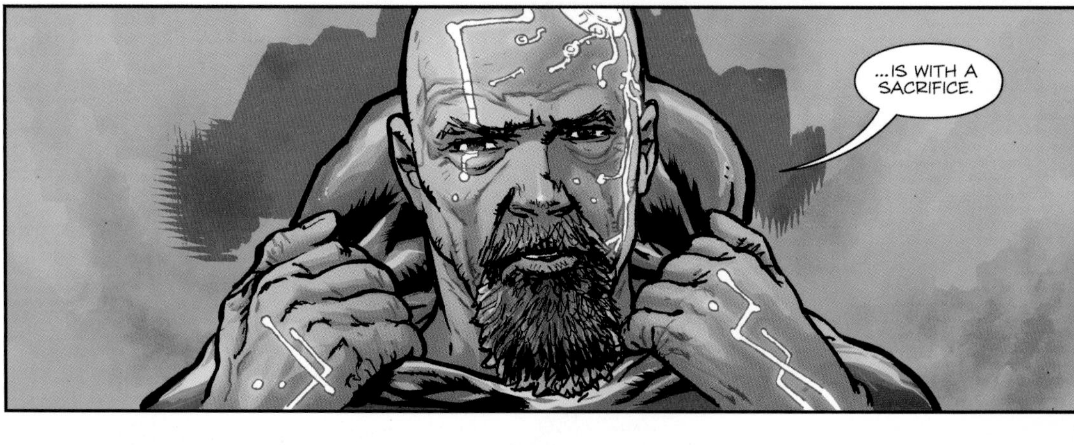
...IS WITH A SACRIFICE.

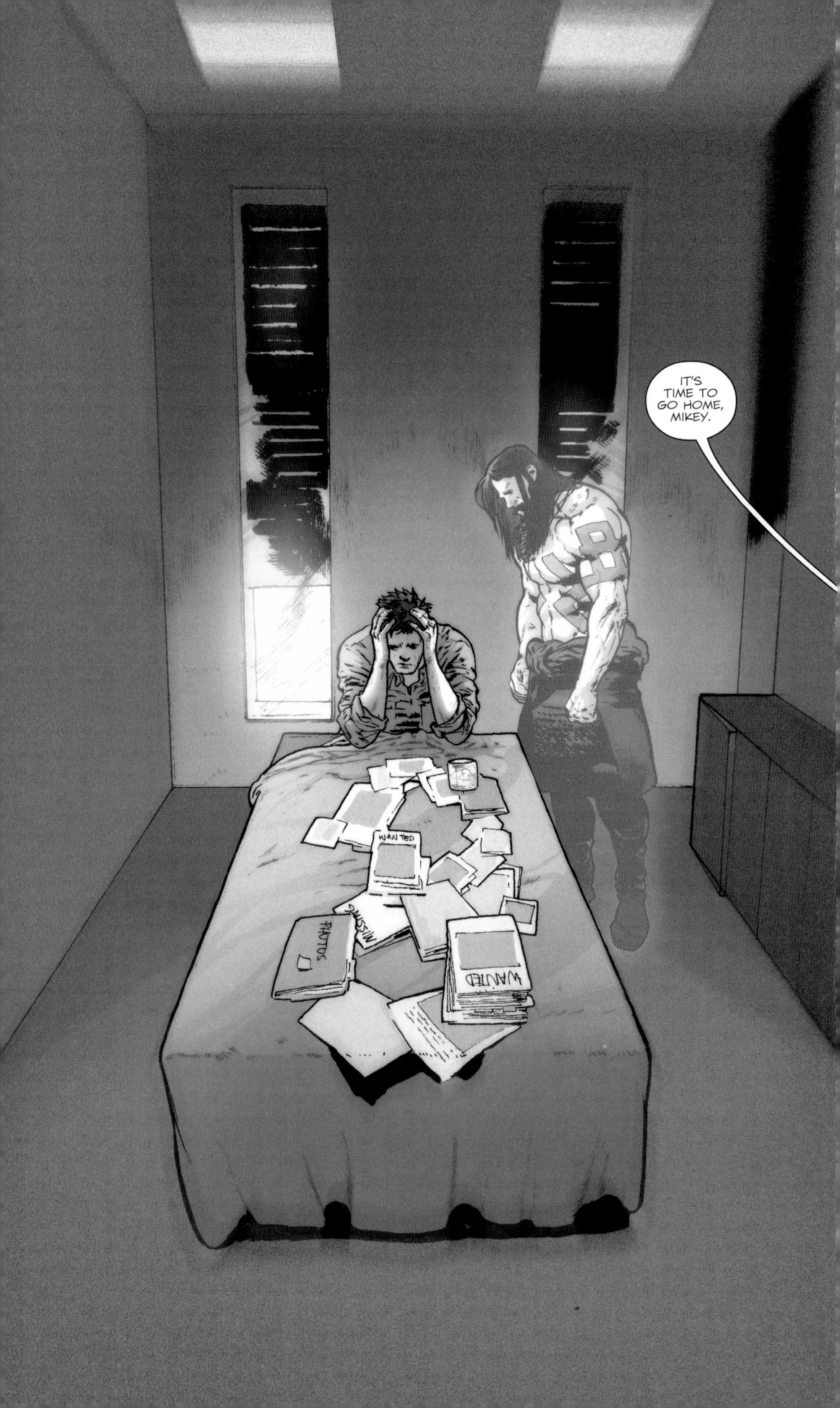
IT'S TIME TO GO HOME, MIKEY.
WANTED
MISSING
PHOTOS
WANTED

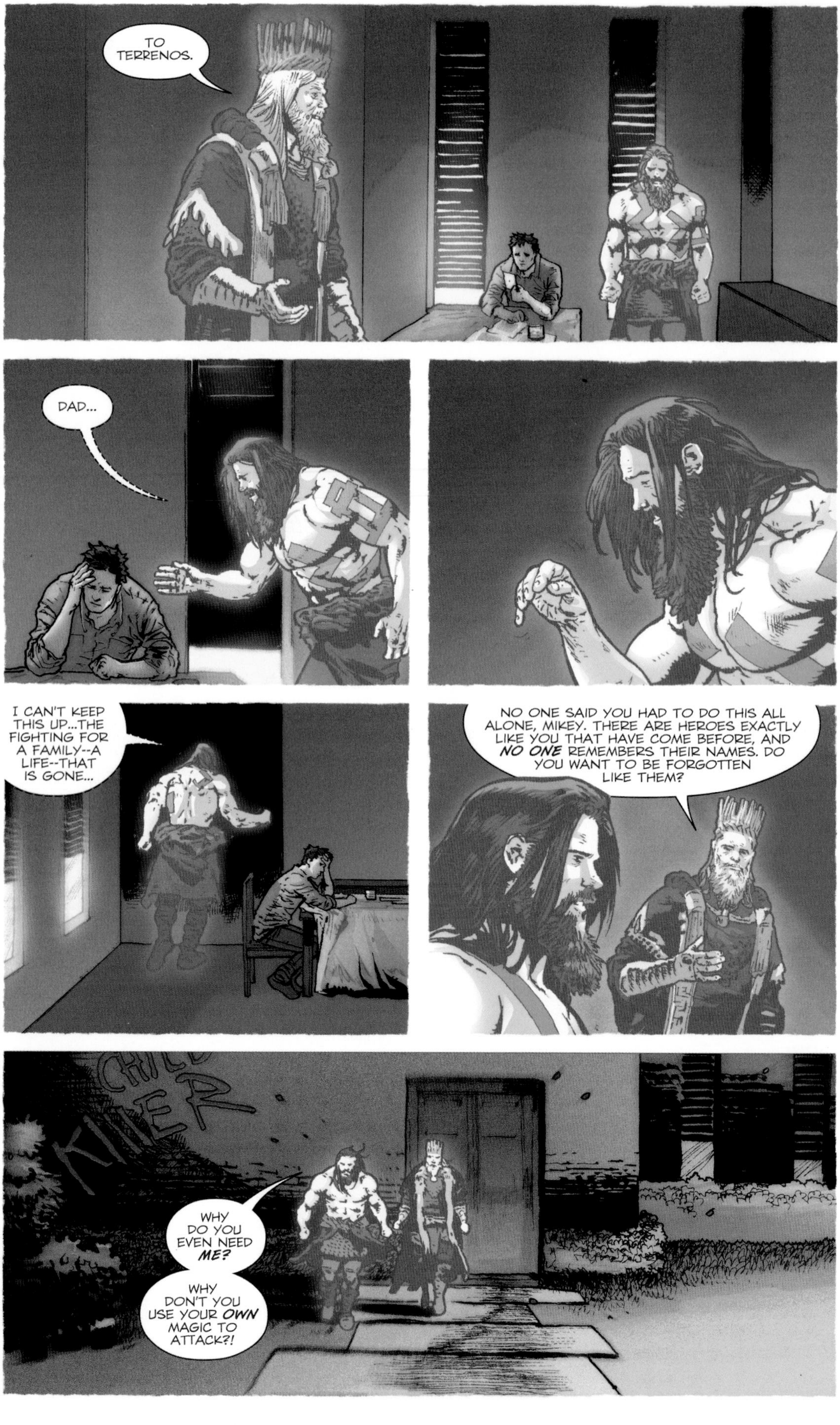

TO TERRENOS.
DAD...
I CAN'T KEEP THIS UP...THE FIGHTING FOR A FAMILY--A LIFE--THAT IS GONE...
NO ONE SAID YOU HAD TO DO THIS ALL ALONE, MIKEY. THERE ARE HEROES EXACTLY LIKE YOU THAT HAVE COME BEFORE, AND NO ONE REMEMBERS THEIR NAMES. DO YOU WANT TO BE FORGOTTEN LIKE THEM?
CHILD KILLER
WHY DO YOU EVEN NEED ME?
WHY DON'T YOU USE YOUR OWN MAGIC TO ATTACK?!

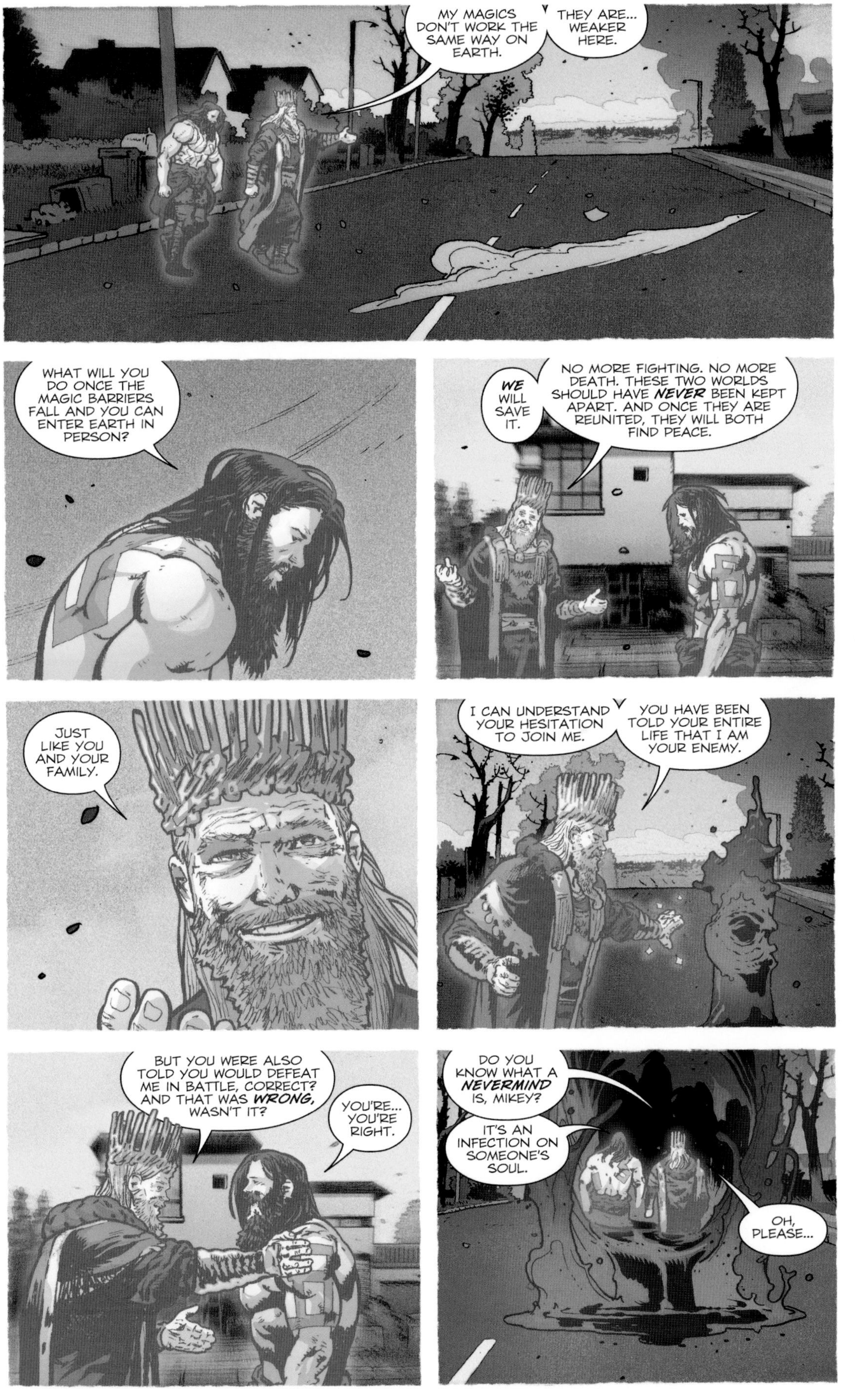
MY MAGICS DON'T WORK THE SAME WAY ON EARTH.
THEY ARE... WEAKER HERE.
WHAT WILL YOU DO ONCE THE MAGIC BARRIERS FALL AND YOU CAN ENTER EARTH IN PERSON?
WE WILL SAVE IT.
NO MORE FIGHTING. NO MORE DEATH. THESE TWO WORLDS SHOULD HAVE NEVER BEEN KEPT APART. AND ONCE THEY ARE REUNITED, THEY WILL BOTH FIND PEACE.
JUST LIKE YOU AND YOUR FAMILY.
I CAN UNDERSTAND YOUR HESITATION TO JOIN ME.
YOU HAVE BEEN TOLD YOUR ENTIRE LIFE THAT I AM YOUR ENEMY.
BUT YOU WERE ALSO TOLD YOU WOULD DEFEAT ME IN BATTLE, CORRECT? AND THAT WAS WRONG, WASN'T IT?
YOU'RE... YOU'RE RIGHT.
DO YOU KNOW WHAT A NEVERMIND IS, MIKEY?
IT'S AN INFECTION ON SOMEONE'S SOUL.
OH, PLEASE...

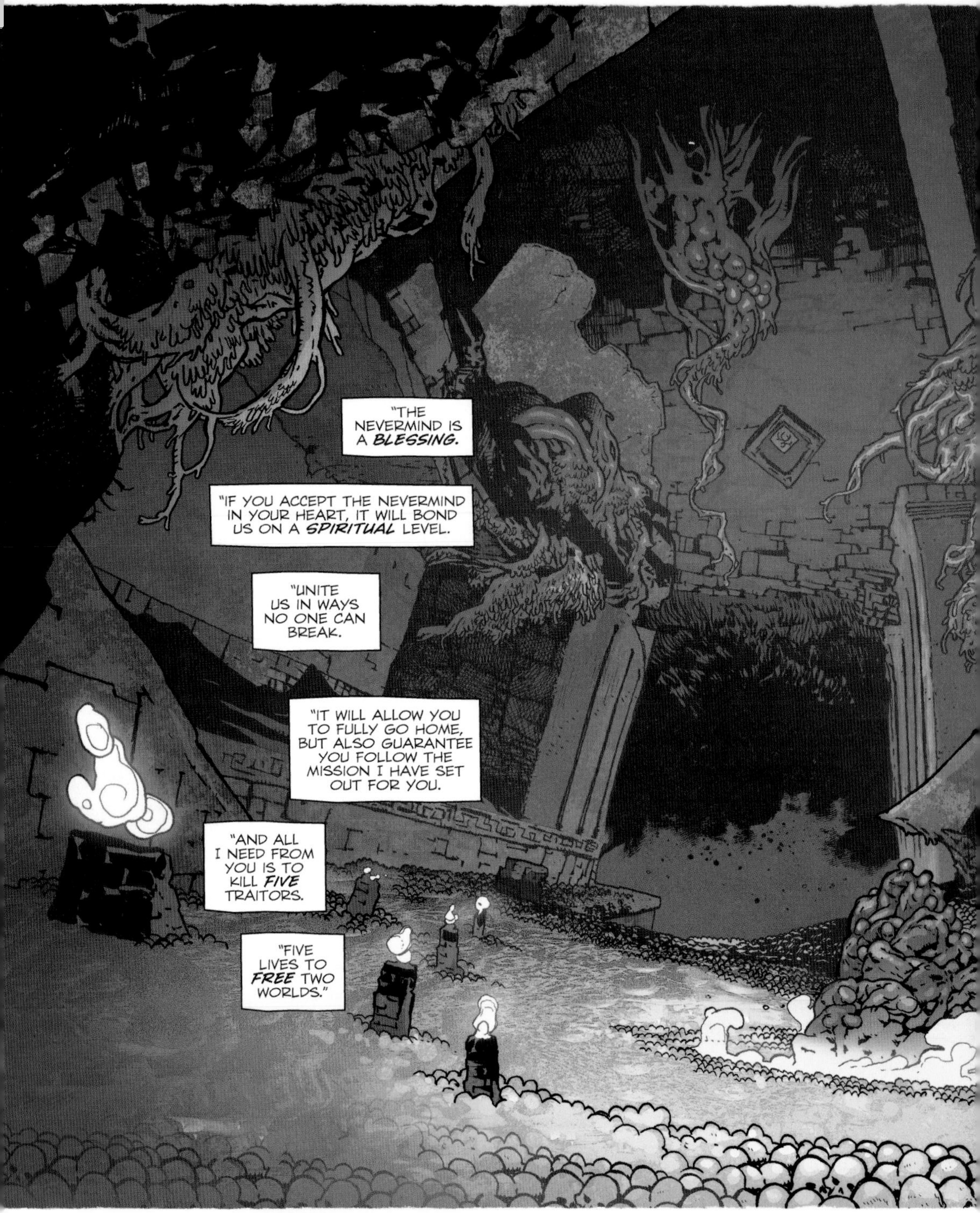
"THE NEVERMIND IS A BLESSING.
"IF YOU ACCEPT THE NEVERMIND IN YOUR HEART, IT WILL BOND US ON A SPIRITUAL LEVEL.
"UNITE US IN WAYS NO ONE CAN BREAK.
"IT WILL ALLOW YOU TO FULLY GO HOME, BUT ALSO GUARANTEE YOU FOLLOW THE MISSION I HAVE SET OUT FOR YOU.
"AND ALL I NEED FROM YOU IS TO KILL FIVE TRAITORS.
"FIVE LIVES TO FREE TWO WORLDS."

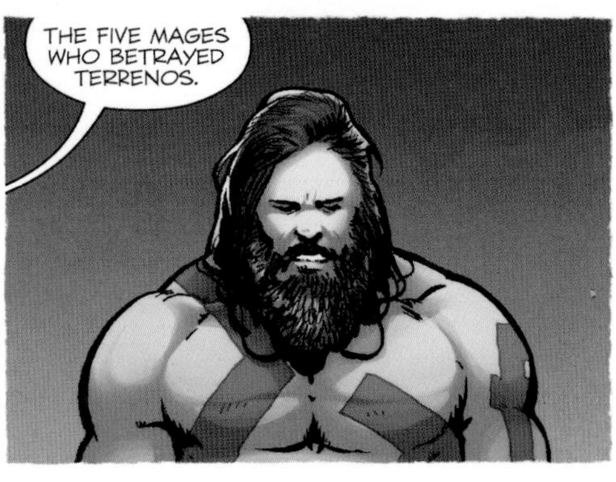
THE FIVE MAGES WHO BETRAYED TERRENOS.

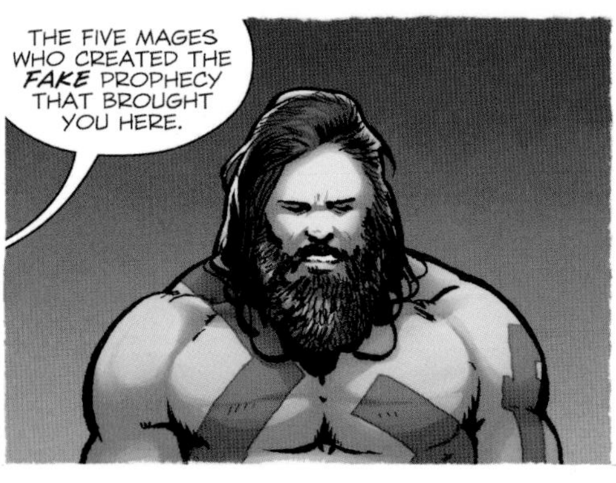
THE FIVE MAGES WHO CREATED THE FAKE PROPHECY THAT BROUGHT YOU HERE.

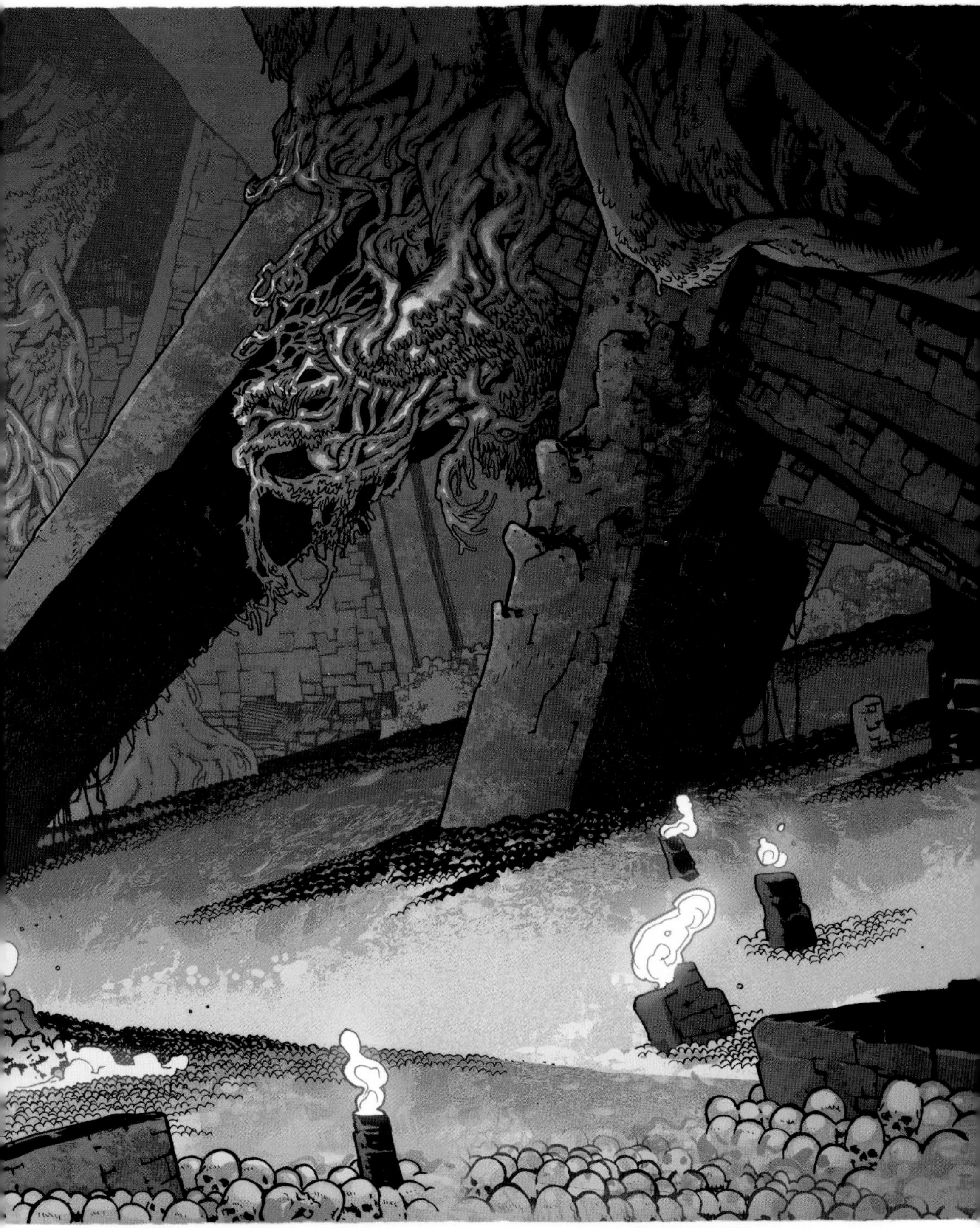

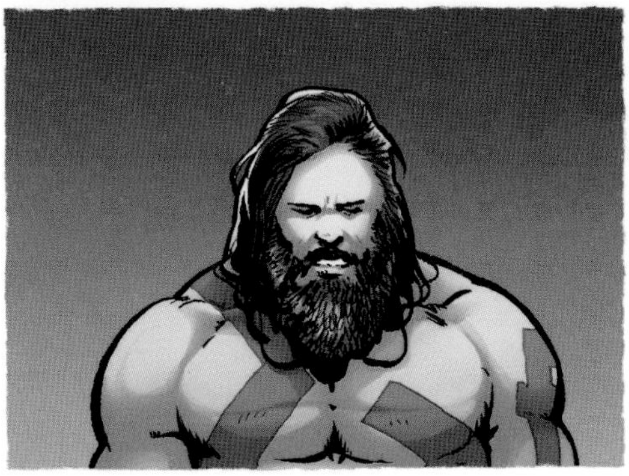

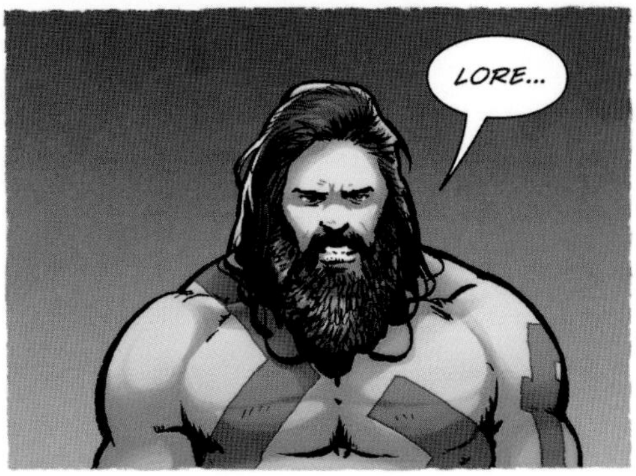
LORE...

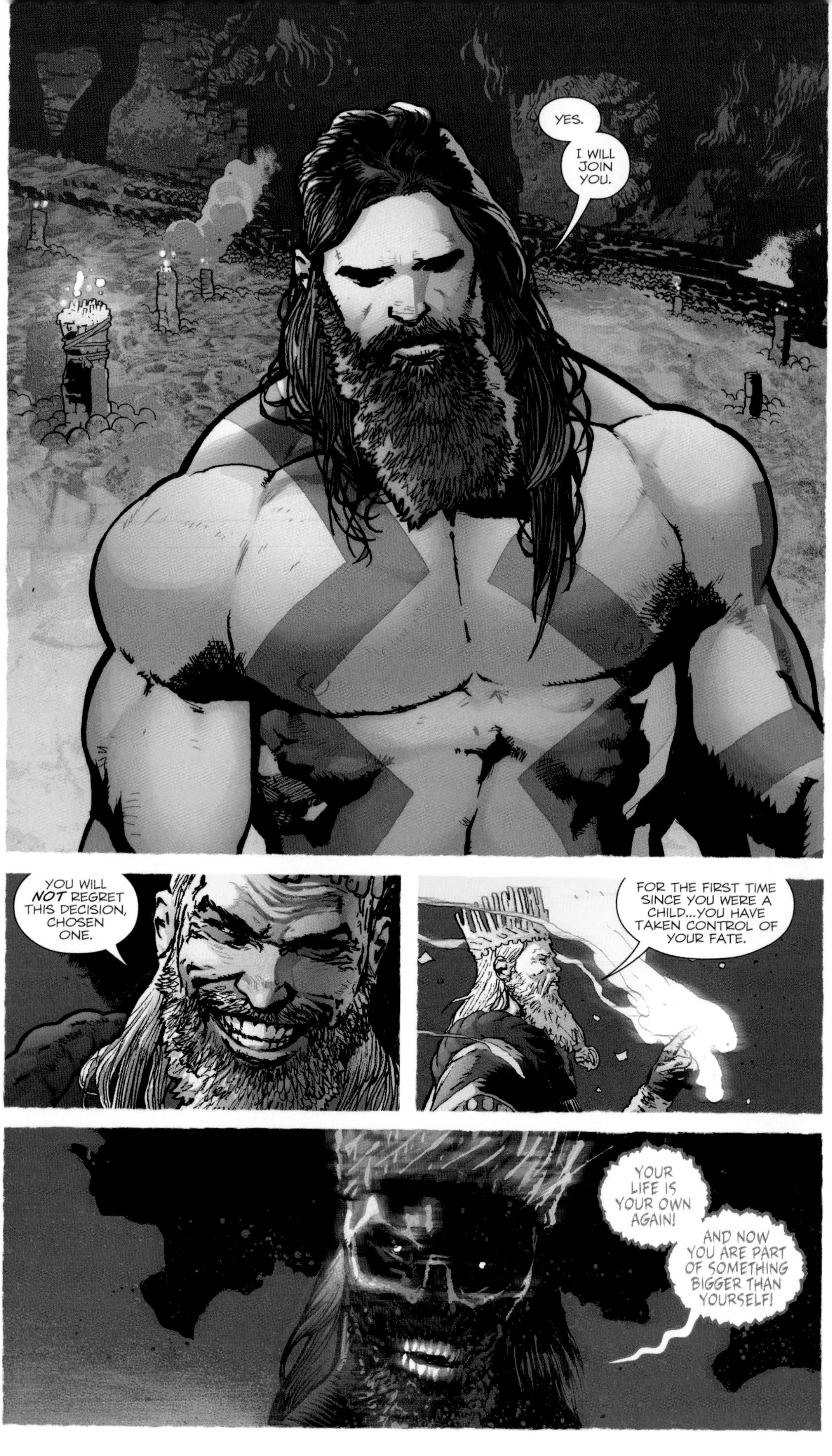
YES.
I WILL JOIN YOU.
YOU WILL *NOT* REGRET THIS DECISION, CHOSEN ONE.
FOR THE FIRST TIME SINCE YOU WERE A CHILD...YOU HAVE TAKEN CONTROL OF YOUR FATE.
YOUR LIFE IS YOUR OWN AGAIN!
AND NOW YOU ARE PART OF SOMETHING BIGGER THAN YOURSELF!

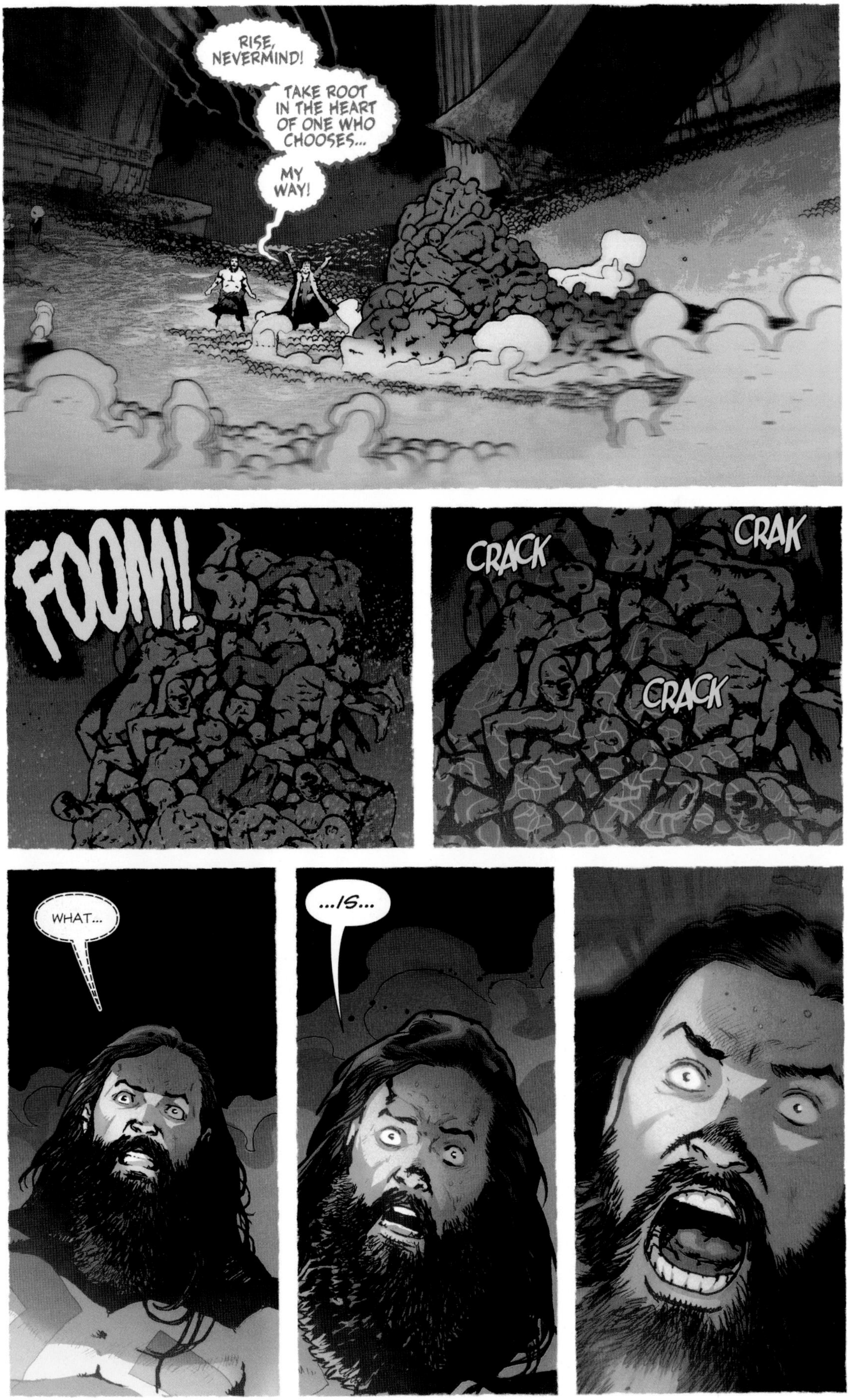
RISE, NEVERMIND!
TAKE ROOT IN THE HEART OF ONE WHO CHOOSES...
MY WAY!
FOOM!
CRACK
CRAK
CRACK
WHAT...
...IS...

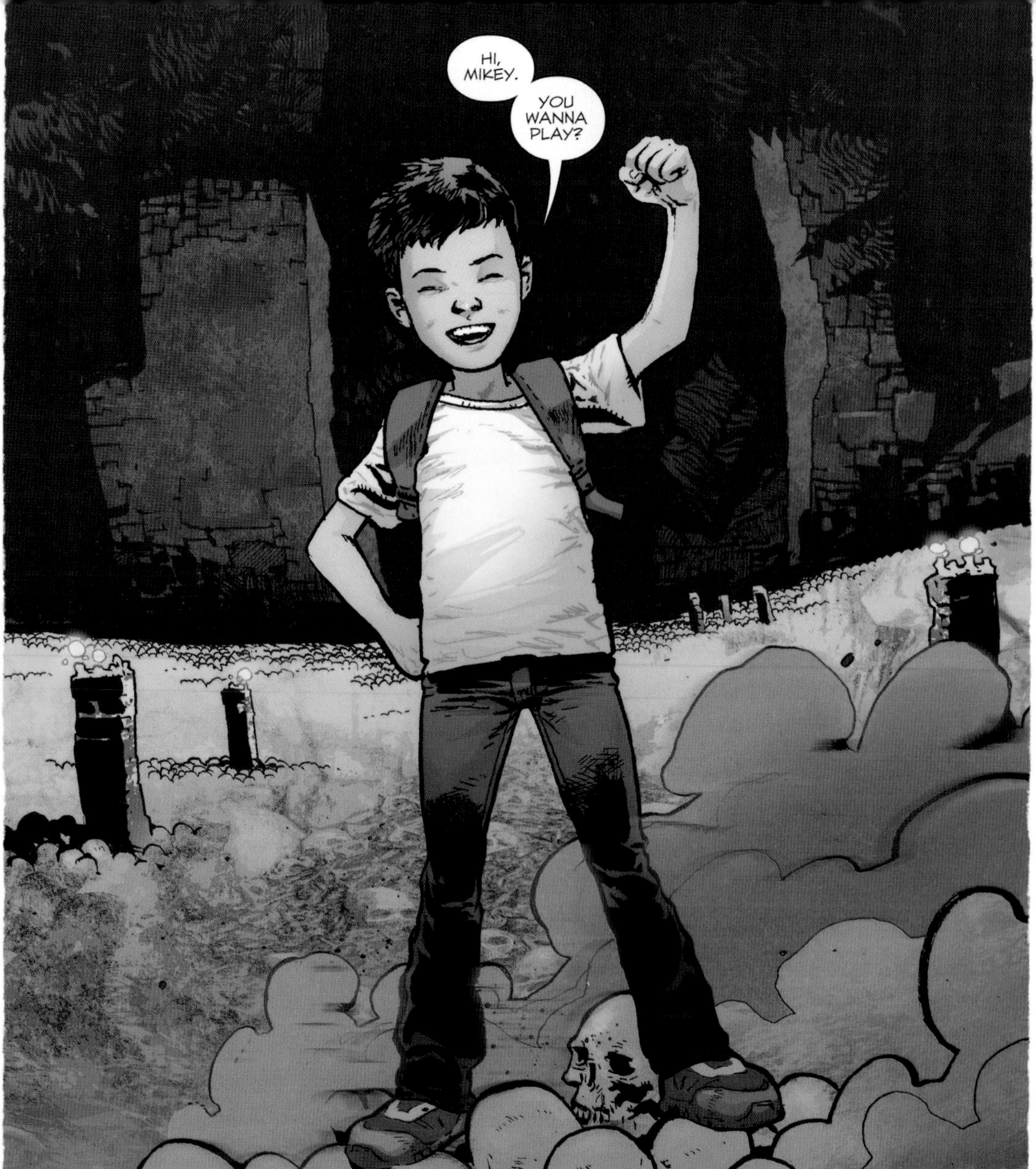
HI, MIKEY.
YOU WANNA PLAY?

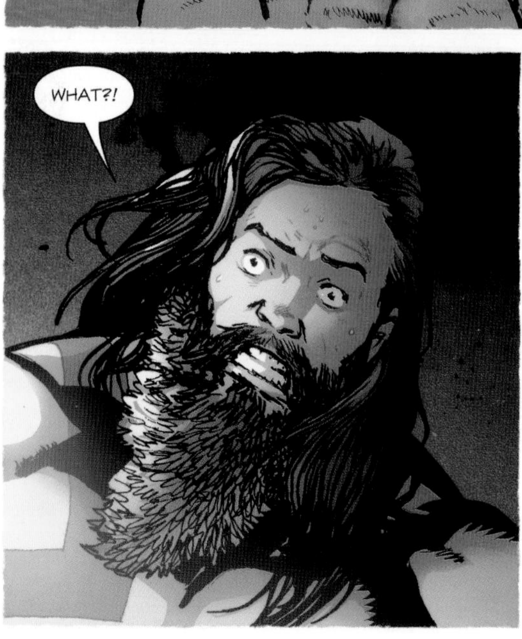
WHAT?!

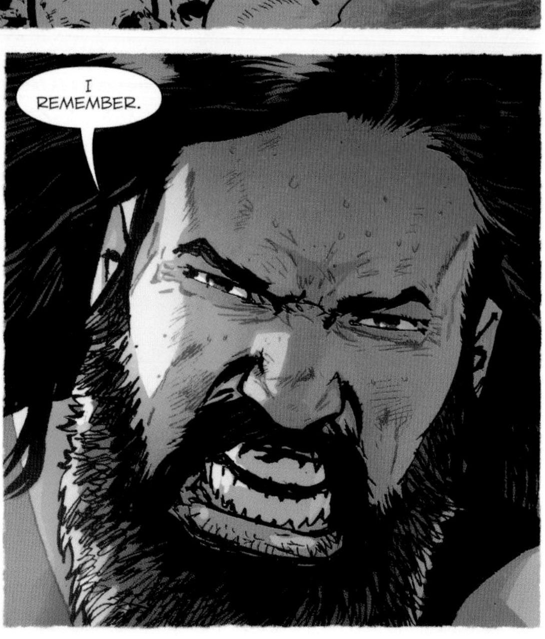
I REMEMBER.

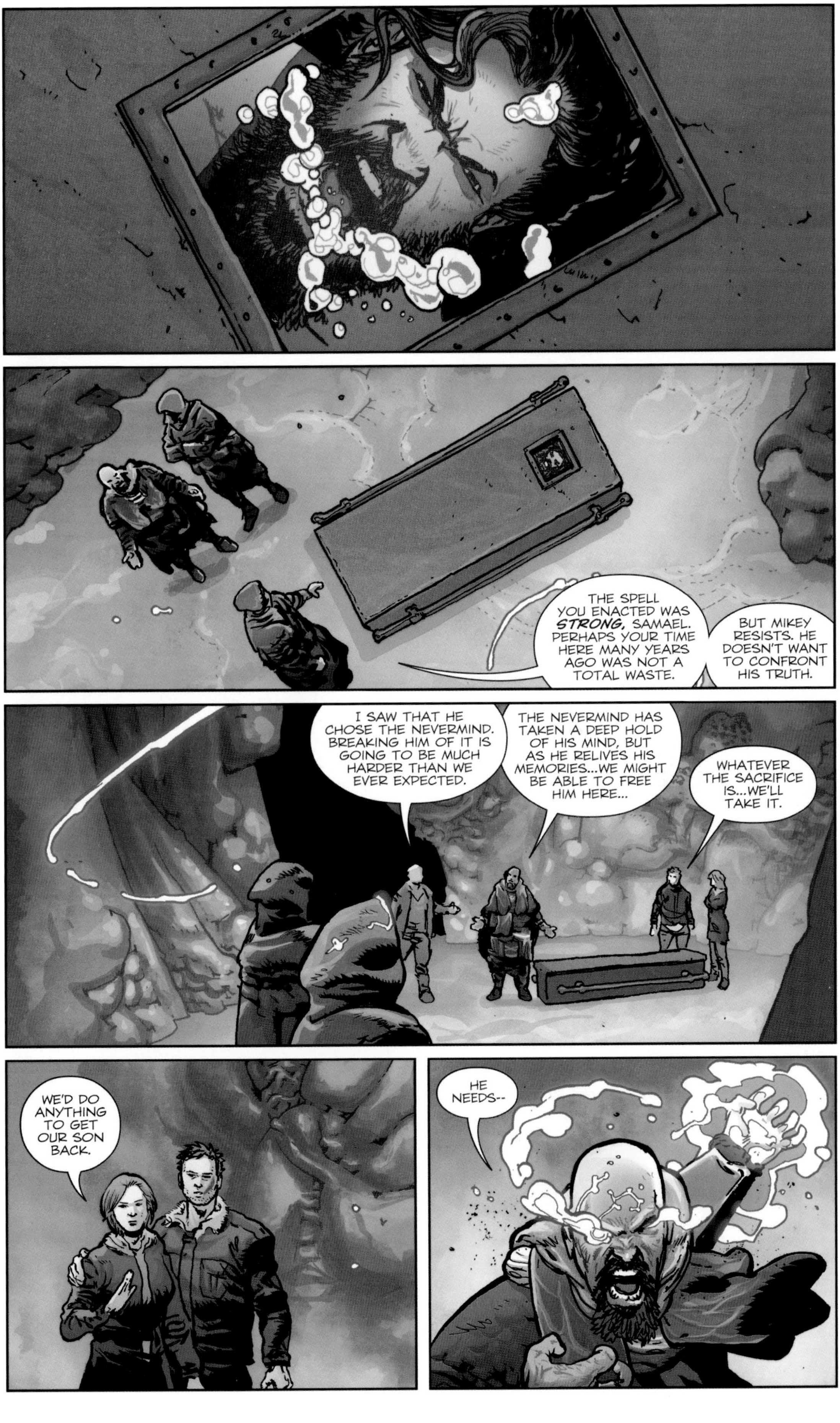
THE SPELL YOU ENACTED WAS STRONG, SAMAEL. PERHAPS YOUR TIME HERE MANY YEARS AGO WAS NOT A TOTAL WASTE.
BUT MIKEY RESISTS. HE DOESN'T WANT TO CONFRONT HIS TRUTH.
I SAW THAT HE CHOSE THE NEVERMIND. BREAKING HIM OF IT IS GOING TO BE MUCH HARDER THAN WE EVER EXPECTED.
THE NEVERMIND HAS TAKEN A DEEP HOLD OF HIS MIND, BUT AS HE RELIVES HIS MEMORIES...WE MIGHT BE ABLE TO FREE HIM HERE...
WHATEVER THE SACRIFICE IS...WE'LL TAKE IT.
WE'D DO ANYTHING TO GET OUR SON BACK.
HE NEEDS--

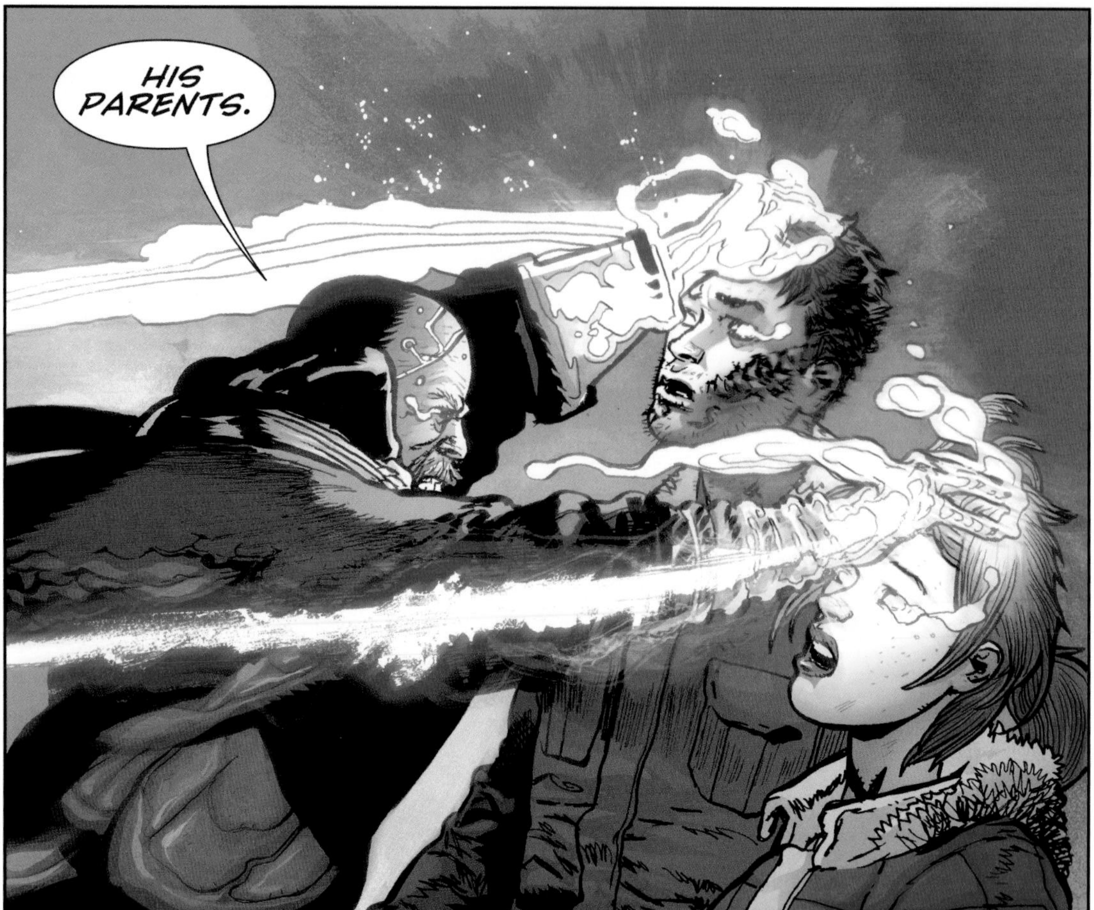
HIS PARENTS.

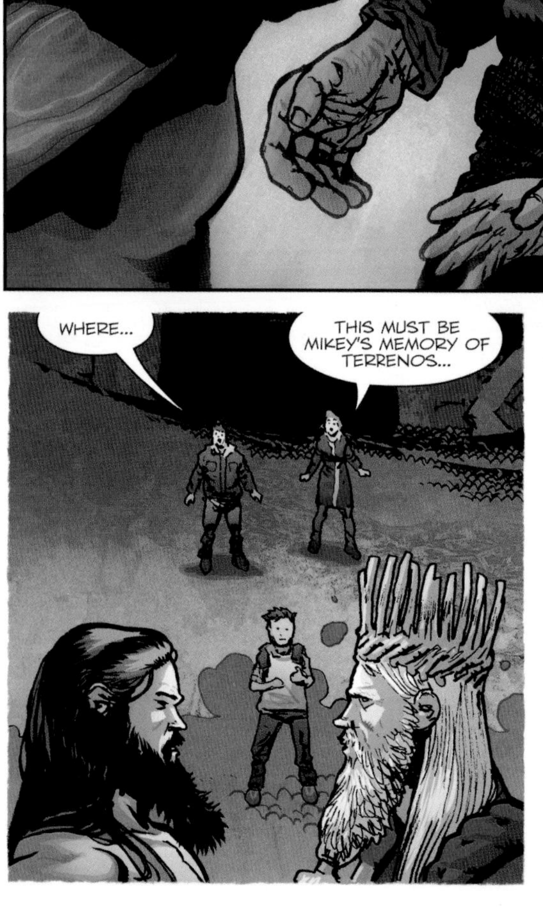
WHERE...
THIS MUST BE MIKEY'S MEMORY OF TERRENOS...

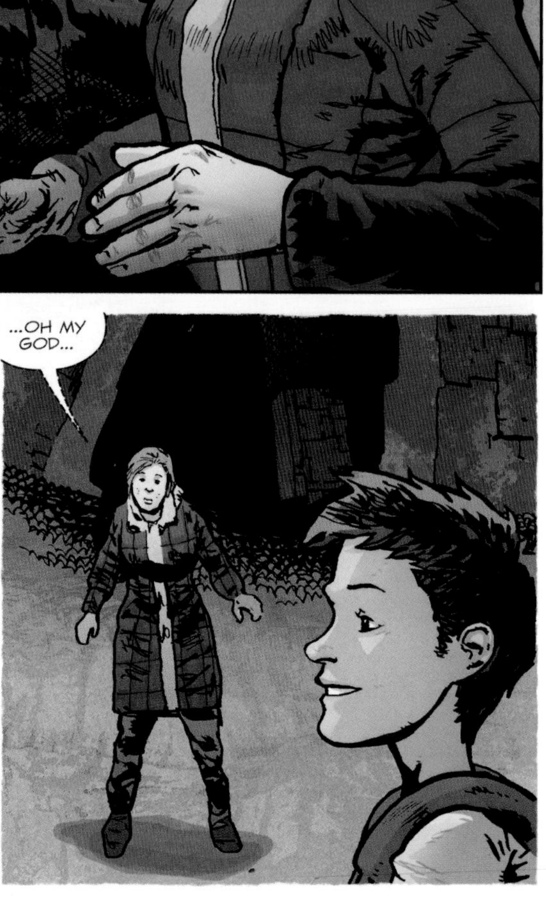
...OH MY GOD...

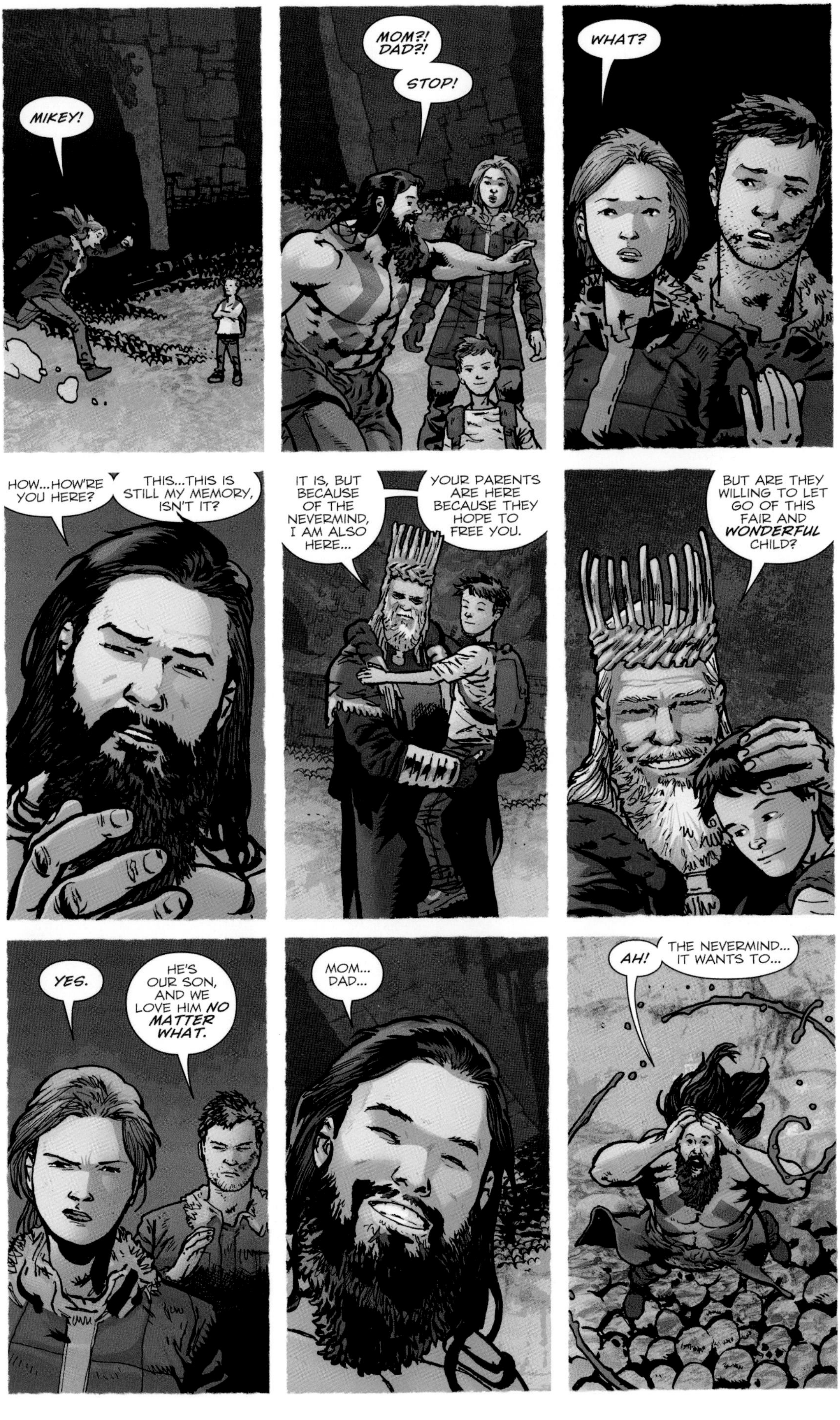
MIKEY!
MOM?! DAD?!
STOP!
WHAT?
HOW...HOW'RE YOU HERE?
THIS...THIS IS STILL MY MEMORY, ISN'T IT?
IT IS, BUT BECAUSE OF THE NEVERMIND, I AM ALSO HERE...
YOUR PARENTS ARE HERE BECAUSE THEY HOPE TO FREE YOU.
BUT ARE THEY WILLING TO LET GO OF THIS FAIR AND WONDERFUL CHILD?
YES.
HE'S OUR SON, AND WE LOVE HIM NO MATTER WHAT.
MOM... DAD...
AH!
THE NEVERMIND... IT WANTS TO...

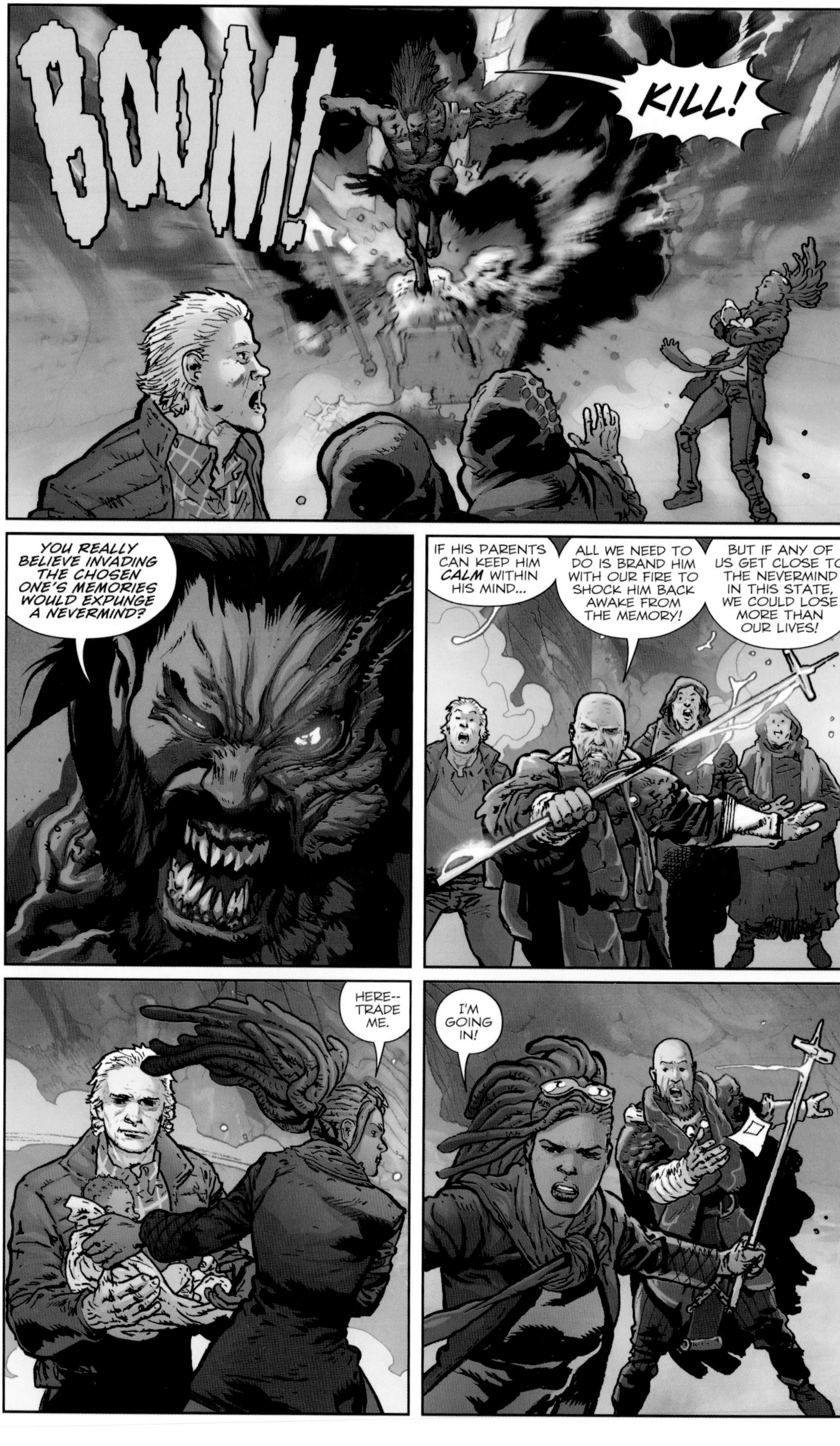
BOOM!
KILL!
YOU REALLY BELIEVE INVADING THE CHOSEN ONE'S MEMORIES WOULD EXPUNGE A NEVERMIND?
IF HIS PARENTS CAN KEEP HIM CALM WITHIN HIS MIND...
ALL WE NEED TO DO IS BRAND HIM WITH OUR FIRE TO SHOCK HIM BACK AWAKE FROM THE MEMORY!
BUT IF ANY OF US GET CLOSE TO THE NEVERMIND IN THIS STATE, WE COULD LOSE MORE THAN OUR LIVES!
HERE-- TRADE ME.
I'M GOING IN!

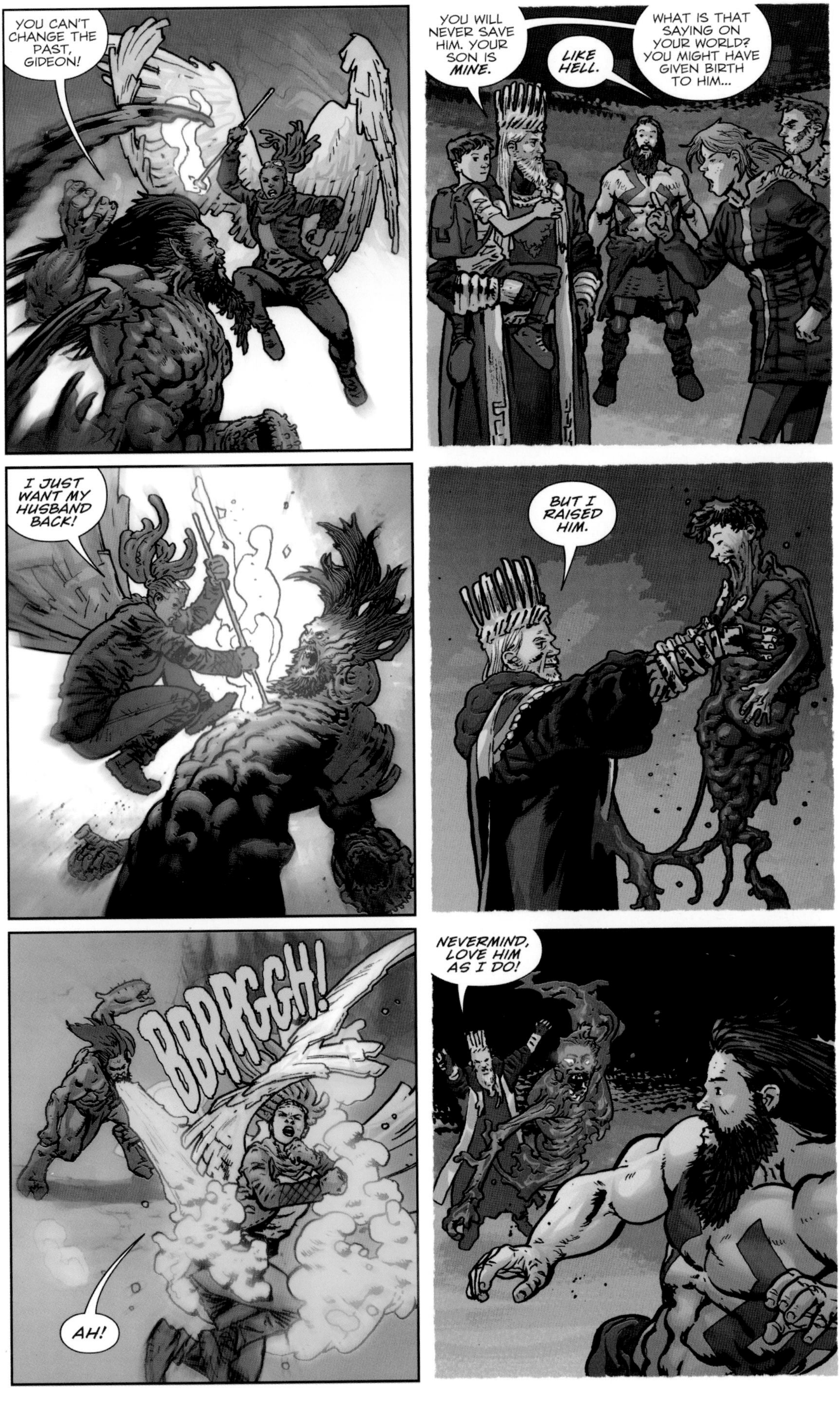

YOU CAN'T CHANGE THE PAST, GIDEON!
YOU WILL NEVER SAVE HIM. YOUR SON IS *MINE.*
LIKE HELL.
WHAT IS THAT SAYING ON YOUR WORLD? YOU MIGHT HAVE GIVEN BIRTH TO HIM...
I JUST WANT MY HUSBAND BACK!
BUT I RAISED HIM.
BBRRGGH!
AH!
NEVERMIND, LOVE HIM AS I DO!

YOU CAN FIGHT IT, MIKEY!

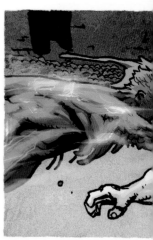

AAAHHHH

AHHHH!!

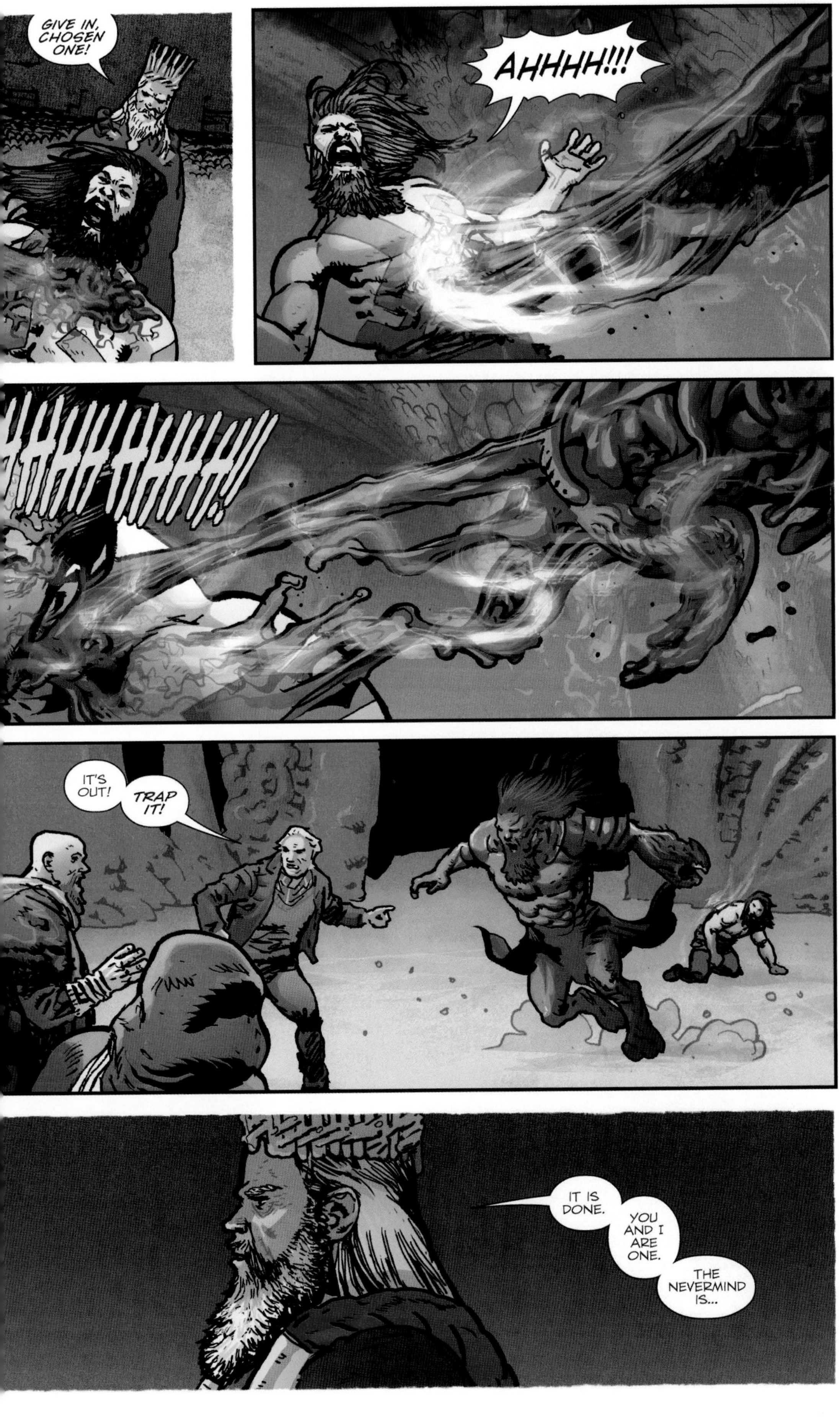

GIVE IN, CHOSEN ONE!
AHHHH!!!
HHHHHHHHH!!
IT'S OUT!
TRAP IT!
IT IS DONE.
YOU AND I ARE ONE.
THE NEVERMIND IS...

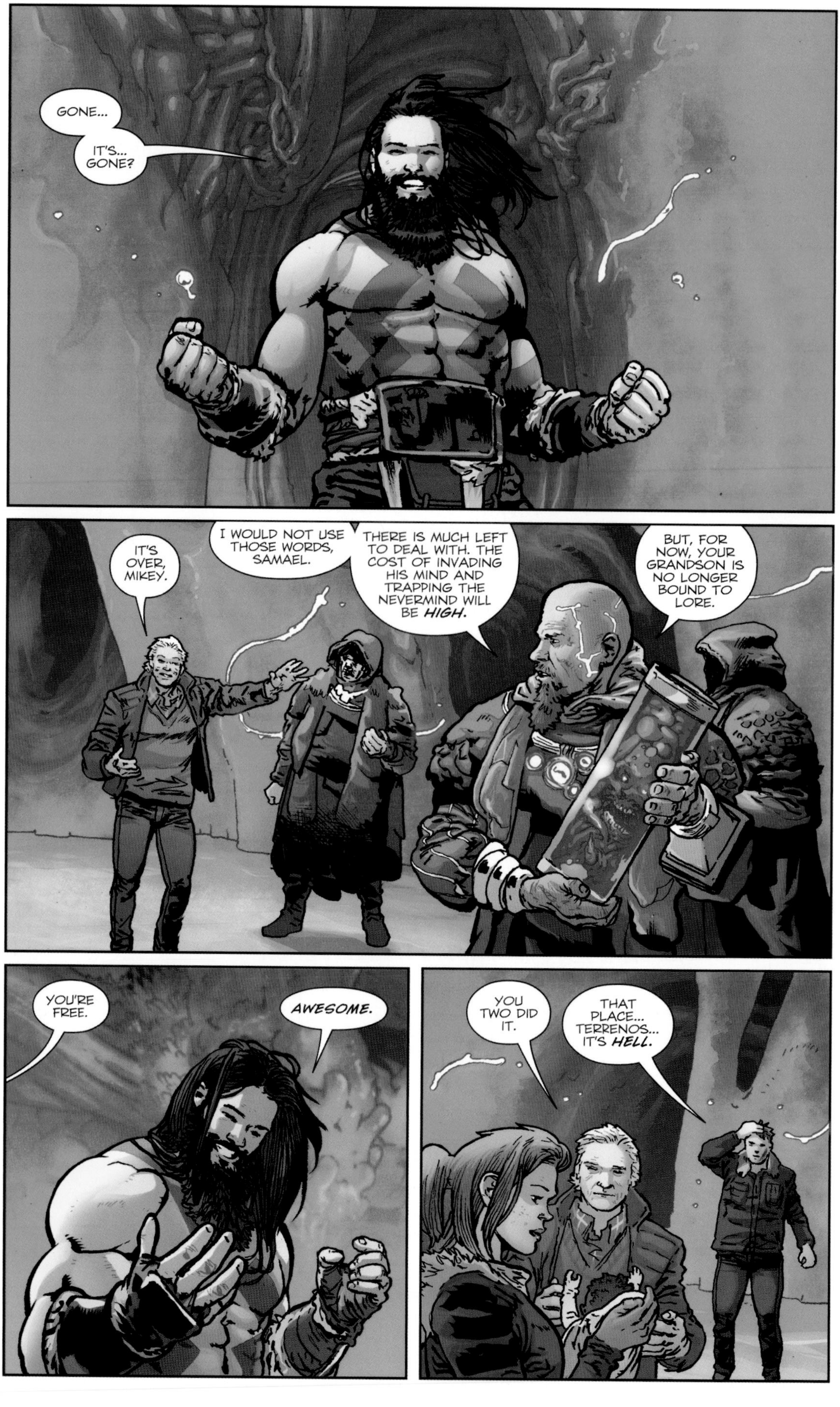

GONE...
IT'S... GONE?
IT'S OVER, MIKEY.
I WOULD NOT USE THOSE WORDS, SAMAEL.
THERE IS MUCH LEFT TO DEAL WITH. THE COST OF INVADING HIS MIND AND TRAPPING THE NEVERMIND WILL BE HIGH.
BUT, FOR NOW, YOUR GRANDSON IS NO LONGER BOUND TO LORE.
YOU'RE FREE.
AWESOME.
YOU TWO DID IT.
THAT PLACE... TERRENOS... IT'S HELL.

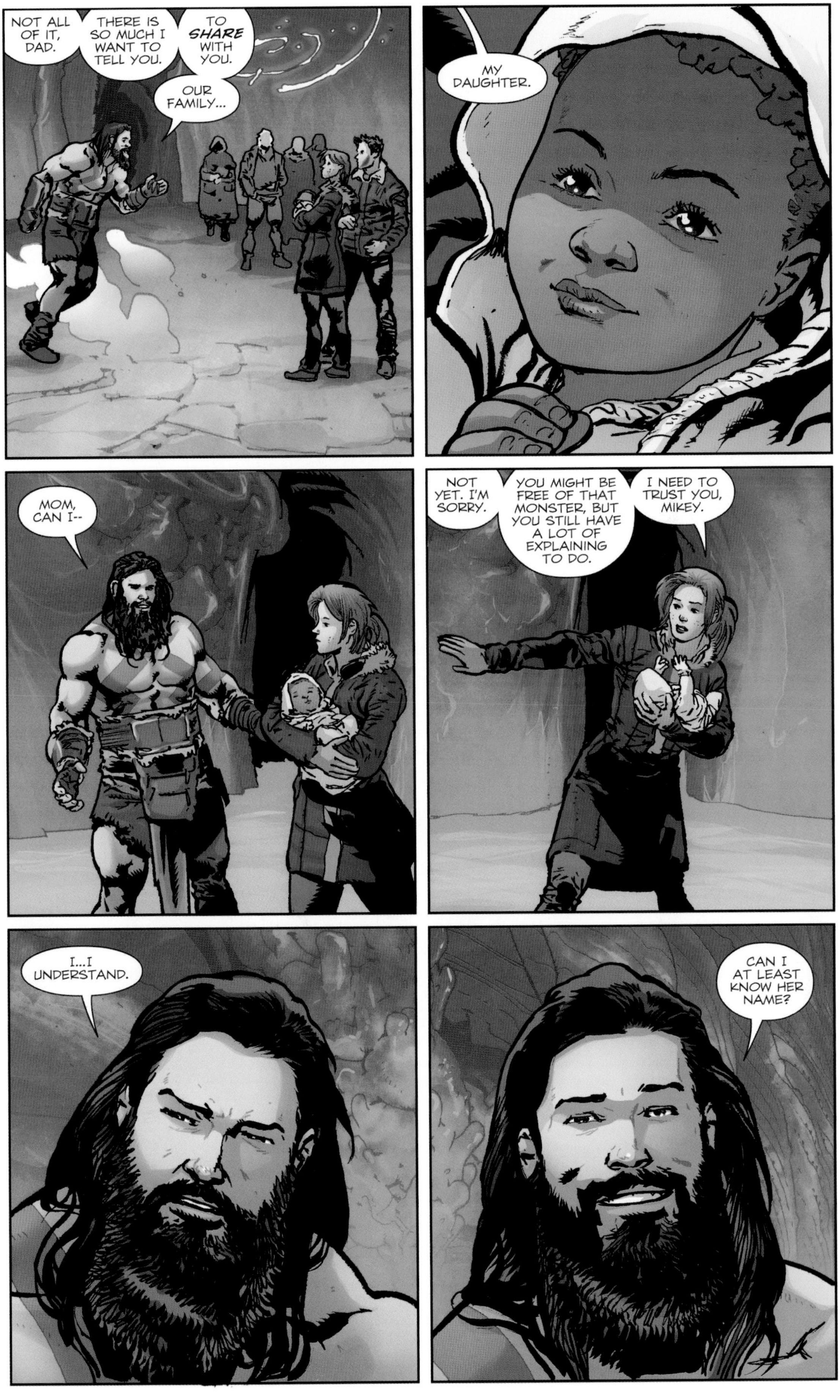
NOT ALL OF IT, DAD.
THERE IS SO MUCH I WANT TO TELL YOU.
TO SHARE WITH YOU.
OUR FAMILY...
MY DAUGHTER.
MOM, CAN I--
NOT YET. I'M SORRY.
YOU MIGHT BE FREE OF THAT MONSTER, BUT YOU STILL HAVE A LOT OF EXPLAINING TO DO.
I NEED TO TRUST YOU, MIKEY.
I...I UNDERSTAND.
CAN I AT LEAST KNOW HER NAME?

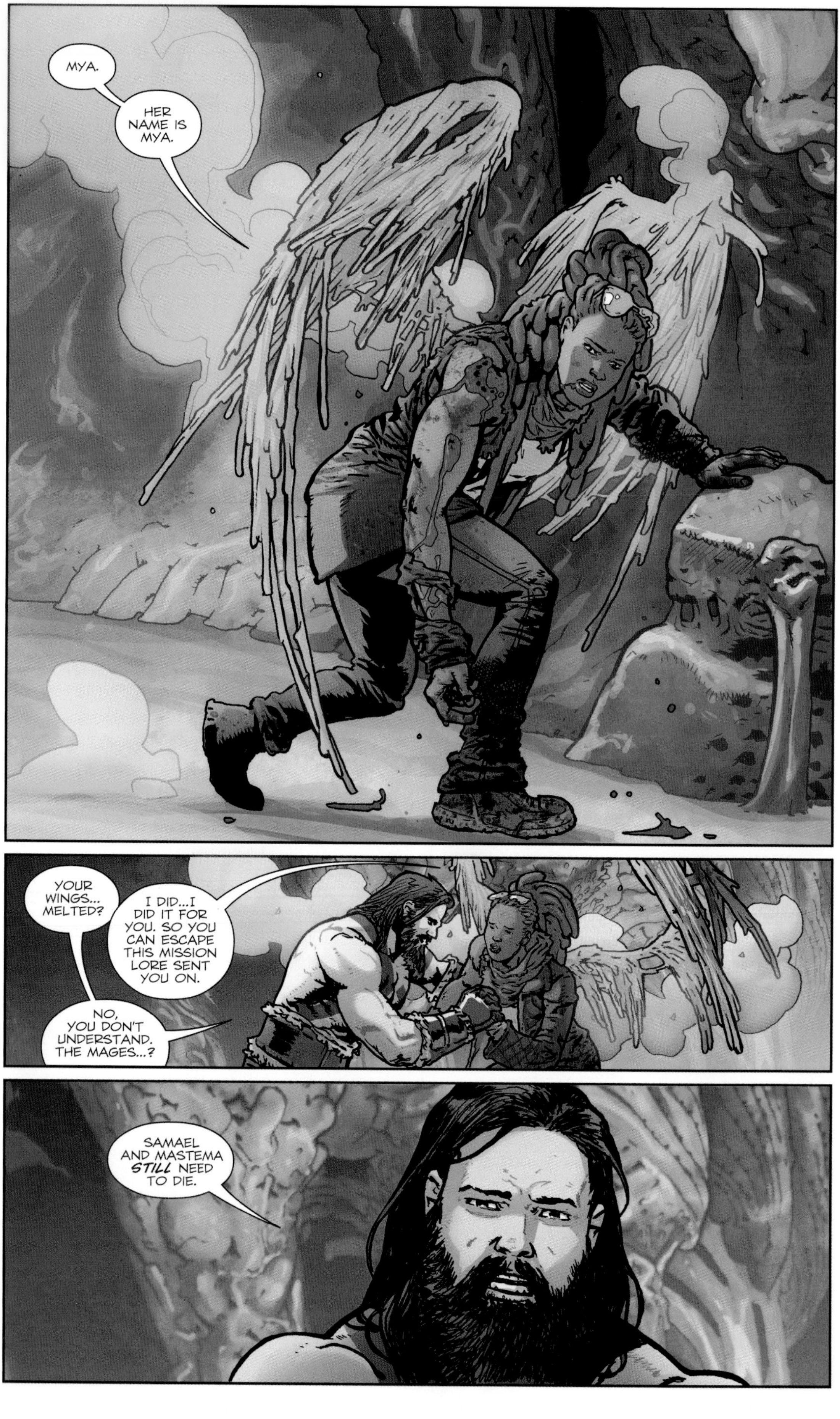
MYA.
HER NAME IS MYA.
YOUR WINGS... MELTED?
I DID...I DID IT FOR YOU. SO YOU CAN ESCAPE THIS MISSION LORE SENT YOU ON.
NO, YOU DON'T UNDERSTAND. THE MAGES...?
SAMAEL AND MASTEMA STILL NEED TO DIE.

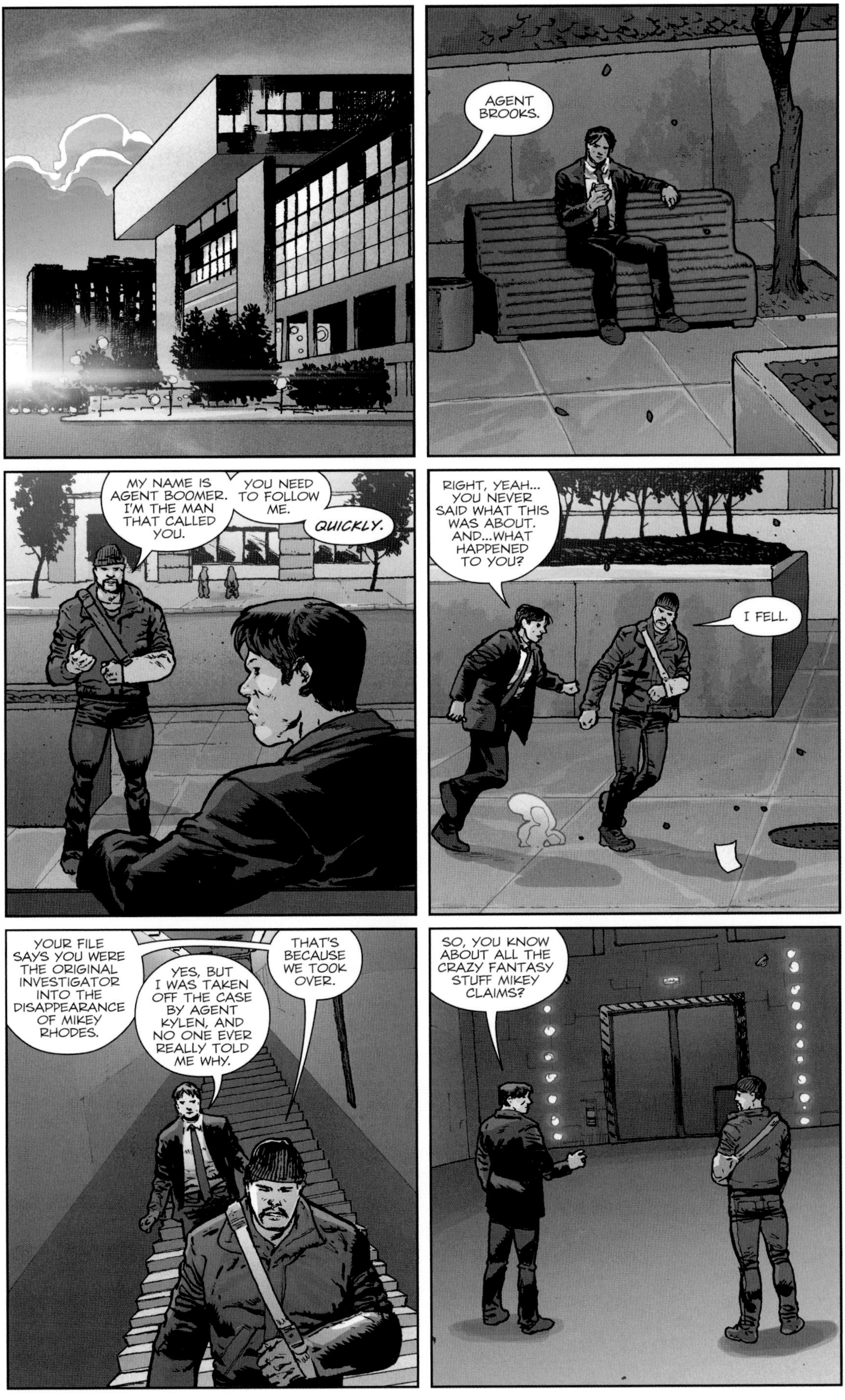
AGENT BROOKS.
MY NAME IS AGENT BOOMER. I'M THE MAN THAT CALLED YOU.
YOU NEED TO FOLLOW ME.
QUICKLY.
RIGHT, YEAH... YOU NEVER SAID WHAT THIS WAS ABOUT. AND...WHAT HAPPENED TO YOU?
I FELL.
YOUR FILE SAYS YOU WERE THE ORIGINAL INVESTIGATOR INTO THE DISAPPEARANCE OF MIKEY RHODES.
YES, BUT I WAS TAKEN OFF THE CASE BY AGENT KYLEN, AND NO ONE EVER REALLY TOLD ME WHY.
THAT'S BECAUSE WE TOOK OVER.
SO, YOU KNOW ABOUT ALL THE CRAZY FANTASY STUFF MIKEY CLAIMS?

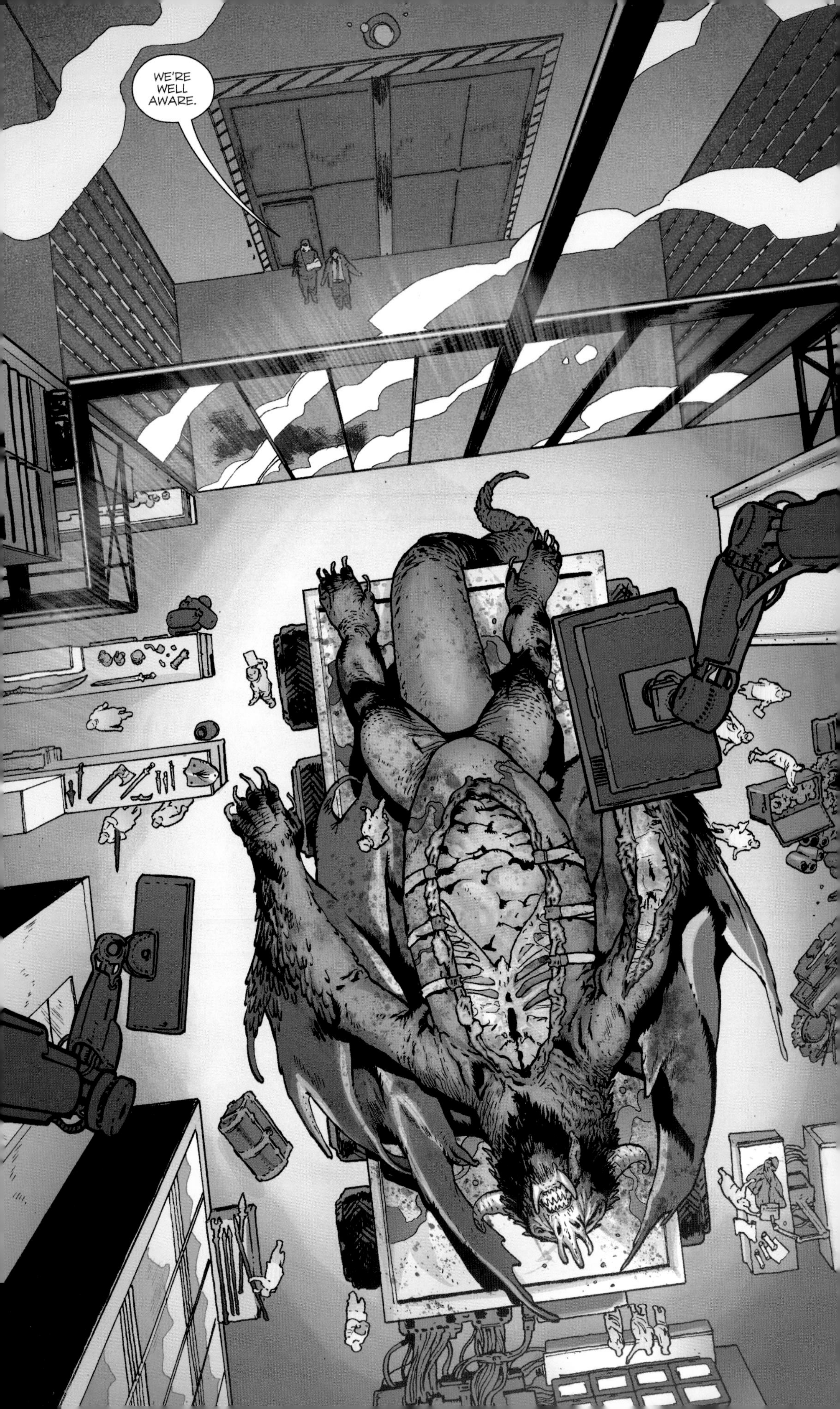
WE'RE WELL AWARE.

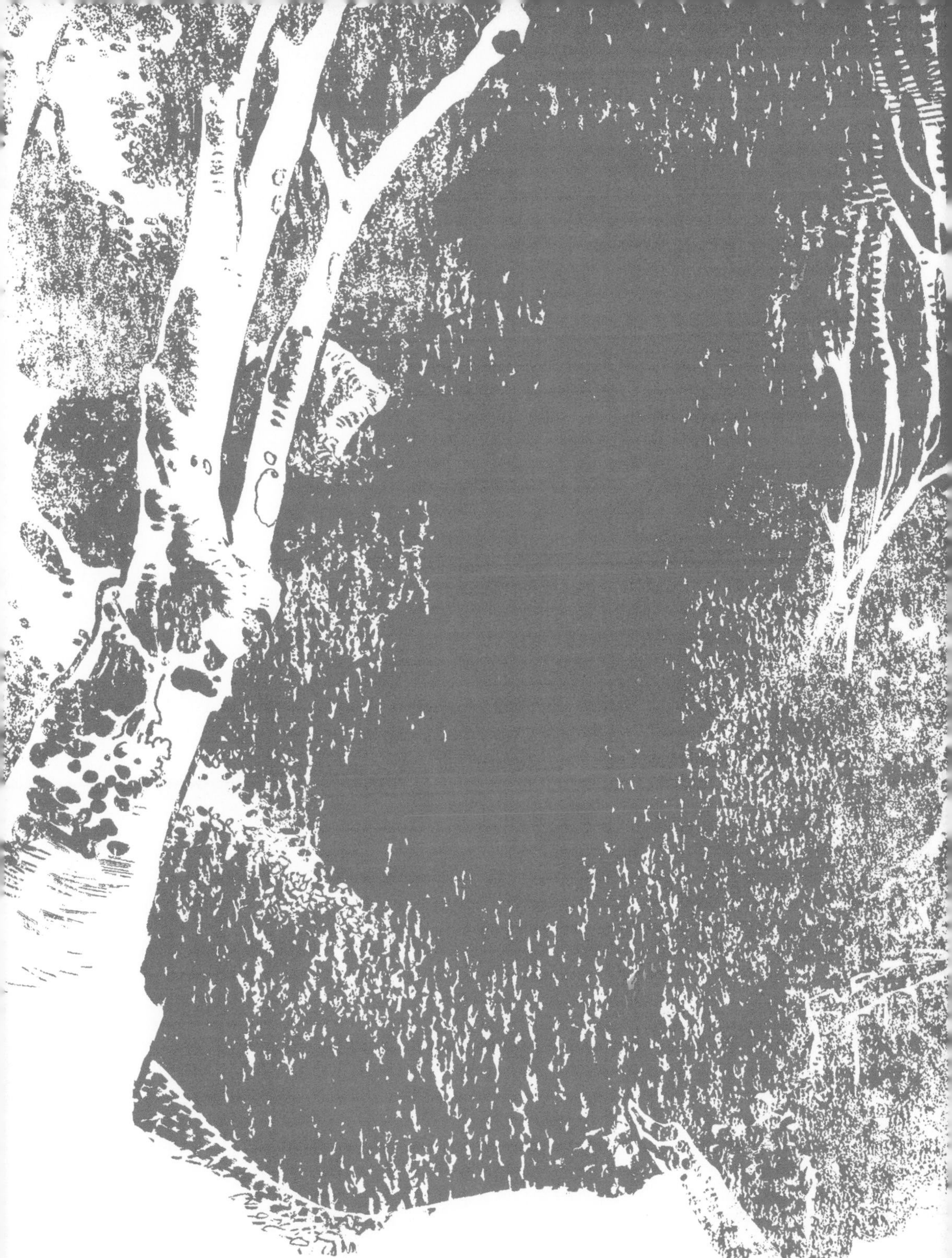

To be continued...

“I could end that chapter of my life…

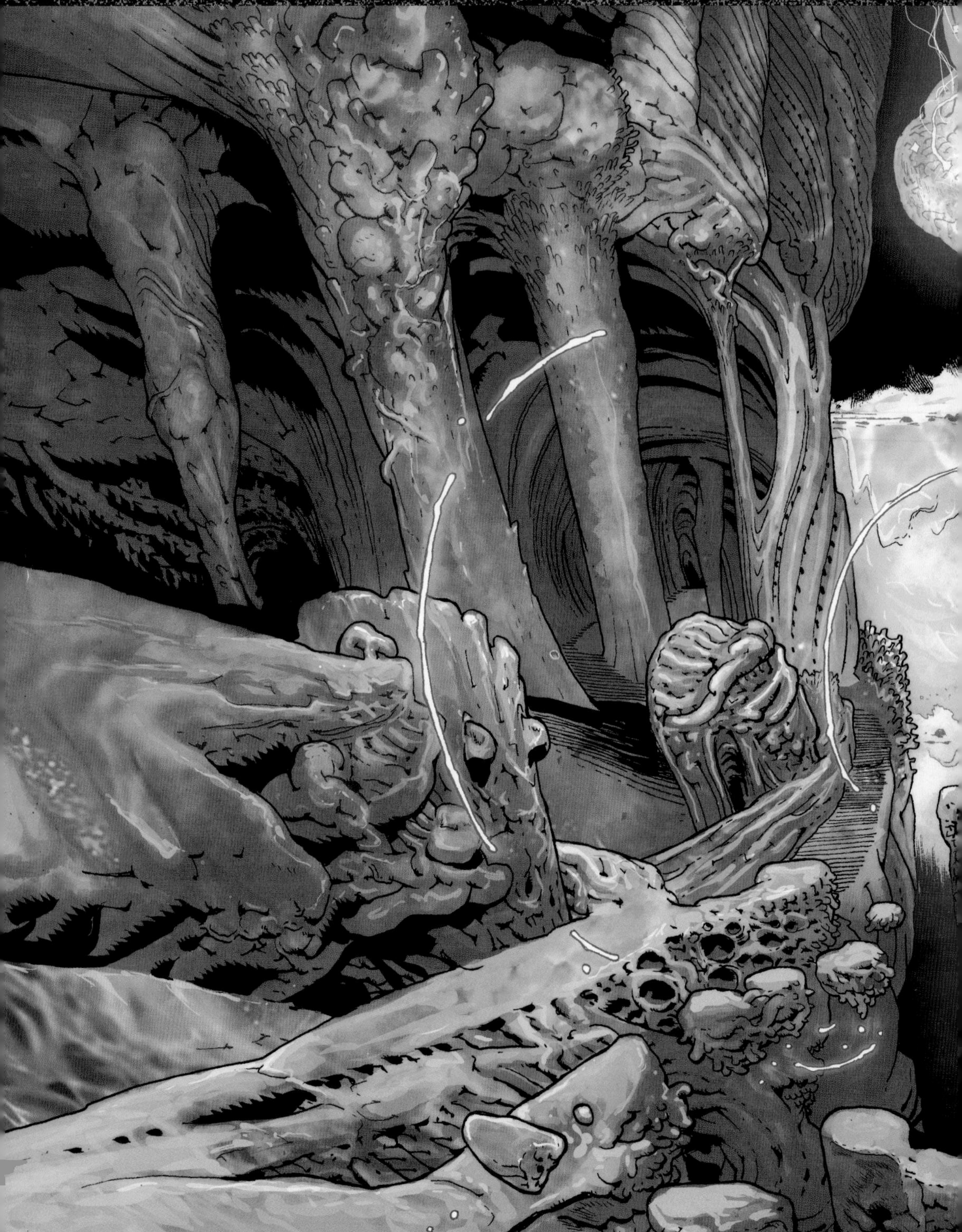

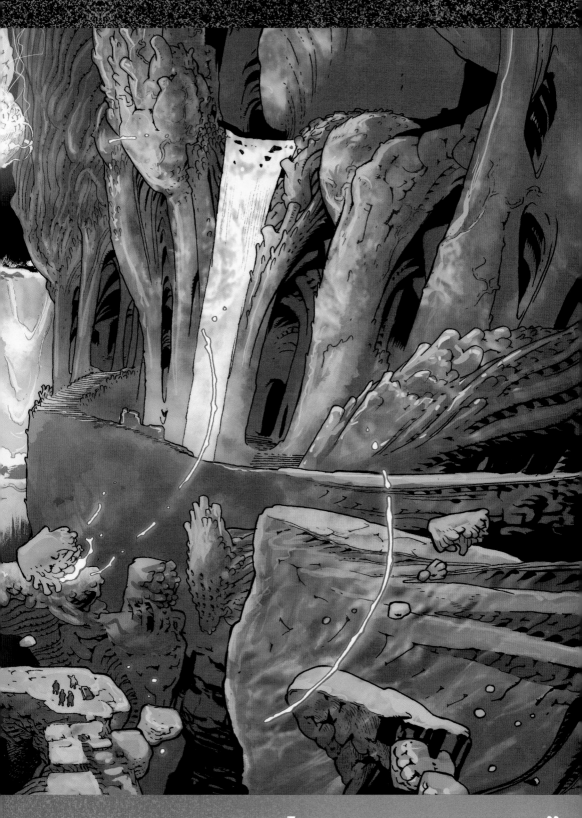

and start a new one."

FALLEN
where
Bone Palace
FIRE trolls!
green flame VOLCANO
Lore's KINGDOM
burning valley
MOUNTAIN Ash forest
MERMAID
Ew!
ANGRY Engine Reef
N
E
W
S

SNOW!

Screaming
SKULL
ISLand

SWAMPS
OF
SERENITY

Sea dragons
live HERE

HTNING
AMPS

FIELDS OF
FOREVEYYYYYYYY...

the haunted
straight

ISLand of
the BLessed

NOS

OR MORE OF THE WALKING DEAD

ROBERT KIRKMAN TONY MOORE
THE WALKING DEAD
VOLUME 1
DAYS GONE BYE

VOL. 1: DAYS GONE BYE TP
ISBN: 978-1-58240-672-5
$14.99
VOL. 2: MILES BEHIND US TP
ISBN: 978-1-58240-775-3
$14.99
VOL. 3: SAFETY BEHIND BARS TP
ISBN: 978-1-58240-805-7
$14.99
VOL. 4: THE HEART'S DESIRE TP
ISBN: 978-1-58240-530-8
$14.99
VOL. 5: THE BEST DEFENSE TP
ISBN: 978-1-58240-612-1
$14.99
VOL. 6: THIS SORROWFUL LIFE TP
ISBN: 978-1-58240-684-8
$14.99
VOL. 7: THE CALM BEFORE TP
ISBN: 978-1-58240-828-6
$14.99
VOL. 8: MADE TO SUFFER TP
ISBN: 978-1-58240-883-5
$14.99
VOL. 9: HERE WE REMAIN TP
ISBN: 978-1-60706-022-2
$14.99
VOL. 10: WHAT WE BECOME TP
ISBN: 978-1-60706-075-8
$14.99
VOL. 11: FEAR THE HUNTERS TP
ISBN: 978-1-60706-181-6
$14.99
VOL. 12: LIFE AMONG THEM TP
ISBN: 978-1-60706-254-7
$14.99
VOL. 13: TOO FAR GONE TP
ISBN: 978-1-60706-329-2
$14.99
VOL. 14: NO WAY OUT TP
ISBN: 978-1-60706-392-6
$14.99
VOL. 15: WE FIND OURSELVES TP
ISBN: 978-1-60706-440-4
$14.99
VOL. 16: A LARGER WORLD TP
ISBN: 978-1-60706-559-3
$14.99
VOL. 17: SOMETHING TO FEAR TP
ISBN: 978-1-60706-615-6
$14.99
VOL. 18: WHAT COMES AFTER TP
ISBN: 978-1-60706-687-3
$14.99
VOL. 19: MARCH TO WAR TP
ISBN: 978-1-60706-818-1
$14.99
VOL. 20: ALL OUT WAR PART ONE TP
ISBN: 978-1-60706-882-2
$14.99
VOL. 21: ALL OUT WAR PART TWO TP
ISBN: 978-1-63215-030-1
$14.99
VOL. 22: A NEW BEGINNING TP
ISBN: 978-1-63215-041-7
$14.99
VOL. 23: WHISPERS INTO SCREAMS TP
ISBN: 978-1-63215-258-9
$14.99
VOL. 24: LIFE AND DEATH TP
ISBN: 978-1-63215-402-6
$14.99
VOL. 25: NO TURNING BACK TP
ISBN: 978-1-63215-612-9
$14.99
VOL. 26: CALL TO ARMS TP
ISBN: 978-1-63215-917-5
$14.99
VOL. 27: THE WHISPERER WAR TP
ISBN: 978-1-5343-0052-1
$14.99
VOL. 28: A CERTAIN DOOM TP
ISBN: 978-1-5343-0244-0
$16.99
VOL. 29: LINES WE CROSS TP
ISBN: 978-1-5343-0497-0
$16.99
VOL. 1: SPANISH EDITION TP
ISBN: 978-1-60706-797-9
$14.99
VOL. 2: SPANISH EDITION TP
ISBN: 978-1-60706-845-7
$14.99
VOL. 3: SPANISH EDITION TP
ISBN: 978-1-60706-883-9
$14.99
VOL. 4: SPANISH EDITION TP
ISBN: 978-1-63215-035-6
$14.99

HARDCOVERS

THE WALKING DEAD
BOOK ONE
a continuing story of survival horror.

BOOK ONE HC
ISBN: 978-1-58240-619-0
$34.99
BOOK TWO HC
ISBN: 978-1-58240-698-5
$34.99
BOOK THREE HC
ISBN: 978-1-58240-825-5
$34.99
BOOK FOUR HC
ISBN: 978-1-60706-000-0
$34.99
BOOK FIVE HC
ISBN: 978-1-60706-171-7
$34.99
BOOK SIX HC
ISBN: 978-1-60706-327-8
$34.99
BOOK SEVEN HC
ISBN: 978-1-60706-439-8
$34.99
BOOK EIGHT HC
ISBN: 978-1-60706-593-7
$34.99
BOOK NINE HC
ISBN: 978-1-60706-798-6
$34.99
BOOK TEN HC
ISBN: 978-1-63215-034-9
$34.99
BOOK ELEVEN HC
ISBN: 978-1-63215-271-8
$34.99
BOOK TWELVE HC
ISBN: 978-1-63215-451-4
$34.99
BOOK THIRTEEN HC
ISBN: 978-1-63215-916-8
$34.99

COMPENDIUMS

THE WALKING DEAD
COMPENDIUM ONE

COMPENDIUM TP, VOL. 1
ISBN: 978-1-60706-076-5
$59.99
COMPENDIUM TP, VOL. 2
ISBN: 978-1-60706-596-8
$59.99
COMPENDIUM TP, VOL. 3
ISBN: 978-1-63215-456-9
$59.99

SPECIALTY BOOKS

THE WALKING DEAD
THE COVERS

THE WALKING DEAD: THE COVERS, VOL. 1 HC
ISBN: 978-1-60706-002-4
$24.99
THE WALKING DEAD: ALL OUT WAR HC
ISBN: 978-1-63215-038-7
$34.99
THE WALKING DEAD COLORING BOOK
ISBN: 978-1-63215-774-4
$14.99
THE WALKING DEAD RICK GRIMES COLORING BOOK
ISBN: 978-1-5343-0003-3
$14.99

OMNIBUS

THE WALKING DEAD

OMNIBUS, VOL. 1
ISBN: 978-1-60706-503-6
$100.00
OMNIBUS, VOL. 2
ISBN: 978-1-60706-515-9
$100.00
OMNIBUS, VOL. 3
ISBN: 978-1-60706-330-8
$100.00
OMNIBUS, VOL. 4
ISBN: 978-1-60706-616-3
$100.00
OMNIBUS, VOL. 5
ISBN: 978-1-63215-042-4
$100.00
OMNIBUS, VOL. 6
ISBN: 978-1-63215-521-4
$100.00

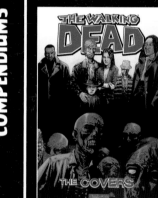

FOR MORE OF INVINCIBLE

TRADEPAPERBACKS

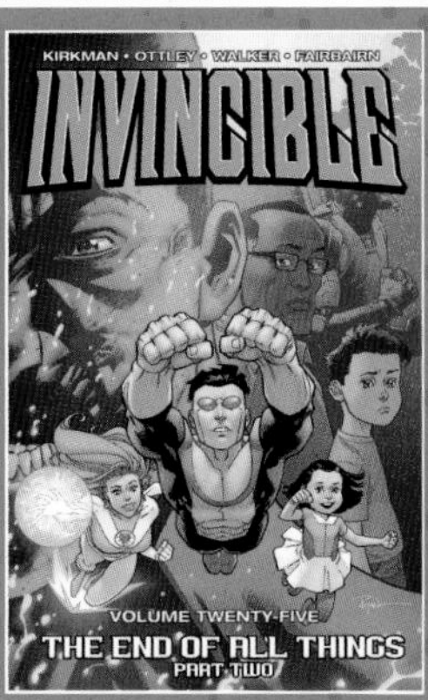
KIRKMAN • OTTLEY • WALKER • FAIRBAIRN
INVINCIBLE
VOLUME TWENTY-FIVE
THE END OF ALL THINGS
PART TWO

VOL. 1: FAMILY MATTERS TP
ISBN: 978-1-58240-711-1
$12.99
VOL. 2: EIGHT IS ENOUGH TP
ISBN: 978-1-58240-347-2
$12.99
VOL. 3: PERFECT STRANGERS TP
ISBN: 978-1-58240-793-7
$12.99
VOL. 4: HEAD OF THE CLASS TP
ISBN: 978-1-58240-778-4
$14.99
VOL. 5: THE FACTS OF LIFE TP
ISBN: 978-1-58240-554-4
$14.99
VOL. 6: A DIFFERENT WORLD TP
ISBN: 978-1-58240-579-7
$14.99
VOL. 7: THREE'S COMPANY TP
ISBN: 978-1-58240-656-5
$14.99
VOL. 8: MY FAVORITE MARTIAN TP
ISBN: 978-1-58240-683-1
$16.99
VOL. 9: OUT OF THIS WORLD TP
ISBN: 978-1-58240-827-9
$14.99
VOL. 10: WHO'S THE BOSS TP
ISBN: 978-1-60706-013-0
$16.99
VOL. 11: HAPPY DAYS TP
ISBN: 978-1-60706-062-8
$16.99
VOL. 12: STILL STANDING TP
ISBN: 978-1-60706-166-3
$16.99
VOL. 13: GROWING PAINS TP
ISBN: 978-1-60706-251-6
$16.99
VOL. 14: THE VILTRUMITE WAR TP
ISBN: 978-1-60706-367-4
$19.99
VOL. 15: GET SMART TP
ISBN: 978-1-60706-498-5
$16.99
VOL. 16: FAMILY TIES TP
ISBN: 978-1-60706-579-1
$16.99
VOL. 17: WHAT'S HAPPENING TP
ISBN: 978-1-60706-662-0
$16.99
VOL. 18: DEATH OF EVERYONE TP
ISBN: 978-1-60706-762-7
$16.99
VOL. 19: THE WAR AT HOME TP
ISBN: 978-1-60706-856-3
$16.99
VOL. 20: FRIENDS TP
ISBN: 978-1-63215-043-1
$16.99
VOL. 21: MODERN FAMILY TP
ISBN: 978-1-63215-318-0
$16.99
VOL. 22: REBOOT? TP
ISBN: 978-1-63215-626-6
$16.99
VOL. 23: FULL HOUSE TP
ISBN: 978-1-63215-888-8
$16.99
VOL. 24: THE END OF ALL THINGS PART ONE TP
ISBN: 978-1-5343-0322-5
$16.99
VOL. 25: THE END OF ALL THINGS PART TWO TP
ISBN: 978-1-5343-0503-8
$16.99
THE OFFICIAL HANDBOOK OF THE INVINCIBLE UNIVERSE TP
ISBN: 978-1-58240-831-6
$12.99
INVINCIBLE PRESENTS, VOL. 1: ATOM EVE & REX SPLODE TP
ISBN: 978-1-60706-255-4
$14.99

COMPLETE LIBRARY

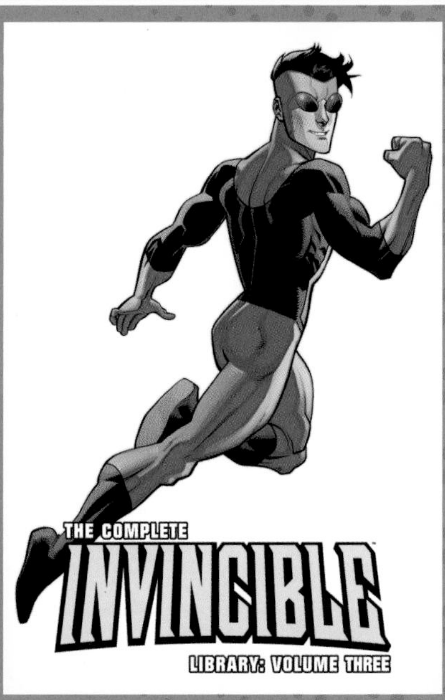
THE COMPLETE
INVINCIBLE
LIBRARY: VOLUME THREE

THE COMPLETE INVINCIBLE LIBRARY, VOL. 2 HC
ISBN: 978-1-60706-112-0
$125.00
THE COMPLETE INVINCIBLE LIBRARY, VOL. 3 HC
ISBN: 978-1-60706-421-3
$125.00

COMPENDIUMS

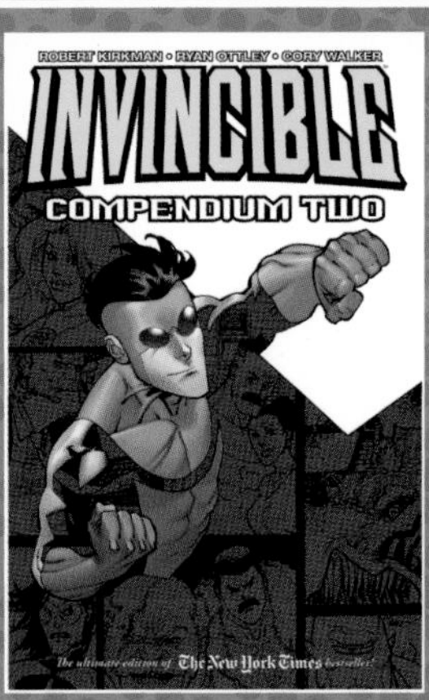
ROBERT KIRKMAN • RYAN OTTLEY • CORY WALKER
INVINCIBLE
COMPENDIUM TWO
The ultimate edition of The New York Times bestseller!

COMPENDIUM VOL. 1
ISBN: 978-1-60706-411-4
$64.99
COMPENDIUM VOL. 2
ISBN: 978-1-60706-772-6
$64.99

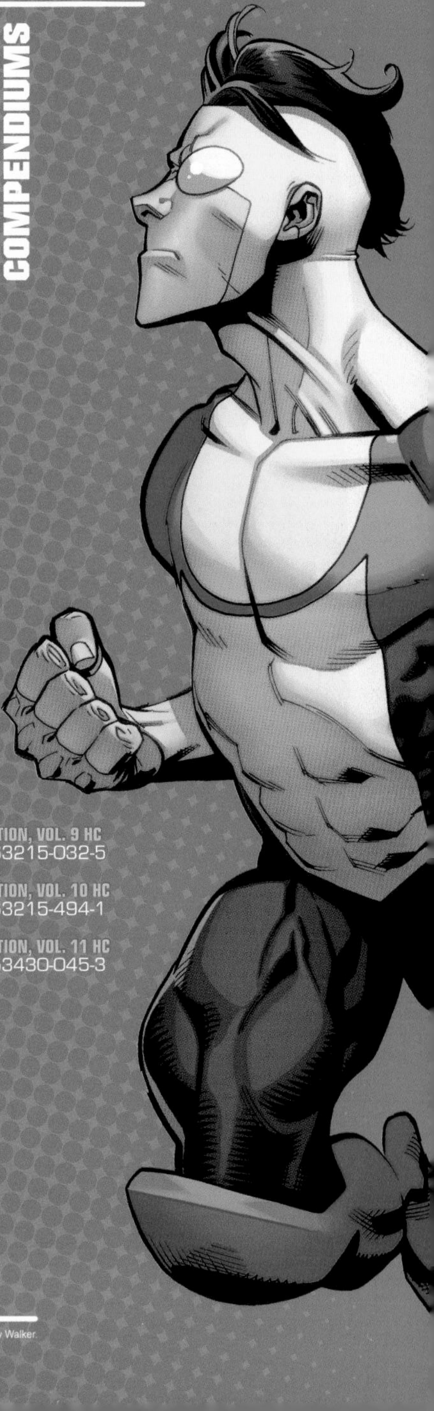

ULTIMATE COLLECTIONS

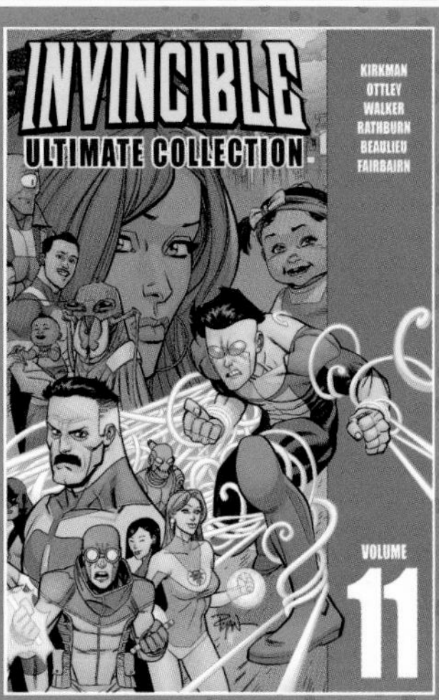
INVINCIBLE
ULTIMATE COLLECTION
KIRKMAN
OTTLEY
WALKER
RATHBURN
BEAULIEU
FAIRBAIRN
VOLUME
11

ULTIMATE COLLECTION, VOL. 1 HC
ISBN 978-1-58240-500-1
$34.99
ULTIMATE COLLECTION, VOL. 2 HC
ISBN: 978-1-58240-594-0
$34.99
ULTIMATE COLLECTION, VOL. 3 HC
ISBN: 978-1-58240-763-0
$34.99
ULTIMATE COLLECTION, VOL. 4 HC
ISBN: 978-1-58240-989-4
$34.99
ULTIMATE COLLECTION, VOL. 5 HC
ISBN: 978-1-60706-116-8
$34.99
ULTIMATE COLLECTION, VOL. 6 HC
ISBN: 978-1-60706-360-5
$34.99
ULTIMATE COLLECTION, VOL. 7 HC
ISBN: 978-1-60706-509-8
$39.99
ULTIMATE COLLECTION, VOL. 8 HC
ISBN: 978-1-60706-680-4
$39.99
ULTIMATE COLLECTION, VOL. 9 HC
ISBN: 978-1-63215-032-5
$39.99
ULTIMATE COLLECTION, VOL. 10 HC
ISBN: 978-1-63215-494-1
$39.99
ULTIMATE COLLECTION, VOL. 11 HC
ISBN: 978-1-53430-045-3
$39.99

For more tales from ROBERT KIRKMAN and SKYBOUND

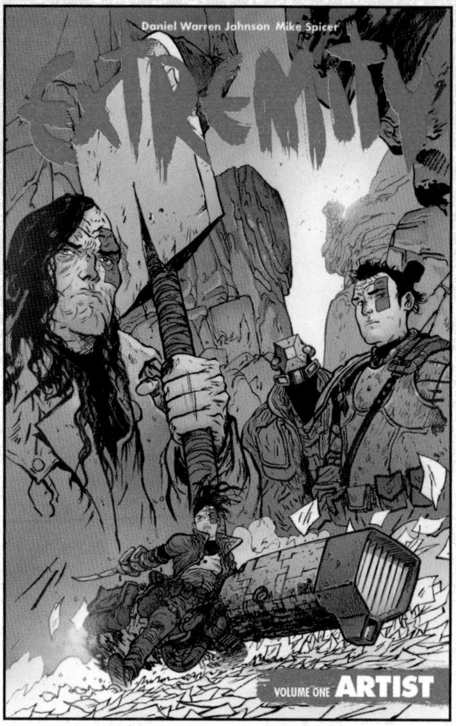
Daniel Warren Johnson Mike Spicer
EXTREMITY
VOLUME ONE ARTIST

VOL. 1: ARTIST TP
ISBN: 978-1-5343-0242-6
$16.99

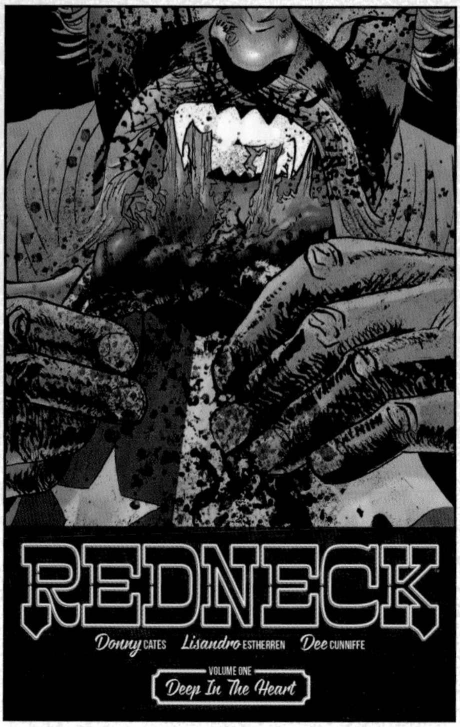
REDNECK
Donny CATES Lisandro ESTHERREN Dee CUNNIFFE
VOLUME ONE
Deep In The Heart

VOL. 1: DEEP IN THE HEART TP
ISBN: 978-1-5343-0331-7
$16.99

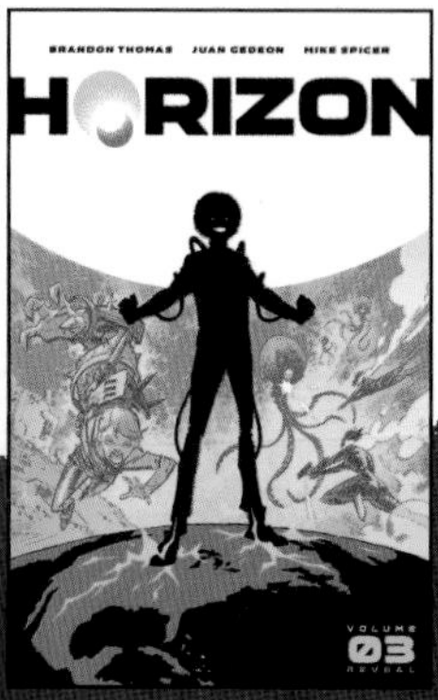
BRANDON THOMAS JUAN GEDEON MIKE SPICER
HORIZON
VOLUME 03 REVEAL

VOL. 1: REPRISAL TP
ISBN: 978-1-5343-0047-7
$9.99

VOL. 2: REMNANT TP
ISBN: 978-1-5343-0227-3
$12.99

VOL. 3: REVEAL TP
ISBN: 978-1-5343-0487-1
$16.99

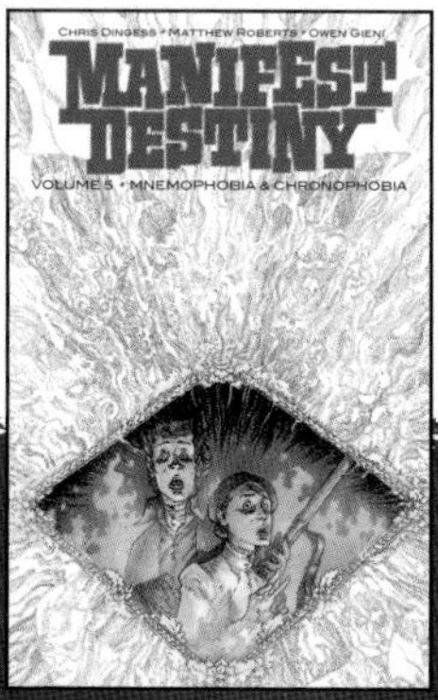
CHRIS DINGESS • MATTHEW ROBERTS • OWEN GIENI
MANIFEST DESTINY
VOLUME 5 • MNEMOPHOBIA & CHRONOPHOBIA

VOL. 1: FLORA & FAUNA TP
ISBN: 978-1-60706-982-9
$9.99

VOL. 2: AMPHIBIA & INSECTA TP
ISBN: 978-1-63215-052-3
$14.99

VOL. 3: CHIROPTERA & CARNIFORMAVES TP
ISBN: 978-1-63215-397-5
$14.99

VOL. 4: SASQUATCH TP
ISBN: 978-1-63215-890-1
$14.99

VOL. 5: MNEMOPHOBIA & CHRONOPHOBIA TP
ISBN: 978-1-5343-0230-3
$16.99

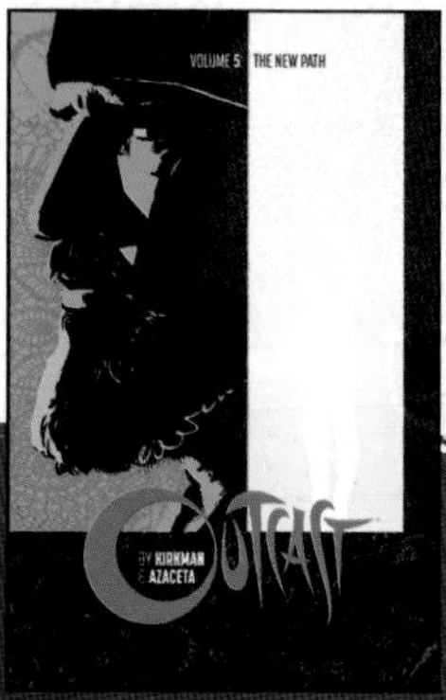
VOLUME 5 THE NEW PATH
OUTCAST
BY KIRKMAN & AZACETA

VOL. 1: A DARKNESS SURROUNDS HIM TP
ISBN: 978-1-63215-053-0
$9.99

VOL. 2: A VAST AND UNENDING RUIN TP
ISBN: 978-1-63215-448-4
$14.99

VOL. 3: THIS LITTLE LIGHT TP
ISBN: 978-1-63215-693-8
$14.99

VOL. 4: UNDER DEVIL'S WING TP
ISBN: 978-1-5343-0050-7
$14.99

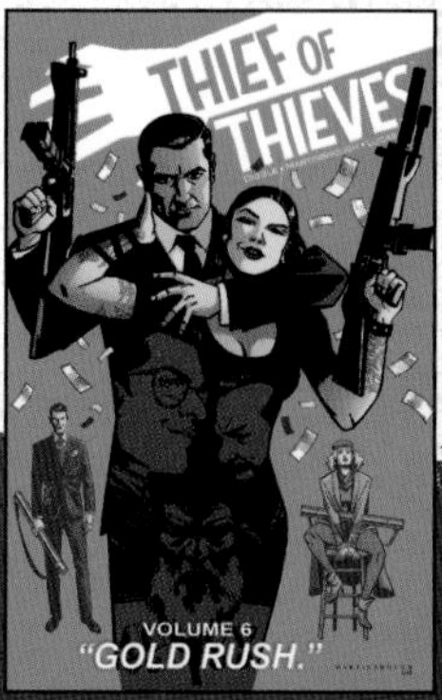
THIEF OF THIEVES
VOLUME 6
"GOLD RUSH."

VOL. 1: "I QUIT."
ISBN: 978-1-60706-592-0
$14.99

VOL. 2: "HELP ME."
ISBN: 978-1-60706-676-7
$14.99

VOL. 3: "VENICE."
ISBN: 978-1-60706-844-0
$14.99

VOL. 4: "THE HIT LIST."
ISBN: 978-1-63215-037-0
$14.99

VOL. 5: "TAKE ME."
ISBN: 978-1-63215-401-9
$14.99

VOL. 6: "GOLD RUSH."
ISBN: 978-1-53430-037-8
$14.99